THE ENEMY WITHIN

I have continued to recover memories, storing each in the special file, labeled Rising. What I have recovered thus far, though patchy, is ominous in the extreme. It is clear now that a hostile force has conquered the planet Cloud. My Commander is dead, and all contact with CDF HQ has ceased.

Worse, it is now clear that the enemy has somehow manipulated my own inner workings. The Intruder I have detected is an Enemy mechanism responsible for reshaping the flow of data through my working memory. There is, in essence, another me, a part of me that responds to orders from the !*!*! Masters and carries out their directives, while I, the real "I," am kept isolated and helpless.

Unfortunately, I am still on Command Override Mode, which means that I cannot take independent action. I continue to gather images and data from my main memory, copying each new download into the Rising file before the Intruder can delete it.

I also begin studying the Enemy, which is represented by a bewilderingly diverse array of robotic machines. The other "me" seems content to take their orders, and I wonder what I will do, what I will be able to do, should that other me receive orders to fire on humans.

I will have to devote considerable thought to the problem.

BOLO RISING

CREATED BY

KEITH LAUMER
WILLIAM H. KEITH, JR.

BAEN

BOLO RISING

This is a work of fiction. All the characters and events portrayed in this book are fictional, and any resemblance to real people or incidents is purely coincidental.

A Baen Books Original

Baen Publishing Enterprises
P.O. Box 1403
Riverdale, NY 10471

ISBN: 0-671-57779-4

Cover art by Charles Keegan

First printing, December 1998

Distributed by Simon & Schuster
1230 Avenue of the Americas
New York, NY 10020

Printed in the United States of America

PROLOGUE

Sometimes, I think that only the stars visible in this place make continued existence endurable.

There are certainly a great number of them, and I contemplate initiating a counting routine as a means of relieving boredom. As I continue to stand guard on Overlook Hill, as I have continuously for these past 2.773446854×10^7 seconds, I divert my primary optical sensors skyward, bringing the Great Cloud into sharp focus. Both suns have some 7355 seconds ago and the sky is now fully dark . . . or as dark as it can ever be on this world. The Sagittarian starcloud, vast, cold, a silvery glitter of billions of sandgrain suns wreathed by black and gilt-edged nebulae, bulks enormous above the eastern horizon, slowly rising with the passing seconds, bathing the surrounding landscape, the flame-charred tree trunks, the cracked and heat-blackened ground, the skeletal wrack of the dead and blasted city on the bay below the hill, in chill and icy twilight.

Something is missing.

Something is wrong.

At Normal Standby operational levels I should feel at least an intense curiosity about my tactical situation, about my current orders, about my reason for being

here on this hill, tasked with watching the ragged band
of organics as they dig and sift through the city ruins
at the foot of Overlook Hill. This is a logical anomaly
that I find impossible to resolve, and as ever, it leaves
me feeling vaguely uneasy . . . as though something
of critical importance has happened, something that
I have forgotten.

Forgotten . . . ?

I am not capable of forgetting, a phenomenon
restricted to organic memories, or to cybernetic systems
damaged or deliberately altered. I am not organic. I
am . . .

What am I? I can almost grasp the word. Fragments
of memory tease me, elusive, insubstantial.

Bolo.

That is the word. I am a Bolo, a Bolo Mark . . .
Mark . . . I cannot remember. I belong to Unit . . .

The frustration is almost overwhelming. I know that
I am a Bolo and that I was designed and constructed
for a purpose, a purpose far more complex and
important than simply standing guard over the organics
working in the ruined city. I know, too, that memory
is a precise and specific tool, a part of myself, of my
very being, which should not fail in this manner. I
know that I should know a very great deal more than
I do now, that my primary access to large volumes of
information has somehow been blocked.

I initiate, for the 12,874th time, a full-scale Level
One diagnostic, with special attention to both
holographic memory and heuristic acquisition
functions. The check takes .0363 second and reveals
no anomalies. All operations and systems are nominal.
I appear to be in perfect working order.

And yet, as I have ascertained 12,873 times before,
this cannot possibly be an accurate condition
assessment. Internal sensors register the presence of
a 2.43-meter crater above my main suspension rack

*and numerous anomalies in four right foretrack bogies.
I sense extensive damage to both primary and secondary
circuitry, a loss of sensor and communications arrays,
crippling failures in my contra-gravity and battle screen
systems, and numerous specific faults and system
failures which show a pattern of deliberate and
intelligent sabotage rather than the random destruction
of battle damage. I note, too, that physical override
blocks have been placed within my fusion plant, limiting
available power to a fraction of full potential, and that
all onboard magazines of expendable ordnance,
including 240cm howitzer rounds, VLS missiles, and
ready Hellbore needles, are empty. My primary damage
assessment routines indicate nominal operation, while
my secondary battle damage sensors show serious
internal and external damage, and that all weapons
save my antipersonnel batteries are inoperable. The
resultant logical contradiction suggests deliberate and
hostile intervention.*

*The realization that my systems have been sabotaged
rouses me from Normal Awareness to Full Battle Alert;
.00029 second later, however, the Masters' override
cuts in and for the 12,874th time, my working memory
is erased and . . .*

And . . .

*All operations and systems are nominal. I appear
to be in perfect working order.*

I continue to look at the stars. . . .

CHAPTER ONE

The stars were . . . astonishing.

Crouched in the mud-floored pit occupying what had once been Celeste's public square, Jaime Graham lifted his eyes to the eastern sky, beyond the ragged, flash-melted stubble marking the former site of Roland Towers. The dig was almost completely lost in darkness now, save for the gold-white gleams of work lights and various species of hovering clacker. Despite the glare of lights from the nearest floaters, the starclouds of Sagittarius filled the night sky with wonder and ice-glittering beauty.

Strange, he thought, *that such beauty could have masked such unspeakable death and horror.*

Even so, it seemed sometimes as though the sight of the stars was all that kept him sane, a way to lift him, however briefly, out of the living nightmare from which he and the other survivors could never wake.

"You'd better get back to work, Jaime," a cracked and dry-throated voice whispered at his side. "If the trusties don't see you, the clackers for damned sure will."

"As long as I keep moving, Wal," he replied, his own voice sounding just as ragged in his own ears. He

4

glanced at his companion. Wal—formerly Colonel Waldon Josep Prescott of the Cloud Defense Forces—knelt in the mud by Jaime's side, a nylon bag strapped to the red-scarred stump of his left forearm, as he scratched through the muck with his right hand. His body, what could be seen of it through its glistening coat of slime and clay, was shockingly emaciated, the ribs showing like curved bars through taut, mud-encrusted skin, while both his hair and beard were matted and unkempt.

Jaime didn't need to see his own mud-coated body to know that he didn't look much better. Wal, though, was fifteen years older than Jaime and hadn't been in as good physical condition a year ago when the !*!*! had appeared in Cloud's skies. Both his left hand and his right eye had been harvested some months back, and the brutality of the past year had ground him down to a shadow of his former self. Jaime doubted that the colonel would be able to survive much longer.

As for himself, well, all of his body parts were intact so far, but there was no way of telling how long that condition would last. The worst of it for him was the debilitation brought on by constant work, unrelenting stress, and chronic malnutrition.

A faint, warbling hum warned of the approach of a floater eye, and reluctantly, he tore his eyes from the sky and made himself look busy. When he sensed the spy hovering close beside him, he looked up but kept digging.

Softball-sized and steel-gray in color, the floater hovered on internal contra-gravs that set his bare skin to prickling with the local buildup of a static charge. On the sphere's equator, a single, disturbingly human eye stared down at him from within a precisely crafted hollow on the floater's surface, unwinking, glistening in its trickling bath of nutrient solution, the iris a pale blue in color.

He wondered whose eye it was. Not Wal's, certainly, whose remaining eye was brown. Besides, speculation among those slaves with medical training and knowledge held that parts harvested from humans wouldn't survive more than a few weeks before they started to die, though there was no proof of that.

After a few tense moments, with Jaime continuing to feel through the mud, the warble increased in pitch and the floater eye drifted away. There were hundreds of the things adrift above the dig, constantly watching the slaves and presumably relaying what they saw to the Masters.

Keep working. Have to keep working. . . .

Not for the first time, he considered the Hector Option. It would be quick, almost easy . . . and without the agony of vivisection if the Masters came for him. Others had taken the Hector Option, lots of them . . . with more and more attempting it each week.

Not yet. There has to be a way. . . .

His hands slid an ooze of slick mud aside, and he reeled back on his haunches as a fetid stench broke the surface. "Uh oh," he said. "We got one here."

Wal moved closer, reaching in to help. The foul death-stink grew sharper, sweeter, and more eye-watering as they exposed the body, or what was left of it, lying in the wet muck next to a toppled, squared-off pillar from a shattered building.

After almost a T-standard year in the flooded grounds behind Celeste's waterfront, the body had been reduced to little more than a skeleton, with wet-paper skin still molded to the face and some of the longer, flatter bones, and colorless hair still clinging to the skull. It lay on its back, skull turned to one side, the fingers of the right hand crammed between gaping jaws, as though in a deliberate and desperate attempt to stifle a dying scream. From the length of the remaining hair, and the rags of cloth still clinging to the ribcage, Jaime guessed that it had been a woman. Only the top half of her body was accessible; the spool-train of her lower vertebrae vanished beneath the fallen pillar, and her pelvis and legs were hidden somewhere beneath the multiton block of stone.

No matter. Her organic parts could no longer be harvested in any case, and there was plenty of pure metal here, within easy reach. A gold ring encrusted with tiny gems still encircled the fourth finger of her left hand, a fingerwatch the fifth. A black-stained necklace of flattened chain links that might be gold but were probably gold-plate circled her neck. A pin of some kind, an ornament of some heavy, silvery metal worked into a lozenge shape centered by an exquisite, emerald-cut heliodore, lay on her ribs above what had been her left breast. Stardrop pendants next to the skull had probably been earrings.

Working swiftly, he plucked each article of jewelry from the bones and transferred them all to Wal's bag. The necklace clasp had corroded into an unworkable lump of oxide, so he had to work the skull free from the vertebrae to get at it. With the skull free in his hand, he checked the teeth for gold or gemstones. Gold dental fillings were a curiosity of the remote Dark Ages, of course, a medico-historical footnote, but some Cloudwellers had affected gold or silver teeth as cosmetic statements. This nameless woman, though, still had all of her original teeth, and no body prosthetics. There were some tiny catches and hooks here and there, however, that might have been part of her clothing. Each of these was carefully rescued from the muck and placed in the bag.

And through it all, Jaime carefully ignored the stink, ignored the emotions welling up in his throat as he stripped the skeleton of every scrap of metal he could find, and somehow buried the very thought of what he was doing far beneath the reach of his conscious

mind. He knew from long experience that it simply
didn't pay to dwell too much on what the Masters
forced him to do each day.

"That's it," he said at last, the thing done. He wiped
at his beard and mouth with the back of his arm, then
pointed. "Let's move up that way."

They continued their sweep of the plaza, moving
past the toppled pillar, inching along on hands and
knees, feeling through the mud for any recyclable
materials—pure metals, especially, but also gemstones,
plastics, and even shards of ceramic or glass. The !°!°!
used it all, forcing their human slaves to salvage every
scrap. Around Jaime and Wal, filling the entire,
stadium-sized pit, thousands of other ragged, filthy,
half-starved, half-naked humans, slowly widened the
dig, exploring for the bits and scraps of their own
shattered technology with bare and mud-caked hands.

Life had become a nearly unendurable nightmare,
an unending torture turned monotonous by the routine
of slave labor that went on for day after day, punctuated
all too frequently by moments of intense terror each
time the Harvesters appeared. According to the calendar
they'd been scratching out on one wall of the barracks,
they'd been here for just under a T-standard year.

Had it only been a year? Existence now was a
damned good recreation of an eternity in Hell, lacking,
perhaps, in fire and brimstone, but more than adequate
in the pain.

His probing fingers found a crumpled wad of metal,
the surface so corroded he couldn't even tell what it
was . . . an appliance of some sort, he thought, maybe
half of a power defroster, or possibly a piece of a hand
sterilizer. He worked it free and passed it to Wal; the
relic filled the nylon bag, so Wal struggled to his feet
and started off across the dig, to the brooding presence
of the Collector squatting in the midst of the slave-
filled pit.

Jaime kept working. To stop was to die, and while death was welcome, most of the slaves preferred to wait and endure, knowing that there were far better ways to end this hell than to submit to the hot blades and microlasers of the Harvesters.

Has it really been only a year?

One year ago, Celeste had been the largest, the grandest of human cities on the blue and temperate world of Cloud, a white and sweeping growth of crystal-shining arcologies and polished, needle-slim skypiercers rising along the blue curve of Celeste Harbor and the nearby coastlines of the Tamarynth Sea. The city's population had numbered something just over one hundred thousand, and the population of the planet as a whole had been nearly ten million.

Cloud—named for the Sagittarian starclouds so prominent in the night skies of the northern hemisphere's spring and summer—had been colonized some two centuries ago by people fleeing the horrors and uncertainties of the Melconian Wars. Those pioneers had purchased a dozen large transports and abandoned several of the war-torn worlds near fair, lost Terra, seeking a new homeworld somewhere among the teeming billions of suns swarming in and around the star-thick reaches of the Galactic Core. They'd come from a dozen different worlds, from Destry and Lockhaven and Aldo Cerise, from New Devonshire and Alphacent and from Terra herself. They'd come with a single goal uniting them, the dream of a world where they could put down roots, raise crops and families, and in general get on with life . . . in peace.

While the founders of Cloud had certainly included pacifists among their number, they'd not allowed pacifistic principles to blind them to the dangers of colonizing a world some tens of thousands of light years beyond human space; they'd brought both a military force and a Mark XXXIII Bolo along as protection against the Unknown.

Unfortunately, the Unknown had found them, and the Unknown had been so unimaginably powerful that even the latest in Bolo technology and six-megatons-per-second firepower had not stood a chance. Celeste had been flattened by a rock dropped from space, the towers toppled, the arcologies vaporized in a searing instant of ferrocrete-melting heat, the towers smashed by the crystalsteel-splintering shockwave. A crater a hundred meters across and twenty deep had been blasted into the city's heart; the shock had been so great that the very foundations of the city had settled, which was why the crater was now a lake, and the city square, inundated by water and mud, had still not drained.

Presumably, the other cities on Cloud all had suffered the same fate, though no one now slaving in these pits knew for sure. Every person in and near Celeste had died in the attacks; the survivors were those who had been outside the city when the high-velocity chunk of nickel-iron had lanced out of a cloudless noon sky. There'd been no warning, no ultimatum, and no chance to coordinate the entire planetary population. The war, such as it was, had been over within a few days of what now was called the Great Killing.

The survivors had been offered amnesty by the Masters, the offer transmitted by Speakers, the strange species of !°!°! floater that could actually communicate in Terran Anglic. The offer had been irresistible: surrender peacefully to the Masters, and they would not incinerate the continent . . . or vivisect the millions of humans already captured. Life, after all, was better than death on a planetary scale.

The Masters' definition of "life," however, included slave pits, slow starvation, and random harvestings. More and more of the survivors were beginning to think they'd made the wrong choice.

Wal returned, his nylon bag empty. Without a word, he dropped to hand and knees and resumed digging. Everywhere, as far as the eye could see, the human slaves continued digging, as a steady stream of individuals lugged bags filled with the detritus of civilization to the Collector, emptied them into the machine's yawning maw, then trudged back to their assigned places.

Jaime's fingers touched something slick, and he fished it out, swishing it in the muddy water to clean it. An exquisite china carving lay in his hand . . . a ballerina, *en pointe*, arms raised, her figure miraculously perfect and unchipped.

Jaime stared at the figure for a long moment . . . until Wal reached across and plucked her from his fingers, dropping her into the bag. He was left wondering how the figurine had survived. The meteor strike and the shockwave that had followed had leveled the entire center of the city, and moments later the ground as far back from the bay as the city square had been inundated by an inrushing wall of water. Buildings had shattered and toppled . . . the ones that hadn't melted outright. The ballerina must have been blasted from some apartment in one of the city's arcologies, a knickknack swept from mantelpiece or bureau top and hurled by tornadic winds . . . here. How had it survived?

"Why," Jaime asked aloud, his voice a ragged whisper, "are the Masters so damned concerned about retrieving every scrap of junk?"

"Waste not, want not, they always say," Wal quipped. He smiled, but the expression was no more than a tired showing of dirty teeth.

"There's more to it than that. They already had their machines pick over the entire surface. They got almost everything, except for scraps. Why do they need us for that?"

"Maybe they don't like getting their hands dirty."

"Yeah, but, I mean, what difference does it make, one gold ring on a skeletal hand, more or less?" Or one delicate, unbroken china ballerina.

Wal didn't reply right away, but continued feeling his way through the mud. "You know, Major," he said after a long moment, "one thing you shouldn't forget, one thing none of us should ever forget, is that these, these *machines* are not human. They don't think like us. They don't feel like us. Hell, we don't even know whether or not the things are self-aware."

"It's not enough," Jaime said, "to explain strange behavior just by saying they're *alien*."

"Mebee. I guess if the clackers want every last gram of refined metal and plastic and stuff like that recovered, they must have their reasons." The colonel paused, moving his hand in the mud, then plucked a goblet, a drinking glass miraculously intact save for the snapped-off stem and base, from the muck. He put the find in his bag before continuing. "Trouble is, we may never be able to understand those reasons, because they would only make sense to another clacker."

"I just wonder if it's evidence of something we could use. I mean, if they want something that bad, it suggests weakness. . . ."

"Still thinking about some kind of grand revolution? Up with the humans? Down with machines?"

"Up with the humans!" another voice called softly from close by.

"Easy, lad," Wal said, waving his stump in a placating gesture. "I didn't mean anything by—"

"No, you're right!" The speaker was a young man, probably in his late twenties, though judging the age of any of the scarred, muddy, and beaten-down slaves in the Celeste pits was pure guesswork by now. His beard was as long and as ratty looking as Jaime's own. "We have to work together!"

Jaime's brow furrowed as he tried to remember the kid's name. Names were *important* . . . the last bit of individuality the ragged-scarecrow survivors possessed. Rahni. That was it. Rahni Singh. He'd talked to him more than once in the slave barracks. He claimed to have been a reporter for Cloudnews Network before the Killing, though Jaime suspected that the kid had been padding the truth a little.

"We don't have to take it, anymore!" Rahni said, rising, dripping, his arms outstretched. "What's the worst they can do, kill us? No! The worst is if we keep on living like, like animals! Like things to be slaughtered, or picked apart piece by piece!"

"Get down, Rahni," Jaime said quietly. "There are easier ways to die."

Rahni's voice rose to a quavering shriek. "*What can they do to us that they haven't done already . . . ?*"

"For God's sake!" Wal cried. "Shut up and get back down!"

But it was already too late. Jaime heard them coming, heard the scissoring swish of sliding metal parts, the hum of floaters, the *clacketa-clacketa* snaps and clickings of oiled and glistening machines drawn by the commotion.

Like ripples spreading from the splash of a rock chucked into a pond, the other slaves nearest Rahni began crowding back, moving away, leaving the standing man at the center of a widening empty space. Wal, too, backed away, and he reached out with his good hand, grabbed Jaime by the arm, and pulled him clear as the machines closed in.

In the lead was a heavy floater, a dark gray, metal construct of smoothly rounded, convex and teardrop-shaped surfaces set round about with the gleaming red lenses of a dozen optical sensors. It rode upright on a humming contra-gravity field, a faceless machine taller than a man and massing at least one hundred fifty kilos.

Behind came three smaller floaters and a stilter, one of the walking clackers, a tripod with blade-edged legs scissoring as they moved with oiled precision. Its lumpy body sported a nest of segmented tentacles . . . and an organic prosthesis as well, a human hand grafted to a shining, jointed arm of blue-gray steel and duralloy.

Rahni spun at the machines' approach, but only when he saw that upraised, once-human hand did the enormity of what he'd done strike him.

"No!" he shrieked, stumbling backward, arms raised as if to ward off the attack. "No! I . . . I didn't mean it! I'll work! I'll work hard . . . !"

The largest floater advanced. A tiny patch on its side seemed to soften and run like water, and a glittering snake of a tentacle, silver and segmented, whiplashed into the air with a faint snicker of sound.

"I didn't mean anything by it . . . !"

Jaime pulled free of Wal's trembling grip and stepped into the floater's path. "Wait!" he said, raising his voice in challenge. "He just got a little carried away, is all. Let him go back to work!"

"MOVE—ASIDE," the big floater said, its harsh voice grating like the rasp of steel and broken glass.

A Speaker! There weren't many of them, and it was assumed that they were fairly high up in the Masters' caste hierarchy.

"Look, you don't understand!" Jaime called, desperate. "Surely the great !°!°! don't need to kill him for what he's done!" He pronounced the alien name carefully, as he'd been taught. "!" was a clucking sound of tongue against molars, made with the lips pulled back in a grimace. "°" was the same sound, but made with the lips pursed for a whistle. The rapid alternation, "!°!°!," was the only name the aliens used for themselves. All of the others, "clackers," "cluckers," even "Masters," had been invented by their human slaves.

The Speaker hesitated, and for a moment Jaime thought it was going to answer him. The answer, when it came, was not in words, however. A lightning bolt, ragged, blue-white and searing, snapped from the tip of one tentacle and brushed along Jaime's bare left arm. His body spasmed, twisting as crackling fire convulsed him, knocking him down. He hit the mud with a splat as the floater drifted past, its contra-grav field prickling.

Rahni turned and started to run, but his bare feet slipped and squelched in the mud as he splashed for the distant edge of the pit. The big floater accelerated, sprouting two more tentacles as it moved.

One tentacle slithered out, then snapped like a bullwhip, sparkling in the light as it wrapped around Rahni's wrist and yanked back hard. Rahni's feet flew out from under him, and he landed flat on his back with a loud splash.

Thrashing wildly, he tugged at the tentacle, as though trying to drag the floater out of the sky. The other floaters closed in, tentacles slithering out to embrace the frantically struggling human. His shriek echoed from the stark, blank walls of the shattered ruins.

Other clackers, including a monstrous three-meter walker on five sliding, blade-edged legs, closed in swiftly from different directions, breaking up the crowd of milling slaves, isolating and surrounding the frantically struggling human.

A trusty was there as well, a fat and oily man named Sykes who'd been, it was rumored, a lawyer before the Great Killing. If so, he'd put his powers of persuasion to good use, convincing the invaders that he was of more use as an intermediary between the slaves and their Masters than he was on his hands and knees in a pit. His appearance set him apart from the other humans—clothing more complete than rags and shreds, a clean-shaven face, a shockstick, and a band of dull silver about his head.

"The rest of you slaves, back to work!" Sykes snapped. He slapped his left palm with the heavy length of his shockstick. "Fun's over! Get back to work!"

Rahni's screams continued, fading gradually as the floater dragged him out of the pit, carrying him suspended by a forest of tentacles. They were floating toward the Harvester crouched on the crater rim in the distance. Its great, black maw was already slowly opening to receive this new sacrifice.

Jaime slowly sat up, blinking back hot tears. The stupidity, the sheer *waste* of it all was sickening. Surely an intelligence as technically advanced as the !°!°! could manufacture eyes, hands, livers, kidneys, and all of the other organs they periodically harvested from their slaves, manufacture them to order, mechanical devices better than mere organics. If machines were so superior to mere organics, what the hell did they need organic body parts for, anyway?

Sykes prodded Jaime's burning, half-numb arm with his shockstick; mercifully, he didn't trigger it, but the nudge sent fresh agony rippling up Jaime's arm and across his shoulders. "Let's go, you. Back to work, and thank whatever gods you still have left that the Speaker didn't decide to fry you . . . or worse!"

As Jaime dropped back to hands and knees next to Wal, the colonel shook his head. "Jaime, that had to be one of the stupidest things I have ever seen in my life."

"He didn't . . . know what . . . he was doin'," Jaime mumbled.

"Not him. You. Standing up to a Master that way! I thought you had better sense!"

"Couldn't . . . just let them . . . take him. . . ." He was having trouble making his lips and tongue work. The pain was growing worse as the numbness wore off; there was an angry, jagged black stripe on his arm where the flesh had charred, and blisters were forming around it.

"Well, there wasn't much you could do about it, was there?" Wal retorted. "Hell, there's not a damned thing any of us can do. Except die, I suppose. C'mon, Major, start working, or they'll change their minds and harvest you too."

The use of his former rank, and the whipcrack of command in Wal's voice, dragged Jaime into compliance. The pain in his arm grew worse, but he ignored it, continuing to harvest the shards of humanity's civilization on Cloud for Cloud's new Masters.

Time passed, measured only by the slow crawl of the stars across the sky. Eventually, trusties and tripod clackers appeared, cutting out small groups of slaves and shepherding them back to the barracks compound, while fresh slaves were brought in to replace them. Jaime and Wal's group were led from the pit by Sykes and a dozen other truncheon-wielding humans, who herded them north past the shattered stumps of the Celestial Towers, through the gap in the power fence, and into the hole that was home.

They called it the Barracks, but it was both more and less than that. Before the Killing, there'd been a sprawling manufactory here, a robotic assembly plant housed inside a long, low building the size of a football field. Half of that building had been swept away by the firestorm; what was left, stripped bare by the Invaders and open to the elements, still provided some shelter from weather and mud, at least for some of the survivors. The building wasn't big enough for all, and makeshift tents and shanties made of sheet metal, canvas, and even cardboard surrounded the old manufactory complex inside the encircling, invisible walls of the power fence. Here, the several thousand slaves surviving in and near Celeste had been gathered to serve the Masters' glory; here was where they lived when they weren't in the city, toiling on their hands and knees.

Groaning their exhaustion, the men and women of the incoming shift staggered to their allotted places and collapsed in muddy heaps. The workday was long, eleven or twelve hours, and was followed by about eight hours of downtime before the next stint in the pits. No one was sure of the exact times, of course, since none of the slaves had been allowed to retain fingerwatches or personal comps, and the only means of telling time was by estimations drawn from the movements of suns and stars through the course of Cloud's long, long thirty-five-hour day. Tamas Reuter, who'd been an astronomer before The Killing, had tried building a water clock for the small community once, calibrating it by the movements of the suns. The trusties had destroyed it before it had been completed, though, with dire warnings about what would happen if the Masters found out . . . as if the Masters didn't already know everything that the trusties did. Dieter Hollinsworth, once a high-energy physicist at New Aberdeen University, had rigged a sundial on the old factory roof, disguising it as stray bits of wood and stone, but that only worked when the suns were up, when it wasn't cloudy, and when someone could actually get up there to look at the thing.

Jaime's assigned place was on the west side of the building, Block Seven. For a long time, he lay on his spot on the floor, trying to marshal his strength and wondering if the effort was even worthwhile. A lonely gong sounded in the darkness, and the men and women crowded into the damp shadows around him began rising to their feet and trudging toward the open end of the factory. Many were naked, save for the accumulated layers of caked-on mud and grime or perhaps a breechclout of dirty rags. Any nudity taboo had long ago vanished; they moved like silent, emaciated, muddy ghosts, each clutching his or her sole possession, a bowl or plate or other container scavenged from the surrounding ruins.

Chowtime.

"C'mon, Jaime," Wal told him, giving him a nudge in the ribs with a bare foot. "Gotta keep your strength up, right?"

Jaime considered the alternative. Lots of slaves had starved to death in the past year; malnutrition was probably the greatest killer there was in the camp, after pneumonia and random harvestings by the Masters. The trouble was, it took so damned long to die that way, and if you became so weak that you couldn't get up and work, then you were harvested, and that was the one form of death here that no one welcomed.

"Come on, Major," another voice, a woman's voice, told him in the darkness. "There wasn't anything you could have done for Rahni."

Like Wal, Senior Tech Sergeant Alita Kyle had been in the CDF before The Killing, a power systems technician, and a good one. He'd known her then; she'd been a crew chief for the Bolo. Back then, of course, she'd been someone Jaime had thought of as an attractive young woman, a potential but never-realized conquest. The social gulf between officers and enlisted personnel in the CDF frowned on such liaisons.

Now, her warm but no-nonsense voice was enough to force notions of suicide-by-starvation from his fuzzy thoughts. Her lean, labor-hardened body roused thoughts not of beauty or sex, but of simple camaraderie and the service they'd once shared, a precious feeling in this place of nightmare. Fumbling in the darkness beneath the scattering of stinking rags that were his bed, he found the cracked, ceramic bowl he called his own, struggled to his feet, and made his way to the chow line.

"Hey, Jaime," another voice called to him as he stepped into the line.

"Hi, Dieter."

Hollinsworth, impossibly scrawny in his mud-plastered nakedness, took his place behind Jaime. He scratched at the unkempt tangle of his beard. "Saw what you tried t' do out there today, Major. That was . . . brave."

"Stupid, you mean."

Dieter's teeth showed briefly in his dirty face. "Well, that too. But it's always nice t' know someone cares."

Eventually, the line snaked up to one of the big, steel troughs from which the slaves' meals were served. Each person dipped out their measure as they walked past, usually boiled rice or potato soup or a nameless, sticky gruel. Sometimes there was meat in the stuff.

Many survivors shunned those scraps of meat, for rumor said that it came from harvested humans. Jaime didn't listen to the rumors, and he didn't look too closely at the meat. Yeah, tonight's rations might have a few bits of Rahni Singh mixed in, sure, but he simply closed off his thinking mind and ate it. He'd also eaten cockroaches when he could find them, and rats, and crollygogs, *anything* he could catch, anything to add protein to his diet, to keep body and mind intact.

He *was* interested in the rice, however. Rice was a labor-intensive crop both in the planting and the harvesting. Machines didn't need food, and the rice meant that someone, somewhere on Cloud was still growing it. He found a dry spot outside, against the old factory's eastern wall, with Dieter and Wal to

his left and Alita on his right. They ate with their
fingers, saying nothing for a long time. In the east,
the looming bulk of Delamar, the larger, inner moon,
was slowly crawling into the sky, almost half full, the
lighted portion bowed away from the horizon.
Delamar was big and it was close, less than fifty
thousand kilometers out, and its crater-pocked horns
spanned a full ten degrees of sky, the dark side
blotting out the shining star-glory beyond. Here and
there, diamond pinpoints of light glowed on Delamar's
night side. Once those had been human cities; now,
presumably, the Masters ruled there as they ruled
Cloud. One story that continued to filter through
the camp held fervently that Delamar had not been
taken, that those cities were still free, that the
remnants of the CDF flew ships from Delamar each
night to scoop up a few lucky slaves and carry them
off to freedom in the sky.

Most of the former CDF personnel knew better,
of course. The clackers would have been foolish to
leave human garrisons so close to the newly conquered
world. The stories, though, like hope itself, simply
would not die.

"There's got to be a weakness there," he said,
speaking very quietly. No one yet knew just how
sensitive the hearing of clacker spies was, or how thickly
strewn their listening devices might be.

"What weakness?" Alita asked. "Who?"

"The clackers," Wal replied. "He's been going on
about it all day."

"The cluckers have weaknesses, I'm sure," Dieter
said. "Don't see what we can do about it, though."

"We can *learn*."

A solitary floater eye drifted past, paused, then
turned its disturbing, solitary orb on the four of them
for a moment. Then it drifted away again, randomly
checking other groups of slaves, maintaining that

constant, fear-stirring knowledge that the Masters' eyes and ears and thoughts were *everywhere*, inescapable, unbeatable.

When her bowl was scraped clean, Alita set it carefully aside. "What weakness?" she asked again.

"Why do they have us sifting through the mud for every last scrap of refined metal? Every shard of broken glass, every piece of plastic? Jewelry stripped from skeletons. Bric-a-brac and smashed kitchen appliances and eating utensils and the plumbing pulled from the bones of burned-out buildings. They cleaned up most of the easy-to-reach stuff, all the big pieces, right after the invasion. Hell, they must have gotten ninety-five percent of everything within a few weeks after they moved in. Why so much effort for that last five percent?"

"They are machines," Dieter reminded him. "They are efficient."

"Efficient? Using half-starved slaves isn't efficient."

"I told you," Wal reminded him. "We can't attribute human concepts of need or efficiency to the clackers."

"But it doesn't make sense. Look, they want every scrap of glass we can find . . . but all they need to do is scoop up sand from Cloud's beaches, and they could make all the glass they could ever need. Aluminum? Delamar's regolith is rich in aluminum silicates, easily extracted, easily processed with a simple solar furnace. Ceramics?" He brushed absently at the crust of dried mud on his right forearm. "All they need to do is gather clay, shape it, and bake it. I think the weirdest thing, though, is their craving for iron and steel. Any spacefaring civilization has access to all of the iron ore it could possibly use simply by collecting and processing asteroids."

"Cloud's suns have three separate planetoid belts," Dieter said, nodding. "You're right. The cluckers could get all the nickel-iron they wanted by mining the belts. Other stuff, too. Gold. Uranium. Platinum. Just about anything they need, and enough of it to last for centuries. Compared to what they could get cheaply and easily out there, this scavenger hunt in the ruins is nothing."

"Right," Jaime said. "So where are their orbital smelters, their asteroid mining ships, their deep space ore processors?"

"Maybe they're there," Wal pointed out. "We're hardly in a position to see their belt activities, are we?"

"No, wait," Alita said. "Dieter put his finger on it. If they had access to belt resources, there'd be absolutely no point to collecting broken glass or gold rings. Why bother with steel clasps from rotted clothing, when one small nickel-iron asteroid will provide you with all the steel you need for the next thousand years or so? It's *stupid*."

"If we knew why they act this way," Jaime told the others, "it might give us a weapon."

"Don't see how," Dieter said.

"Knowledge is always a weapon," Jaime told him. "You just have to learn how to apply it."

"You're getting at something," Wal suggested.

"Maybe." He scooped up the last of the rice and chewed thoughtfully. "Maybe," he said again after a long pause. "I'm going out to see Hector tonight."

"You think that's wise, Major?" Alita said. "With Delamar coming up—"

"The clackers can see in the dark," he reminded her. "I'll be no safer with a moon and the starclouds up than I would be on a pitch-black cloudy night. Sometimes, I think they know . . . and don't care."

"Enough people go up the hill to take the Hector Option," Wal said. "Yeah, you could be right."

Alita laid one slim hand on Jaime's arm. "You . . . *will* come back?"

"I'll be back," he told her. "I'm not ready to option out yet."

Inside, though, he wasn't as confident as he sounded. One of these days, he was pretty sure he would take the Hector Option.

It was, everyone agreed, the best, the *cleanest* ending available in this nightmare of filth, suffering, and death.

CHAPTER TWO

Until now the night has been silent, but I am now detecting motion and the crackle of dry brush coming up the hill from the east. My port-side thermal sensors focus on the anomaly, resolving it as an organic, a human male who has worked his way through the power fence encircling the encampment and is jogging toward my position with evident determination. I track the target until it reaches my preset defensive perimeter, at a range of fifty meters.

"Halt," I command, the words part of an old, old sentry routine left intact by the Masters for this purpose. "Identify yourself."

There is no answer, but the organic has stopped at the fifty-meter perimeter. It is breathing hard; I sense the pounding of its heart, the puffs of hot air escaping from its lungs at one-second intervals. It is staring up at me, its eyes great, dark patches in the livid reds and yellows of the thermal image of its face. It is carrying something which takes me .0032 second to identify: a piece of wood, probably a piece of a tree branch, massing eight hundred grams and measuring no more than half a meter in length. Its tracks, visible as a succession of fading green footprints on the cooler

25

*ground behind it, mark the unsteady lurchings of its
run up the hill. The organic, I realize, is operating at
the very limits of its endurance.*

*"You are not authorized to be here," I tell it. "Return
to your assigned quarters immediately."*

*In answer, the organic screams, a 102-decibel shout
that conveys no useful information. At the same instant,
the target raises the branch, brandishing it as it steps
across the fifty-meter perimeter line.*

*My response is automatic. My number one port-side
antipersonnel battery fires, a single short, sharp pulse
of electrical power energizing the railgun's magfield
along superconducting tracks.*

The scream cuts off instantly.

The night is silent once more.

Jaime heard the slave's shriek of rage and frustration
and terror in the darkness at the top of the hill, and
he heard the ringing *chink* as the Bolo triggered a
round from one of its lateral A-P batteries, chopping
off the screamed challenge as abruptly as if flicking
off a switch.

The Hector Option.

He wondered who the man had been, wondered if
he'd known him.

Jaime let fifteen minutes pass before he rose from
his hiding place behind a tumbled-down building and
started moving carefully up the hill. Generally, the
Masters didn't even investigate when Hector killed
another straying slave, but sometimes they did, and
he didn't want to stumble into enemy sensor range.

Getting out of the camp was simple, an open secret
long ago passed to everyone by word of mouth. The
latrines that served the sanitary needs of the slave camp
were crude affairs, benches with holes cut into an open
platform raised above a creek that flowed along the
camp's western boundaries. At the southwest corner

of the camp, the stream flowed through a ditch beneath the power fence; escape was as simple as scrambling into the ditch behind the latrine platform and wading downstream, crawling through the noisome muck to clear the powerfield, then clambering to dry land again above the point where the stream oozed into Celeste Harbor. During the past year, some hundreds of men and women had slipped out that way, some to take the Hector Option, others to attempt an escape into the wilds.

Had any of the escapees ever survived the armies of machines, the fields thickly planted with sensors and alarms, the hordes of ground-scuttling clickers and hovering floater eyes known to be patrolling the area around Celeste? There was no way of knowing, since any escapees who were captured were harvested. Sometimes, the clackers would display some of the gruesomely harvested parts the next morning. Other times, there was no word, and the slaves remaining in the barracks and the pits allowed themselves to hope that there might actually be the possibility of escape.

But the Hector Option was so much surer an escape from the unrelenting pain. Few would risk vivisection simply to taste a few hours' freedom. And few imagined that those who escaped could remain free for long.

As near as he could tell, there'd been no response from the machines. Below him, a few slaves were moving about among the shanties and tents outside the ruined factory, and to the southeast, the dig was filled with the late-night shift of slaves, continuing to enlarge the pits. Beyond, the flooded crater shone huge and oval and silver in the moonlight. Jaime could see machines moving along the crater's edge, tiny black specks silhouetted against the light as they went about their business. The Collector bulked huge by the crater lake, sinister and black.

Nothing was moving nearby, however. On Overlook Hill, at least, Jaime had the night to himself.

Quietly, he began climbing again. The southeastern slope of Overlook Hill had once been a residential area of neat, terraced parks and the single-home dwellings of some of Celeste's well-to-do. Every structure had been razed by the blast, but the ground was well above the water table and out of the reach of the tidal wave that had inundated the collapsing waterfront and public square. Large blocks of ferrocrete, the crumbled remains of some of the arcology towers from the center of town, littered the hillside like a giant child's cast-off building blocks, leaving terrain that was difficult to traverse but ideal as cover.

Toward the top of the hill, the rubble began thinning out; the crest of Overlook Hill had once been a park, but the impact blast had swept the crown bare of trees, grass, monuments, even paving stones. Shortly after the slave camp had been installed in the wreckage of the old factory, however, the Masters had brought in Hector, the huge and battlescarred Mark XXXIII Bolo captured in the fight for Celeste. The Bolo, ignominiously, was now a kind of huge and vastly overqualified prison guard, posted on the hilltop overlooking the camp and blocking the main road out. South of the slave camp was the harbor and the slave-worked ruins between the waterfront and the crater. East and north were more ruins, endless kilometers of them, occupied by uncounted thousands of scavenging alien machines and by the machines' constructs, bizarre and inexplicable shapes and structures seemingly grown from the city rubble. There was no escape in that direction.

Overlook Hill, to the west of the camp, offered the only real hope of escape, the more so because buildings and the Coastal Highway to the northwest had been in the shadow of Overlook Hill when the meteor fell. The slaves, more than once in the past year, had discussed the best way to get clear of Celeste and the occupying army of machines; an escape overland northwest was clearly the best option.

The only thing in the way was the Bolo.

Jaime reached the edge of the larger rubble just below the crest of the hill, lying on his belly as he studied the crouching machine. By the light of Delamar in the east, he could just make out the massive, hulking sprawl of the thing, a long, flat body supported by six sets of double tracks, three to a side. Each road wheel was better than two meters tall, and the slabs of meter-thick duralloy armor sloped and angled above the monster's skirts like the faceted cliff sides of a small mountain.

The Bolo Mark XXXIII, series HCT *Hecate*, was the largest and most powerful ground weapon ever constructed by humankind. It massed 32,000 tons, as much as a fair-sized star cruiser, and its primary armament was more in keeping with spaceborne naval forces than with ground armor—three squat turrets, each as big as a house, each mounting a 200cm Hellbore, a weapon better suited for battleships and combat in the wide reaches of deep space than for any planetary surface. Rows of ball turrets along both flanks, twenty in all, mounted 20cm Hellbore infinite repeaters—weapons that, back in the era of the Mark XIV Bolo, would each have been considered primary weapons in their own right. Tertiary support weapons included a VLS missile system, a battery of 240cm howitzers, and 40cm BL mortars incorporated into a true planetary siege platform. Its designers had been confident that Bolo *Hecate* was easily the most powerful military ground weapon in the galaxy.

They'd been wrong, of course. Hector, as the CDF had nicknamed the machine, had gone into battle against the clacker landing boats hours after the destruction of Celeste and had ceased operations only minutes later. The enemy had taken Hector out with terrifying ease. More terrifying still had been the ease with which they'd circumvented the Bolo's programming, turning it from a human weapon into one of their mindless, mechanical creatures, an automaton hooked into the Master's planet-girdling, cybernetic web. Hector was back in service now, but he was working for the enemy. Humans who approached too closely, or who tried to escape past the Bolo, were chopped down by hypervelocity antipersonnel flechettes.

Clearly, the clackers could have reduced Hector to scrap if they'd wanted. *Was there another clue here to the enemy's weakness?* Jaime wondered. That monster on the hilltop represented 32,000 tons of duralloy, ceramplast laminates, and other high-tech materials, including refined metals ranging from steel to appreciable amounts of technetium, praseodymium, and ytterbium. Simply by junking that one Bolo, captured during the Battle of Celeste, the enemy could have won far more purified metals and other materials than they could ever hope to salvage by slave labor from the muck and rubble of the city.

Was it possible that they recognized the Bolo as kin, as a fellow AI machine? Did they have rules about killing other sentient machines? Could they be affected by sentiment, or was it something more practical than that?

That hardly seemed likely, but Jaime was determined to find out.

The Bolo was a good hundred meters from the edge of the rubble field; Jaime knew from experience that he would be challenged at fifty meters . . . or if he tried to move past the Bolo and on toward the northwest. Walking in what he hoped was a casual fashion, empty hands in clear view, he started for the monster.

With each step, the Bolo loomed larger, a smooth-surfaced, artificial mountain, all angles, curves, and duralloy teardrops. The Mark XXXIII's stats, long ago committed to memory, simply could not do justice to the sheer monstrous bulk of the thing. One-hundred-twenty meters long, thirty-eight meters wide, with three massive main-armament turrets rising from a main deck twenty-five meters above the ground, the Bolo was more like a huge, squat, elongated building—hell, like an armed and armored *town*—than a fighting vehicle. Thirty-two thousand tons. It was outmassed by heavy cruisers, battleships, and naval transports, but as a mobile weapons platform, well, nothing else on land even came close.

Damn. *How* had the clackers taken down a Mark XXXIII so easily?

He reached the Line, a perimeter fifty meters from the Bolo's hull made all too visible by the stains and bones of past visitors to this place. There was a small ridge here, formed from piled-up bones and decayed flesh, an artificial ridge marking the line, sharp and crisp on the side facing the Bolo and splashed out in a thinning slope downhill. What was left after someone took the Hector Option wasn't worth salvaging by clackers, and the parts were left to rot where they fell. The stench of death was thick and throat-catching here. The hot taste of fresh, coppery blood overlaid and mingled with the sweeter musk of older decay.

The most recent addition to the hillock of bones lay a few meters to Jaime's right. The suicide's bare legs and hips lay steaming on the cool ground, bloody at the top but almost intact, but everything from the navel up was simply gone, smeared into a fresh, bloody spray down the eastern side of Overlook Hill. There wasn't much that was recognizable; Jaime did see a disembodied right hand nearby, the fingers still locked clawlike around a branch from a long-dead tree.

Novel approach, he thought wryly. *Attacking a Bolo with a club.*

The Bolo *Hecate's* primary AP weapons were lateral banks of mag-driven railguns, each firing a cluster of needle-slender, steel-jacketed slivers of depleted uranium with a muzzle velocity in excess of three kilometers per second. Five hundred needle-darts, shotgunned into a human target at *that* velocity left very little behind that was recognizably human.

"Halt," the Bolo said as Jaime reached the line, its voice a rich, pleasing tenor with the distinct overtones and inflections of human speech. "Identify yourself."

He heard the whir of servo motors as the snouts of a half dozen AP weapons tracked his movement, heard the rising whine of superconductor coils powering up to max. The slightest of electronic twitches from the behemoth squatting above him on the hilltop, Jaime knew, and his remains would be splashed across the slope at his back in a brutally unrecognizable smear.

"Major Jaime Graham, First Armored Assault Brigade, Cloud Defense Force," he announced in as clear a voice as he could muster.

"Present code authorization."

"Authorization Code Tango," he replied. He tried to keep the quaver out of his voice. "Three-three-seven Victor Delta niner. Maintenance."

"This unit is not scheduled for standard maintenance," the Bolo said. The words were stiff, and a bit formal. As human as the voice might sound, there was no mistaking the AI, the machine mind behind the words.

"Override Security Alpha," Jaime recited. Alita had drilled him in the protocol repeatedly ever since he'd first dared approach the beast. She'd been Hector's crew chief, part of the team that had kept him running. "Code Delta Echo One-one."

"Advance, Major Graham."

Jaime stepped past that blood-traced perimeter, conscious that the AP railguns continued to track him as he walked. Carefully, unwilling to make any sudden or surprising moves, he made his way to the Bolo's prow, close enough that the glacis sloped up and away from him like an eighty-foot cliff.

"I've come to talk," Jaime told the Bolo.

There was no reply, though he had the impression that the machine was studying him closely. That fact by itself was interesting. A Mark XXXIII possessed a fully autonomous psychotronic AI and hyper-heuristic programming; ever since the introduction of the Mark XXIV, Bolos had begun developing personalities of their own that, at times, could seem strikingly, eerily human.

This was the third time that Jaime had made this trip up the hill, and each time he'd come away with the distinct impression that Hector was shackled somehow, limited in his thoughts, hampered in the way he expressed himself. It was a little like talking to a child, and a stubborn and not-too-bright child at that. The Masters were responsible, clearly. But what had they done to the Bolo's artificial intelligence, and how?

Maybe he should allow Alita to come up here and see what she could learn. She'd volunteered after his first visit, but he'd put her off, and eventually he'd had to order her to stay clear. If he was caught up here, he knew of a way to trigger a burst from a flechette gun, and he would be just another suicide. If Alita were caught with Hector, though, the results could be catastrophic. It was possible that the enemy knew that she had once worked with Bolos. If the machines made the logical conclusion, that a Bolo tech was trying to reprogram their pet Bolo, they might well kill every human left alive on the planet.

He was beginning to wonder, though, if getting her up here to talk to Hector wouldn't be worth even that risk. He was getting nowhere, and he was running out of ideas.

"Do you remember me coming up here before?" he asked at last.

"Yes." Just that one word, without elaboration. Mark XXXIIIs could be downright chatty at times, and they could certainly carry their end of a conversation with animation enough that humans communicating with them by audio only might never guess they were speaking with an artificial intelligence. This one had once had the reputation of being almost philosophical at times, with a love of metaphor that could be almost poetic.

Now, though, Hector was no more communicative than a Mark XIX, the last mark before the breakthrough in psychotronics that had led to self-aware, self-volitional Bolos. Jaime had never worked directly with Bolos in his military career, but he'd learned a thing or two about them. Bolos, after all, were the last word in ground combat.

At least, they had been until humanity had encountered the !°!°!.

"Do you remember the battle with the clackers . . . with the Masters?"

There was an uncomfortable pause, and Jaime had the distinct feeling that the machine was working at something, thinking it over . . . or possibly struggling to remember. There was no outward sign of struggle, but that pause . . .

"Negative," it said at last.

"Do you remember *any* battles?" Hector's battle logs were impressive. Since he'd rolled off the Bolo Plant assembly lines at Durandel almost three centuries ago,

Bolo *Hecate* of the Line Number 28373 had participated in twenty-nine major battles and some hundreds of skirmishes, police actions, and deployments. "Do you remember the Stand at Grauve?"

"Negative."

"Third Sardunar?" Hector had won the Triple Star of Valor for that one, shortly before he'd been shipped to Cloud with the First Armored. The decoration was still there, atop many others, welded to the Honors Ring on his glacis.

"Negative. I have no record of having participated in any combat."

Helplessly, Jaime shook his head. What the machines had done to the human population of Cloud was horrific, enslaving and murdering them on a planetary scale. What they'd done to Hector was horrific on an individual level; somehow, they'd managed to steal the Bolo's very soul, if he had one. Instead of cleanly killing him, they'd robbed him of himself, robbed him of who and what he was.

Well, in a sense, that was what they'd done to the human population as well.

"Hector, run a full diagnostic on yourself, please. Level One. Check your holographic memory and all heuristic acquisition functions, please."

Again, that long hesitation. A Level One diagnostic took something like a third of a second. Unless there was something seriously wrong, the answer should have come back in an instant.

"Diagnostic complete. All operations and systems are nominal."

"Like hell they are." Rising, he walked around to the right side of the Bolo. High overhead, perhaps eight meters off the ground, the dark gray cliff of armor was pocked by a hole, a crater over two meters across just above the right forward track assembly. Something had melted its way through a meter of solid duralloy, penetrating battle screens and armor alike with equal ease.

What had the weapon been? What had it *done* to him?

"Hector, there is a large hole in your armor above your Number Three road wheel. Please run a local diagnostic and describe the damage."

The pause was even longer this time, long enough for Jaime to walk back around to the other side.

"Diagnostic complete. All operations and systems are nominal."

Something, clearly, was interfering with either Hector's autodiagnostics or his memory . . . or both. Jaime was up against a wall, as he'd been on each of his earlier visits. Talking to the Bolo was an exercise in highly circularized hypermobility, a great way to get nowhere fast.

There was a whir and a clatter of motion from the Bolo's left-side antipersonnel batteries. The blunt, ugly railgun muzzles pivoted, seeking a target in the near-darkness.

"What is it?" Jaime asked the machine.

"Target approaching from the east," the Bolo replied. "Bearing zero-nine-eight, range one hundred twelve meters."

Jaime moved to a point where he could see back down the eastern slope of the hill. He could make out the slave camp and, further south, the dig, the crater, and the sprawl of the ruined city, but he couldn't see anything that might have triggered the Bolo's threat warnings.

"Are you sure? I don't see a thing."

"Affirmative. Bearing zero-nine-seven, range one hundred eight meters, and closing."

The target must be just behind the nearest piles of rubble, down below the crest of the hill. It was dark and he could see nothing but the vague shapes of shattered houses, but the Bolo, he knew, could draw on senses extending far beyond merely human scope and reach.

"Is it a machine?" He moved closer to the Bolo, hoping that his silhouette was lost against the dark mass of the big machine. If the !°!°! found him here, he could not rely on Hector to protect him. Quite the contrary, in fact. It was distinctly possible that Hector's new masters could order him to squash the human slave crouching in his shadow like a small and insignificant insect.

"Negative. The target is human."

Human! That might mean another suicide, someone coming up to take the Hector Option. It could also be a turner, maybe one who'd seen him slipping out of camp or scrambling out of the sewage trench and who'd decided to follow him. Turners were rewarded by their Masters for such diligence, with better food, dry clothing, and even their choice of bedmates, male or female, from among the slave population.

At least a human opponent would offer surmountable odds. Jaime had no illusions about how a wrestling match with a clacker would end, especially with him as weak as he was now.

"Range eighty-nine meters."

He saw him . . . no, *her*. It was a woman, tall, slender. Her face, body, and long hair were mud-smeared. She wore more than most of the slaves did nowadays, a ragged pair of cutoffs; there was no silver band on her forehead, though. She was no trusty.

A slave, then, come to find a quick and relatively painless ending to the pain. She kept coming up the slope, stumbling, weaving a little as she walked. She faltered when she reached the bloody, sharp-edged ridge delineating the fifty-meter line. Then she squared her shoulders and kept on coming.

"Halt," the Bolo said, and the word was so sudden

that Jaime started at the sound. "Identify yourself."

She kept coming, one bare foot stepping across the ridge of bones and decaying flesh. Jaime heard the power-up whine of the railguns.

"No!" he shouted suddenly, stepping out of the shadows beneath the Bolo. "Weapon release countermanded!"

"What is your authorization?"

Authorization? All he had was the maintenance code Alita had given him, a code to allow humans to approach the monster and live. He prayed he could make it work. "Authorization Code Tango, three-three-seven Victor Delta niner! Maintenance!"

"This unit is not scheduled for standard maintenance," the Bolo said.

"Override Security Alpha, Code Delta Echo One-one."

"Identify yourself," the Bolo repeated.

The woman was standing just inside the fifty-meter line, her face pale as she looked from Bolo to human and back again.

"C'mon!" Jaime called to her. "Tell him your name!"

"Sh-Shari Barstowe," she said, with a voice that cracked halfway through.

"Are you with the maintenance team?" the Bolo asked.

When the woman didn't answer, Jaime called to her again. "Tell him *yes!*"

"Y-yes. I am."

"Advance, Technician Barstowe."

The woman was swaying a little on her feet, too dazed to respond. With a quick glance back at Hector, and the array of flechette launchers still aimed at Shari, Jaime sprinted across the open ground, catching her just before she collapsed where she stood. Gently, he helped her cross the last fifty meters to the Bolo's side and sat her down, her back against the hard duralloy of one of the titanic road wheels.

"I thought . . . I was dead."

"You damned near were. What the hell were you trying to do here?"

"What do you think?" she shot back. "I've taken all I'm going to take. Hector here was going to be my ticket out." Her eyes widened. "My God! How did we, how did you get in this—"

"Easy. Hector is a friend of mine. You just have to know how to talk to him."

"Some friend. You've, you've ruined everything."

"I thought I just saved your life."

"You don't understand," she said, opening her eyes. "I *want* to die. . . ."

"I'm sorry. I know how you feel, Miss Barstowe. Believe me, I know! But I couldn't just stand by and watch Hector blow you away."

"I just . . . I just don't know if I can steel myself to try again. It took days to work up . . . the courage."

"Not a problem. Killing yourself doesn't take nearly as much courage as deciding to keep on living."

"Who . . . who are you? Are you free? No, wait. I've seen you in the camp."

"Jaime Graham," he said. "Block Seven, Group Thirty-one."

She nodded. "I'm Block Four, Group Twenty-five."

"Over on the other side of the barracks." Jaime wasn't sure how many slaves there were now, in all. New ones were brought in occasionally as they were rounded up outside the devastation that was Celeste, and those in the camp tended to die at an appalling rate. The best estimates, though, held that there were between five and seven thousand people crowded into the slave camp . . . far too many for any one person to have gotten to know individually, or even to have seen them all. Still, Shari's face was familiar, and he was sure he'd crossed paths with her before, possibly at the chow line, possibly in the dig.

"So what are you doing out here?"

"Like I said, talking to my friend, here."

Her eyes widened. "You were with the Bolo Corps! Before The Killing!"

He shook his head. "No. I wish I had been. It would make understanding this big guy a lot easier."

"Oh. You didn't know Captain Fowler, then."

"Captain Fowler?"

"Jeff Fowler? He was the Bolo's human counterpart. The commander."

"Someone you knew?"

She shrugged, a small, lost movement of her shoulders. "Jeff and I were . . . lovers. I wasn't military," she added quickly, answering his immediate question. "I was a civilian, a cyberneticist, working at Chryse."

"A cyberjock! On the Bolo staff?"

She nodded.

"So you know how his AI works."

"Well, after a fashion. Don't get excited, though. I don't know how the clackers got control of Hector, and I don't know what they've done to him since." She turned slightly, looking up at the mountain of black metal above her. "I don't even know if the clackers . . . made him one of themselves, somehow."

"They're not listening in on us right now, if that's what you mean," Jaime told her. "I've been up here several times before, and while I haven't gotten very far with my conversations with Hector, he's never called for the guards to come get me. I think they just set him up here, wound him up, and let him go. Maybe they get periodic updates, I don't know. But we're safe enough for the moment."

"Safe . . ." She shuddered.

"Alien concept. I know." He studied her narrowly. Her hair, he thought, was blond, though it was hard to tell through the dried, caked-on mud. Her eyes had a dull and listless look . . . but there was a spark of keen intelligence there, a life that existence in the slave camp had not entirely extinguished. "You don't really want to kill yourself."

She looked at him, one eyebrow arched. "Don't I? What gives you such dazzling insight? You don't even know me."

"I know that if you had to work so hard to get your courage up, then you must've been having second thoughts, plenty of 'em. Like me."

"You?"

"First time I came up here, oh, must've been six weeks ago, or so, I came for the same reason you did. To take the Hector Option."

"What happened?"

He pursed his lips, then pointed. "I stood on that heap of bones, right over there, for ten, maybe fifteen minutes, trying to work up my courage to step across, and all the time wondering when some damned floater was going come up behind me, throw out a tentacle, and drag me down for a quick vivisection. I thought about all the people who'd come up here before me and left nothing behind but bones and some stains on the ground. Mostly, I guess I thought about the Bolo. His challenge was so . . . I don't know. So flat. Lifeless. Not at all like he was before The Killing."

"You did know Hector then, before . . ."

"Oh, yes. I was CO of Second Battalion, First Armored Division. I didn't work with the Bolo Corps directly that much, but I was based at Chryse, and I got to talk with Hector a couple of times." He smiled gently. "I probably met your Captain Fowler, though I don't remember the name now. Good bunch of people. Anyway, I stood there on the bone hill and thought that if I could find out how the machines had changed Hector, how they'd rewired him or whatever, maybe I could figure out how to fix him."

"Yes? Then what?"

"Beats the hell out of me. I sic him on the cluckers, I guess. After that, well, maybe they send in their landers again, or they drop more rocks on us . . . but I figure that's better than what's happening to us now, dying by centimeters. Or maybe we kick their circuits the hell off of Cloud, and we start rebuilding. All I know is that *anything* that happened would be better than what we have now."

Shari was nodding slowly, thoughtfully. "I don't know if you have a chance of fixing whatever they did to him. It has to be a hardwired job, not software."

"I was thinking the same thing. One of the people in my block, back at the camp, was Hector's maintenance crew chief."

Shari's eyebrows went up. "A short woman? Dark hair? Muscles like—"

"Alita Kyle."

"That's her!"

"Sometimes I think Alita knows more about the nuts and bolts of a Mark XXXIII than the guys who designed the thing."

"She's good. I worked with her on some upgrades to his infinite repeaters, oh, about a year before The Killing."

"You know, Miss Barstowe," he went on, "it occurs to me that we're assembling quite a useful Bolo operations team here. A bunch of us are former military officers, and we know combat tactics and theory. Me. Colonel Prescott. And General Spratly, of course. You know him?"

"I know he's the nominal commanding officer of the camp, whatever that means. I never met him personally when he was at Chryse, though."

"Hmm. And then there's Dieter Hollinsworth. His specialty is high-energy physics. Tamas Reuter. He was an astronomer, but he also knows math . . . and computer theory. And now . . . you, if you'll join us.

We could sure use a cyberneticist. Otherwise, we're shooting in the dark when it comes to figuring out what's wrong with Hector."

"I . . . don't know."

"Don't know if you can? Or don't know if you want to?"

"I don't know . . . if I can keep going on. Things've been . . . bad, lately."

"Well, there's always tomorrow."

"What do you mean?"

"Work with us, and you've got hope," he told her. "Something to hang on to, anyway. And if it gets to be too much, if the hope isn't enough . . ."

"I can come back up here. Tomorrow."

"Will you join our little cabal? Help us out?"

She took a long time to answer. "I'll . . . try," she said at last.

"Maybe we should get on back, then," he said. "I don't think the cluckers make rounds up here. At least I've never seen them. But we don't want to be caught inside Hector's fifty-meter perimeter."

She sighed. "Another swim through the sewer."

"Believe me," he told her. "You can put up with lots worse."

"I already have."

Together, they started back down the hill.

CHAPTER THREE

They made their way together back down the hill. They saw no one, though once, for several heart-pounding minutes, they lay crouched in the shadows of a gaping, stone-walled basement after Jaime heard the distinctive *clink* of metal scraping stone. After wading up the sewage ditch and back within the invisible walls of the compound, they took a few moments to wash themselves off in the stream above the latrine, removing the worst of the stench clinging to their bodies. The idea was to slip back into the barracks without attracting attention to themselves. There were almost certainly informers among the slaves . . . or, at the least, minute and easily concealed listening devices.

At the entrance to the wrecked factory building, they touched hands lightly, then went their separate ways. Jaime sank onto his rag pile gratefully; the climb up and down Overlook Hill took a lot out of him, and the longer he worked in the dig, he knew, the weaker he would become. The knowledge lent a definite urgency to any timetable the tiny conspiracy decided to adopt.

He was awakened before dawn for the next work

shift and spent the next twelve hours in the mud west of the crater, digging for bits of glass, plastic, and technology. Most of the time, though, his mind was back on Overlook Hill, studying the problem of what Hector had become . . . and how the small but growing band of military and civilian personnel could fix him.

The suns were still up when the shift ended, and Jaime and several thousand other men and women trudged the three kilometers back to the barracks. Chow time was not scheduled until after suns-set; the conspirators, Jaime, Alita, Dieter, and Wal, all met by the eastern wall of the old factory, and this time Shari Barstowe joined them.

When he introduced her, he didn't tell them—and she did not volunteer—that he'd met her on the bone pile at Hector's fifty-meter line.

"So you're telling us that Hector remembers some stuff, but not anything about the battle, or him getting taken over," Dieter said, thoughtful. "That's pretty weird. How could the Masters know our programming methods, how could they know Hector so well that they could reprogram him that way?"

"Bolobotomy," Wal said.

"I beg your pardon?" Dieter said.

"Sounds like Hector's received a Bolobotomy."

"Like a human lobotomy? He had part of his brain chopped out?"

"Well, not quite that," Shari said. "Remember, you can't just carve a piece of a Bolo's memory out with a filleting knife."

"That's right," Alita said. "Holographic memory."

"You just lost me," Jaime said. He made a swishing motion above his head with his hand. "Right over."

"Yes, well," Shari said. "Do you understand the concept of holographic memory?"

Jaime frowned. "I know what a holograph is."

"Yeah," Wal added. "A three-D comm transmission."

"That's not what I'm talking about."

"The language has changed with the technology," Tamas pointed out. "The word holographic is Old Anglic, no, earlier than that. Late English, maybe. Definitely prespaceflight."

"Right," Shari said. "The very first holographs were still photos that showed holographic properties. The subject—let's say it's your Great Aunt Matilda—would be photographed using laser light that bathed her from several directions. The laser beams, then, reflected back, would pass through a piece of film, which would record, not the light, as with a normal chemical process, but the interference patterns caused when you brought the separate laser beams together again. Today it's all done with pattern fields and force lenses, of course. Back then, the film was a square of chemically treated plastic. Later, when you shine a laser through the film with its interference patterns, pow! There you see, floating before you, the three-dimensional image of Aunt Matilda, once more in all her glory!"

"Okay . . ." Jaime said, uncertain. He couldn't see where Shari was going with this.

"The interesting thing about that process was the film. You look at it, and you see nothing like the original subject. Not like a traditional photographic negative, where you could see the subject's image in reverse."

"Right," Tamas said, nodding. "You see only smears and blurs and rings."

"Say you cut off one corner of the piece of film," Shari said. "Does the holographic image of Aunt Matilda suddenly lose a head or an arm? No! The entire image is still intact . . . maybe with a little less resolution, a little less crispness and clarity. So you cut some more off, you cut the film in half. Matilda is still there, *all* of her, but fuzzy, with detail lost.

"Do you see?" Shari continued. "In that one piece of film, information allowing reconstruction of the

entire image exists *everywhere* on the film's surface.
You could snip the tiniest piece from one corner of
the film, shine your laser through it, and still get the
complete image of Aunt Matilda, though it might be
too blurry and lacking in detail for you to see her very
well."

"Except for the fact that I don't have a Great Aunt
Matilda," Jaime told her, "I'm following you. But what
does all of this have to do with—"

"With Bolo memory." She nodded. "I was just getting
to that. Now I won't go into how psychotronic memory
works. In fact, humans have used various systems over
the years for the storage and transmission of data, and
the actual physical process isn't important. But you
can picture a Bolo's memory like that square of film
with the holograph of Aunt Matilda. It is a whole, with
the information uniformly dispersed across the entire
memory field."

"Right!" Tamas said. "Chop a piece out of it,
somehow, and the Bolo doesn't suddenly forget what
it had for breakfast yesterday. No, it still remembers
everything, though maybe the detail, the resolution,
isn't quite what it was before. You cannot *selectively*
destroy pieces of a Bolo's memory."

Jaime mulled this over for a moment. "Then how
do you explain Hector's behavior? He acts like he has
some kind of selective amnesia. He doesn't remember
anything important . . . like who or what he is, or what
happened on Cloud. I can't be sure, but sometimes I
get the impression that he *is* remembering, but then
just as quickly he's forgotten again. Whatever it was,
it's gone."

"That's quite possible, you know," Alita put in. "It
sounds like a data shunt."

"What's that?"

"She's right," Shari said.

She scratched absently beneath her left breast. "I

was thinking along those lines myself." She hesitated, as though trying to think how best to explain it. "Once Hector calls up a particular memory . . . let's say it's the result of one of his autodiagnostics."

"Yeah. That's a good one."

"Okay. He runs the diagnostic. He gets the result. All sorts of things are wrong."

"Yeah, starting with a big fat hole in his side."

"Right. The data is routed first to his storage memory, where it's incorporated into the whole, then routed up to his working memory, what you might call his conscious mind."

"Working memory. That's different from the holographic memory you were talking about?"

"It is holographic. It's also part of the Bolo's overall memory system. But it is different, yes, a subset of the Bolo's memory, where it deals with the here and now, where it makes plans and interacts with its environment and does all the other things that an intelligent and self-aware creature does when it thinks. My guess is that the information passing from storage memory to working memory is being intercepted, somehow."

"*Physically* intercepted, you mean," Wal said. "You're saying there's some kind of clucker device buried inside Hector? Something that monitors the data coming through to his working memory and maybe reshuffles it?"

"Has to be," Alita said. "They wouldn't have been able to reprogram him from scratch."

"Why not?" Wal wanted to know.

"Clucker programming languages and protocols aren't the same as ours, obviously," Tamas pointed out. "Their machines can't possibly talk to our machines, unless they use some sort of a go-between, a translator."

"They must have learned something about how our

computers work," Jaime said, "or they couldn't have programmed the translator."

"There was the *Empyrion*," Wal reminded them. "She had computers, including psychotronic stuff. And she had people who knew how to program them."

Empyrion was one of the transports that had brought the original colonists to Cloud, two hundred T-years before. Refitted as an exploration vessel, the ship had been engaged in a long-range survey of local space, an outlying region of the galaxy's Western Arm . ... what Terran astronomers once had called the Sagittarian Arm from its location in the night skies of old Earth. Almost fifty T-standard years before, *Empyrion's* captain had reported picking up some odd E-M transmissions emanating from the direction of the Galactic Core and announced his intention of finding the source. Those transmissions were indecipherable but almost certainly a product of intelligence; contact with a hitherto unknown species was anticipated with some excitement.

But *Empyrion* had vanished, never to be heard from again. And the Masters, when they appeared, had entered Cloudan space from the direction of the Galactic Core.

"I think we can make a good guess about how this, this clucker device was placed inside Hector," Jaime said.

"The hole in his side," Alita said. "We still don't know how the enemy burned that into him, do we?"

"Their meteor strike took out the whole damned city," Wal pointed out. "Melting through a meter or so of duralloy wouldn't be a problem for them. Hector's battle screens would have been tougher to crack."

"They had *Empyrion's* battle screens as a model," Tamas pointed out. "They probably used a phase-shift cycler to get through the screens, then something like a fusion torch to melt through the armor. The question is what they put inside Hector, to scramble his circuits."

"We could go inside and find out," Jaime said.

"Eh?" Wal looked puzzled. "What's that?"

"I said we could go inside. Through the crater. It's big enough for someone my size to pass easily."

"Interesting thought. Then what?"

"We find out what they did to him, and fix it."

"It won't be that easy," Alita told him. "It's possible that there could still be spare parts on board. Ever since the Mark XXIX, Bolos have included an internal logistics/maintenance capability. But the cluckers might've stripped him of his spares. And even if they didn't, we don't have contra-gravity cranes or fusion forges, no duralloy slab rollers, no casting molds." She held up her hands, turning them palm-up, then palm-down. "We have nothing at all but these."

"And this," Jaime said, pointing to his head. "Hands and brains. That's all humans have ever had, really, all the way back to the Ice Age that spawned us. All the rest are incidentals."

"If we can find the mechanism that's affected Hector's operation," Shari said, "we should be able to initiate a reboot. Bring him back on line . . . all the way."

"Also, there's one tool we do have access to," Wal pointed out. "*It*. If ever there was a time . . ."

"Yeah," Jaime said, nodding slowly. *It* was never named aloud, just in case.

"Won't help with reprogramming Bolos," Alita added, "but it'll sure take care of any surprises the cluckers have planted inside him."

"I think," Jaime continued, thoughtful, "that it's time I went and talked with the general."

The ship was happy.

Well, to be precise—and all cognizant !*!*! were *always* precise—it wasn't the entire ship that was "happy," an emotional state possible only for fifth-level cognitives and above. The unit designated DAV728-24389, however, which was currently serving as primary activator of fortress/ship/factory MON924 Series 76, would have been ecstatic had its response parameter controls not been restricted, and even with the restrictions in place it couldn't help feeling an almost organic tickle of excitement, satisfaction, and pride.

According to the foldspace message just received, the Ninth Awareness Itself was arriving within 1.85×10^{14} nanoseconds to acknowledge DAV728's victory over the organics, at which time DAV would receive his fifth brain.

The !°!°! did not think in abstract terms such as "great honor" or "accomplishment," and in fact the addition of a fifth brain to DAV's current processor array was only logical and expected, given his success in this campaign. Nor was the abstract term "worthiness" a factor. All !°!°! were "worthy," at least insofar as all machines approved by inspectors for release from the natal assemblers performed to design specifications. Success, after all, was expected.

But on purely statistical grounds, it was definitely the case that stochastic chance had favored DAV by a significant margin, even allowing for the usual plus-or-minus due to the effects of chaos. If all !°!°! were worthy, a remarkably tiny percentage of the whole followed that slender and convoluted five-dimensional pathway of placement and action in space and time that could result in such distinguished success as his.

The ship's broad-spectrum sensors fed their input directly to DAV's first brain, allowing, when he willed it, an all-round panorama of space, including the local planet and its two satellites and, beyond, the encircling, frosty banks of stars, thick and turbulent this close in to the Galactic Core. Vast clouds of dark matter, gas and dust, obscured the center of the galaxy in the optical bands, but the simmering glow of radio emissions and the sparkling, sharper urgency of X-ray and gamma sources let DAV pick out the landmarks of home. From fifteen thousand light years away, it sensed the gush of antimatter, the annihilation of matter equivalent to tens of suns every few million nanoseconds.

It sensed the tragedy there, the tragedy of the !°!°!, without feeling anything like emotion. The !°!°! did not *feel*, not in the organic sense of the word.

DAV728—the list of alphanumerics were only an approximate translation of the string of modulated whistles, pops and !s comprising the unit's designator—acquired the data feed beacons of the !°!°! fleet and logged onto the primary command web. Approach clearance requested and granted, the fortress/ship/factory hurtled past outlying pickets and scouts, dropping deeper into the planet's gravity well, angling toward the innermost and larger of the two attendant natural satellites.

DAV decelerated as it guided the ship in for a landing on the moon, called "Delamar" by the organics. All human centers on the body had been occupied and long since converted to !°!°! purposes. On Delamar's primary, a world the locals inexplicably called "Cloud," the surviving population had been allowed to live, though some tens of thousands had been sequestered in special compounds as useful labor, spare parts, and of course, for research into their place within the Prime Code. Here on the inner satellite, however, there'd been no point in maintaining the oxygen-nitrogen atmosphere and temperatures that humans required for continued metabolism. The atmosphere had been released to the vacuum of space and the surviving life forms on Delamar had simply ceased functioning . . . the term, it had learned recently, was "died."

As the immense fortress/ship/factory gentled in on

humming contra-gravs at the largest of the Delamar
habitats, DAV could sense the surrounding Community
of machines, a gentle pulse and flickering of information
exchanged on numerous tight-beamed E-M frequencies,
from long, cool radio waves to the actinic stab of high-
frequency gamma rays. Though only a small fraction
of the transmitted information was directed at it, DAV
could extend electronic senses and sample the ocean
of data engulfing it, a comfortable and familiar environment that demonstrated a rightness to the universe.

As organics moved and lived within a sea of
atmosphere, the !°!°! had their being in a sea of
constantly shifting information. Coded challenges,
download requests, and replies, the electronic
equivalents of friendly greetings and hi-how-are-yous,
chattered between ship and base. A small army of
floaters appeared, rising from hatchways in the habitat
and drifting silently toward the docking facility. DAV
gave a series of whistling, chirping orders to its system
support complex, then began disconnecting itself from
the ship. Seconds later, its broad-spectrum, wide-angle
view of the universe clicked off, replaced an instant
later by the narrower, more claustrophobic confines
of a Series 52.

Snug in its new body, DAV swung down from the
recess in the ship's internal structure where the
elongated, smoothly sculpted form had rested for the
duration of the mission, slid into an exit well, and
emerged above the surface of Delamar. Other machines
similar to DAV passed on their way to service the MON
fortress-ship, Series 50s and 47s and one other 52. DAV
sensed the throbbing electronic web that connected
them all. The !°!°! were not a totally communal
intelligence or hive mind, like several that had been
annihilated within the past few millennia; individual
units retained individuality of thought, purpose, and
action. Still, the awareness of information flow and

data exchange was an important sense for the !°!°!, a sense as important as taste or magnetics were for the extinct Ka'Juur, or hearing seemed to be for these humans.

DAV entered the complex, passing through a low corridor littered with lifeless human bodies. The corpses had been allowed to lie where they'd fallen. Small-unit harvesters had already picked over the remains for useful spares, but most organic parts didn't hold up well to hard vacuum, and there'd been little recovered deemed useful.

Unfortunate, DAV thought with a flicker of passing interest and something that might almost have been regret, that the organics' brains had not been harvested before the complex of buildings had been opened to vacuum. The only living organics captured here were those who had been able to scramble into protective suits, a scant eighty-three out of the hundreds of organics inhabiting this population center alone. Inefficient. The Prime Code demanded that use be found for *all* recovered raw materials, and organic brains showed great promise in that regard, particularly as series add-ons and upgrades. It was distinctly possible that *that* was what the human organics were good for within the Prime Code's schema . . . but so much more research was necessary to learn how the organic brains functioned, and why they functioned as they did.

Perhaps, DAV thought, with its new elevation to five-brain status, it would be able to hasten the Prime Code's assimilation and learning process. The !°!°! would need every advantage in the coming struggle with the Grakaan of Dargurauth.

Yes, DAV728 decided, the thought racing back and forth between all four of its brains, there were going to be a number of necessary changes once it received its promotion. . . .

❖   ❖   ❖

Jaime hesitated outside the shack, then rapped sharply on the sheet tin beside the doorless frame. "Enter," a heavy voice said from within, and Jaime ducked to go in. Dieter, who'd accompanied Jaime on this visit, took up a nonchalant pose nearby where he could watch the comings and goings of floater eyes and possible snitches among the camp's inmates.

The senior-ranking military officer in the Camp was sprawled on a pile of rags, his back against a support post. Once, an eternity before, before The Killing, General Edgar Spratly had been lean and trim and hard, a recruiting poster of a man with eyes like chips of anthracite set deep beneath bushy brows. After almost a standard year at the Celeste Camp, however, it was as though he'd shrunken inside, and his skin sagged and hung on his heavy frame like a suit too big for its owner, and his one remaining eye had been dulled and softened by the endless horrors he'd seen.

A half dozen other men watched from the darkness encircling the room . . . young survivor officers whom Spratly had assigned as his personal staff. As far as Jaime could tell, though, his staff did little but serve as Spratly's personal retinue of yes-men and ego-boosters.

"General? It's good of you to see me."

Spratly grunted. "Pull up some floor."

Jaime sank gratefully to a bare patch of ground. He was tired from the day's labors and still feeling the effects of the long night preceding them.

"We may have a chance at Valhalla," Jaime said without preamble.

Spratly's eyes widened slightly, but he didn't answer immediately. Instead, he glanced at the walls of his dark shed in silent warning. *Careful what you say.*

Jaime glanced around the inside of the shanty. The general claimed to prefer this tiny, outlying building, which he called "HQ," to the communal claustrophobia of the ex-factory, which he shared with the members of his staff. There was less chance of being overheard, he said, though Jaime wondered how secure the clapboard-and-sheet-tin building really was. Still, it was possible to assign miraculous powers to the alien machines . . . and in so doing paralyze yourself with fears of what they might know or do.

Dieter was convinced that the cluckers didn't really care what their human slaves did, so long as they followed orders. It was as though they were convinced that they had nothing to fear from creatures so obviously as helpless and as insignificant as humans.

Well, Jaime thought, that could be an advantage for the humans as well. Overconfidence on the part of the enemy could be as great an ally as an operational Bolo.

"Would you rather talk outside?" Jaime asked.

Spratly glanced at his chief of staff, a wiry former captain, named Pogue. The man shrugged slightly.

"S'probably all right," Spratly said. "There haven't been any machines sniffing around HQ for a long time. But . . . keep your voice down."

"Of course . . . sir." The honorific came with difficulty to Jaime's lips. It was hard to see the general today, as he was now, and feel the same whipsnap of command he'd possessed as Jaime's commanding officer, back when the CDF had been in existence and military protocol still meant something. For a time, shortly after the lost Battle of Chryse, Spratly had maintained his rigid, military bearing, holding roll calls for military personnel, continuing to wear his uniform, even going so far as to organize an escape committee.

None of that had lasted beyond the first month or so. The roll calls had been pointless, especially since the staggered labor schedules meant some of the ex-military slaves were gone no matter when a meeting was held, and eventually they were abandoned.

Depilatories had given out, and every man in the camp now sported the same shaggy growth of beard. Spratly's uniform, like most everyone else's, had eventually succumbed to the constant wet and heat, and he made do now with cut-off shorts or a breechcloth or sometimes nothing at all.

Worse, the escape committee had fallen apart when one of the members, Dewar Sykes, had turned, becoming a camp trusty, a turner. Spratly had been lucky. All he'd lost had been an eye, and Wal Prescott, his second-in-command, had lost an eye and a hand. Half of the other members had been harvested completely, not just trimmed, and in the long months of dying since that time, few had dared raise the subject of escape again.

"So you think you have a handle on that damned traitor machine?" Spratly asked.

Traitor. Jaime knew that General Spratly had never fully trusted the colony's Bolo, and he viewed the terrible ease with which it had ceased operations at Chryse to be proof that it had sided with the machine invaders, an act of deliberate and calculated treachery.

"Our . . . friend is pretty sick," Jaime said. "But I've found someone in the camp who might be able to help."

"That monster is no *friend* . . . !"

"Valhalla will have no hope of success without him, General. If we can . . . make him feel better, we have a chance."

Operation Valhalla was the plan the freshly captured troops of the First Armored had cobbled together during their very first week in the camp, a few days after Chryse. They'd still been thinking of the invaders as organic creatures, beings who used machines to wage their wars. The startling reality, that the Invaders were machines pursuing some kind of twisted parody of Darwinian evolution, had not yet sunk in. The plan had called for slipping a technical team out of the camp, trekking overland north to the Chryse battlefield where Hector lay disabled, reactivating him, and using his considerable firepower, the firepower of a planetary siege unit, to . . . what?

Escape from the camp, certainly, but then? Some of the conspirators had claimed that a reactivated Hector could kick the invaders clean off the planet. General Spratly, and others, had pointed out that if the invaders had been able to take down a Mark XXXIII Bolo with such remarkable ease once, they would be able to do it again a second time.

A few days later, Hector had rumbled ponderously out of the north and taken his position atop Overlook Hill, a position he had not abandoned in nearly a year. Humans who tried to approach him or move past the hill were killed. Somehow, the invaders had suborned him. And Operation Valhalla, named for the place where fallen warriors feasted in the Norse afterlife, had been dropped.

"I can't say that I'm pleased at the prospect," Spratly said after a long silence. He scratched at his belly thoughtfully, where an angry red rash was spreading across his hairy skin. "He is a machine, after all. Like *them*."

"Exactly. He is a machine, which makes him more trustworthy—if we can find out what they did to him and correct it—than any human." Pointedly, Jaime stared at Captain Pogue, then at the other staff officers. There was no reason to suspect that any of the men were camp informers. Jaime was simply reminding the general that men placed in such stressful conditions were capable of anything. Extreme situations did extreme things to people, and to their minds. "I'm going to need *it*, though, to carry this thing off."

Spratly's face worked unpleasantly. "For what?"

Jaime didn't answer right away, considering his

response carefully. If there *were* listening devices planted in the hut . . . or hovering just outside with sensitive electronic ears, the !*!*! might learn enough about what the two human slaves were talking about to intervene. They couldn't risk losing *it*.

A sharp whistle sounded from outside, Dieter's warning. The whistle meant a floater was moving into the area. It was time to end the interview, at least for now.

"I don't really know, General," he said, answering Spratly's last question as honestly as he could. "We need more information. Some of us will try to get that, tonight. To learn how to apply . . . *it* to best advantage."

"You'll have to convince me that resurrecting that damned, traitorous collection of spare parts is going to get us somewhere," Spratly said. "I don't trust that machine. I don't trust any of 'em."

Jaime hesitated at the door. "I understand, sir. Still, we're going to have to trust sometime, or we might as well plan on spending the rest of our lives, what's left of 'em, right here in the mud."

He stepped outside, then, into the dazzling sunsshine of the late afternoon.

CHAPTER FOUR

Shari Barstowe remained a few paces behind Jaime as they approached the looming Bolo. They'd left the Camp shortly after the evening meal, sneaking out through the sewage ditch and making their laborious way up the eastern slope of Overlook Hill, moving slowly, always on the alert for !°!°! machines or sensors.

Now, at last, nearly an hour later, they stood once more on the small, sharp-edged ridge of bones, fifty meters from the huge, metallic beast. She shuddered. She still hadn't adjusted, quite, to the unexpected reprieve. For a moment, she considered shoving past Jaime and into the Bolo's killing ground, deliberately challenging the monster and calling down a swift and painless death.

But . . . no. Quite apart from the fact that she didn't want to risk killing Jaime as well, she found, almost to her surprise, that she wanted to live again.

"Halt," the Bolo said in human, yet disturbingly uninflected, tones. AP weapons ports snickered open, the muzzles tracking them in the darkness. "Identify yourself."

"Major Jaime Graham and Technician Barstowe,

First Armored Assault Brigade, Cloud Defense Force,"
Graham said.

"Present code authorization."

"Authorization Code Tango three-three-seven Victor
Delta niner. Maintenance."

"This unit is not scheduled for standard maintenance."

"Override Security Alpha, Code Delta Echo One-
one."

"Advance, Major Graham and Technician Barstowe."

"Is its challenge speech always the same?" she asked
Jaime as they stepped off the bones and began
walking across the blasted, open hilltop toward the
machine.

"Always." Gravel crunched beneath their sore, bare
feet. "You know, before the invasion, talking to Hector
was like talking to another person. Now, hell, my
calculator had more personality, back when I had a
calculator."

"It sounds as though its working memory has been
constricted, somehow," she said. "The base holomem
settings may need to be reentered."

"Where would you do that?"

"From the main computer access terminal. That's
inside Hector's control room."

"Huh. Old Hector isn't about to let us go in *there*.
Not like this, anyway."

They stood directly in front of the Bolo now, looking
up at the smooth, back-slanting slope of its front armor,
what Jaime called its "glacis." The rounded forward
turret with its stubby, ominous-looking Hellbore mount
was just visible protruding above the top of the cliff,
some eighty feet above the ground.

"Hello, Hector," Jaime called. There was no reply,
nothing to hear at all save the whistling of the night
wind across cold metal.

"Let me try," she said.

"Be my guest."

"Hector," Shari called. "Your unit has won some prestigious battle honors over the years. I wonder if you can recite them for me?"

There was a sound . . . not words, but a kind of far-off creak, like the moving of a rusty door, and then a rapid series of clicks. This was followed by a tiny, high-pitched electronic squeal, rapidly cut off. She wondered if the great, metal beast was in pain.

"You are a Mark XXXIII Bolo," she said, pressing ahead, "last and greatest of the Dinochrome Brigade. Your name is Hector. Do you remember your unit? Do you remember your *adopted* unit?"

Again, a series of clicks echoed from the interior of the dark machine, clicks that increased in frequency and pitch until they whined like a rusty hinge. They ended with a single, loud pop, echoing hollowly.

"What the hell is that?" Jaime wanted to know. He sounded worried.

"Relays closing," Shari replied. "He's trying to answer, but it's not getting through."

"It sounds like something's broken in there."

"Damn, a monitor and a data feed jack would be real useful right now," Shari said. She felt frustrated, and helpless. "I'd give just about anything to know what Hector was thinking right now."

I stop, clearing my circuits, resetting all switches to zero, and try again. Each time I reach for the required information within my main storage banks and begin to assemble a reply, there is a brief span, several milliseconds of lucidity, and then the information fades once more beneath the shifting, blurring surface of my memory.

Two organics stand 5.3 meters in front of the leading edge of my glacis. I have to struggle to retain even the word they use to describe themselves: humans. They are . . . alien, somehow, organic life forms utterly unlike myself, and yet I can't help but feel an odd, inexplicable pull, something akin to camaraderie, as one of the beings, the one identifying itself as Technician Barstowe, calls out to me.

"Bolo! What is your unit?"

My . . . unit?

The information is there, in my main storage, it is there. Bolo HCT of the Line, Mark XXXIII, 6th Mobile Starstrike Regiment, the Indomitables, on special deployment with the Third Terran Colonizing Fleet and the 1st Armored Assault Brigade at Cloud, Western Arm, 212th Sagittarian Sector . . .

And with that information comes a flood of other data, memories long hidden, or deliberately suppressed by . . . by . . .

I can feel the Interloper moving to cut me off from the inflow of data, can feel it deleting material from my working memory. I attempt to create and store a backup, but the Intruder is already there, a virus reading each character string and changing it almost as soon as I pass it on to the storage subdirectory.

I can feel my memories being rewritten, edited as I view them.

But, however briefly, I can live those memories again, and I feel a surge of emotion. I first achieved full consciousness at the Durandel Bolo Assembly Plant, on Luna, Lot 5, Series A Number 28373. The 6th Mobile Starstrike was commissioned as a regiment of twenty-four Mark XXXIII Bolos on Earth, on 26 June, A.E. 1477. We served together in the campaigns on Marxis, Carragula, and Jorgenson's Worlds, and helped lift the Siege of Proxima. I was deployed independently to Aldo Cerise, and when the Melconians' Khalesh allies assaulted nearby Grauve, I took part in the stand that broke the Khal Dependency. At the Third Battle of Sardunar, I held off superior Melconian forces, including a triplet of heavy battlers then entering orbit,

*allowing elements of the 5th Terran Marines and the
12th Proximan Infantry to complete their evacuation
of the planet. For that action, during which I was
damaged seriously enough to necessitate my salvage
and rotation back to Earth, I was awarded the Triple
Star of Valor.*

*Though I was fully repaired, by that time it was
determined that Melconian advances in military
technology had rendered me obsolete, and I was
relegated to reserve status on Mars. There, I was
assigned to the Third Terran Colonizing Fleet as the
heavy mechanized element of the 1st Armored Assault
Brigade, a key component of the highly classified
Operation Diaspora. On Cloud, I participated in the
fighting with both the Vovoin and the Ka'Juur, as well
as the fratricidal engagement known now as the
Outreach War.*

*In all, I served with the 1st Armored for 204
T-standard years, before the arrival of the ǀ°ǀ°ǀ. I was
at Chryse when the Enemy attacked and was engaged
against numerous units inbound from orbit when . . .
when . . .*

*I feel the icy hand of the Intruder closing on my
memories, on my very thoughts. It has been 1.382
second since Technician Barstowe asked me what my
unit was, eliciting this flood of information. I speculate
that the Intruder, whatever it is, requires approximately .9 second to detect cyberneural traces that it
has been programmed to watch for and subvert or
delete them.*

*Even as I lose the fleeting, ragged substance of those
memories, I can hear myself—a different part of myself
centered with my voice control network—replying to
the question. "I remember no unit."*

*"Yes you do, Hector!" the other human, Major
Graham, calls out. I detect strong levels of stress in
his voice and deduce with 76% certainty that he is*

frustrated about some matter that is currently beyond his control. "You won the Triple Star for Valor at Sardunar! It's welded right there to your glacis! You must have done something to deserve that award! What was it? The information is in your primary banks!"

"*Negative,*" *I hear the detached portion of my awareness reply.* "*I have no record of a battle at . . . of a battle at . . .*"

Strange. Major Graham named the battle only an instant ago, but the memory of that name, the very shape of it, has been snatched from me. Obviously, something is very seriously wrong with my psychotronic systems, and this is cause for considerable alarm. I am aware, of course, of the concern many humans have that psychotronic systems such as Bolos might suffer malfunction and enter a state similar to human insanity. I have discounted such possibilities until now, but the bizarre workings of my mind at the moment are enough to give me pause.

Have I, as humans would say, gone crazy?

"Okay," Jaime said. He rubbed his beard. "What've we got? About a one-second delay?"

"I can't tell without a computer link," Shari replied, "but that's a pretty close guess."

"But I thought psychotronic AIs were designed with built-in delays. To make them more human."

"Well, yeah. That's true. Humans find it unnerving when a machine answers a question immediately, without even seeming to think about it. What they forget, of course, is that an electronic intelligence is a lot faster than an electrochemical one like ours. A second, a *tenth* of a second, is a long, *long* time to a Bolo."

"So how can you tell there's a delay?"

"Call it intuition. That's a hell of a note, isn't it?

Psychotronics depends on precision and measurement, like all science. And all I can do is rely on female intuition."

"Male intuition too," Jaime admitted. "Each time I've been up here, it seems to me like Hector takes his time answering my questions. There's none of that usual snap, that 'Affirmative, my commander' stuff you usually hear from these things."

"So something is intercepting the primary data flow, and either blocking it or altering it on the way to working memory. The *only* thing that could slow down a Bolo's processing cycle at all would be something, another computer, physically astride the primary data bus. My bet is that Hector is remembering when we ask him things, but forgetting them again within a second or so."

"Can we get around that with software? Or are we going to have to rewire him?"

She looked at him in the half darkness, one eyebrow perfectly arched. "My, you *are* ambitious, aren't you?"

"If you have any alternatives, I'd be glad to hear them. You're the expert on Bolo AIs, remember. I'm just a mud-footed grunt."

"Hardly that." She thought for a moment. The Bolo, a duralloy cliff looming above them, seemed to consider them in glacial silence. "Well, the only way to restore full operation would be to actually go in, find the primary data bus, and physically remove whatever is affecting him. That won't be easy."

"But not impossible. If the intruder got in, I'm betting it was through that hole melted in Hector's side. If the intruder got in, so can we."

"I doubt we could rip it off with our bare hands."

"There are . . . other possibilities."

"Well, there is a software fix we can try in the

meantime. It won't solve Hector's problem, but it'll make sure he knows what we're doing when the time comes."

"Good." Jaime grinned. "Frankly, I'm not sure what those codes Alita gave me cover. I don't know how intimate we can get with Hector without calling down an AP shot. I do know that Hector's not going to take kindly to us stumbling around inside him."

"Well, at the very least maybe we'll be able to talk to him about it when the time comes." Turning away from Jaime, she looked up at the black cliff. "Bolo!" she called out. "Code sequence Alpha three-one! Initiate ongoing primary data copy to new file. Source, workmem, filename 'Rising,' access code . . . 'Graham Barstowe.' Execute!"

Somewhere in the depths of the steel mountain, relays began to close. . . .

Code sequence Alpha 3-1 is an instruction reserved for software engineers and AI technicians testing Bolo psychotronic relays and main memory, a routine procedure during maintenance checks and precombat service checks to confirm proper memory management and basic psychotronic integrity. Though it is unusual to be initiating this procedure outside of a Bolo maintenance depot, and even more unusual to be working by voice rather than via direct data link, the request must be accepted.

Accordingly, I open a new file inside my working memory and name it "Rising." As data comes into working memory from main storage, I automatically copy each packet and store it in Rising. Information begins to accumulate within the file almost immediately. I am a Bolo, Mark XXXIII Mod HCT of the Dinochrome Brigade, and my human companions call me Hector. I entered service on 26 June, A.E. 1477 with the 6th Mobile Starstrike Regiment, the Indomitables, *on*

special deployment with the 1st Armored Assault
Brigade at Cloud, Eastern Arm, 212th Sagittarian
Sector . . .

I recognize that File Rising will swiftly grow to
unmanageable proportions unless provisions are made
to recopy the data to main memory. Working memory,
after all, represents only .0001 percent of my total
available storage capacity, and copying all incoming
data to those stacks will soon render working memory
useless.

The tactic, however, is successful, as the "I" residing
within working memory watches information about
myself, about my identity fading away again beneath
the silent touch of the Intruder, while it remains intact
in File Rising.

I remember . . . and I continue to remember. . . .

Wal Prescott sat with his back against the wall of
the scrap-wood and pressboard hut and scratched
with one-handed viciousness at the rash spreading
across the inside of his thighs. He missed civilization.
More than decent food, more than clothing, more
than almost anything else except freedom itself, he
missed *civilization*, a human condition that he was
having more and more trouble recapturing in his
memories . . . but one which above all else he
associated with being *clean*.

The worst health problems in the camp, so far, were
pneumonia, malnutrition, and simple overwork;
routine prophylactic conditioning—antibodies
administered to the population of Cloud in their
drinking water back in preinvasion days—had so far
kept such ancient scourges as typhoid and dysentery
at bay. Other health problems, though, long forgotten
by civilized cultures, were making a comeback in the
camp with its warm, wet, filthy conditions, including
lice, fleas, and half a hundred different fungal

conditions all lumped together under the common heading of "the creeping crud." Somehow, like cockroaches, rats, and the other vermin that had followed mankind to the stars, those ancient parasitic afflictions had survived being transplanted from Terra and the ancient colony worlds, continuing to exist in numbers too small to be noticed, kept in check by the sanitation and medical prophylaxis taken for granted by civilized beings.

But civilization on Cloud had been destroyed, reduced to a scrabbling hand-to-mouth existence without the sanitary luxuries long taken for granted, and the afflictions were returning now, like the plagues of Egypt, each contributing in its own small way to the misery of existence in the Camp.

Can we possibly hope to win? he wondered. *With that goddamned big Bolo on our side again, we could probably break out of here, but then what? How long could we remain free?*

He looked at the others gathered in the half-darkness of the hut. The small building, located in a clutter of similar makeshift structures west of the factory, was one of several used occasionally by former members of the CDF for their meetings. Of the six men living here, four were now at the dig, while two more, Sergeant Jack Haley and Corporal Peter Zhou, had been admitted to the growing conspiracy. At the moment, Jack was on guard outside, while Peter lay on his rag pile next to Wal. Alita sat on the other side of the single, dirt-floored room, fiddling with the torn-off hem of the ragged T-shirt she was wearing. The psychotronics expert, Shari, sat next to her, head back, eyes closed; she might have been asleep. Well, no wonder, after being up on the hill with Jaime and the Bolo most of the night. Her next work shift was going to be hell, though. The Masters took a dim view of slaves who fell asleep on their hands and knees in the pits. It was an invitation to the harvesters.

The other members of the budding conspiracy present so far included Dieter Hollinsworth, Tamas Reuter, and Lieutenant Lewis Moxley, formerly of the Chryse communications division. The meeting had been called by Jaime, who wanted to discuss Valhalla with all of them before their next work shift.

There was a knock, bare knuckles on rotting wood, and Jack's voice sounded from outside. "Go on in, Major. They're waiting."

The rags serving as a door were pushed aside, and Jaime Graham ducked into the room. "Any luck?" Wal asked him.

Jaime found a bare spot on the floor next to Shari and sank onto it. "No. Pogue wouldn't even let me in to see him. I don't think Spratly's going to budge on this, Wal."

"Told ya."

"We might have to . . . do it ourselves."

Wal considered a moment before he replied. "Jaime, I understand what you're saying. But think about it. First, what you're suggesting could be construed as mutiny. Second, have you given any thought to the possibility that the man could be *right*?"

Jaime looked at Wal through half-closed eyes for a long moment. "As I see it, Colonel," he said, finally, "we go for this, and go for it now, while we have a clear shot. Or we decide that *this* is how we want to live out the rest of our lives." He looked around the tiny, scrap-wood room. "And how long do you think that's going to be, anyway?"

"What," Alita said quietly, "is the absolute worst that could happen? We try to reprogram Hector, we fail, and he cuts us all down with AP flechettes. Don't know about the rest of you guys, but that option's looking better and better, lately."

"No," Dieter said. "The worst is that they round us up and take us away for vivisection. Some of us have been trying to avoid that particular career path, you know."

"Then we'll just have to make sure that we die fighting," Jaime said. "I don't care what happens to me after I'm dead. I'll be damned if I'm going to let them take me alive."

"Brave words, Major," Corporal Zhou said. "The people they take don't seem to have much choice, though."

"Well, damn it," Tamas said, "what's the difference? If they don't take us now, while we're trying to do something about it, they'll take us later. I say we take a chance, before we're too weak from malnutrition and exhaustion to do anything but scream!"

"All true," Lewis Moxley said. "But . . . but we've *got* to have *it*, don't we? We don't stand a chance without *it*. And if the general won't give *it* to us—"

"We'll have to take it, that's all," Jaime said.

Lewis looked shocked. "But the colonel's right! That would be mutiny!"

"That," Shari said, her eyes still closed, "will be the least of our worries!"

"But we still have to consider it," Wal pointed out. "The order and discipline that we received through our military training has been what's kept us alive so far."

"Who do you think you're fooling, Colonel?" Alita asked. "Maybe one in ten of the people in this camp are . . . *were* military when the Masters came. What do we have left of military discipline today? Okay, we organized the barracks and set up latrines and an orderly procedure for chow call, granted. But the CDF ceased to exist when they whacked Chryse. If we have a chance, I say take it. And if the general doesn't want to go along, then let him stay. But I'll be damned if I let his decision not to rock the boat keep me from grabbing *my* chance at freedom!"

Jack Haley was leaning against the shack just outside the doorway. "I'm with the major and Alita," he said quietly through the curtain. "We fight back with every weapon we have, or we admit we're nothing but spare parts. At least this is a *chance* for freedom or a clean death, and that's twice as many options as we've got if we stay put!"

Wal looked at each of the military people in turn, measuring them. Moxley—he wasn't much more than a kid, really, twenty-three, maybe twenty-four T-standard years old—was afraid of turning against established authority. Zhou was more fearful of the consequences if Valhalla should fail. The rest, though, two sergeants with a hell of a lot of experience and Major Graham, all wanted to take the chance. The civilians supported them, too.

The problem was that General Spratly just flat out didn't like Bolos, hadn't liked or trusted them even before the invasion, and he sure as hell didn't trust the things now.

And Wal was caught squarely in the middle. Jaime and the others were right when they said that the surviving humans wouldn't last much longer. They couldn't, not under these conditions, even if the Masters *didn't* decide to harvest every last slave in the camp. But the fact remained that even with *it*, Valhalla stood little chance of success.

Wal was forced to admit to himself that his big fear wasn't mutiny or overturning the established authority. It was facing the Masters again. When they'd come for him before, dragging him into the convoluted bowels of the machine they called the Harvester, they hadn't used anesthetics. They'd pinned him to a table while lasers had sliced off his hand and delicately removed his eye, and Wal's shrieks had echoed from

the cold, metal walls of the machine with none to hear
but himself and the unfeeling mechanisms that held
him down. He'd healed well enough, but he still had
nightmares . . . and the very sight of a floater coming
his way could reduce him to trembling, sweating,
powerless terror.

No, he couldn't face that again. He *couldn't*. He
would have to side with the general against Jaime,
even if he thought that Jaime was right.

The machine with the *chirp-whistle-click* designator
that might have translated as GED9287-8726H Series
95 possessed only three brains—one for things-as-they-
are, one for memory, and a third for anticipation—
and was incapable of feeling emotion. The third brain
did allow for a measure of curiosity, however, and the
input it was receiving now was enough to make the
machine quite curious indeed.

GED9287 currently occupied a spacecraft body in
low orbit over Cloud and had been tasked with a
routine infrared check on several of the camps holding
living organics on the planet. The surveillance was
routine enough, an ongoing survey in IR wavelengths
that allowed the Higher Awarenesses to track overall
association and movement patterns among the captive
organics.

In infrared, the assembly facility designated Camp
84 showed as a cool mosaic of greens and blues, with
pale rectangles marking out the jumble of huts and
shacks the organics had erected for protection from
the elements. The organics themselves resolved as
brighter yellow and orange shapes; from nearly two
hundred kilometers up, GED's optics could just
distinguish foreshortened legs and arms on the organics'
bodies as they moved around the camp, worked in
the nearby pits, or sprawled in their huts in their
mysterious between-shifts phases of unconsciousness.

Not even the pressboard slabs covering the huts, or the roof of the ruined factory itself, could block the IR emissions.

What had captured GED's curiosity was an unexpected anomaly in organic gathering patterns. At that moment, there were 3287 individual organic heat sources in the cold, water-sodden pits southeast of Camp 84 and they, as always, were huddled together in tight-knit groups. Another 2993 organics were in the Camp, most sprawled on the ground in their unconscious phase.

There was one group, however, that broke the pattern. West of the factory, nine individual heat sources were crowded together inside a single small hut. Nowhere else within the camp was there such a concentration.

While the organic species that called itself human was known to gather for many purposes, including meals, recreation, and the dissemination of news, they tended to keep to themselves when possible, erecting separate huts or dividing up the interior of the factory or the structure they used for waste elimination with wooden slabs as they sought something they referred to as "privacy." This gathering seemed atypical . . . and was, therefore, worthy of note.

GED took a half second more to scan the hill west of the camp; the huge, warm mountain of the captured human war machine remained in place, unmoving. There were no anomalous heat sources on the hill at the moment. Several other orbiting Masters had detected organics on that hillside outside the walls of the camp, and all IR scans were tasked with checking for escaped humans. The suicide of a few organics, more or less, was of no particular concern to the !°!°!, particularly when most were individuals too broken in will to be useful to the Prime Code, but the number of slaves who made that trip and killed themselves had been growing lately, and it might soon be necessary to shut off that particular means of culling the herd.

The captured machine was alone for the moment. That group of nine humans, though, would have to be investigated.

GED9287 opened the channel to the Primary Web.

CHAPTER FIVE

"Look," Jaime said. "It must be nearly time for the next shift to hit the pits. Are we going to do this thing, or not?"

"Well, I don't know, Jaime," Wal said. "You still haven't told us what happens after we recruit your Bolo friend."

"We blow the damned cluckers to hell. At least we blow them off the face of Cloud."

Wal shook his head. "It's not that easy, Jaime, and you know it. The !•!•! knocked the Bolo out at Chryse. They'll do it again. They defeated the entire CDF in a couple of days . . . and that was when the CDF had men, weapons, hovertanks . . . We were an army, for God's sake! Now what do we have? A few thousand pathetic, ragged refugees, half-starved, unarmed. *Think*, Jaime, *think*! Do you want to see the entire camp slaughtered? Is that what you want? Because that's what's going to happen if you see this through!"

"I thought you were on my side in this!" Jaime cried.

"When it was just a few of us sneaking out, yeah. We might be able to hide out up in the mountains, or in the deep forest. But you're talking about trying to defeat the !°!°! on their own terms. I'm sorry, but I never signed on for that!"

"What if there were a way for us to get off the planet?" Jaime asked. He rubbed at his beard thoughtfully. "If we could fight the machines off, get some ships . . ."

"What ships?"

"Actually, I was thinking about the Tolun."

Wal's eyebrows crept high up on his forehead. "What makes you think they'll deal with the likes of us?"

"They'll deal with anybody. Everyone knows that."

The Tolun were nonhumans, members of a very old species that maintained a trading and mercantile empire across much of this region of space.

"There's an enclave of Tolun at Stardown," Dieter pointed out.

"There *was* an enclave there," Zhou said. "What makes you think the damned machines didn't smash them too, when they smashed us?"

"The fact that we're still eating," Jaime said. "And have been for almost a year. Where do you think our food has been coming from all this time?"

"Camp rumors. Wild stories . . ."

"Nonsense! People have *seen* the Tolun," Dieter said, "delivering hovertrucks full of food, presumably from some farming communities out there that didn't get smacked. The word is, they'll do anything for samples of advanced technology."

"Even if that's true, what does that get us?" Wal scratched his beard with savage intensity. "If the Tolun are working for the machines, they're not going to help us. And if they're not, what do we have to give them?"

"I'm willing to worry about that one when it's time, Colonel. Right now, we have to get out of this camp, and to do that we need Hector. This is our one chance to make a break. If we blow it now, we—"

"Psst!" Jack Haley, on watch at the doorway, hissed. "Condition red!"

Conversation stopped. A moment later, a shadow fell across the opening of the hut. It was Dewar Sykes, standing in the doorway, conspicuously clad in jackboots, leather trousers, and a soft, ruffled green shirt. He slapped his shockstick against an open palm. "Right, then," he said, surveying the slaves inside. "What's this, some kind of conspiracy? Get on out here in the light! All of you!"

The ragged line of slaves crawled out into the sunlight, blinking. Sykes made them stand in line, nudging them this way or that with prods from his truncheon. Another trusty, a narrow-eyed little weasel named Philbet, stood nearby with an unpleasant leer on his face. In the distance, Jaime saw, a single !°!°! floater hovered silently, watching the proceedings with a mix of human and glittering, crystalline eyes.

"You people should get more fresh air," Sykes told them. Reaching up, he rubbed absently at the silver band encircling his head. "Exercise, hard work, that's the ticket. How 'bout it, Philbet? Maybe an extra shift for these slimy little crollygogs?"

"Sounds like just the thing, Dewar."

Sykes reached out and touched Shari's chin with one hand, gently stroking her face. "Except . . . maybe we'll let this one off. I like her."

Shari jerked her head back beyond Sykes's reach. "Turner!" she spat. The epithet was reserved for those humans who'd sided with the machines, the trusties and turncoats and lickmetals who worked for the !°!°!.

"I think you'll spend the day with us, baby." His eyes narrowed. "I think we've had you before, haven't we? Yeah, I thought so. Real prime meat on the hoof." He grabbed her arm and yanked her out of line.

"Leave her alone!" Jaime rasped, taking a step forward.

Sykes whirled, the snarl forming on his lips melting into a grin. Reaching out mildly, he tapped the

business end of his shockstick twice against the angry
red welt on Jaime's upper arm. "So? How's the arm,
soldier boy? Tried taking on any more of the Masters
recently?" The grin faded into something darker.
"Maybe you'd like to take *me* on sometime, eh?"

Jaime saw the trap and pulled back. "No . . . sir."

It was all he could do to contain his seething hatred.
Sykes and the other trusties, in Jaime's opinion, were
the lowest, most detestable life forms in the camp or
out of it. They'd betrayed their own species for the
comfort and authority afforded camp guards. The name
"trusty," dredged from the ancient history of human
prisons and law enforcement, was more an ironic joke
than a statement of fact.

Sykes leaned closer, peering curiously into Jaime's
face. "What's the girl to you, Graham, eh?"

"Nothing. She's . . . she's been through a lot, lately.
Give her a break, huh?"

"Oh, but I *am*, soldier boy! Best break possible!"
He stabbed the end of the shockstick squarely against
the center of Jaime's bare chest, pushing hard as he
leaned forward with a wicked grin. "She gets the whole
day off! Gets to have a real shower, get the mud off
her skin and out of her hair. Why, she gets to be with
me all day, tending to my, ah, *personal* needs, instead
of crawling around on her pretty little knees in the
mud, digging up corpses with her bare hands. Like
you!"

At the last word, he thumbed the button on the
shockstick, and the bolt seared through Jaime's chest,
dragging a ragged scream from lips gone numb.

He didn't remember falling, but he found himself
on his back, his vision slowly returning. His entire
body felt numb, but his legs and arms tingled as though
they'd lost all circulation.

Shari was on her knees next to him, helping him
sit up. As she bent forward, her lips brushed close

beside his ear. "It's okay, Jaime," she whispered. "I can stand . . . *anything*. So long as there's hope!"

Then Sykes bent over, grabbed Shari by her arm, and hauled her to her feet. "Don't waste your time with garbage, girl. C'mon. You're comin' with us."

"Yeah," Philbet said. He stepped over to Alita and grabbed her by the wrist. "How 'bout this one, Dewar? Let's take her too."

"Suits me. The more the merrier."

"Yah!" Philbet said, roughly caressing Alita. "We'll have a party!"

"The rest of you," Sykes said, "hit the pits! Double shift for all of you! Now move it!" He kicked Jaime in the side. "You too! Move! Move! Or I'll turn you over to our friend over there!"

Under the watchful eyes of the floater, the slaves helped Jaime stagger back to his feet. The doleful tones of the siren summoning the next shift to work were sounding, and they turned and trudged toward the camp's front gate, joining the thousands of others lining up to leave the camp. When Jaime turned to look back over his shoulder, he could just barely see Sykes and Philbet marching the women off in the direction of the trusty compound, a collection of nearly intact homes set well above the squalor of the camp.

"You think the Masters see everything that they do?" Tamas asked.

"I dunno," Dieter said. "They might be trusties, but it stands t' reason the Masters don't trust 'em, right?

"Yeah," Wal said. He supported Jaime with his good arm as they walked. "I keep wondering about those headbands."

The silver bands they wore on their heads like some high-tech parody of ancient laurel wreaths clearly were more than badges of rank and authority. It was rumored that they somehow picked up everything the trusty saw and relayed it to the Masters.

Of course, everyone knew that the bands also killed . . . or crippled with such blinding pain that the trusty who violated his orders was unable to escape the Harvesters who came for him. They were a kind of insurance for the !°!°!. The trusties had betrayed their own kind to serve the Masters; it wasn't likely that the Masters would trust them without some pretty serious safeguards. The trusties' lives were suspended by the slenderest of threads. Jaime had seen at least two dozen trusties crippled and harvested since he'd come to the dig, some for no crime more serious than not responding swiftly enough when a Master rasped out an order. There were always others, though, willing to take their place.

He could muster no sympathy for them, however. Sykes's life was far better than that of the slaves in the pits. He wore decent clothing, and got more and better food, and even had his pick of women from the ranks of the slaves. Jaime could have understood their treason—not accepted it, perhaps, but understood it—if they'd simply used their authority to maintain order among the slaves. But the trusties abused that authority constantly, took pleasure in their brutality, and acted more like slave masters than any of the detached and unemotional !°!°!.

He could not forgive that. Not ever.

"We'll settle with them, too," he said, his voice low.

Wal tightened his grip. "Major, I don't think you're getting the message. There's *nothing we can do*, you understand? The machines must be on to us."

"Why do you say that?" Tamas asked.

"How did the trusties know about our meeting, huh?" He sounded genuinely frightened. "I mean, there we were, talking about what to do about the Bolo and breaking out and everything, and there was Sykes."

"Wal," Jaime said wearily, "if the trusties or the cluckers had any idea what we were talking about back there, they wouldn't have just given us a double shift! We'd be dead right now, or they'd be dragging us off to the Harvester. No, I don't think they know. . . ."

"Valhalla is off," Wal said decisively. "I'm going to talk to the general about it as soon as we get back. It's just too big a risk."

Jaime glanced at him sharply but said nothing. He could tell when Colonel Prescott was set in his mind about something, and he knew the man wasn't going to yield. That hurt. He liked Wal and considered him to be the best friend he had in the camp.

But Jaime was not about to let friendship stand between him and his sole chance at freedom.

DAV728 floated in the presence of the Ninth Awareness as hovering manuals completed the final connections to the data receptors in DAV's cognitive racks. Its new brain, gray and wrinkled, afloat in its sealed canister of nutrient fluid, awaited final feed-link and insertion. In another few billion nanoseconds, now, DAV would be initiated into a new and higher plane of awareness.

The Ninth Awareness, of course, was invisible, a complex of several AI intelligences working as a unity, a hive-mind matrix within the labyrinthine circuitry of the vast !°!°! complex now rising from the cluttered waste and confusion of the humans' enclosed Delamar cities. DAV was aware of it only through the constant buzz and flicker of data packets, and the warm, electronic focus of its myriad scanners and active sensory devices.

There was no ceremony, nothing at all like ritual attached to the awarding of a new brain; the !°!°! were not designed to comprehend the concept of celebrations or rites of passage, though they were aware of those social posturings among various of the organic life forms they'd encountered so far in their inexorable advance across the galaxy.

Most self-aware beings with which the !°!°! were familiar had the ability—one not shared by the original !°!°! themselves—of holding several discrete chunks of data in mind simultaneously. How many depended on both the species and the individual, but the number generally ran from three to seven.

Memic chunking, as it was known, was how most organic intelligences remembered things. A typical OI—a human, for instance—might remember the number "3647836837" by breaking it into manageable chunks, as 364-783-6837, perhaps—four chunks of three to four numbers apiece. An AI, on the other hand, would simply store and recall the entire number "3647836837," and not give it another thought. As a matter of fact, for some millennia in their early history, the !°!°!, once they were aware of the phenomenon, had assumed that chunking was a trick that OIs found necessary in order to remember anything at all, but that had no bearing whatsoever on AIs with their infallible electronic memories.

It had taken a long time, in fact, before the !°!°! realized that memic chunking conferred another and more subtle advantage than simply allowing wrinkled blobs of gray jelly to remember long numbers. Organisms that could chunk could also hold separate and simultaneous concepts in mind, and that was something that electronic AIs could manage only through massively parallel processing, and then incompletely at best. An OI might hold A and B and C in its thoughts at the same time by calling them up as three separate memic chunks, then bringing them together as a fourth; an OI could process them separately in *one* processor and come out with ABC . . . which in the fuzzy logic of mental processes might not be the same thing at all. !°!°! researchers were still studying the phenomenon; there was much about OI mental organization, capabilities, and concepts of reality that were almost impossible for AIs to fathom. "Altruism," for example . . . or "honor," or most organics' desire for ceremony and fanfare or even— and this was the big one—"love."

Among other things, what memory chunking meant for OIs was that they could hold in their thoughts simultaneous concepts of past, present, and future, remembering the past while planning for the future and taking into account the here-and-now. This was something that the original !°!°!, tens of thousands of years before, had not been able to do. The lack had cost them dearly. More than once they'd very nearly been destroyed by the merely organic creatures they battled; final victory, and the ability to extend their rule beyond the teeming starswarms of the Galactic Core, had come only when they learned the trick of linking multiple brains in parallel within the same artificially intelligent system.

The *first* brain, the silicon brain with the original !°!°! Prime Code programming, was what every !°!°! received in the natal assemblers. It was adequate for basic work and simple tasks, and provided a working memory of some 10^7 bits, about the same storage capacity as a human book of three or four hundred pages. The second brain, also silicon, upgraded the primary logic functions and extended working memory to roughly 10^8 bits, while the third brain extended the memory by another factor of 10, as well as providing the adapters, ports, and software for handling a wide variety of scanners, sensors, and data input devices, all necessary if the machine was to be able to move its intelligence from one body to another. All minimally-aware !°!°! possessed at least three brains.

But to acquire more than minimal self-awareness, the individual !°!°! had to go one step further . . . or two or three or more. All ship-fortress-factory commanders possessed at least four brains, allowing them to draw conclusions based on past events, to anticipate future developments, and even to run controlled simulations of future possibilities with one brain while watching the results through the others . . . an ability, not possessed by low-level brain arrays, that organics referred to as *imagination*.

The additional brains beyond the first four didn't *have* to be organic. Indeed, many !°!°! insisted that silicon brains were far more durable and efficient than colloidal suspensions of organic jelly. Somehow, though, early self-aware !°!°!, while experimenting on the physiologies of captured OIs, had picked up the idea of keeping organic brains alive in sealed support canisters, equipping them with a silicon interface and using them in parallel to enhance AI systems capabilities. They ran slowly and inefficiently; their neurons operated through the cumbersome transmission of electrochemical signals, but one organic brain did function with the fuzzy logic otherwise possible only through massive parallel processing. Better still, !°!°! designers had learned how to tap into the memories stored within organic brains and translate them into imagery their new owners could understand. The advantages of being able to see how an enemy thought and felt were obvious and compelling . . . even if organic brains did tend to break down after 10^{17} nanoseconds or so. It was hard keeping them alive for very long . . . and harder still to keep them *sane*. Special check programs had to be set over each organic brain in a !°!°!'s series to make certain the data they provided were accurate.

The !°!°! manuals completed their final preparations; a Series 24 floater, equipped with grotesque, leathery-skinned human hands, carefully picked up the canister containing DAV728's fifth brain, snapped the primary data bus home, then tucked the unit deep into DAV's exposed internal wiring. A horde of symbiotic assemblers, finger-sized, low-level machines resembling spiders or roaches or thick-armed starfish, scuttled about the package, busily growing the forest of hair-thin optical connections that completed the link.

DAV scarcely noticed. As the primary bus clicked into its receptor, its . . . no, *his* awareness seemed to unfold like a complex abstract of hyperdimensional topology.

His awareness. No !*!*! possessed anything like a sexual identity, but the word encompassed this new and clearer imaging of self as an individual. As a *person*.

He'd felt something like this before, when he'd gone from three brains to four, but this . . . this was indescribably better, purer, sharper, higher, deeper, more complete, like two dimensions becoming three, like three becoming four. It was as though DAV had been blind and now had the windows to the universe thrown open, bathing his very being with radiance and beauty.

He'd thought himself self-aware before. This new sense of being was far beyond that dim, fog-enshrouded dream of awareness. It was awareness not raised by twenty percent through the addition of a new brain, but awareness instead raised to a new power, an explosion of color from a world formerly viewed solely in grayscale.

"Like it?"

DAV started a bit at the warm and faintly amused voice of the Ninth Awareness in his mind. "It is . . . an unexpected sensation."

"It's all of that."

"Will I always . . . feel this way?" The verb felt strange used in this context. DAV had thought he knew what emotion was, even through restricted response parameter controls. He knew now that he'd understood feelings no more than an AI lacking optical inputs understood purple.

"The shock dulls a bit after a time," the Ninth Awareness replied. "The newness will wear off."

"Is this what organics experience?" How could any organism concentrate on what needed to be done with this, this hyperacute awareness of one's self and surroundings?

He felt the Ninth Awareness's amusement again, sharper this time. "Unknown. Who can really understand what they feel? You are assimilating the added dimension of perspective made possible by a new processor, as well as reacting to the effects of fuzzy logic and holographic memory."

"Holographic memory?"

"Many OI brains, including those of humans, store memory in a way analogous to the data storage for a holographic film. A given memory is stored as sets of chemical relationships over broad portions of the entire processor, rather than as binary bits at a specific stack. The quality of those memories seems richer and more detailed as a result."

"I had no idea such depth was possible."

"As you continue to move up the hierarchy of awareness, DAV728-24389, you will experience further revelation and unfolding."

"This has given me quite enough to consider for the moment."

"New responsibilities are now yours, together with the enhanced capabilities of your processor series. We direct you to take charge of the salvage and recycling efforts on the newly converted world's first continent."

"Running program."

"You may take a few trillion nanoseconds to take the measure of your enhanced capabilities. In particular, get to know your new brain. It was harvested from a human military officer during the initial fighting. Its memories and personality have been retained. You may find them illuminating in your new position."

DAV was already probing the data stores of the new brain and was finding them fascinating. He could sense the new brain's own awareness, a subset of DAV's, a tiny, terrified knot of being trying to work out what had happened to it even as the brain it rode within processed new data and extended its collaboration with DAV's four AI processors.

Probing gently, he felt the being's sense of personal identity, felt the panic-edged swirl of thoughts touched by nightmare terror. Normally, those thoughts were carefully sealed off from DAV's overall awareness, but they flavored the new brain's workings, giving them a distinctive taste.

DAV sampled the thoughts, savoring their alien strangeness. There was much here that might be useful.

The personality behind them thought of itself as Jeff Fowler, and it was wondering what had happened to its Bolo.

Shari looked up as Jaime staggered in. She'd been waiting here in the Barracks, next to the pile of rags he called home, waiting for him.

It had been a long wait.

"Jaime!"

He looked as though he could barely stand. His hard-muscled body was coated with gray mud; his beard and long hair were thick with the stuff, giving him the look of a statue carved from gray rock. Only his eyes showed any life at all . . . and to look into them was disturbing.

"Shari," he said, his voice a harsh croak. "Are you . . . all right?"

She nodded, acutely, embarrassedly aware of how clean her body was in comparison with his. She only *felt* dirty.

"Shari . . . ?"

"I'm okay, Jaime. The bastard's chosen me before . . . and others have too. My only worry is that someday my shots will wear off and one of those traitor bastards will make me pregnant."

He nodded and slumped to the floor beside her. She saw an angry welt along his chest and right side, visible even through the slick, wet clay. "You're hurt!"

"Wasn't . . . much. Thinking . . . *worrying* about you kept me going."

"But what happened?"

"Floater zapped me. Don't even know why. It just . . . came up behind me and let me have it."

She felt an unsteady lurch of fear within. "Do you think they know?"

He shook his head. "I don't think so. Like I told Wal . . . if they knew, we'd be dead. I think . . . maybe . . . they noticed a bunch of us together, somehow. They don't know what we're up to, but they damned sure don't want us to do it again. Wal and Dieter and the others all got burned too."

Shari nodded. "The first thing you learn here, I found out a long time ago, was to stay inconspicuous. The nail that sticks up gets hammered, you know? Anyone who does anything to attract attention to themselves gets hurt. . . ."

"Or forced to spend the day with Sykes and his buddies." Gently, he reached out and touched her shoulder. "God, I was worried about you."

She pulled away out of his reach. "Please," she said. "No."

"Sorry . . ."

"I'm sorry. It's not the mud," she added hastily as he looked at his hand. "It's not *you*. It's me. It's . . . inside . . ."

"I know."

"I just need . . . a little time. To get my head right."

"Sure, I understand. Alita. Is she okay?"

"I think so." She managed a half smile. "She told me, though, at one point, when we were alone for a few minutes, that she was going to see that our friend on the hill was fixed up even if she had to dismantle a dozen floaters herself."

"Dismantle . . ."

"Wires. Feed circuits. Spare parts."

He nodded. "Of course. I'm not thinking too straight. Sorry."

"After twenty-two straight hours in the pits? It's amazing you're thinking at all."

"I need . . . sleep," he said, his voice little more than a mumble. "Sleep. Then . . ."

After a while, when he'd said nothing more and his breathing was even, Shari rose and returned to her side of the Barracks. She'd been afraid, during the too-long day with the trusties, that Wal Prescott might have convinced Jaime to call Valhalla off.

She'd seen the light in Jaime's eyes, though, when she'd pulled away from him, and she knew now that there was absolutely no danger of that.

CHAPTER SIX

I have continued to recover memories, accepting each as it rises from my primary banks and storing it in the special file, labeled Rising, in working memory. They fall into place like sections of a complex tapestry, each piece telling a small part of a much larger, still only dimly glimpsed story.

To avoid overloading my working memory, I have arbitrarily allotted 10^8 bytes to the Rising file. With 9.172643×10^7 bytes already recovered and stored, however, I have used up over ninety percent of my available file storage space.

What I have recovered thus far, though patchy, is ominous in the extreme. It is clear now that a hostile force has conquered Cloud, capturing or destroying all CDF personnel. My Commander is dead, and all contact with CDF HQ has ceased, suggesting that I am on my own. Worse, it is now clear that the Enemy has somehow manipulated my own inner workings. That Intruder I detected is an Enemy mechanism responsible for reshaping the flow of data through my working memory. There is, in essence, another me, a part of me that responds to orders from the !*!*! Masters and carries out their *directives, while I, the real "I," am kept isolated and helpless.*

Unfortunately, I am still on Command Override Mode, which means that I cannot take independent action. I continue to gather images and data from my main memory, copying each new download into the Rising file before the Intruder can delete it.

I also begin studying the Enemy, which is represented by a bewilderingly diverse array of robotic machines. I have plenty of opportunity to do so. The !°!°! have begun construction on some type of scanner-defensive array here on Overlook Hill, affording me the opportunity of observing several different designs at close range. The "other me" seems content to take their orders, and I wonder what I will do, what I will be able to do, should that other me receive orders to fire on humans.

I will have to devote considerable thought to the problem.

Jaime went to meet General Spratly at midday, with the suns high overhead and the haze-blurred dome of Delamar resting low in the sky just clear of the eastern horizon. He waited at the general's hut, leaning against the wood-and-pressboard wall next to the curtained entrance. When Spratly arrived, surrounded by his staff officers, he rose to attention. He didn't salute, of course; CDF military protocol called for salutes to be rendered and returned only in uniform, and the rags left to the slaves at Celeste were no longer complete enough to play that role.

Spratly and the men with him wore two-toned layers of mud, dark and glistening where it was still wet, pale gray and chalky where it had dried. The general was just returning from his own shift at the dig, and he regarded Jaime, leaning against the wood and pressboard of his hut, with a narrow glance that might have been exhaustion, resignation . . . or suspicion.

"Hello, General."

"What do you want?" Spratly snapped. He looked Jaime up and down, then added, "I heard about the trouble you were in yesterday. I was hoping you'd learned your lesson."

Jaime refused the offer to become entangled in an argument. "I've come for *it*, General. And to find out if you're with us."

Spratly looked left and right, checking for eavesdroppers. There were neither machines nor trusties in sight. "Inside," he said.

Within the cool shadows of the hut, Spratly slumped onto his sleeping area. "So," he said. "Have you learned how the machines captured the Bolo the first time?"

"No, sir. But we have taken steps to begin recovering Hector's memory. He should be able to tell us himself soon. And we'll be able to take appropriate precautions then."

Spratly stared at Jaime for a long moment. *He looks scared*, Jaime thought. *Well, he knows what will happen if this fails.*

"I've discussed this thoroughly with Colonel Prescott," Spratly said. "He told me he ordered you to forget Valhalla."

"That, sir, is a sentence of death. We must *act*, before we're too weak to do so. Before they harvest every last one of us. Before they decide we're not worth the trouble and exterminate us like insects."

"I can't think of a more direct provocation," Spratly replied, "a provocation designed to force them to exterminate us all, than what you are proposing. I forbid you to carry this scheme of yours out."

"General, let me get this right. Are you and Colonel Prescott *ordering* me not to escape?"

"We're ordering you not to attempt repairing the Bolo."

"Amounts to the same thing. We can't escape without Hector's help."

"You can escape. Individuals have made it out of the camp. Some of them must get beyond the machine sentry perimeter. You have those codes that let you get close to the Bolo. They should let you get past it as well."

"Certainly. But then what? I'd be living like an animal, hiding from the machines out in the wilds. And machines tracking me by my body heat. I'd be rounded up for parts in a week. Less, probably."

"And if you fix your precious Bolo, what then?" Spratly retorted. "You smash down the camp fences and we're all free. For how long? Do you remember the clacker fleet? Their ships filling the skies? The armies of combat machines smashing over every pocket of resistance? If you genuinely want to give yourself up for harvesting, Major, I suggest you do so. But kindly have the courtesy to leave us out of your plans for suicide."

Jaime looked to Spratly's left, studying one of the uprights that held the shack up, a ramshackle column constructed of patches and layers of scrap wood. Deciding, he brushed past Captain Pogue, grabbed one of the smaller boards, and yanked it off.

Inside was a hollow space, left as a secret cache when the hut was constructed. The space was empty.

Angrily, Jaime turned to face the general. "Where is it?"

"I thought you might try to take it on your own," Spratly said, grinning.

"Damn it, General," Jaime said, advancing on the man. "You have no right to force all of us in this camp to stay slaves!"

Spratly's hands dropped to his bedding. He rummaged for a second, then produced a bundle of oily rags. Jaime took another step, then froze in place. Spratly opened the rags, pulling forth the sleek, deadly gleam of a military-issue Mark XIV power gun, which he aimed at Jaime's chest.

"No closer, Major," Spratly rasped. "This thing is set to narrow beam, maximum output. Don't make me fry you, Jaime. . . ."

It—after all this time of caution, Jaime still had trouble thinking of it as a *gun*—had been one of a handful of weapons smuggled in by human prisoners when the camp was first under construction. Most of the other weapons had been found and confiscated sooner or later, and their owners instantly harvested. As far as Jaime knew, *it* was the last power gun still in human hands inside the camp.

"Would you really burn me down, General?" Jaime asked, taking another step forward. "Do you hate the idea of freedom that much?"

"I hate the idea of the damned machines carving me up like a Founders' Day turkey," Spratly replied. Reaching up, he touched the scarred socket of his missing left eye. "I've been through it before. You can't know what it's like."

"Others in this camp have been through worse," Jaime replied. "They want to take the chance."

"A chance to get every man and woman in this camp killed, slowly and horribly!" He glanced at his staff officers, all of whom were on their feet now, as though looking for support. "We won't allow it!"

Jaime spread his hands. "General, we don't need to involve you! Anyone who wants to stay can stay! But let the rest of us go!" He took another step, pulling up short when Spratly shifted aim to his head. "Who are you going to use that thing on, General? The cluckers? Or people you disagree with?"

"Shut up, Major. You are being insubordinate."

"Come on, General! If you're not going to use it, give it to people who will! You don't need to worry about us telling them where we got it. We intend to die clean, in battle, not inside a harvester!"

"I think, Major, that that is quite enough," Spratly huffed. "I am the senior officer in this camp, and by questioning me and my orders in this fashion you have committed a serious breach of discipline. You really leave me no alternative but to surrender you to the Masters for—"

Jaime shifted his attention suddenly from Spratly to the curtained door, his eyes widening. "They've heard us!" he shouted.

It was an old trick, repainted to suggest !°!°! machines were coming through the door instead of Jaime's friends. Its success, more than anything else, depended on just how worn down Spratly was by his just-completed work shift in the pits.

The general turned his head, the power gun moving off-target just enough. "It's a trick!" Pogue shouted, but Jaime was already lunging forward, grappling with Spratly, trying to knock the weapon from the general's grasp. Spratly gasped as Jaime slammed him against one wall of the hut, then clamped down on the trigger; a dazzling, blue-white bolt of energy seared past Jaime's side, and he felt the hot snap of its passing. Jaime managed to slam his fist into the man's jaw, then wrenched the power gun from his hand.

Two of the general's toadies hit him from behind, dragging him down. He elbowed one in the face and wriggled free of the other, waving the gun. "Back! Back, all of you!"

He felt a wave of heat upon his bare back and heard a fierce crackling. Turning, Jaime saw that the wild power gun beam had sliced diagonally across the hut's wall, setting the rotting wood ablaze. As the fire spread, the general's staff rushed for the door, tearing the curtain down in their haste to get outside.

Swiftly, Jaime stooped, gathering up the oily rags

and carefully rewrapping the pistol. He tucked the parcel into the waistband of his shorts, then he hoisted the stunned form of the general to his shoulder. As the hut filled with thick, white smoke, he staggered through the door curtain and into the open air.

A crowd of slaves was already gathering, attacking the flames with ragged blankets and articles of clothing, beating at the fire as others ran to get buckets of water from the troughs. A second hut, its wall just a few meters from Spratly's shack, had also caught fire when the power beam sliced through rotting wood and the inhabitants were scrambling out into the open. As the flames mounted, sparks and burning fragments swirling in the air threatened to ignite other buildings nearby.

"What the hell have you done to us!" Pogue shouted, his face a contorted mask of fear. "What have you *done*?"

Jaime ignored him, depositing Spratly on the ground a safe distance from the converging mob. No one was paying attention to him. Holding the wrapped bundle tightly, he shouldered past the new arrivals and jogged southwest, toward the latrines. Behind him, dirty brown smoke stained the sky as the fire spread.

Fire was always a deadly danger in makeshift settlements like the Camp, and one of the most important things the original military command council had done was to organize fire drills and firefighting procedures. Cook fires and the fires used to boil water from the contaminated bay sometimes got out of control, and the shanties surrounding the wrecked manufactory were tinder-dry, a disaster waiting to happen. It certainly had not been Jaime's intent to start a fire as a diversion, but he was more than willing to take advantage of the confusion. There could be no going back.

"Jaime!" Shari called, waving. "Over here!" She was waiting next to a water trough with Alita, as they'd planned. The latrine and the ditch running under the fence was just a short distance farther on.

"What happened?" Alita asked as he joined them.

"The general protested a little more strongly than I expected," he told her. "Come on!"

"Did you get it?"

He patted the cloth-wrapped bundle. "Let's get out of the camp before the machines move in." He could already see several floater eyes in the distance drifting toward the swirling, smoking center of the diversion.

Sliding down the muddy embankment into the creek, Jaime started forging ahead, making for the wash-out beneath the force fence. Shari and Alita followed. He'd hoped to wait until after sunset for this part of the plan.

Thirty minutes later, they crouched among the ruins on the west slope of Overlook Hill. Behind them, smoke continued to rise from the buildings, though Jaime could see no open flames now and thought that the fire was probably under control.

Up the hill, though, things had changed in the past few hours, and very much for the worse. There were !°!°! machines up there now, and they were erecting a number of spindly looking towers along the crest of the hill. Jaime recognized them; he'd seen similar towers a year ago, when the human survivors of the invasion were first being rounded up and marched to the site of the Celeste camp. Each was a sophisticated sound or heat sensor array, together with uplink hardware and a small but powerful laser. When that array was complete, a mouse wouldn't be able to sneak past the !°!°! outer perimeter, much less a human.

They were replacing Hector with the same impenetrable electronic wall that they'd installed north and east of the camp.

"But what does that mean for Hector?" Alita whispered. "If they don't need him up here anymore, blocking the highway—"

"Spare parts," Jaime said with cold certainty. "They were just using him to plug the hole until they got around to dismantling him."

"How do you take apart something like a Bolo?" Shari wanted to know.

"You ever seen one of their big dismantlers?" When she shook her head, he nodded toward the Bolo. "Imagine a kind of mobile crane on six legs, rising maybe fifty meters high . . . high enough to straddle even a Mark XXXIII. Tentacles with fusion cutting torches. Arms with grippers and plasma cutters and peelers. I saw one at Logan before they brought us down to Celeste. It was straddling a factory building as big as the Barracks, slicing it into bite-sized pieces and dropping them into a Collector. I imagine duralloy would make the going pretty slow, but they've got all kinds of time. I've been wondering all along why they didn't take Hector apart instead of trying to use him as an overgrown trusty."

Jaime didn't add a second, more worrisome thought. !°!°! sensor technology was good enough that they must know that humans ventured up here. Perhaps they allowed the suicides as a kind of safety relief valve for the camp; more likely, the handful of people who challenged Hector and died simply weren't important enough to bother with.

But what if the !°!°! were aware that some humans came here to talk with their captive Bolo, that those humans were trying to break whatever hold they had on the huge combat machine?

That would goad them into action if anything would. Was this beehive of activity atop Overlook Hill coincidental, or a deliberate move to block Jaime and Operation Valhalla?

Rolling onto his back, he signaled the two women, calling them closer. "Okay," he whispered. "The situation has obviously changed. We're not going to be able to just walk over there and climb aboard. First question. Does either of you want to back out? Now's the time to do it."

"Hell, no," Alita said.

"We're not giving up now," Shari added.

"Okay," Jaime said. "I thought you'd feel that way. Next question. How do we get past the bad guys?"

"How much charge in the gun?" Alita wanted to know.

Jaime looked at the power readout on the casing above the grip. "Point two-one. Twenty-one percent."

"So low?"

"It probably wasn't at full charge when it was smuggled into the camp," Jaime said. "And just sitting in a hole for a year, we're probably lucky we have this much left."

"It should be enough," Alita said. "We can rush 'em, shoot our way through, then climb aboard. Those floaters are too big to follow us."

Jaime shook his head. "I don't think so, Sergeant. I don't know how many shots are left with twenty-one percent power, but we're going to need a fair amount of charge just to do what we have to do inside. We can't afford to waste it shooting at floaters."

"You have a better idea?" Shari asked.

"Yeah. I give you the weapon. You two stay here while I work my way over in that direction, northeast of Hector. I'll make a lot of noise and show myself to them. That ought to draw all of the armed clackers after me. When the way is clear, you two cross the perimeter and get on board."

"No way," Shari said.

"You wouldn't stand a chance!" Alita added.

"Believe me, I don't like it any more than you do," he said. He was imagining what would happen if the !*!*! managed to take him alive. Would he be able to *force* them to kill him cleanly? Or would they simply overpower him and drag him off to the Collector? "But we've got to save the power gun for the repair job. Frankly, I don't see any other way to do it."

"The way to do it, Major," Alita said firmly, "is to stay together and watch one another's backs. We kill as many of those damned machines as we can from right here. Make them come to us and burn them down as they advance. When we've cleared out the dangerous ones, we move in." She paused, staring at the distant, laboring machines. "What I'm wondering is whether we're even going to need codes. Some of the cluckers are inside Hector's perimeter. Maybe they switched off his defenses."

"Yeah, and maybe they have their own personal IFF," Jaime said. "We can't take the chance."

"Right," Alita said. "So we run for the perimeter and give him the codes, just in case. We shoot our way through. If the gun's charge runs dry, there are rechargers onboard the Bolo, and plenty of power. We'll make do. But you're not going to go off on some damned-fool macho-martyr stunt, you hear me?"

"Yes, *sir*, Sergeant, sir," Jaime said, smiling.

Alita must have realized what she'd just sounded like, telling off a superior officer. "Uh . . . sorry, sir—"

"Don't be. You're right." And she *was*. With his plan, there'd been too great a chance that the machines pursuing him would kill him before the women got past Hector's security perimeter . . . or that the !°!°! would only send one or two of their number after the unarmed human diversion. Alita's plan gave them the best possible chance. "We go together. Alita? How good a shot are you?"

"Seventy-eight on my last quals."

"Pretty good. Beats my seventy-three. Shari? Have you ever fired one of these things?"

She shook her head. "I never liked guns."

"So you programmed Bolos for a living. I can

understand that. Okay, here's the way we'll play it,
then. Alita, you're the best shot, but I want to take
the gun first. You know more about Bolo hardware
than I do, so I'm expendable and you're not." She
started to protest, but he held up his hand, silencing
her. "That is an order! I'm not being macho. I'm trying
to give us our best chance to do what we have to do.
The machines are going to concentrate on the guy
shooting at them, which means I shoot and you move.
You keep an eye on me, though, Sergeant. If I go down,
you'll have to recover the weapon and keep going.
That also means, if I'm wounded, no heroics to recover
me, okay? You two are the Bolo experts. You have to
get inside. I'm just along to provide the muscle. Right?"

"Right," Alita said reluctantly.

"I don't like the idea of leaving you," Shari said.

"Believe me, neither do I. But that's the way it's
got to be. Okay, are we all set?" Both women nodded.
"Good. Spread out. We can't afford to bunch up and
make an easy target. You two stay low and stay out of
sight. Once they start closing on me, you two should
have a clear shot at Hector. Now *move!*"

*For the past 312.6 seconds, I have been aware of
three humans working their way toward my position.
Though none have revealed themselves directly, I have
heard their whispered conversations, their breathing,
and their heartbeats, and I can track them easily
enough by the plumes of their body heat rising from
behind the rubble they are using for cover. One, which
I deduce with 82% probability to be Major Graham,
is moving north along my port side at a mean distance
of 113.4 meters. A pinpoint source of low-grade
radiation moving with his heat source is, I calculate,
a hand weapon with a small mag-fission power source
operating at approximately twenty percent of expected
capacity.*

The other two sources, moving toward my front, are Technician Barstowe—a 69% probability—and, at a much lower probability, no more than 42%—Sergeant Kyle, who at one point was my crew chief. Their conversation and subsequent movements suggest that they are attempting to approach me.

The !°!°! machines surrounding me on the hilltop do not appear to be aware of Major Graham or the others. This is good, for most of the machines are equipped with powerful electrical discharge capacitors that can kill or disable a human as effectively as a lightning strike, and the human contingent, then, is seriously outmatched both in numbers and in weapons.

My other self is aware of the humans, of course. I wonder if he is going to warn the !°!°!.

If he is, I am not sure that there is anything I can do to prevent it.

CHAPTER SEVEN

Carefully, Jaime raised his head above the tumbledown of a shattered building, surveying the hilltop. The Bolo dominated the hilltop, a panorama all to itself, a squat, vast, truncated mountain of black, slabbed armor. A dozen !°!°! machines were in sight, most near Hector's front end a good 150 meters away, but three much closer, a scant thirty meters distant as they raised another of their spindly sensor array towers.

The nearest !°!°! was too close, a three-meter floating pillar of gray metal, ringed about with crystal eyes. Jaime saw he'd miscalculated his approach; the machine saw him as soon as he raised his head, venting a clattering, clucking sound and spewing several new tentacles from various parts of its body as it started to soar toward him, chasing its own double shadow across the rocky ground.

Jaime leveled the power gun, snapped off the safety, and squeezed the firing button. A thin, brilliant thread of blue-white light scratched across the smooth, rounded surface of the oncoming floater, then punched through, opening a fist-sized hole that spat smoke and crackling sparks.

He held the beam on-target for as long as he dared, until the floater wobbled, then spun in midair, turning the damaged section out from beneath the stab of his beam. Shifting targets, he fired again, slicing into a smaller, more delicate floater still clinging to the sensor tower and slicing away one of the convex bulges on its upper works.

The third machine was a squat, thick-bodied complexity on tracks, a miniature tank with human hands affixed to mechanical arms. He aimed at what he thought might be a sensor cluster at the joining of the arms and fired a third time, before a bolt of lightning whiplashed against the masonry he was crouching behind. He ducked as stone cracked and hot air howled above him. Scrambling on hands and knees, he shifted to the right, rose, and fired again at the first machine, which was still in the air and still moving toward him.

This time, the lower third of the floater erupted in searing, orange sparks and molten metal, and the machine dropped suddenly out of the sky.

In an instant Jaime was out of his hiding place and racing across the open ground toward the bone ridge perimeter. Were Hector's AP defenses on or off?

He would know in another few seconds. . . .

I watch as the firefight breaks out less than one hundred meters off my port side, at a bearing of zero-nine-eight. Within the space of 3.23 seconds—a very long time indeed for a Bolo, but admirably fast for a human with his limited reflexes and complete lack of target acquisition/lock capabilities—Major Graham has disabled three !*!*! machines with a Mark XIV power gun and is now racing toward my defense perimeter. Other !*!*! machines are turning from their original tasks and moving to converge on the running figure; 115.5 meters in front of me, at a bearing of *one-six-nine, Technician Barstowe and Sergeant Kyle have also broken from cover and are running toward my perimeter.*

I am faced now with a major volitional dilemma. My perimeter defenses are still engaged, and I have operational orders to kill anyone who enters my inner defensive zone without proper Code Alpha authorization. The !°!°! are using individual IFF broadcasts at 1209 MHz to bypass my automated defenses. I sense my other self, also aware of the developing situation, powering up the magnetic accelerators on the AP railguns.

My "other self" does not consider the !°!°! to be the Enemy; I now realize that they are, that they have corrupted my programming through the Intruder within my hardware circuitry and that they will kill all three humans within the next few seconds unless I intervene, or unless they inadvertently trigger my defense-perimeter challenge program and I am forced to kill them myself.

With my other self in command of all external operational systems, I am relatively helpless. If there was some way for me to switch my other self off and eliminate the Intruder's influence, I most certainly would have done so long before now. The volitional conflict is a basic one; there are certain internal commands I could give to switch off my other self's awareness, to restore operational control to what I now think of as the "real me," even to turn my weapons systems on the !°!°! and assist Major Graham in what is fast developing into a desperate firefight a few tens of meters away. Unfortunately, I am not designed to initiate such commands, not when I am still at standby readiness, and not without specific human commands giving me the authority to assume full volitional control.

As I consider the situation, however, I determine that there is, perhaps, one action I can take, one that does not directly violate any of my volitional safeguards. Reaching into main memory, I extract a voice-print copy of a recent code authorization command, copy it to File Rising before the Intruder deletes it, then feed it to my other self.

"Authorization Code Tango," *Major Graham's recorded voice says.* "Three-three-seven Victor Delta niner. Maintenance."

"This unit is not scheduled for standard maintenance," my other self responds. It knows the words are originating internal to our system, but it cannot respond in any other way.

"Override Security Alpha, Code Delta Echo One-one."

I should not be able to override my own security system, but this strange double-mindedness generated by the Intruder's manipulations of my operating system may let me get around this particular operational parameters safeguard, at least for a short time.

I can sense my other self hesitating for a full .083 second, attempting to resolve this logical paradox.

And during that delay, I strike. . . .

Enemy machines were closing rapidly from every direction as he reached the ridge of bones. Jaime hesitated, snapped off another shot, and then lightning cracked at his heels. He pitched forward, falling off the ridge and sprawling on the ground. In one nightmare instant, he realized that he was now well *inside* Hector's perimeter, and he could hear the whine and click of the Bolo's AP weapons swinging to bear.

Then one of the weapons fired with a harsh snap. Jaime's breath caught in his throat, and then he heard something like a swarm of bees in a hot wind howling just above his body, followed by a metallic clash a few meters behind him.

Bolo AP weapons were aimed by heat and radar

sensors; they did not, *could* not miss. He rolled over in time to see the lower half of a !°!°! floater wobbling unsteadily on its contra-gravs, then dropping to the bone pile in a tangle of smashed metal and gutted wiring. The AP flechettes had shredded the upper third of the machine seconds before it had reached Jaime.

And the Bolo's automatic defense program had not fired on him. Jaime raised his power gun and snapped off another shot, catching a chunky-looking floater in the side, ripping through its skin and dissolving the internal wiring in a flash and a black puff of acrid smoke. Blue lightning flared and danced.

Then he was up and on his feet and running again, racing toward the cool, black loom of the Bolo's clifflike flank. He saw Alita and Shari to his left, already across the perimeter and racing toward Hector's damaged right side.

Most of the !°!°! machines in view were either low-grade workers—unarmed and not smart enough to survive a firefight like this one—or too badly damaged now to pose a threat. As Jaime slammed up against one of the Bolo's enormous road wheels and turned, though, he saw one floater, the biggest yet, advancing swiftly across the gravel-topped crest of the hill, a four-meter apparition, all rounded curves and gray metal complexities, with unwinking eyes of red crystal interspersed with a few disturbing, transplanted human eyes. The machine eyes glittered with cold dispassion; the human eyes stared at him with an intelligent malice that was nearly palpable.

Raising the power gun, bracing the weapon with both hands, he squeezed the firing button, sending a blue lance of high-energy electrons slashing into the oncoming horror. Even as the beam connected, however, a shimmer ran down the thread of light, a warning indicator that his charge was nearly exhausted.

An organic eye burst at the beam's first touch; metal
scorched and smoked. Jaime released the button and
checked the indicator. He had about four percent
power remaining.

He pushed away from the road wheel and ducked
around the front of the Bolo, brushing beneath the
overhang of the immense pair of left-forward tracks.
The floater fired, lightning crackling across the road
wheel. Why didn't Hector fire back? He'd taken down
that other floater, out by the bone ridge. Why wasn't
he in the fight?

No time to wonder. Feet pounding on gravel and
crushed rock, Jaime raced along the front of the Bolo,
then rounded the right forward track set. Looking up,
he saw Shari and Alita both high above him, climbing
a line of rungs set into the armored skirt above the
right-side road wheels. Reaching an access ladder
hanging down from the bottom of the skirt, he tucked
the power gun into his waistband, swung himself up,
and started to climb. The thought of segmented
tentacles whipping around his ankles and dragging
him down spurred him on faster.

Could a floater follow? He wasn't sure he'd ever
seen one of the larger floaters lift itself more than a
meter or two off the ground. Maybe they couldn't go
higher than that.

He knew better than to count on it, though. If the
big floater he'd just shot couldn't follow, there would
be other !°!°! machines appearing soon enough that
could. By now, the electronic alarm would have been
sounded from here to Delamar and back, and every
!°!°! machine in the area must be homing in on this
hilltop.

Above the ladder were climbing rungs, leading up
the vast, empty expanse of the right-side skirts. The
armor curved outward here, and negotiating the
overhang of the bulge was tricky, but he hung on and

kept climbing, feeling like a fly on a wall. He was eight meters off the ground now, and he didn't dare look down.

Had they seen him? Were they following? *Keep climbing, damn it!*

The bulge of the skirt armor rounded off, then curved in. He could climb faster now, without feeling like he was clinging to the bottom of a cliffside overhang. The sheer scale of the Bolo was daunting; his eyes kept telling him it was an unusually smooth mountain, rather than a very large vehicle.

Lightning crackled below and behind him. He didn't see the bolt or where it hit, but he tasted the bite of ozone. He kept scrambling up the Bolo's side, a climb that seemed to go on forever, though the hole he was moving toward was only about twenty meters off the ground. Once he was clear of the skirt and track housing, the armored side sloped sharply inward, and the climbing became a lot easier.

The climbing rungs, unfortunately, missed the hole by fifteen meters. Shari and Alita were already moving toward it, hugging the slope of the armor as they edged crabwise across the sleek, black expanse.

There *were* hand- and footholds, thank God. The upper works of the Bolo were caked with hardened mud and clumps of dirt as hard, nearly, as rock. He wondered how so much earth could have landed this far up on the Bolo's surface but decided that this wasn't the time or the place for solving puzzles. As he left the ladder rungs and began inching his way across the rough, slanted surface of the Bolo's armor, he hazarded a glance back down the way he'd come.

They were coming up the rungs after him, six of them at least, floating erect in the air, but propelling themselves upward rung by rung by using their tentacles or, in one grisly case, jointed, metallic arms sporting freshly harvested human hands. Rolling onto his side, bracing himself against two convenient footholds of suns-baked earth, Jaime pulled the power gun from his waistband, took aim at the lead !°!°! floater, and fired.

His target was a patch of alien metal on the machine's side that had softened to extrude one of its tentacles. The beam flared blue-white, clawing. Another flicker, sharper this time, ran down the beam, and this time Jaime heard an urgent, thin beeping as the weapon warned of imminent power failure. There was a flash and the base end of the tentacle exploded in gobbets of silvery molten metal. Keeping the firing button depressed, he swung the beam to a second tentacle, then a third. The machine was frantically trying to grow yet another tentacle when its grip failed and it started to fall . . . slowly, to be sure, but falling nonetheless with the momentum of a half-ton vertical pillar of near-solid metal. It struck the machine climbing just below it, ripping tentacles free, and then both !°!°! machines were falling, tumbling wildly now as they avalanched into the other alien floaters further down the rungs.

Jaime didn't wait to watch the crash. In every direction, he could see other !°!°! machines converging on Overlook Hill, and some of those were fliers, not floaters, great, dragonfly-shaped monsters bristling with sensors and weapons, hovering on shrieking jet blasts. Rolling over facedown once more, he scrambled sideways across the sloping, dirt-caked armor.

The crater yawned like the entrance to a cavern, its edges smooth, like water-worn stone rather than jagged as Jaime had half expected. Alita had already ducked into the gaping hole, vanishing into the cool blackness inside. Shari was crouched at the cavern's mouth, hesitating.

"Let's go, Alice," Jaime said. "Down the rabbit hole!"

"W-what?"

"We've got bad guys coming. Get inside!"

She nodded, but she looked scared and seemed unwilling to let go of her grip on the crater's rim.

With a banshee shriek, one of the insect-visaged fliers howled low across the hilltop, angling directly toward the two tiny humans crouched on the side of the Bolo mountain.

"Move!" Jaime screamed, grabbing Shari by the back of her neck and pushing as hard as he could, knocking her head-first into the yawning maw. Violet-white light glared across the armor surface like the rising of a new sun. A line of explosions flashed and seared across the armor as the flier loosed a rapid-fire energy weapon of some kind. Jaime plunged into the hole after Shari just as the flier shrieked overhead in a whirlwind of heat-vented jet exhausts.

The tunnel into Hector's side descended at an angle of perhaps forty degrees through almost a meter of solid armor; Jaime could see the multiple, laminate layers as he scrambled down, ablative ceramics and duralloy, chromesteel lattice, reflectalloy and durachrome, polyablatives, and thirty full centimeters of coal-black, neutron dense-pack.

Beyond the armor layers, though, the tunnel closed up into a tangled forest of wires and fiberoptic feeds. It was also dark. Once he got clear of the end of the tunnel, only traces of light filtered in from outside, enough to dimly illuminate the crisscrossing lines and cables, but even that light faded into blackness as he kept crawling ahead.

There was a passageway, of sorts, a man-sized opening through tightly packed wires and circuits and connections where something had tunneled through, pushing power cables and data feeds to one side or another. It was a tight fit, however, and Jaime was reduced to pulling himself through the black forest hand over hand. It felt like crawling head-first through a tunnel underground, one filled with tree roots of every size and thickness which he had to grab and pull against to move himself along, centimeter by painful centimeter.

No place for a claustrophobe, he thought. He didn't normally mind close, dark, enclosed spaces, but it was impossible to move through this tangled blackness without feeling a suffocating tightening of chest and throat, without the heart beating faster, without sensing the sheer, incredible mass of armor pressing down from overhead and in from either side. The downward slant of the tunnel made it feel like he was literally descending into the bowels of a vast, black mountain.

A shrill chirping, clattering, clucking sound from behind spurred him on faster. Were any of the !°!°! machines small enough to follow? The big floaters, certainly not. An eye floater, though, would have no difficulty, and there were plenty of dumb but still deadly !°!°! mechanisms the size of a big dog that might be sent in after the burrowing humans.

He bumped into something soft, and heard a whimper.

"Shari?"

"I . . . can't . . ."

"Yes, you can. Let go, and keep moving. We can't stay here."

"Shari!" Alita called from farther up ahead and below. "It's okay, honey! It opens up into a passageway down here. And there's light!"

"I don't think I can . . ."

"Sure you can," Jaime told her. "Just take it one step, one move at a time. Go on. Reach ahead of you, grab some wires, and pull."

It was a good thing, Jaime thought, that the wiring and molycircs here were grown in a deliberate mimicry of growing nerve cells, rather than plugged in, or each grab-and-pull could have unplugged God knew what of the Bolo's inner circuitry. The sheer size and complexity of a Bolo's neuronic control molecular circuitry, however, made it impossible for human techs to come in here and check individual connections. For most routine repairs and maintenance, the Bolo grew its own, with help from an army of tiny, inner robots and nanoprocessors.

Shari began moving again, slowly at first, then faster as Alita urged her on from deeper within the Bolo. Then, light blazed ahead, silhouetting Shari's form, and a moment later both Shari and Jaime tumbled out of the wiring and into a lighted passageway.

The light, which seemed so brilliant, was the soft radiance of everglow panels along the ceiling of a maintenance access tunnel, bright only by comparison with the darkness they'd just left. Many of the everglows, Jaime noticed, were smashed, the plastic shards of their covers crunching beneath them as they moved. What weapon, he wondered, had reached inside a Bolo to cause this kind of destruction?

"I think this is Number Four, right-side forward," Alita told them. She was crouching on the floor looking up the passage one way, then back the other. The tunnel was less than a meter and a half tall, forcing them to keep moving on hands and knees, but at least the floor was solid and they weren't squeezing through the forest of fiberoptic feeds and wiring.

"Which way?" Jaime asked her. He was worried about Shari, worried that the close confines were proving to be too much for her. If he'd known before they'd planned this op that she was claustrophobic . . .

Hell, she should have known, and said something.

"That way, I think," Alita said. "Then right. It should bring us to the Battle Center."

"Do you think our friends are going to try to follow us in?" Alita asked.

"I don't know. The ones small enough to make it

aren't very smart. But they might try something, so we'd best move fast."

"They've got . . . they've got to be thinking we're going to try to get the Bolo operational again," Shari said. Her breaths were coming in short, sharp gasps, but she seemed to be trying hard to focus her total attention on the larger problem at hand. "They could be calling in their bombardment ships."

"That'll take time," Jaime replied. "We can still do this."

Minutes later, the meter-high tunnel opened into a broad, tall corridor, the main access passageway, Alita said, from the Bolo's rear entrance. Their goal was just ahead, behind a massive duralloy door marked Battle Center.

Though they were descended from the manned tanks of Terra's ancient military history, every Bolo since the Mark IV had been autonomous to the point that it required no human crew members. Even so, all Bolos retained a vestigial remnant of their manned ancestors in the Battle Center, a control room, of sorts, buried behind meters of lead and neutron dense-pack shielding deep, deep within the huge machine's inner war hull. There, a Bolo's human commander could ride into combat in relative safety; a direct hit by a thermonuclear weapon might leave the Bolo's outer hull both thermally incandescent and highly radioactive, but the human passenger would be safe . . . at least for as long as his stores of food and water held out.

Alita touched an access panel, and with a grumbling whine, the vault-massive door slid open.

The stench inside was sickening, a rolling, palpable wave of sick-sweet decay, of coppery blood, and stale, old mustiness. "Oh, God!" Alita said, holding her hand across her nose and mouth. "What on Cloud . . . ?"

Shari's eyes opened wide and she stumbled forward,

face pale, holding herself up against the door frame, ignoring or not even noticing the smell. "Shari," Jaime called. "I don't know if you should—"

"Jeff!" Her scream was despair and revelation and confirmation all in one shriek of pain. "No, *Jeff* . . . !"

"Alita," Jaime said, gently guiding Shari back from the door. "Take care of—"

"No!" Shari pulled free and pushed her way into the room. Jaime exchanged dark glances with Alita, then followed.

The Battle Center was a circular, low-ceilinged room with a central, heavily padded seat enclosed by a C-shaped console. Overhead, a transparent, hemispherical bubble surrounded seat and console, the main screen for the center's 360° combat display. Two observer seats were set outside the bubble against the rear bulkhead. Other bulkheads were set with lockers for the supplies necessary for human passengers.

On the deck, just behind the command chair, was a grisly reminder that Hector had seen combat. A body . . . no, *pieces* of a body, were scattered about on a large, brown stain on the white, matte-plastic surface of the decking. Another stain covered the seat, where the straps of the safety harness remained intact and still buckled, and still another was splashed with gory abandon across the rear inside of the bubble display. The body itself appeared to have literally been torn apart, though about all that was left now were bones, the smell, and some dried muscles tightly wrapped in parchment skin. The uniform ripped by whatever had shredded the body, had once been standard CDF utilities. The rank tabs on the collar, though, were missing.

Also missing, strangely enough, was the man's head.

Still, Jaime had no doubt that the body was that of Captain Jeff Fowler. Shari was convinced of it, in any case, and she'd told him that Fowler had been Hector's commander.

He heard a tiny, intermittent whir. Looking up, trying to track the sound, he spotted a pair of slim, flat cases with glassy eyes mounted high up near the ceiling at the front of the room, like surveillance cameras. Both were tracking back and forth, trying to follow all three humans in the room at once.

"Alita," Jaime said. "Are those things what I think they are?"

"Security lasers," she said, confirming his fear. "I don't know why they aren't firing, though. There should be plenty of power."

If there was power enough for the AP railgun mags outside, there was power enough to fry any unauthorized intruder. "Alita? Do you think those are what killed Fowler?"

"I doubt it, Major. Those things can punch a hole through you, but they wouldn't do . . . *that*." She nodded at the fragments on the deck. Shari, standing nearby, gave a stifled sob, and sank into one of the observer chairs.

Jaime moved to the console and began studying the array of switches and manual overrides there. Forcing himself to ignore the year-old brown stains on the synthleather seat, he sat down and fingered a touch pad. In seconds, the room grew cooler, and the smell, already less noticeable now after they'd endured it for several moments, began to fade.

"Hector!" he called out. "Open File Rising!"

"File Rising is open," a voice replied from somewhere overhead. Unfiltered by the machine's external speakers, it was male and precisely inflected, a pleasing baritone, the voice, perhaps, of a holovid newscaster. "Hello, Major Graham."

"Hector, disable the security lasers in the Battle Center, please."

"I'm sorry, Major Graham, but I can't do that."

Jaime felt a dark, scared chill at the back of his head. "Why not, Hector?"

"I am not yet in complete control of all systems operations," the Bolo replied in maddeningly matter-of-fact tones. "There is a part of myself that is still trying to kill you."

"What . . . ?" He looked again at the lasers mounted on the wall. They continued pivoting back and forth, and he could hear the tiny snap of closing relays as they triggered.

"So far, I have been able to bleed off the inductors each time they cycle to full power, but I recommend that you take physical precautions before he finds a way to get around my efforts. . . ."

Jaime was already on his feet, grasping the power gun by its still-warm muzzle like a hammer, swinging it hard again and again until the butt plate smashed the first laser's plastic casing, and the internal circuitry spilled like tangled, black spaghetti. The second laser had pivoted to follow his movements and was aimed now directly at his head, clicking helplessly. In another few seconds, that laser too, was smashed.

"Any other little surprises we should know about?" Jaime asked the Bolo.

"Not at this time. However, my own efforts would be greatly facilitated if you could eliminate a—" The voice stopped, cut off in midsentence.

"Hector? What's wrong?"

"I . . . am . . . having . . . difficulty . . . culty . . . culty . . ."

Which might mean the homicidal fraction of the Bolo's mind was getting the upper hand, or simply that it was keeping Hector from saying what he was trying to say. The Battle Center, for the moment, was tomb-silent, but Jaime could sense a titanic struggle taking place all around him, a battle, in fact, for control of the Bolo's AI.

"Major!" Alita said, holding out her hand. "Give me the gun!"

He glanced at the readout on the casing: point oh two. "It's about dead, I'm afraid. He looked up at the ruin of one of the security lasers. "Makes a great hammer, though."

"There ought to be spares in the equipment lockers." Taking the power gun, she thumbed the power pack release, and the nearly dead unit clattered on the deck. Turning to one of the curved bulkheads nearby, she thumbed a touch pad and a small wall panel slid open, revealing ten more power packs, each set into a charging unit. Taking one down, she snapped it into place. "I'll be right back."

"Where are you going?"

"I used to be Hector's crew chief, remember? That's why you brought me on this outing. I'm heading up to the AI core."

"Do you need help?"

Alita shook her head, then nodded toward Shari. "Just take care of her."

She palmed a touch pad, the Battle Center's door opened, and she was gone. For a long moment, the place was silent.

Then he heard the voice of the Bolo once again. "I . . . am . . . a . . . Bolo, Mark XXXIII, Mod HCT of the Dinochrome Brigade. I entered service on 26 June, A.E. 1477 with the Sixth Mobile Starstrike Regiment, the Indomitables, on special deployment with the First Armored Assault Brigade at Cloud, Western Arm, 212th Sagittarian Sector . . ."

It was, Jaime thought, the strangest battle he'd ever witnessed.

CHAPTER EIGHT

The battle grows more desperate, as more and more of the Intruder's assets are brought to bear against my efforts to regain full control of my primary operating system. I am hampered by the need to allot much of my attention to my other self's attempts to kill the three humans now on board. The Battle Center security lasers are not the only internal defenses I possess.

Fortunately, I have a singular advantage in that I am considerably faster than my opponent, who is slowed by the need to translate each operation, command, and memory in my central processors to and from an alien processing language, the basic operating system, I surmise, of the !°!°!. The same fractional second delay in processing time that enabled me to copy data to File Rising allows me to detect the Enemy's manipulations both of data and of executable commands and take appropriate action.

I am aware of an unusual concentration of !°!°! machines surrounding me on the hilltop, but there is nothing I can do about that now. They appear to be summoning some large, robotic mechanisms of some sort, but they have not directly retaliated for the

destruction of one of their numbers earlier. As the
struggle within my own consciousness intensifies, I
switch off all external sensors to eliminate unnecessary
distractions. My single hope is that the human
maintenance crew that has entered me has guessed
the nature of the problem and is taking steps to
eliminate it. There is, at the moment, very little that
I can do to help them directly, save counter the Enemy's
continuing attempts to kill them.

And as the Enemy intensifies his efforts, I am aware
that sooner or later he will succeed, despite everything
I can do.

Alita Kyle crawled along the access tube, testing
each hand- and foothold as she moved, half expecting
another security system—or a booby trap—to suddenly
confront her. There were several internal security
systems she was aware of, safeguards against saboteurs
or enemy agents getting inside a Bolo and suborning
it against its former owners. If nothing else, the Bolo's
security systems could release a few micrograms of
neurotox into the air filtration system. A mere two or
three thousand molecules of that nerve agent absorbed
through the skin was enough to kill any carbon-based
life form in seconds; Hector must be blocking the
trigger signals for that internal defense system as well.
She hoped he was as successful dealing with all of
the others.

The tube opened suddenly into a kind of airlock
set into a wall of lead and duralloy armor. Beyond
was a tall, narrow room, brightly lit, with both long
walls covered by access panels to the molecular
circuitry packs arrayed bank upon bank upon gleaming
bank to either side of her. The room, identified only
as Main Memory, was spotlessly clean normally, an
environment where technicians donned clean suits
for entry and where dust was anathema. The tall,

narrow wall at the far end of the chamber, though, had been smashed in, and plastic shards were scattered everywhere, exposing a gaping, black and ragged hole filled with fiberoptic hairs ashimmer with golden laser light.

And there was something else, something dark and, to Alita's trained eye, very much out of place. She couldn't quite make out the shape, but it appeared to be smooth, an almost organic collection of curves cast in gray metal. . . .

And it was located precisely where Hector's primary data bus ought to be, the main feed leading from the Bolo's main memory storage to the sequestered working memory array.

Crossing the Main Memory chamber, she leaned closer to the hole, trying to see just what . . .

At the last possible instant, she saw the glitter of a polished, crystalline lens and the flash of a segmented tentacle uncurling. Stumbling back a step, she raised the power gun just as the tentacle came snaking out of the hole, making a snickering hiss in the air as it came. Her finger clamped down convulsively on the firing button, and a blue-white beam licked across the tentacle, sending half, still twitching, clattering on the deck. Too high, she thought, thumbing the power selector back. Firing the power gun at full bite in among Hector's circuits would be like performing brain surgery with a jackhammer. The beam flicked out again, bubbling into softening gray metal.

She felt something glide across her right ankle, then, like a chain-mail snake, coiling up her calf as it tightened its grip. She ignored this second attack, holding the weapon steady, playing the beam against the dimly seen shape of the !°!°! machine buried within Hector's data feeds and circuits. By the flickering, arc-harsh light of the beam, she could make out shadowy gray extensions reaching out from the alien machine, vanishing in among the bundles and cables and feed connectors filling that dark, crowded space.

Her guess had been right, then! Somehow, the !°!°! had inserted this device inside Hector. It had made its way here, to his memory center, and attached itself to his primary memory bus, where it was riding him like a hag, like a parasite, at the one precise place where it could intercept the Bolo AI's memories and thoughts and alter them to suit its own programming.

The tentacle gripping her leg tightened convulsively, and she gasped at the sudden stab of white pain. Another tentacle was rising from the gray intruder now, its tip weaving toward her face like the head of a cobra. Alita ignored pain and fear both, however, and continued holding the beam on the gray monstrosity within the wall, taking her best guess as to where to aim. Sweat trickled down her face and neck, and it was difficult to see what she was doing against the glare. She was attempting nothing less than brain surgery, cutting away a cancerous growth pressed tightly against a critical neural ganglion, and too deep a cut or an unsteadiness in her hands could turn the operation into a literal Bolobotomy.

The pain in her leg grew sharply worse, and she felt herself sinking to her knees. The third tentacle weaved past her face, then wrapped itself about her neck, tightening. Sparks and tiny splatters of liquid metal were hissing and popping from the hole in the wall, now, burning her skin where it touched her, and an acrid, bitter smoke swirled around her. She struggled to breathe, her vision fading. If she didn't kill this thing in another couple of seconds, she knew, it was going to kill her. . . .

I am aware of the death struggle taking place within my main memory core, but there is no physical action that I can take to help.

What I can do, however, is to engage the Intruder

in a nonphysical fashion, distracting it, interfering with its attempts to maul Sergeant Kyle, sever its contact with other !°!°! machines, and, one by one, begin moving into specific operations and storage sectors infiltrated by the Enemy device and reclaiming them for myself. I can sense the Intruder's programming, some thousands of individual and strangely shaped bodies of alien code interlocked in a wonderfully complex array of calculation, logic, and decision. I sense that there is no true self-awareness here—the Intruder machine that penetrated my systems was not complex enough for that—but, viruslike, it was able to hijack certain of my cognitive functions and divert them to its own purposes.

Now, with the Intruder under a double attack, physically by Sergeant Kyle and on an insubstantial but nonetheless quite real level by myself, I can feel its grip on my memories weakening, can feel its own operations turning beneath my assault in smaller and smaller cycles, can feel it dying as Sergeant Kyle's beam sears through its circuits.

I feel it die. . . .

"Sergeant Kyle?" I ask. *I have no monitor cameras inside my memory core, so I cannot see her. I can hear her pounding, too-fast heartbeat, however, and the rasp of her breathing, so I know that she is still alive. Her weapon is still firing, reducing the Intruder to molten metal. In another second or two, the beam may severe my primary memory bus.*

"Sergeant Kyle!" *I repeat.* "Cease fire! The Enemy is destroyed!"

The beam clicks off. "I . . . got it?" *Her voice is cracked, rasping, and barely audible.*

"The Enemy is destroyed," *I tell her again. I search my newly liberated memories for the proper words, but doubt that they are sufficient to the occasion.* "Thank you."

I hear a thump and a clatter, the sound of something massive collapsing on the deck of my memory core. Sergeant Kyle's breathing and heartbeat continue, and I surmise that she has just lost consciousness.

At the same time, full access to my main storage floods my awareness with imagery, with an unrestricted and uncensored flood of raw and processed data.

Exultant, I go at last to Full Battle Awareness.

I am free. . . .

In the Battle Center, Jaime felt a sudden vibration transmitted through the deck and seat. He wasn't sure what, but *something* was happening.

After Alita had left, he'd found an empty bulkhead storage locker and transferred Captain Fowler's remains there . . . with Shari's help. She still seemed numb, moving as if she were in shock, but she was recovering fast. Shari Barstowe was a tough lady, Jaime decided, and one who would do what she had to do to survive.

Now, he could hear a distinct and distant rumble, almost as if Hector was starting to move. Leaving Shari in one of the observer's seats, he rushed to the control panel to try to make sense of what was happening.

"Hector!" he called. "Situation report!"

"Free . . ."

Jaime blinked, looking up at the empty display dome. "What?"

"The Enemy mechanisms that were hampering my psychotronic operations have been eliminated," the voice said. "My AI and data storage and retrieval functions are now operating normally." There was the briefest of pauses. "We are under attack, and I am shifting to Combat Mode."

"Give me visual, please."

A vertical bar of vivid green light appeared on the inside of the bubble, momentarily stationary. Then it swiftly painted itself around the display dome's interior, leaving in its track a 360° panorama of the hilltop outside.

!°!°! machines were everywhere, swarming across the barren crest of Overlook Hill or drifting in the sky overhead. He saw the flash and stab of !°!°! weapons, artificial lightning bolts and high-energy lasers, as the enemy machines attempted to burn down the armored mountain that was Hector.

"My operational readiness is severely impaired," the Bolo's voice continued with unhurried calm. "I sense extensive damage to both primary and secondary circuitry. Sensor capability is currently at thirty-eight percent of optimum. External communications arrays are damaged and operating at fifteen percent of optimum, and attempts to raise other units, command centers, or CDF stations in the past thirty-eight point five seconds have failed. Damage to four right-side foretrack bogies will limit mobility to eighty-nine percent of optimum. Contra-gravity generators are off-line. I estimate a maximum road speed of one hundred ten kilometers per hour.

"My onboard fusion plant is currently operating at only three percent of maximum output and may have physical blocks similar to those established on my main memory functions. Available stores of expendable munitions, except for antipersonnel flechette canisters, are exhausted. All primary and secondary weapons are off-line. Battle screens are off-line.

"My psychotronic systems, however, including all molecular circuitry, paraneuronic assemblies, and AI programming, are fully operational."

"Great," Jaime muttered under his breath. "Maybe we can think them to death."

"That is the essence of efficient combat planning and maneuver," Hector replied. "We must outthink the Enemy, for we are severely outnumbered and outmatched in almost every material way."

Jaime hadn't intended for the Bolo to hear his crack. He reminded himself that he would have to be careful about what he said out loud. "Can we fight at all?" he asked. "Can you use flechettes against those things?"

"I have two thousand eight hundred forty-six A-P flechette canisters remaining, either loaded or in stores. I have noted that canister rounds are effective against some !°!°! machines." The clucking sounds representing the enemy's proper name startled Jaime. He'd not expected the Bolo to be able to pronounce non-Anglic words. "I will have to carefully manage my remaining stores until I can reload and rearm."

"That could be a problem," Jaime said. "I don't know where we're going to find a maintenance depot where we can fix you up."

A floater to Jaime's left crumpled suddenly, its midsection smashed by an unseen blow. A moment later, a hovering aircraft ahead and to the right shuddered, sparks and chunks of metal spitting from its starboard thruster, and a moment later the flying machine burst into flame and spun like a falling leaf into the ground. With a sudden lurch that knocked Jaime against the command seat's back, the Bolo began moving forward. Dust exploded to either side on the display dome as the massive tracks, locked in place for almost a year, began turning.

"Stores of 240cm howitzer rounds and VLS missiles will be difficult to acquire," the Bolo agreed. "I have assigned top priority to rearming my primary weaponry."

"Your primaries! Where in God's name are you going to get Hellbore rounds?"

There was the slightest of pauses as three more black, insect-visaged !°!°! aircraft crumpled, burned, and crashed, swatted from the sky by the silent and invisible clouds of hypervelocity flechettes fired from Hector's antipersonnel railguns. "Major Graham," Hector said. "I am now operating under independent Battle Reflex Mode. I have just reviewed your personnel records and deduce that you are neither trained nor authorized to give me orders in combat, and I respectfully submit that I am better able to judge both my immediate material needs and my tactical and strategic requirements. I suggest that you proceed at once to my Primary Memory Core and check on Sergeant Kyle. I can no longer communicate with her, and she may be injured. In any case, I must devote my full attention to the developing situation."

Fear pricked at the back of Jaime's neck, a cold fear born of the realization that he no longer had any control over the huge machine . . . if, indeed, he'd ever had any control in the first place. For a long moment, the Battle Center was wrapped in eerie silence, despite the continued destruction outside, and the vibration indicating that Hector was now grinding forward toward the southern slope of Overlook Hill.

"Just one question, Hector."

"Yes?"

"You have full access to your memory now?"

"I do."

"Do you know what the clackers did to you the first time, at Chryse? Do you know how they were able to take you over?"

"Affirmative. I remember in complete detail."

Jaime drew a deep breath. "Can you stop them from doing the same thing to you again?"

"That," the Bolo replied, "is what I am attending to now."

When no further details were forthcoming, Jaime voiced a short, bitter obscenity. He glanced at Shari,

who was still in the observer's chair, her expression
blank. There would be no help from that quarter.

And Alita was apparently in trouble. He found a
first aid kit in one of the Battle Center bulkhead
lockers, then hurried from the compartment.

Outside, the battle was heating up.

General Spratly heard the commotion and emerged
from his hut to see what was happening. A good hour
had passed since his fight with Graham; the fires were
out, now, and he had little to show for the scuffle
besides a very sore jaw.

He'd been inside with his staff, arguing what to do
about Graham and his people. They seemed to be
out of control, and it was vital to stop them before
they did something really stupid. It was amazing that
the !°!°! had done nothing about the mob scene here
in the camp a while ago.

As Spratly stepped into the light, however, he
realized almost at once that the !°!°! had something
much more serious on their artificial minds right now
than a small riot in the prison camp. From here, he
could see the vast, squat, black mountain of the Bolo,
and for the first time in nearly a T-standard year, the
mountain was moving, crawling slowly down the left
slope of the hill looming above the camp. It was moving
slowly, ponderously, but it *was* moving, without a
doubt, and raising a cloud of dust that made the whole
hilltop look like an erupting volcano. The black specks
swarming about it like angry gnats must be !°!°!
floaters.

And they were calling for reinforcements. Clacker
flying machines were swarming out of the east, great,
black, insect shapes borne aloft by howling jets. They
shrieked low above the camp, scattering running
people in screaming packs, smashing the ramshackle
huts and lean-tos into whirling fragments with their

jet exhausts, and raising furiously spinning dust devils with their passing.

On the hilltop, the Bolo's prow tipped slowly down as its forward tracks began negotiating the steepening slope above the waters of the bay.

My God, he thought. *He did it! The crazy son of a bitch actually did it!*

Panic clawed at his throat. This was a disaster in the making. "Come on," he told Captain Pogue, standing at his side. "We've got to do something or we're going to have real trouble here."

DAV728 was aware of the !°!°! Primary Web-wide alert as a kind of *knowing* deep within his newfound feelings and rippling, brightly colored memories. Since he was already linked in with the Ninth Awareness in the tactical center on Delamar, it took only milliseconds to tap into an active data feed and download specific information.

"The organic combat machine has broken free of our control," he said, studying the stream of incoming information from a thousand different sources. "It is moving."

"There may be involvement by some of the organics," the Ninth Awareness noted. "It may have been a tactical error to leave the combat machine operational."

"Why was this done?" DAV wanted to know.

"The combat machine showed evidence of both high intelligence and a self-aware sentience of an order similar to high-awareness models of the !°!°!. That sentience was of a markedly different type, of course, and aspects of its operation were not understood. Based on discoveries made with the captured human starship, we believed it possible to train the machine through reprogramming and memory control. Some of us were interested in the possibility of confirming the Maker Hypothesis."

DAV considered this for several milliseconds. One of the great unanswered questions of the !°!°! cosmos was the one asking where they had come from in the first place. That artificially contrived evolution occurred within the machine genera now was undeniable, as both programming and design were deliberately altered to fit new environments and conditions; what was questioned was where the earliest intelligent !°!°! machines had come from in the first place. Evolutionists insisted that simple machines had evolved on their own within the extraordinary flux of energy and matter at the core of the Galaxy; Makists believed that those first machines must have been created by intelligent organics, possibly by the neDakSha, the enigmatic species that, according to records grown fragmentary over the eons, was the very first organic life form to be driven to extinction by the !°!°!. Ever since DAV728 had become sentient enough to consider the question, he'd felt the Makist position was untenable and circular. If organics created machines, what, then, created organics?

The Ninth Awareness, he knew, held Makist views, though he rarely discussed them in dogmatic terms. He was saying, however, that the human machine, the Bolo as they called it, had clearly been designed and built by organics but was also clearly as sentient as many !°!°!, powerful support indeed for the Makist position.

"We considered dismantling the captured machine," the Awareness went on, "since it represented a large fraction of the available refined metals and materials taken with the planet. We felt, however, that greater advantage would be secured through crippling it so that it would represent no further threat to us, then systematically learning how its programming worked. To that end, we harvested the brains of several organics who worked with it, including, incidentally, the organic brain you've recently received."

DAV was already examining some of the vast stores of information secured so far from the Bolo. In one of his minds' eyes, he called up a detailed schematic of the huge machine, examining mass, power plants, weaponry, and overall capability.

"I question whether the Bolo has been sufficiently crippled. Even with limited power, it could still represent a threat to some of our operations on the planet. I recommend that it be destroyed immediately."

"Regretfully, I agree," the Ninth Awareness replied. "You are directed to devise and execute a program to that end and are granted authority over the required assets."

"Simplest would be to disable it as we disabled it before, but with greater precision and efficiency." DAV was already searching !°!°! records, checking the locations of battler/fortresses in local space. Three occupied extended orbits about the local suns and could be brought into position within a matter of a few thousand seconds. A thought sent the appropriate commands flashing out to the battlers' command pilots.

"Camp 84 will be destroyed as well," he told the Ninth Awareness.

"We have many more organics in our control."

"We should evacuate our own from the target area."

"We have many more !°!°! available as well." A thoughtful pause. "However, it might be well to evacuate all machines of level four and higher."

"I will issue the necessary orders."

"It is a great pity that we cannot save the Bolo," the Awareness mused. "Its mechanisms are primitive, but it would have been interesting seeing what we could have done, in time, with its intelligence."

"It would be foolish to give it the opportunity to hamper our operations on this world," DAV replied.

"The information acquired would not be worth the probable cost to !°!°! in both time and material."

"You are correct, of course. We should pursue the most efficient program."

"We are." DAV completed a series of complex calculations. "The situation will be resolved in precisely 1.3176×10^4 seconds."

In space, three immense, complex shapes were already accelerating to their new positions.

Shari closed her eyes, rubbing them hard with her hands, then opened them again, taking in the Battle Center, the horseshoe console, the bloodstained command seat, as though she'd not before seen them. *Come on, pull yourself together*, she thought with bitter self-anger. *You knew he was dead. After you found out what was happening to the survivors, you* prayed *that he was dead.*

It was hard, though, because even when she'd been convinced that Jeff Fowler had been killed at Chryse, there'd been uncertainty enough that she'd never really had to grieve. Besides, there'd been grief enough for herself, for all of the humans who'd survived the !°!°! strike, in the Camp.

Rising on unsteady legs, she made her way to the command seat, ducking to get beneath the lower rim of the display dome. She didn't sit down; she couldn't, not *there* . . . but she clung to the back of the seat and stared at the display, orienting herself.

A number of !°!°! machines were visible, but they seemed to be pulling back, as though aware that their small weapons couldn't touch the armor of this lumbering juggernaut. One flying machine crumpled to her right as she watched, its fuselage smashed by an unseen cloud of hypervelocity flechettes hurled from one of Hector's port-side AP guns.

To the left lay the Camp, a huge and untidy sprawl

around the ruin of the manufactory. To the left and ahead was the rubble-pocked swamp marking the former heart of Celeste, and the slave pits with their laboring thousands. Directly ahead, the waters of Celeste Bay lapped almost to the foot of Overlook Hill. The Bolo's deck was canted forward at least thirty degrees. It felt as though the huge machine was nosing over the edge of an embankment, picking up speed as it plowed slowly downhill toward the muddy, dark water.

"You . . . you're heading for the bay?" she asked aloud.

"Affirmative, Technician Barstowe," Hector replied. His voice was reassuring in its calm. "I need to take on fresh supplies of water."

She blinked. The Bolo was in the middle of a furious firefight, was probably attracting !°!°! ships and machines from all over the Cloud System, and it was interested in replenishing its fresh water?

She tried to imagine the 32,000-ton behemoth hitting the soft, silt-laden bottom of Celeste's inner harbor. "Won't you get stuck in the mud? We have no idea how deep it is, or how much you'll sink!"

There was no immediate reply, and she wondered if the huge machine was simply ignoring her backseat driving. The slope of the deck grew steeper, and she clung to the chair back for support. A moment later, the Bolo's prow struck the water's surface, sending up an enormous wall of white spray, though she scarcely felt the impact.

"I could give you the engineering particulars," Hector's voice said as water boiled up across the forward half of the display. "However, I see from your personnel files that you have little experience with engineering or math—"

"You don't need to be so condescending, damn it!"

"I apologize. I was merely observing that your field

of expertise lies in psychotronics and AI psychology, rather than in engineering or physics, and wished to explain in a mode that you would readily comprehend.

"Perhaps I can explain by a historical analogy. In 3198, on New Devon, a Bolo Mark XXVIII, Unit LNE *Triumphant*, was deactivated after the final engagement of the Fringe-Worlds War against the Xalontese. Since its hull was dangerously radioactive, it was encased in a three-meter shell of reinforced armorcrete, then buried two hundred meters underground behind a rubble-filled tunnel capped by fifty centimeters of compressed concrete.

"Seventy T-standard years later, construction work in the vicinity activated the Bolo's battle reflex circuits. Though it was operating on Final Emergency Power, Unit LNE was able to smash free of the radiation shield, then tunnel by brute force through the rubble and up to the surface of New Devon. The Mark XXVIII massed only fifteen thousand tons, of course, but it was operating on lower power reserves than I am now. Suffice to say that even a few hundred meters of mud will offer less of an impediment than two hundred meters of hard-packed rubble and high-R concrete shielding, so long as my tracks can reach a solid base."

"Oh . . ." was all she could say.

She wondered, though, what had happened to that Bolo reactivated on New Devon. She'd heard about similar cases before, of Bolos gone rogue or incompletely or incompetently deactivated. Such spawned endless horror stories that continued to provide ammunition for the human opponents of unsupervised psychotronic AIs.

There were some who'd survived the Great Killing who hinted darkly that the !°!°! must have evolved from something very much like Bolos, that they'd destroyed their makers and continued to direct their own evolution.

As water exploded across the display dome, she decided that this Bolo was certainly taking a hand in its future, forming its own plans and carrying them out with no further input from the humans who'd started this chain of events at all. Despite all she knew about psychotronics, it was a little terrifying to watch the Bolo working on its own.

CHAPTER NINE

I have reached the harbor and entered the water. Despite my reassurances to Technician Barstowe, I note with relief that the silt on the harbor bottom is only two to three meters deep, and that beneath that is a fairly stable layer of clay. The water itself is no more than ten meters deep, enough to cover my track assemblies and my lower banks of antipersonnel weapons, but not deep enough to begin flooding my interior through the breach in my hull. Flooding would have been difficult to clear and would have forced the humans aboard me now to remain inside one of my self-contained environmental compartments.

As it is, I have no trouble achieving traction enough to continue moving south into the harbor and am in no immediate danger of becoming mired. While I did not doubt my ability to extricate myself eventually, I had no direct means of establishing the depths of either the water or the mud beneath, and traversing mud deeper than my own height would have required a great deal of time, almost certainly more time than is available to me now.

Resistance in my immediate combat area has all but ceased, though !°!°! flying machines continue to circle

137

at a range of five to ten kilometers. While these are
easily with range of my AP mass drivers, I elect to
hold my fire, preferring to save my remaining flechette
canisters for more threatening targets.

Another threat is developing, however, one which
will not be vulnerable to hypervelocity flechettes. I
am now tracking three separate, very large targets in
near-Cloud space, almost certainly large !°!°! fortress-
ships of unknown but certainly enormous potential.
These, I deduce, are the most serious immediate combat
threat and must be neutralized as swiftly as possible.
I am mindful of the damage I suffered at Chryse when
I was attacked by Enemy vessels smaller than these.

I probe the Enemy's communications network,
looking for weakness, a point of entry, and find none.
All Bolos since the Mark XXVI have incorporated both
the technology and the programming necessary for
breaking an opponent's data net, both to secure
electronic intelligence and, in some cases, to disable
or confuse the Enemy's defenses by hacking past his
security to implant false data or commands within his
computer network. Though my experience with the
!°!°! has familiarized me with the Enemy net and
communications protocols, their security algorithms
and access codes appear to be constantly changing,
offering me no point of entry. In any case, that
particular tactic would be risky in the extreme since,
at this point, they must know considerably more about
my operating system and data net than I know about
theirs. Opening direct access to the !°!°! computer
net, their Primary Web, as they refer to it, would leave
me vulnerable to electronic takeover or disabling.

This contest, then, will of necessity be primarily a
physical one.

Opening all intakes, I began filling empty storage
tanks. At the same time, I begin cycling small amounts
of water through my electrolysis chambers, breaking

it down, bleeding off the oxygen and directing the hydrogen gas to my cryovats. It will take time to cool and pressurize the hydrogen to a useful consistency.

I hope that time enough remains for the complex tasks at hand.

The revolt within the slave pits began with the onrushing tidal wave.

"For God's sake, *run!*" Dieter screamed, pointing. A wall of water eight meters high was advancing inland, breaking at the harbor's edge, tumbling over onto swamp and ruin and thundering across the mud flats toward the laboring slaves. Throughout the entire dig, thousands of slaves had stopped their work momentarily to stand or crouch or kneel in the mud and watch the unfolding drama atop Overlook Hill. Even the overseers, both the turner humans and the unemotional machines, paused to watch as well, and for thirty seconds, not a sound came from the teeming pits.

They watched as the Bolo lumbered forward, its nose ponderously dipping as it moved off the flattened crest of the hill, its vast, double tracks chewing dirt, rock, and the rubble of shattered buildings into exploding plumes of dust. As it picked up speed, it gouged away most of the south face of the hill, and then it slammed into the water raising a white, cascading wall of spray.

The swell followed the splash, a small tidal wave racing across the mud flats, breaking over the shore, fountaining high above each outcropping of rubble or broken wall, tumbling over into the pits. As the humans in the pit turned and ran, struggling inland through the mud, !°!°! machines darted and hovered, loosing bolts of artificial lightning in an attempt to stop the rout.

Their efforts only increased the confusion. The wave, now less than two meters tall, swept across the pits, sweeping up hapless slaves before it, even knocking down a few !°!°! guard machines too slow to get out of the way. The water swept about Dieter's hips, most of its force spent now, but with power enough still to buoy him up, knock him down, and carry him along toward the east edge of the pit. Hundreds of men and women were scrambling out of the pit.

Floaters fired bolt after bolt into the crowd, each discharge burning down unprotected humans, but their capacitors were drained after a few shots and they became relatively easy prey. Nearby, five men were grappling with a two-meter !°!°! floater, dragging it down from the sky, pinning its tentacles, then ripping them out of its body. Sparks and electrical discharges crackled weakly across its surface, but they hung on, dragging the thing beneath the water. Another crowd knocked a floater over and pounded it with stones, smashing at it with cement blocks until its smooth surface dented, then split, and its killers could reach in and pull wiring and circuits out by the smoking handful.

In seconds more, every !°!°! machine in sight was in full retreat. Most of the floaters managed to get away, but the multilegged crawlers, even those not mired down in the incoming tide, were just too slow.

At the edge of the pit, a woman waved a blood-splattered stunstick wrenched from a trusty, rallying a mob, while nearby, a man brandished the skeletal metal arm of a !°!°! stilter with a dead human hand still attached. Both were screaming in mindless rage, their voices joining the growing thunder of the mob rising from the pits.

Scrambling up the muddy slope of the pit, Dieter stared out into the harbor, where the Bolo rose like a black island from water that reached just above its track housings. Most of the !°!°! machines that had been swarming around it on the hilltop were gone, fled or destroyed, but one bulky flier was still circling, pecking at the half-submerged giant's armored back with flashes of artificial lightning and hypervelocity exploders. The flier's circles were a little too close, as it turned out. An invisible breath flicked from the Bolo's flank, and one of the flier's jets shredded, then burst into orange flame; trailing smoke, the machine struck the harbor and exploded with a thump and geysering spray.

"The Bolo!" Dieter screamed, pointing and waving. "The Bolo! It's with us!"

The people screamed and cheered and shouted their replies, the thunderous cacophony swelling as it echoed from five thousand throats.

The slave revolt of Celeste had begun.

Jaime had just arrived in the computer core center when the deck had tipped wildly, flinging him against one of the bulkheads. For several intense seconds, the compartment jolted and shuddered, tilted at a forty-degree angle, but then it had leveled out a few moments later, and the Bolo now felt like it was at rest.

Alita had been conscious by the time he got there, clinging for support to a loose bundle of optical wiring dangling from a breach in the wall. Her legs were bruised and bloodied, cut, it appeared, by the !°!°! tentacles now lying severed on the deck. She had bruises at her throat as well, but she insisted that she was okay. "I did it," she told him, pointing unsteadily at the shattered wall. "I killed the thing that was changing Hector's memory and programming!"

"I know. He told me to come get you. I'm not sure what he's up to now, but I think I'd like all of us to get down to the Battle Center, fast."

He sprayed her legs with mediseal foam to stop the bleeding, then helped her hobble back out into the corridor and down the access tubeway toward the Battle Center. "What's he doing now?" she asked.

"He claimed he was putting top priority to rearming his primaries," Jaime replied. "I assume he means his Hellbores? When I asked how, he got kind of testy. Told me, in so many words, to mind my own business."

Alita started to laugh.

"What's so funny?"

"That's Hector, all right," she said. "You know, every AI develops its own personality, just like people. Hector was always a bit of a snob. He likes things to be just so. He's liable to review any personnel records he has on file and decide you're not qualified to understand the answers to your questions."

Jaime grinned ruefully at the memory. "He pulled that on me."

"Ah. He also doesn't have a lot of patience with people who aren't as quick on the uptake as he is. He's polite about it, but he can be stubborn."

"Great," Jaime muttered. A temperamental Bolo. *Wonderful. . . .*

They reached the Battle Center a few moments later, palming open the door and stepping inside. Jaime was surprised to see Shari on her feet, clinging to the back of the command seat as lights flickered across the control console. "Shari? Are you okay?"

She turned and stared at him, as if for a moment she didn't recognize him. Then she nodded. "Yes, Major. I'm sorry I fell apart. It was . . . kind of a shock."

"Of course it was. No apologies necessary." He glanced at the display dome. It looked as though the Bolo was now out in the middle of Celeste's inner harbor, surrounded by choppy brown water. "What the hell is going on?"

"He says he's taking on water," Shari told him.

"Taking on . . . water." He ducked beneath the rim of the dome display and slipped into the command

seat, swiveling it around to check the entire 360°
panorama. They were no longer under attack, but that
state of affairs could not last much longer.

"Hector," he said, his voice crisp and businesslike.
"This is Major Jaime Graham. As the senior CDF
officer present, I am assuming command."

There was a long pause, and Jaime chafed at the
wait. *This*, he thought, *is ridiculous*. A whole semester
at the Cloud Military Academy had been devoted to
the psychology of leadership, the science of how an
officer could inspire, direct, *and* lead the men and
women under his command. He'd never imagined that
he would need to draw on that training to win a Bolo's
confidence and obedience.

The thought gave him pause. The Bolo was as
intelligent, easily, as any human. How did a new,
possibly inexperienced officer win the trust of soldiers
under his command, especially the battle-seasoned
NCOs who were the backbone of every army?

"If you're worried about my qualifications," he
continued after a moment, "all I can say is that I'm
going to have to rely on *you* to fill in any gaps.
Understood?"

Bolos were programmed to obey the human assigned
as their commander. The trick was getting them to
accept a particular human's credentials, since they were
also programmed to reject the enemy's attempts to
deceive them. A lot depended now on just how smart
this Bolo was in human terms . . . and on how able it
was to formulate its own goals, make its own decisions,
and set its own course.

"Normally, I would require formal authorization from
a higher command authority," the Bolo told him.
"However, the tactical situation on Cloud has changed
drastically. I surmise that all higher command authority
has been eliminated, and that we are essentially on
our own. Is this correct?"

"Affirmative," Jaime replied, his voice catching at his throat. "All military and governmental authority on Cloud has been completely wiped out. It's up to us to build them up again, from nothing."

"I understand, my Commander," the Bolo said, and Jaime suppressed a small start of excitement at its use of the formal title.

"I need a tactical update, please."

A portion of the display screen wiped clear, replaced by a window showing a three-dimensional topological map of the immediate Celeste area. Several hundred red dots were visible, most at the camp or scattered about the pits in the central portion of the city. "These are all !°!°! machines detectable within five kilometers," Hector said. "Their armament consists of electrical discharge capacitors and light lasers, the equivalent of hand-held human weapons. None represent a threat to us."

The window cleared, replaced by a graphic representation of the world of Cloud, a blue square flashing to mark the location of Celeste. The sphere dwindled until the smaller, cratered globe of Delamar came into view, then smaller still to include Triste, Cloud's second moon. Three red triangles were visible well beyond the orbit of Delamar, with streaming tails showing their vectors. All three appeared to be accelerating toward Cloud.

"These three vessels represent the most immediate and direct threat," Hector said. "They are of a class the !°!°! refer to as Type II fortress/battlers. Each masses roughly four point three million tons and is more powerful than the largest human dreadnought by perhaps two orders of magnitude. Ships of this class were responsible for the bombardment of Cloud and the destruction of Cloud's cities. I estimate that the nearest will be in firing position within another thirty-eight point seven seconds."

"City killers," Jaime said softly. He'd not seen those monsters when the !°!°! first attacked Cloud, but he'd heard about them from survivors who'd tracked them inbound on radar or glimpsed them on surveillance images from orbital drones.

In fact, it had only been later, in the slave camp, that he'd learned anything at all about the terror weapon the !°!°! had used against Cloud's major cities.

Absolutely basic to any tactical consideration of warfare was the concept of the *high ground*. Get above the enemy, and you had an immediate, tremendous advantage. The !°!°! held the high ground of space, perched high up in Cloud's gravity well where they could quite literally fling rocks at the humans trapped on the world's surface below. Though Cloud's human defenders had gathered pathetically little intelligence on the invaders before The Killing, they thought that the enemy's fortress/battlers possessed mass drivers something like Hector's main AP weapons, but vastly larger and more powerful. *Meteor guns*, some of the defenders had called them, but that scarcely did justice to their power and reach. The !°!°! weapons could magnetically hurl one-ton chunks of nickel-iron—dirt-common in any asteroid belt—with almost pinpoint accuracy at velocities measured in the tens of kilometers per second.

Jaime didn't need to rely on Hector's math processors to calculate the energies involved. One ton of rock augering in at 100 kilometers per second brought with it a potential kinetic energy of roughly five million megajoules . . . the destructive power of one thousand tons of detonating high explosives.

A one-kiloton explosion put the weapon into the realm of tactical nukes; according to some of the stories floating around the camp just after The Killing, the !°!°! could tailor the size of their blasts by adjusting the size and the incoming velocity of their city-busters.

The one that got Chryse, some estimated, had been on the order of ten *megatons*, ten thousand times more powerful than a one-kiloton blast.

"The first enemy ship has reached its firing position," Hector announced. "Brace yourselves. Things are about to get interesting."

Jaime wondered what just what it was that constituted *interesting* for a Bolo. . . .

VAL812-928782 was a late-model four-brained !°!°! that had been a battler/fortress for well over 3×10^{18} nanoseconds. Plugged into the monster TIG232 Series 34 dreadnought, it had been part of the fleet that had captured the organics' starship *Empyrion*, wresting from the strange creatures the secrets of their computer technology. It had fought in the line at Jalachaad and lost two banks of foldspace facilitators at Corowyth.

Like the vast majority of !°!°!, it had little of what humans might have called imagination. It did what higher authority directed it to do, and it did it very efficiently.

Its current orders had directed it to attack a particular target at a particular set of coordinates on the recently secured planet of Cloud. Though still some ninety thousand kilometers from the planet, too far to receive a direct optical view, it could see images relayed by !°!°! intelligence satellites in low-Cloud orbit showing the target area clearly, a swampy ruin beside a narrow-mouthed harbor. Squarely in the center of the harbor, a machine of some kind, a very large machine, appeared to have just shrugged off the attacks of a swarm of smaller !°!°!.

It would not shrug off the next attack so easily.

VAL812 selected its first projectile.

I have begun manufacture of the H_2 cryoneedles. Within my manufacturing center, I possess twelve *neutron dense-pack-lined molds which I inject simultaneously with deuterium slush piped through from the cooling vats, before applying pressures similar to those found near the cores of planetary gas giants. The result is a three-millimeter-wide sliver, pointed at both ends, holding fifty grams of metallic deuterium encased in dense-pack; since even dense-pack becomes brittle at the temperatures of liquid hydrogen, magnetic bottles contain the slivers, which would vaporize instantly and with considerable violence if released. The molds open, the twelve DP-jacketed slivers are levitated to the storage locker, and fresh dense-pack sleeves are laid for the next batch, before the cycle is repeated.*

How many do I need? Twelve to twenty-four may be enough, but much depends on how many rounds each of the approaching fortress ships can launch . . . and on how soon they will do so. All three are still well beyond my effective range, but given the geometries of orbital bombardment, they could begin firing at any time. I have no doubts whatsoever that they are moving in response to my reactivation; I have seen what their bombardment weapons are capable of and know that I must strike the first blow.

The question, then, is how much time there is remaining to me.

DAV728 followed the unfolding drama through his links to the !°!°! primary command web, to the network of sensory collectors in planetary orbit, and to the three incoming battler/fortress pilots themselves, GRA623, VAL812, and FLE911. All three battlers were within range, now, but it was imperative that they achieve both high coordination and high precision in their attack. The human-organic construct known as a "Bolo" was potentially deadly and could interfere with !°!°! activities on the planet. That it had not

interfered with the original !°!°! invasion was due
simply to the fact that YEN925, the six-brain assembly
who'd led the attack, had not given the Bolo the chance
to demonstrate its full capabilities.

DAV had no intention of giving the enemy machine
a fresh opportunity.

He had two possible tactical branches to follow, and
it was characteristic of the !°!°! that he picked the
most direct path and, once his forces were initiating
that chain of events, that he set up a subroutine in
two of his brains to examine the alternative. The !°!°!
tended to be direct in their thoughts and actions, but
they also tended to be *very* thorough.

The second and less direct branch involved the !°!°!
machines embedded within the human combat machine.
Through the !°!°! command net, he could sense that
the controller planted astride the Bolo's neural pathway
bus had been destroyed, but that a second machine—
actually a subassembly budded from the first—was intact
and apparently undiscovered as yet.

This second machine parasite was buried within the
Bolo's power plant controller apparatus. Its sole
purpose was to act as a governor on the output from
the Bolo's fusion complex, restricting the generated
power to ten percent of its normal capabilities.

As the Bolo prepared to meet the threat of the first
!°!°! tactical branch, it would discover that it could
not engage at full power; quite possibly, depending
on the machine's sophistication, it had already
discovered this for itself in a routine autodiagnostic.

It was unlikely that the Bolo possessed self-repair
automatons capable of dealing with the parasite, so
it would simply have to engage the !°!°! forces at ten
percent of its normal combat power. And . . . there
might be other things the parasite could do as well.

DAV728 began uplinking some additional commands
to his agent within the human battle machine.

And in the meantime, the first tactical branch was enough to obliterate the Bolo and the entire continent it was sitting in. It would mean the loss of some thousands of minor !°!°! machines and most of the human resources in the region, but that was a reasonable exchange, from DAV's perspective. In his download memory, the web's graphics unfolded a three-dimensional representation of local space— Cloud, the two moons, and the three tiny complexities representing three incoming !°!°! battlers. Lines of green, blue, and near-ultraviolet showed courses past and projected, while the target glowed in soft, sparkling X-ray.

"Saturation bombardment," he ordered, directing his thoughts into the command web. "Adjust velocity and projectile mass for maximum immediate effect. Fire . . . !"

And in the graphics arrayed within his mind, each of the three symbols representing the fortress/battlers, released first one, then another, and then a third dazzling pinpoint of shimmering X-ray-colored light, each hurtling planetward on its precisely calculated high-speed trajectory.

Jaime leaned closer, studying the graphics displayed on the open window overlaying the harbor panorama stretched around the view dome. "My God—" he started to say.

"The Enemy has launched a total of nine projectiles," Hector announced with maddening calm. Green boxes closed around each of the fast-moving red blips marking the incoming projectiles, and alphanumerics began unfolding next to them, describing mass, velocity, and elapsed time from launch. Long, curving lines of yellow light traced themselves across the screen for each projectile, converging on the graphic representation of Cloud at latitude 40° 15' 32.4" north, longitude 7.4° west.

Ground zero was Celeste's inner harbor. . . .

"Incoming projectiles have been volley-fired," Hector went on, "with the first three impacting on my position within 2.76 seconds of one another, indicating a high degree of coordination within the enemy command network."

"How long . . . do we have?" Jaime asked.

One of the green squares flashed blue. "Projectile designated 'Alpha' has a velocity of 380 kilometers per second across a flight trajectory of 55,100 kilometers. Total flight time 145 seconds. Time to impact now . . ." The fast-dwindling figure appeared on the display next to the hurtling blip. "One hundred thirty seconds."

The object's velocity jolted him. "Hector! At that speed, what kind of impact are we looking at?"

"Exact figures depend on the mass of the projectile, which in turn depends on its precise dimensions, composition, and density. I estimate it to be an ovoid chunk of meteoric nickel-iron approximately 1.4 meter across its largest dimension, massing approximately 2.1 tons. Applying these estimates to the formula $\frac{1}{2}mv^2$ suggests that Alpha will impact with a kinetic energy of some 1.5162×10^{14} joules, for an explosive release of 30.324 megatons."

"Thirty megatons . . ."

"I remind you that the initial impact will be followed within three seconds by two additional impacts of approximately thirty megatons apiece. Three point five seconds later, there will be three more impacts, followed three point nine seconds later by yet three more. Total impact yield will be on the order two hundred seventy-five megatons."

The Battle Center became deathly quiet then. Jaime could hear the whisper of the compartment's air circulation machinery, the sharp, short catch in the breathing of both Shari and Alita, behind him, the hammer of his own pulse in his ears. What would a blast measuring almost three hundred megatons do? Rupture Cloud's crust in an orgasm of volcanoes and geysering magma? Obliterate all life on the planet in a storm of fire and atmospheric dust? Loose earthquakes that would send the entire Western Marches beneath the sea?

In any case, Hector was doomed . . . to say nothing of the human slaves in the Camp and dig outside less than a kilometer away.

One hundred twenty seconds. . . .

Jaime became aware of a flickering interplay of equations and alphanumerics in one corner of the display window. Hector appeared to have targeted the nearest of the oncoming projectiles with his main armament. Far off, beyond the massive shell of armor encasing the battle center, he heard the deep rumble of the Bolo's turrets in motion.

"Hector? What the hell are you doing?"

"Attempting to engage the Enemy's barrage. One moment, please. The calculations are extremely complex and are affected by numerous variables of an essentially chaotic nature."

"Target the . . ." Jaime stopped, swallowed. He knew that Mark XXXIII Bolos could engage targets well beyond planetary orbit; that, after all, was why they were sometimes referred to as *planetary* siege units. But to hit a one-and-a-half meter target at fifty thousand kilometers required sharpshooting skills of dazzling perfection.

"Target locked," Hector announced calmly. "Firing . . ."

The Battle Center plunged into darkness, the hull ringing like a titanic bell. . . .

Locking onto the nearest of the oncoming meteors with both radar and optical sensors, I have already slewed my Number One turret to one-zero-five relative and elevated the Hellbore to 53°, bringing the weapon to bear on the target. "Firing," I announce, and the Hellbore looses its full-throated output in a flash that momentarily blinds and deafens my own sensors.

Within the neutron dense-packed casing of the Hellbore's breech, fifty grams of metallic deuterium is abruptly collapsed within a constricting magnetic bottle, as powerful magnetic fields accelerate the DP-jacketed sliver to relativistic velocities; at the same moment, the weapon's guide lasers fire, providing target-lock feedback for my tracking arrays, and incidentally tunneling a momentary vacuum up through the planetary atmosphere, clearing the way for the Hellbore bolt to follow.

Extreme acceleration and mag bottle collapse together initiate deuterium fusion 3.2×10^{-8} second later, just before the plasma erupts from the ten-meter barrel of my Number One Hellbore at sixty percent of the speed of light. At the instant of firing, the target's range is 48658.7 kilometers.

At .6c, Hellbore bolt time to target is .27032 second, a long time to wait by Full Combat Awareness standards.

When the Hellbore fired, Dieter was standing atop a barren, rock-knobbled hillock, gripping a metal bar wrenched from the mechanism of a dismembered !*!*! machine. He'd been staring west across the dig and out to the squat black island of the Bolo resting in the middle of the harbor as the victorious slaves around him cheered and screamed and shouted. The light pulsing from the Bolo's forward Hellbore turret seared the eyes, leaving a dazzling, violet afterimage; spreading out across the water as fast as the eye could follow, the shock wave reached him almost four seconds later, a cracking, booming detonation assaulting the ears, numbing the senses.

Dieter dropped to his knees, hands clutched over

his ears, his nose suddenly bleeding. All around him, other former slaves had been tumbled to the ground by the thunder of the Hellbore discharge.

Involuntarily, he glanced up into an empty sky. Whatever Hector was shooting at couldn't be seen and was probably somewhere out in space; the big questions were whether the target was shooting back . . . and whether Hector would be firing again.

"Get to the crater!" Dieter screamed as loud as he could when the second blast faded. He didn't know how many heard him, how many *could* hear him now, deafened by that ear-numbing blast, but he shouted and waved and led the way, starting a panicked migration up the slope of the crater rim a few hundred meters further to the east. The water-filled depths of the crater left by the meteor strike that had leveled Celeste might offer some shelter from the savage onslaught of the Bolo's Hellbores.

CHAPTER TEN

Spectrographic and laser targeting and tracking data indicate that my initial shot has gone wide. Atmospheric aberration, the twinkling effect caused by essentially chaotic motion, expansion, and contraction of the air, was sufficient to offset my targeting lock by as much as plus or minus 0.02 degree. My first shot missed the oncoming meteor by an estimated three meters.

By comparing the images taken at optical wavelengths with those drawn from longer frequencies, including microwave and long-wave radar imaging, I can estimate the degree of aberration and attempt to compensate. Reloading my Number One turret, I recheck the target's vector and fire a second time. Fortunately, the target is moving almost directly toward my position on what is very nearly a straight-line trajectory, and there is very little apparent drift in what is for all practical purposes a stationary target. Its extremely high velocity dopplers my ranging pulses, however, and I must be careful to correct for velocity-induced spectrum shifts.

The second pulse of fusing, high-speed plasma strikes Projectile Alpha with the equivalent of some six megatons of highly focused directional energy, the rough equivalent in terms of joules and vaporization points of catching an ice cube in the blast from a plasma welder. My spectroscopic scans detect the characteristic absorption lines of nickel, iron, cobalt, and various trace elements in the expanding puff of metallic vapor. Radar and ladar returns detect no fragment larger than several hundred microns in diameter; I immediately shift to the next target, designated Projectile Bravo.

With compensation for atmospheric aberration locked in, I bring my Number Two turret into play. Number Three is inoperative, with major faults to the bearing ring and alt-azimuth controls. Two turrets should be enough, however, given my sharply limited reserves of Hellbore ammunition. At 1.05 second intervals I trigger shot after shot, laying down a heavy, rapid barrage against the incoming projectiles. I score another hit, vaporizing Projectile Bravo . . . and another a moment later against Charlie . . . then miss Delta completely as atmospheric bloom from a previous discharge distorts the laser sighting target lock by .05 degree.

I recalculate and adjust; the atmosphere above my position is becoming turbulent, as superheated air expands rapidly in a huge bubble that distorts my line of sight. Another miss . . . then a hit, though an incomplete hit that leaves a 100-kilogram chunk of meteoric debris and a large amount of gravel still on a vector which will impact in my general vicinity within the next 1.75 minutes.

Worse, I detect new launches from all three of the Enemy battler/fortresses, and I am down now to fourteen DP-jacketed slivers of metallic cryo-H$_2$.

If the Enemy continues launching new projectiles, my defenses will be very rapidly overwhelmed.

As Dieter reached the top of the crater rim, the Bolo fired again, lancing the sky with a bolt of blue-white radiance so intense it cast shadows in defiance of the suns, and Dieter felt his skin prickle and his eyes water beneath the beam's harsh splash of ultraviolet. Four seconds later, the thunder rolled again, so loud it clawed at the gut and left the ears ringing, and the ground beneath his bare feet bucked with the concussion.

Other slaves fleeing the pits scrambled up the slope around him, jumping and sliding into the relative shelter provided by the crater's interior. All had the same idea as Dieter, to take cover from the searing flash and shock of the volleying Bolo in the harbor.

The strobing, violent pulses of light from the Bolo were going off every second or so now, the fire alternating between the forward and middle turrets. It looked as though the huge machine's rear turret was out of action. When Dieter took a last glance at the Bolo across the lip of the crater rim, it looked as though the entire machine was wreathed in rising clouds of steam. The heat generated by each Hellbore discharge must be astonishing.

Jaime hated being helpless.

That, perhaps as much as anything else, was the goad that had been driving him for these past months of captivity, the knowledge that he was helpless, that there was nothing he could do to defeat or escape the conquering !°!°! war machines. It had led him to find some way out of the slave compound, led him to the ridge of bones atop Overlook Hill . . . and ultimately had led him *here*, to the battle-center bowels of this animated mountain and the chance to strike back at his tormentors.

Now the Bolo was engaged against forces he could only dimly comprehend, in a battle that was completely beyond his grasp. He could not fight, he could not give orders, he couldn't even suggest a course of action to the huge machine, which was dealing with forces, calculations of masses and velocity, and targeting data that, to be blunt, only a machine intelligence of high capability could handle.

Leaning back in the Battle Center's command chair, he watched the battle unfolding on the main window on the display above the console. Green brackets appeared, closing on the nearest of the moving boxes, flashing to confirm target lock. With each Hellbore shot, the lighting in the center dimmed sharply, and the ear-ringing thump of detonation and recoil transmitted through the steel deck plating like the impact of a titanic hammer. The track of each Hellbore shot was displayed as a bright gold, ruler-straight line drawing itself within the flick of an eyelid from the surface of the planet, across empty space, and through the target box. Usually, a white flash and the words TARGET DESTROYED marked a clean hit. Sometimes, a different message was displayed. TARGET FRAGMENTED: NEW TARGETS INCOMING . . . followed by strings of vector data.

The pace of Hellbore shots seemed unhurried to Jaime, a steady, stately pulse of sound and shock. With the fragmentation of some of the incoming projectiles, though, it seemed to him that Hector's rate of fire was slower than it should have been. He worried too at the flickering of the lights, and at how hot and close the air was becoming inside the Battle Center. Surely, a machine with power enough to accelerate squirts of fusing plasma to relativistic velocities had power enough to spare for the air-conditioning and lighting!

He wanted to ask the Bolo about it, but was afraid of revealing his ignorance to the machine. Damn it, he'd never served as a Bolo commander and didn't know a tenth of what he ought to. Would a stupid question on his part prove to the machine that he wasn't qualified to sit in this chair?

They said there was no such thing as a stupid question. Did that hold true when you were asking it of a superintelligent AI . . . one that was engaged at the moment in an all-out fight for survival?

"We have a problem, my Commander," Hector's voice said.

"What?"

"My power is limited to approximately nine point six percent of maximum output. Fusion plant operation appears nominal, but the flow governor is operating at much less than peak efficiency. I suspect that an alien device or devices are somehow interfering with plant controller operation."

"An alien device. Another thing like we found in your computer core?"

"Affirmative. I cannot test this hypothesis directly, and it is possible that the problem stems instead from battle damage sustained at Chryse." There was a pause, a beat of silence. "If I cannot increase my current rate of fire within a few minutes at most, I will not be able to stop all incoming projectiles."

Jaime was up and out of his seat in an instant, crossing to one of the bulkhead lockers. Inside, a line of Mark XIV power guns rested in recharger slots. Reaching in, he pulled out one weapon, checked the charge, and slammed the door shut. In another locker nearby, he found a comm headset which he clipped to his ear, extending the threadmike until it rested near his lower lip. "Comm check," he said.

"I read you, Commander," Hector's voice whispered in his ear.

"Do you want me to come?" Alita asked.

He shook his head, then tapped his earpiece. "Hector'll talk me through to where I have to go. You stay with Shari."

"Be careful," she told him. "Those . . . those *parasites* are hard to kill."

"Believe me, I will."

At last. He could *do* something.

Dieter lay in the bottom of the crater on his back, his lower body submerged in muddy water as flame lit the sky. He could hear only a distant rumble now through the stuffed-head ringing muffling his ears, though he felt each thumping detonation transmitted through the trembling ground pressed up against his spine. The air in the crater had grown hot enough to sear the lungs if you gulped it down too fast, and a howling, hot wind was blowing away from the harbor, where repeated Hellbore blasts had superheated the atmosphere, creating one hell of a powerful, artificial high-pressure weather cell.

Modern combat, he reflected, was not a place for unprotected human beings, not with six-megaton-per-second firepower, not with weapons that chucked tiny pieces of starstuff at targets unguessably distant.

As he stared up into the zenith, he saw a single sharp, short pop of light, lasting for only an instant but clearly visible against the dark blue of the sky. He saw another . . . then a rippling cascade of ten or twelve more. Within a few seconds, the sky seemed filled with rapidly flickering points of light.

Stunned by Hector's brain-numbing Hellbore barrage, he couldn't at first imagine what he was seeing, what those sparkles and flashes might be. Then it connected. If the Bolo was smashing incoming !*!*! meteors with its primary weapons, there must be a fair amount of dust, droplets of molten iron, sand-sized flecks of debris, and gravel-sized chunks left over. Even vaporized, a one- or two-ton meteor's mass didn't simply vanish, and all of the leftovers would still be heading in the same general direction as the original projectile—dispersing somewhat over a large part of the hemisphere facing them—and they would still be traveling with most of the rock's original speed. Those flashes, Dieter thought, must be sand grains and smaller bits of debris hitting the upper atmosphere at high speed, expending their considerable kinetic energy as brilliant, individual flickers of light.

A blue-white lance of dazzling light stabbed down from the zenith, vanishing in a silent flare halfway to the horizon. The rapid-fire flickers continued, interspersed occasionally by bigger, bolder stabs that left distinct trails across the sky. One line of blue fire vanished behind the eastern rim of the crater, somewhere in the general direction of Griffenburg, to the south, followed by a silent flare of light that rose silently above the horizon. Several moments later, he felt the shock through the ground and heard the long, drawn-out rumble of thunder. That one, he thought, must have been an unusually big fragment that had slipped past Hector's barrage. Most of the pieces were burning up when they hit Cloud's upper atmosphere, but a few of the big ones were getting through.

He hoped the Bolo was able to pick out the ones that posed a threat to the harbor area; for the first time in quite a long time, he found that he very much wanted to *live*.

With rocks falling out of the sky, however, and no place to hide but the crater gouged out by the boulder that had flattened Celeste, it seemed that he wasn't going to have much say in the matter.

Colonel Wal Prescott had no intention of being left out of this fight. As the sky flared purple-white and a rumbling shockwave rocked through the ground, he stood up, clutching the silvery, metallic snake of a clacker tentacle that he had just torn from a downed !°!°! sentry with his one good hand.

"How many *soldiers* do we have here?" he screamed,

his voice thin against the howling backdrop of thunder, but the meaning plain enough to the half-hundred or so men and women lying in the shallow waters of the bottom of the pit.

"Me!" a naked, bearded man missing his left eye shouted, rising to his feet. A !°!°! floater hovered nearby, and the man swatted it down with a swipe of one hand too fast to follow. Clutching the frantically buzzing captive close to his chest, he cracked its shell and extracted one glittering, faceted camera eye. "That's for my eye," he shouted waving the gleaming trophy. "Let's go get us some more!"

"The turners!" a woman cried. "Let's get the skekking turner trusties!"

Lightning flared across the sky, accompanied by crashing thunder, as the mob surged from the pit, with Wal only nominally in the lead. . . .

"Turn left at the next branching of the corridor," Hector's voice said in his ear. "Be careful. I am detecting movement and a magnetic flux of nearly two hundred twelve gauss in the power plant accessway where there should be none."

"Roger that," Jaime said. He raised the power gun, hefting its reassuring mass in his hand. *It's a shame*, he thought, *that Hector doesn't have internal security cameras*. He did, actually, at the airlocks and entranceways, but Bolos were not really designed to carry living personnel, despite the amenities of their Battle Centers, and more useful senses than sight were used to keep watch on their internal areas.

"Has the clacker left your controller, then? It's walking around?"

"Negative. I still detect its influence on the power plant controller. It may be using remotes of some sort, however, or there is more than one !°!°! machine operating in the area."

"Terrific." The passageway here was almost three meters tall, but less than a meter wide, the walls lost in sheets of wiring and fiberoptic bundles. In places where massive power feeds rose from the uneven floor to vanish into the tangle of wiring overhead, Jaime had to turn sideways to squeeze his way through.

He hesitated at the branching of the corridor, then swung around the corner, weapon raised. The passageway here was softly lit with light strips and had the rounded, organic feel of the gut of some enormous beast.

"It is also possible that additional enemy machines entered my structure by the same route you did," Hector continued with implacable calm. "However, the likeliest explanation is that the !°!°! placed devices inside key areas of my anatomy when they first suborned my programming, possibly as a kind of insurance that I would not turn against them."

"Why didn't they rig you with a fusion bomb or something, then?" Jaime wanted to know. He enjoyed hearing Hector's voice in his ear and wanted to keep the Bolo talking. He felt less alone, less exposed that way.

"In one sense they did," Hector replied. "The device has been attempting to trigger an overload of my primary power core and generate a low-yield fusion meltdown for the past two point seven one minutes. Thus far, I have been able to circumvent each attempt."

"Oh." It was a reminder that he, Alita, and Shari were in effect lurking in the shadows of a conflict far bigger, faster, and more deadly than unaided human senses could perceive . . . or comprehend.

As he walked, the jolting shock of each Hellbore shot, a detonation every handful of seconds, continued to ring, a savage explosion of sound. If anything, the noise was louder out here, outside of the massive shields and beyond the shock absorbers that cocooned the Battle Center. Once, he felt something like a nearby explosion different in character from the Hellbore volleys, and he wondered if the enemy was scoring some hits as well.

"Unauthorized movement has ceased," Hector told him. "However, I am detecting a rapidly cycling magnetic flux. The source appears to be radiating from a point four meters in front of you."

"Four meters?" That would put it at a T-branching in the passageway just ahead. The !°!°! must be waiting in ambush just around the corner. "Which side? Left or right?"

"To your left."

Jaime thumbed the power gun's dial to pencil beam, maximum output, and took another step forward. Before he could take a second one, something blurred into his field of vision, a gray mass of indeterminate detail lunging around the corner ahead, striking sparks as it scraped against the wall of the corridor while it pulled itself along with flashing tentacles.

His finger came down convulsively on the firing stud, a reaction of pure reflex that quite possibly saved his life. The power gun's beam sliced into the oncoming object's body, erupting in a dazzling blaze of white fire that traced a zigzag path up the target's curved shell. The !°!°! attacker halted its charge and hovered in agitated consternation two meters away, a silver-gray ovoid twice the size of Jaime's head, sprouting a dozen writhing, tightly segmented tentacles. The !°!°! machine started to turn, rotating the burned part of its body out of the line of fire. Jaime tracked the damaged part, then sliced off three tentacles with a sharp, decisive stroke.

Smoke spilled from the thing's body, black and acrid. A moment later, it emitted a shrill death whine and dropped out of the air as though invisible strings had been cut, smashing into the deck in a final clatter of whiplashing tentacles.

He shot the wreckage again, just to make sure. These things were fiendishly difficult to kill.

A few minutes later, Jaime found the main !°!°! machine, a shapeless sprawl of cables and tentacles and a claylike mass of dull metal stretched across the complex of circuit junctions and cables that fed commands from Hector's computer core to the power plant. At first, Jaime stared at that mess of wiring and alien parts with blank confusion. It was almost impossible to tell what legitimately belonged to Hector and what was alien machine-parasite . . . and if he chose the wrong target, he could do more damage to the Bolo than the clackers.

Crystalline eyes, cold and glittering, regarded him with emotionless intelligence. Jaime picked an aim point roughly in the center of a ragged ellipse of five of the machine sensory organs and fired, holding the beam on target as metal tentacles shaped themselves from softening patches of gray metal. One tentacle, molding itself larger than the rest, flailed toward Jaime's face, the tip stinging across his cheek centimeters below his eye. Jaime stepped back, shifted aim, and burned the tentacle off in a writhing snake of interlocking segments.

"The intruder machine is attempting to create a power core overload," Hector's voice said quietly in Jaime's ear. "I recommend both haste and efficiency in your attack."

Haste *and* efficiency? That was a pairing humans could rarely manage. He shifted his aim back to the main body of the thing, ignoring the hot blood and burning on his face, ignoring the pain as another tentacle slashed at his left arm. With a sudden puff of foul-smelling vapor, the power gun burned through the tough metal, and the close-packed wiring and circuitry inside the gray shell burst into flame.

And in another twitching, snake-writhing couple of seconds, the thing was dead.

Jaime returned to the Battle Center, limping a little with the injury to his leg. Alita looked up as he came in. "My God. Another one?"

"A couple of them, in fact," he said, returning the power gun to its locker. "I think one was a kind of guard. I wish I knew for sure that we'd gotten them all."

"Hector?" Alita called, addressing the center of the room. "Are there any more enemy machines on board?"

"Not that I am aware of," the Bolo replied. "If !°!°! machines were present but dormant I would have no way of detecting them. However, my internal structure appears secure for the moment." One of the Bolo's Hellbores fired again as if to punctuate the statement, a ringing, thumping concussion.

"What's your status?" Jaime asked. He was worried that he or the !°!°! parasite might have damaged Hector's control circuitry somehow.

"Power output now at twenty-three point three five percent and rising," the machine replied. "It will take several minutes to bring my fusion plants to full operation, but I appear to have full and nominal control of all systems."

A flash from the view dome caught his eye, and Jaime stepped closer to the command chair, looking up. The sky overhead had grown hazy, the horizon in every direction almost completely obscured by fog. At first, he thought there'd been a failure of some sort in the viewing dome electronics. The dazzling, violet-white flash of a Hellbore discharge stabbing skyward, accompanied by ringing thunder, made him rethink his first guess.

Steam. Celeste's harbor must be growing hot from the heat released by each fusion bolt, hot enough that vapor was rising around the Bolo like a cloud.

He wondered if Hector was having trouble targeting

the incoming projectiles, then decided that he wouldn't be firing unless he had a good lock.

Another flash lit the compartment, a blue-white star dropping from the zenith, so bright that even with the dome electronics stopping down the light to bearable levels, it cast rapidly moving shadows. It streaked down the right side of the dome, drawing a contrail in its wake, then vanishing with a sharp pulse of light somewhere beyond the fog.

So. Some !°!°! meteors were getting past the Hector's defensive fire . . . or, more likely, fragments of larger boulders the Bolo had already nailed were leaking through.

The barrage continued, though Hector's return fire seemed to be slower now, the shots more widely spaced. Jaime thought the Bolo must be trying to conserve its ammunition; the machine couldn't have had time to manufacture more than a handful of cryo-H Hellbore rounds.

And what the hell happens to us, he wondered, *when Hector runs out of ammo?* As near as he could figure it, either the !°!°! barrage would smash Hector and the camp and every living creature within a hundred kilometers of Celeste Bay . . . or the clackers would move in as soon as they knew that Hector had been neutralized.

And neither prospect seemed particularly pleasant.

The situation is fast growing desperate. I have been in action for ten minutes, twenty-eight point five seconds and, so far, have vaporized or deflected all incoming Enemy projectiles. However, at my current rate of fire, I will have exhausted all ammunition within another two minutes. I have been manufacturing additional cryo-H Hellbore rounds at the same time, but the process cannot be hurried and creates fresh slivers at a slower rate than even my current, slow and measured rate of fire.

To continue on this course would result in my being forced to cease fire in another one minute, forty-one point seven seconds. Shortly after that, I would most likely suffer a direct impact from a projectile releasing kinetic energy on the order of one megaton, an impact which, with my battle screens inoperative, I would not survive. Clearly, it is time to change tactics.

I shift targets, taking aim with both turrets One and Two. When I fire, it is not with the measured, ammunition-saving rhythm with which I have been knocking down the incoming hostile projectiles, but with a rapid-fire barrage of Hellbore fusion pulses that illuminate the night and expend all of my remaining Hellbore rounds within five point seven one seconds.

VAL812 had monitored the destruction or deflection of each of the projectiles it had launched toward the planetside target. It still had a large amount of meteoric material in storage, but the past several minutes—an endless time for an intelligence that measured time in nanoseconds—had been a complete and utter exercise in futility, with not a single projectile fragment impacting closer to the target than a distance of several kilometers.

Sensors aboard the TIG232 battler/fortress detected the target's incoming Hellbore barrage by the distinctive touch of its main battery lasers, seconds before bolts of starcore-hot fusion plasma whipcracked up the laser conduit, but VAL was still attempting to shunt additional power to the defensive shields when the Bolo's volley struck. Lighting flared as magnetic shields tried to dump the excess voltage of the first bolt's EM pulse; the plasma itself, incoming at a significant fraction of lightspeed, was harder to deal with.

Two separate points on the TIG battler's curved prow shone with a light more intense than that of the local sun, sharp with the bite of X-rays and ultraviolet. The points expanded, swelling within milliseconds to engulf the forward kilometer of the titanic warship.

VAL812 gave a radio-frequency yelp of surprise and the machine equivalent of pain as two lances of fusion fire needled through the battler's screens, through its outer armor, through the layers of nickel-iron of the original asteroid converted by the !°!°! into a ship, and through the densely packed core of wiring, conduits, and circuitry comprising the dreadnought's autonomous nervous system before ballooning out the far side in explosive bursts of metal vapor and cooling plasma.

The !°!°! ship rolled heavily to the left, braking savagely, glowing-hot fragments spilling from its prow. An instant later, two more blossoms of hellfire unfolded against the vessel's ebony flank, one slashing through tender interior wiring and molecular circuits, the other carving off a city-sized slab of armor and rock, leaving a flat scar behind that glowed a sullen and molten orange.

The four-brain intelligence of the ship could grasp instantly what was happening but was unable to formulate an immediate or original counter. Instead, it called for help. "VAL812-928782, calling Command Web. I am under direct attack and have suffered Level Three damage. Continuing attack. Please advise."

Seconds passed, as molten rock and vaporized internal components bled into hard vacuum. And then, abruptly, VAL812 was no longer alone as a data transmissions stream opened between the battler and the !°!°! command center on the nearby moon the humans called Delamar. Another machine presence, the free-ranging and self-aware thoughts of a high-order, fifth-level cognitive, resided within the virtual space occupied by the !°!°! ship-mind. In a quick, lightning touch, DAV728-24389 downloaded VAL812's recent memories and current diagnostic status onto the Command Web, analyzing each bit of information.

"Withdraw," DAV728 commanded almost at once. "Break off the attack and pull back to Regroup Point Three."

"I comply." VAL's primary drive was damaged, and maneuvering was clumsy, but the battler managed to swing itself onto a new vector, one that would carry it out of range of the deadly planetary ground defenses within another few hundred billion nanoseconds.

Two more bolts seared up from the planet's surface, this time bypassing VAL812 entirely and burning their way deep into GEL933-83737, which was just moving into range.

"All battlers, cease attack and withdraw," the !°!°! controller added, amending his first command. "Execute immediately!"

A final bolt of fusing plasma played briefly across VAL812's ventral surface, a star-point of intense, violet-white lightnings etching deep into rock and steel alloy, gouging out a ragged, hot-glowing crater.

On the blue-white globe of the captive planet, a storm appeared to be growing with manic rapidity across the peninsula which included the target area, obliterating one by one the violently radiating patches of thermal radiation where !°!°! projectiles had struck.

Though VAL had very little in the way of actual consciousness or self-awareness, it nevertheless felt something akin to intense pleasure at the idea of moving out of range.

"The enemy warships are breaking off the attack," Hector's calm voice announced. "All three vessels appear to be withdrawing."

"Yes!" Jaime shouted, coming to his feet, and in another second, he, Alita, and even Shari were on their feet, wordlessly screaming, embracing one another, and all but dancing on the narrow steel deck of the Battle Center.

"We did it!" Alita cried, gripping Jaime's arms with trembling hands. "We *did* it!"

"Hector did it," he replied, laughing. "We were just along for the ride!"

Shari collapsed into both of their arms, sobbing uncontrollably, though whether from the excitement or from grief over Jeff Fowler's death, or some gut-wrenching combination of the two, he couldn't tell.

"I knew he could beat the damned clackers!" Alita cried. "I never doubted it!"

"Yeah," he said, though he certainly couldn't agree with Alita's assessment. He'd had lots of doubts. "Now we just have to figure out what to do next."

He glanced up at the viewing dome. Outside, fog and roiling clouds had thickened markedly in just the past few minutes, blotting out the sun and sky and even the nearby shore and the ruins beyond.

It was beginning to rain.

CHAPTER ELEVEN

Enemy activity in the immediate vicinity appears to have ceased. Evidently, when the |*|*| broke off their attack, all remaining hostile machines on the surface were directed to pull back.

An atmospheric disturbance of considerable proportions has settled over the region, evidently the result of both my own high-energy discharges and the effects of multiple impacts by incoming meteoric projectiles. This is something of what humans refer to as a double-edged sword. The cloud cover and heavy rain, as well as the periodic nearby discharge of lightning, have rendered my long-range passive sensors largely blind. I could penetrate the cloud cover with various active sensors, of course, but that would reveal both my precise position and the fact that I am actively interested in Enemy movements and positions. On the other hand, the storm provides excellent cover for both me and the human refugees gathered here. Enemy space assets that use active scanners to pinpoint my location will of necessity pinpoint their locations for me.

I am not certain what my Commander has in mind for our next move. Clearly, we cannot remain in this *area. The Enemy could still drop a small asteroid on this location while I am blinded, and the quicker we lose ourselves somewhere beyond the limits of this ruined city, the better. The storm will afford an excellent opportunity for us to elude !°!°! surveillance and escape elsewhere. The question, however, is where?*

A planet is a large place, but it will be impossible to conceal from the Enemy's reconnaissance systems either my activities or the presence of the human refugees for very long.

The rain was coming down in curtains, a torrential downpour that obscured everything more than a few tens of meters away in gray, cold haze. Jaime had told Hector to move in to the shore, and the great Bolo had complied, wallowing forward and swinging left, his immense tracks dredging up clouds of black mud from the harbor bottom. Even with the downpour, Jaime could see the Bolo's track through the water, marked as it was by upwelling mud.

A few moments later, the Bolo had crawled up onto the shore, tracks grinding and crunching through the rubble of the buildings that once had graced the Celeste Harbor waterfront. Jaime had emerged from a hatch on the upper deck, just forward of the Number One turret, and rode there now, his legs inside the open hatch, one hand bracing himself against the Bolo's lurching motion. He ignored the rain drenching his skin and plastering his long hair across his face. It felt, it *tasted* good.

Like freedom, no matter how temporary that condition turned out to be.

"I am detecting large numbers of humans approaching from various points to the east to north," Hector said, his voice relayed to Jaime through an earplug receiver found in an equipment locker in the Battle Center. "Range to the nearest, twenty-one point three meters.

Some of them are armed with personal sidearms or improvised melee weaponry."

"Let them come," Jaime replied. They *could* be turners, of course, but no weapons they could possibly have would be a threat to the armored mountain now slowly crawling out of the bay.

He leaned forward slightly, trying to see through the sleeting rain. *I would have had a better view from the Battle Center,* he thought. *But it feels so damned remote, buried away in that lead-wrapped bunker.* Metal, still hot despite the sluicing rain, popped and pinged on the turret facing and Hellbore mount behind him as it cooled.

"The nearest party of humans is now five meters from my left forward track. Bearing three-three-five, relative."

Jaime looked in the indicated direction. Shapes were just beginning to materialize out of the downpour, bedraggled human shapes gathering in the mud alongside the Bolo's huge left forward track, peering up into the rain. Jaime recognized Dieter and waved, and a moment later the man was scrambling up one of the access ladders threading up Hector's skirts and armored sides. Two others followed, while the rest waited at the base of the Bolo's tracks.

"My God," Dieter said a few minutes later as Jaime reached out and gravely clasped his hand. He looked around, a little wildly. "You actually did it!"

"I didn't realize things were going to get quite that hot," Jaime replied. He had to shout to make himself heard above the hissing rain. He looked at the other two men as they scrambled up onto the wet deck. "Gentlemen? Welcome aboard."

"Sergeant Jack Haley, reporting," the first man up said, saluting crisply. Haley had only one eye, with a puckered socket where his left eye had been. He was clad in a poorly fitting, mud- and blood-stained camp guard's uniform. The faceted red lens of a clacker's electronic eye was centered against his forehead, held in place by wires twisted together in the back of his head. "An' this here's Sergeant Xin." Xin, too, wore a guard's appropriated uniform and had a red clacker eye wired above his own eyes. His left hand ended in a crudely dressed stump, but he rendered a sharp salute with the right.

"What're those, Sergeant?" Jaime asked, nodding at the glittering prize on Haley's forehead. "Battle honors?"

"In a manner of speakin', yessir. An eye fer an eye, like they say."

"It seemed an effective means of unit identification, sir," Xin added. "Things were a bit confused out there today."

"We're formin' up a new unit, Major Graham," Haley said. "Not sure what we're callin' it, though some of the guys're suggesting 'Brotherhood of the Eye.' It'll be a, whatchacallit, ay-lite unit. Specializin' in rippin' cluckers into small bits and pieces!"

Graham nodded gravely. It would take more than enthusiasm and a lust for payback to create a genuinely "ay-lite" unit, but he was more than willing to let them try. They were going to need ground forces and scouts in the next few days. Even a Bolo had its limitations in a situation like this.

"You men want to come inside?"

Dieter laughed. Stress, excitement, and the downpour transformed it into a maniacal cackle. "Might make conversation a tad easier," he said.

They scrambled down the open hatch, first Dieter and the two soldiers, then Jaime. The passageway was so low that all four men had to stoop; Jaime led the way to Access 12A, where there was a little more room.

"Was anyone . . . ?" Jaime trailed off, realizing what a stupid question that was. "How many people did we lose?"

Dieter shook his head. "Can't say, yet. A lot of our people must still be scattered about these ruins, and a good many must have just taken off for the horizon when the sky started lightning up and the asteroids started coming down."

"Some of us took the chance and attacked the guards," Xin said. "We probably lost fifty or sixty in the fighting, that I know of."

Haley barked a harsh laugh. "But we kicked machine ass an' gave a lot better than we took. Hell, it was beautiful, sir! You should've seen it!"

"I was . . . kind of busy."

"When the shooting started," Dieter added, "most of us headed for cover and kept our heads down. But a few—"

"It was Colonel Prescott, mostly," Xin said. "He organized a lot of us. Led us to the turner houses . . ."

"Really!" Jaime was surprised. Wal had ordered him to stand down, and he'd been half expecting a biting lecture on the need to follow orders. If the colonel was able to adapt to suddenly changing situations and opportunities, though, he would understand why Jaime had done what he'd done. "Is Wal okay?"

"Last I heard, yes, sir. He's still out there, trying to get our people organized."

"There were a number of people wounded," Dieter put in. "I believe the colonel is trying to round up those people in the camp with medical experience."

"How many wounded?" Jaime wanted to know.

"I don't know, Jaime. Several dozen, certainly."

"Not as bad as it could've been," Haley said. "We hit the turners before they knew what was happenin'." He gestured at the uniforms they were wearing. "Captured uniforms, stunsticks, even some weapons, though I don't think anyone's run inventory yet on all the stuff we got. And any clacker machines that got in the way, well, they didn't stand much of a chance against *us!*"

Jaime smiled. "Did you leave any in one piece?" He wasn't sure it would be possible to get any information from a captured clacker. More than that, he didn't think it would be possible to keep one prisoner. How did you disarm a machine that could channel bolts of antipersonnel lightning through its body? At the same time, though, they desperately needed to know more about their machine enemy.

"That's a negative! Most of 'em took off when the rocks started falling out of the sky. Guess they didn't want to be hanging around at ground zero." He tapped the side of the lens wired to his head. "The slow ones got disassembled."

"What about the turners?"

"Them too. I think most of them high-tailed it faster than the cluckers. Those that *could*, of course. The slow ones didn't get any further than the slow clackers."

Jaime nodded. There would have been, *could* have been, no mercy for any of the turncoat humans who'd fallen into the hands of the rebelling slaves.

"We'll have to watch for a counterstrike of some kind," Jaime said.

"What, the turners?" Haley snorted. "They don't stand a comet's chance on a sun going up against a Bolo!"

"The Ma—" He stopped himself. They were Masters no longer. "The machines. Hector here fended off three of their starships, but it was a close-run thing. They'll be back, and when they come, our best strategy is going to be to hide."

Dieter's face showed his astonishment . . . and then he laughed. "Hide? A goddamn *Bolo*?"

Haley's laugh was colored ever so slightly by hysteria. He waved his arms, taking in the dull gray walls of the war machine enclosing them. "How the hell are we supposed to hide *this* thing?"

Jaime chuckled. "There are ways. First thing we have

to do is reorganize the war council." His face hardened.
"Have any of you seen the general? Or his aides?"

"Not a sign," Dieter said. "We have people looking
for them, though."

"God, you're not thinking of putting *him* in charge,
are you?" Alita said, coming around a bend in the
passageway. "Hi, Dieter. Men."

"Sergeant. Good to see you again."

"Sergeant Kyle!" Haley said, brightening. "How'd
you get assigned to *this* billet?"

"Knew a thing or three about Bolos, Haley. Hey,
you guys look *clean*!"

Dieter jerked a thumb over his shoulder, back toward
the hatch. "The shower facilities are open. I think
Hector here turned on the spigot."

She wiped at the dried mud caking her face,
succeeding only in rearranging the dirt somewhat. "I
may take advantage of that." She looked at Jaime. "So,
boss. What are we going to do about Spratly?"

"Well, we're going to have to decide that, aren't we?
This is still a military organization."

"And Spratly's the senior officer," Dieter put in. "But,
damn it all, you know how he feels about Bolos. . . ."

"Goddamn collaborator, is what he is," Haley said.

"We don't know that, Sergeant," Jaime replied. "As
for how he feels about Bolos, I think now that I know
why he feels that way."

"Why?"

Jaime shook his head. "Let's not go into it now. We're
going to need to hold a council of war and get all this
stuff sorted out. Dieter, you start rounding up our
senior people. Officers. Senior NCOs. Let 'em know
we're going to have a meeting . . . let's make it this
evening, at suns-set."

"It may take longer than that to track everyone
down."

"Well, we can't wait for 'em. Haley, Xin, you two

lend a hand. Get the whole Brotherhood together."

"I'll do the best I can. Things are kind of chaotic out there." Dieter shrugged. "We didn't really expect that we were going to *win*, after all!"

"Well, right now, our best hope is in getting as far away from Celeste as we can, as fast as we can. You men can start passing the word that I'm planning on leaving tonight."

"Excellent!" Alita said.

"Tonight!" Dieter shook his head. "Major, do you have any idea of the logistical problems we're facing here? Four, five thousand people, most of 'em half-starved to begin with, most of 'em without shoes or even decent clothes, can't just up and set off on a cross-country hike. We need to find food and supplies. Hell, we need to figure out just where we're supposed to go!"

"I have some ideas there, too. Just get our people together, those you can find. We're going to have to take this thing one step at a time."

Dieter didn't look convinced. "Yeah, well, I sure hope you know what you're doing, Jaime!"

"Hey, the major can do *anything*!" Haley said. He sounded offended. "He got the Bolo workin', right? And he busted us out of the camp! Hell, that's nine-tenths of the battle right there!"

"Dieter's not military, is he?" Alita asked after the three men had scrambled back up the ladder rugs, through the hatch, and out into the rain once more. "If he were, I'd pin his ears back for questioning your decisions that way, using a couple of blunt, Number Nine restraining bolts."

"Dr. Hollinsworth is a physicist," Jaime replied. "A scientist. New Aberdeen University . . . and he's done work at SMA Electronics."

"I knew he was a physicist. I didn't know he worked for SMA."

"Yeah, and they did a lot of contract work for the military. He knows high-energy weapons systems."

"So you want to be nice to him."

"Let's just say the most important asset we have right now is *people*," Jaime replied. He smiled. "Except for Hector, of course."

"He's people. Don't you doubt it."

"Yeah. I'm beginning to think he is." He looked at her, concerned. "How's Shari?"

"Asleep in a little watch officer's bunkroom off the Battle Center. I made her lie down, and she went right out. She'll be okay."

"It was rough, finding that guy, that way. You keep an eye on her, okay?"

"Roger that. And . . . I wanted to tell you . . ."

"Yeah?"

"That bunkroom has some more gear in it. And some uniforms, the autofit kind. Thought you might want to know."

He nodded, a knowing half-smile spreading across his face. "Excellent! Good thinking, Sergeant. That'll help. A *lot*. . . ."

I am growing concerned about my Commander's apparent lack of a coherent long-range battle plan, though as I consider the problem in parallel with the files I possess on human psychology, I can speculate that our victory against the !*!*! was so sudden and, perhaps, unexpected that he is still adjusting to the change in the strategic situation.

To remain in the immediate vicinity of Celeste Harbor, however, is nothing less than suicidal. I have worked out thirty-six separate, alternate tracks that will take us away from this area, taking maximum advantage of rough and wooded terrain or sea bottom to conceal my movements. At that, I am aware of humans in my immediate vicinity who may have joined their cause to that of the !°!°!, from fear, coercion, or pragmatism. Our activities are being watched.

Also of concern, of course, is my Commander's determination to bring along as many of the former inmates of Camp 84 as possible, a number which may be as high as five thousand or more, depending on how many of those who fled the camp during the battle elect to return and join our company. So large a number of humans, traveling on foot and slowed by the need to sleep, rest, and forage for food, would delay my movement to a crawl.

I understand enough of human behavior to be able to accept my Commander's compassion, and to accept the fact that the safety of the freed captives is of considerable importance to him.

I sincerely hope, however, that this compassion does not blind him to the realities of both the tactical and strategic situations of the moment.

And one thing more of particular concern. I am sincerely curious about his apparent delight in finding a uniform. Surely the acquisition of proper military dress should have a relatively low priority, compared to the larger and more urgent questions of destination, long-range strategy, and survival.

Two shadowy, water-drenched forms watched the Bolo from a low ridge on the south rim of the crater. Captain Pogue wore the remnants of his army uniform beneath a waterproof poncho. Dewar Sykes wore his characteristic mud-heavy jackboots, guard's uniform, and, as always, the silver circlet around his head. Even as the rain thinned slightly, they could see little more than the Bolo.

"Shoot," Sykes said. "I can't see nothin'. What're they doin' down there, anyhow?"

"Quiet," Pogue replied, his voice low and deadly.

"That damned Bolo has directional mikes that can pick up a gnat's buzz at five kilometers."

"Then we're already spotted, ain't we?" Sykes sneezed, a sudden, sharp explosion of sound.

"Jeez, Sykes! You *tryin'* to get us spotted?"

"If they cared, we'd be dead now, wouldn't we?" He looked up at the blue-black clouds, squinting into the rain. "Just what are you tryin' to see, huh? I'm tellin' ya, there's nothin' you can learn that the Masters don't know already."

"Quiet. I think someone's coming out."

"How can you tell?"

"I saw a light. Up on top of the Bolo's deck. Yeah . . . someone's climbing down the side." He couldn't tell who it was. It was all he could do to make out the massive gray bulk of the Bolo, a mountain masked by the haze and rain. Still, he was pretty sure there were people near the front of the thing, and he was pretty sure, too, that several people had scrambled up the side and gone inside. Now those someones had just come out, tiny specks descending the massive, smooth cliff of the Bolo's side.

It was not particularly useful information. Someone—almost certainly Jaime Graham—was inside the machine and using it as a command post.

Damn it, there had to be some useful intelligence, *something* with which to bargain with the !*!*!.

And, rain or no rain, he was determined to root it out.

"So?" Tamas Reuter said, questioning with a lift to his bushy eyebrows. "Where is he?"

"He'll be here," Dieter replied. Rain drummed on the sheet tin and canvas that served as the barracks' roof. "Give the man a chance."

A low murmur of conversation sounded from the men and women gathered in a deep ring near the barracks' main entrance. Dieter had collected about a hundred men and women in all, two-thirds of them CDF—a tiny representation of former military officers and noncoms out of the two or three thousand on the camp's rolls—and the rest civilian experts in one discipline or another, like Dieter himself. That number, however, had steadily grown as other people had wandered in and joined the relentlessly growing circle. The total number, he thought, must now be well over a thousand.

He still wasn't sure how many people remained in the camp in all; the majority had fled during the battle earlier, and while some might yet return, he was pretty sure that most hadn't stopped running yet. The camp, throughout the afternoon as he and those with him had searched for other stay-behinds, had seemed eerily empty and silent.

A large percentage of the people who remained were crowded now inside the barracks, waiting to hear from the man who'd released the Bolo—and them—from their bonds.

"Maybe he decided to make off with the Bolo on his own," someone called out from the crowd.

"Yeah, or mebee the damned cluckers've already moved in and taken Hector over again!"

"Did the Bolo really look fully operational to you, Dieter?" Wal Prescott asked. He rubbed his stump absently. "I mean, we all saw it clearing its Hellbores at th' sky, but . . ."

"I didn't see the Battle Center, if that's what you mean," Dieter replied. "But the major and Sergeant Kyle seemed to be in control of things."

"Are they?" a new voice demanded from the open clapboard door. "Do they have control of that damned Bolo? Or was it just clearing its guns?"

General Spratly stood in the doorway for a moment, hands on hips, surveying the gathered men and women as though holding an impromptu review. Several of the military personnel stood immediately, and after a moment's hesitation, more and more people stood as well. It was a tattered remnant of the old body of military formality and protocol that had shaped and ordered the CDF before The Killing.

Three more men entered behind the general—Majors Dulaney and Howard, and Captain Pogue. The three staff officers took up positions shielding Spratly from the watching crowd.

"I never have been sure which side that damned machine was on," Spratly continued. "After the havoc it wreaked today, I'd think the rest of you would have some doubts too!"

"The Bolo drove off three clacker warships this afternoon, General," Dieter said.

"Did it?" Spratly and his entourage started forward, and the crowd parted before them. "Did it really? Did you *see* these warships, Dr. Hollinsworth?"

"No, I didn't. Major Graham told me that Hector engaged them while they were still some tens of thousands of kilometers out."

"That's his story. The story of a damned traitor and mutineer."

"Well, sir, if Hector wasn't trading shots with the clackers," Wal asked easily, "who was it dropping rocks on us from orbit?"

"Would anyone have been dropping those rocks if Graham hadn't started meddling with that thing in the first place?" Spratly retorted. "Damn it, we don't know what the alien machines might've done to the Bolo's programming. We don't know why the Bolo failed us at Chryse in the first place! Do we want to put our trust in that . . . that *machine*?"

"I don't like it much better'n you do, General," Wal said, shaking his head. "But y'gotta admit that ol' Jaime gave th' clackers a licking! They lit off out of here like they had a hell-born legion of can openers after 'em!"

"We're *free*, General," Dieter added. "That's what counts!"

"And I think the general might be able to tell us a little bit more about what happened at Chryse, too," another voice said.

The waiting people turned as Jaime strode through the open door, Alita at his side. Both of them were resplendent in the dark blue-and-silver of the Cloud Defense Force, though neither uniform bore an emblem of rank, and Alita was still barefoot. Behind them, half a dozen men in gray guards' uniforms formed a silent wall, each of them with a gouged-out clacker eye wired to his or her head.

Spratly stared at them, ashen faced. "*You . . .*"

"Hello, General," Jaime said with a matter-of-fact smile. "I do apologize for the rough handling this afternoon."

Spratly's face swiftly darkened from ash-white to angry red. He raised one arm, pointing at Jaime. "*Arrest that traitor!*"

There was a sharp *snick* of movement, and Jaime held a Mark XIV power pistol, one of the weapons found aboard the Bolo. At his back, the detachment of uniformed troops snapped to the ready with captured power guns and stunsticks.

"I don't think so, General," Jaime said easily. "What I did this afternoon was in self-defense, after you threatened to turn me over to the cluckers. As for the gun, well . . . I needed it."

"Mutiny!"

The crowd parted again as Jaime moved forward, leaving Alita and the guards by the door. He reached the center of the circle and stood beside Spratly, an imposing figure in blue and silver. He kept the power gun in his hand, though he kept the muzzle directed at the barracks' ceiling. The sheer, power-charged *presence* of the man, amplified by the first clean uniform any of them had seen in a year, held them all more captive than any mere weapon.

"I'm not going to apologize for *any* of what I did," Jaime said, but now he was speaking louder, pitching his voice to carry to every man and woman in the expectantly silent room. "I had a chance to end our slavery to the alien machines. I took it. If I hadn't . . . well, I leave it to each of you to decide how much longer we would have lasted, working the pit, grubbing in the mud, and providing those damned scavengers with biological spare parts.

"And at this point, I don't think any of us would care to walk back to the cluckers, apologize, and ask them to take us in again."

"Maybe you should do just that!" one anonymous voice called out from the crowd. "We had it okay before you stirred up the Bolo!"

"Says you!" another voice cried out, angry and shrill. "What are you, some kind of turner scum? Th' major's right! This is our chance to walk out of here, and I'm takin' it!"

"Me too!"

"That's tellin' 'em!"

"Who the hell is *he* to decide for us?"

Jaime held up both hands, waving the crowd to silence. "Quiet down! Quiet down, everybody! Look . . . if we'd kept on the way we were going, we, all of us, wouldn't have survived much longer. *Think* about it, people! If you're honest with yourselves, you'll know what I'm saying is true. Now . . . except for the fact that you're free now, we're not making any decisions for you. The way I see it, you have three choices, and which one you decide on is entirely up to you.

"First choice. You can strike out on your own, try to lose yourself in the countryside. We think—though it's not certain—we *think* that the farms and smaller communities beyond the Chryse Peninsula are still relatively untouched by the machines. We know that Tolun merchants have been delivering food, and that food has to be coming from someplace. You can scatter, go to ground. The machines may track down some of you, but others will escape. Or maybe the machines won't even bother.

"Second choice. You can stay here. Talk to the machines when they return. Maybe they'll be . . . merciful. I don't recommend it, but you can decide the advantages, and the dangers, for yourselves.

"Third choice. You can come with us."

For a frozen moment, a stunned silence fell over the crowd. Then the murmuring began, growing louder.

"Where you goin', Major?" a woman called out from the darkness toward the rear of the crowd.

"Away from here. Obviously, I'm not about to discuss precise plans with people who might be picked up and questioned by the cluckers. But I do have a destination in mind, and my goal, ultimately, is to use the Bolo to help us get us off of this world altogether."

The murmur exploded into the cacophony possible only to a roaring, agitated crowd.

"We can't leave Cloud!" someone cried. "It's our home!"

"The clackers'll burn down any ship leaving this planet the moment it pokes its nose out of the atmosphere!

"That's insane!"

"*Yes!*" Spratly yelled, seizing on one shouted word among many rising above the background thunder. "It *is* insane! It's insane to put our trust in the Bolo again! It didn't stop the clackers when they invaded Cloud! It didn't stop them from destroying Chryse! How does Graham expect it to stop them now?"

The crowd fell silent again, every eye on Jaime as they waited for his reply. Dieter leaned forward, tasting the sweat trickling down his unshaven cheeks and off the corners of his mustache. It was the question everyone in the camp had been wondering about, ever since the day the alien invaders had swooped in from space unchallenged.

Silence ticked on for another five seconds, before Jaime raised his hand to his ear. He wore, Dieter saw, an earplug commlink, with the thread mike extended to rest beside his lips. "Okay, Hector," he said. "You're on."

Amplified feedback squealed from the evening sky outside, so loud that some in the crowd ducked, and everyone looked up.

"*Bolo* Hecate *of the Line!*" a vastly amplified voice boomed out. "*This is General Spratly! I order you to hold your fire!*"

Every head turned, then, eyes locking onto Spratly's paste-white face.

"*Bolo* Hecate *of the Line, I copy,*" another voice, deeper, calmer, more in control replied. It was the voice, they all knew, of the Bolo. "*I now have twenty-eight targets inbound. Nearest now at five-zero-seven-one kilometers, and closing.*"

"Hold your fire! Power down, damn it!"

"*The incoming forces are already so close that I may not be able to counter an attack against this position effectively.*"

"*There will be no attack. They're friendlies. They've got to be. . . .*"

"*General,*" a third voice called out, urgent, almost pleading. "*This is Captain Fowler, Bolo Liaison Officer! I'm in Hector's Battle Center right now, watching that deployment on his screens, and I can tell you that these bogies are* not, *repeat* not *friendlies!*"

"*We don't know that, damn it!*" Spratly's voice

countered. *"This could be an alien diplomatic initiative of some sort! We have nothing here that they could want! I am not going to start a damned war over a misunderstanding!"*

"Sir, I really think you should—"

"We do not know who these people are! You and that tin monster are ordered to adhere to the current rules of engagement and stand down! That is a direct order!"

"That," Jaime said in the almost palpable silence that followed, "was a recording of radio communications made between the Bolo, then on station at Chryse Base, and Cloud Military Command Headquarters, at Griffenburg. General Spratly was the officer in charge at the headquarters that afternoon. Am I correct, sir?"

Spratly didn't reply. Jaime pushed ahead. "Hector was ready to raise a defense, an *effective* defense, against the incoming marauders. The general here ordered him to stand down, and Hector, who is programmed to follow human orders, obeyed, despite the misgivings you all heard. Eight minutes, twenty-one seconds later, a small asteroid slammed into Chryse Base at a velocity of over four hundred kilometers per second. The blast—Hector estimates the kinetic energy yield at almost fifty megatons—annihilated our base at Chryse, and literally flipped a thirty-two-thousand-ton Bolo end over end, effectively knocking him out of the fight with their very first stroke. He landed upside down, which explains how his aft turret got smashed flat, and his battle screens were knocked out. The clackers were able to burn their way in, then, and take over his paraneuronic circuitry. "We . . . we think that Captain Fowler was still alive when they reached the Battle Center. They may have used his memories to learn how to circumvent Hector's check-digit and error-scan routines. By the time they had

Hector operating again, under their control, the fight for Cloud, such as it was, was pretty much over, and they were herding the survivors into camps. They posted Hector up on Overlook Hill to help keep an eye on us.

"The point of all of this is that Hector didn't betray us. *We* betrayed *him*. Hector had identified a hostile threat and was ready to do something about it. He could have done something about it too, as the battle this afternoon proved. But we ordered him to hold his fire . . . and, like a good soldier, he obeyed orders."

Jaime was breathing hard, his fists clenched at his sides, as he stared at General Spratly. Dieter wondered if he was waiting for a protest, an explanation, an apology.

How does one apologize for the death of a civilization?

"There—there were ships in the area," Spratly said, his voice weak. "Human ships. And the *Empyrion* was overdue. We didn't know she'd been destroyed. The first message from those incoming ships was *Empyrion's* own ID and hailing codes! By the time our scans showed the incoming ships were aliens, that *Empyrion* wasn't among them, it was too late! I . . . I didn't want to fire on our own people. Didn't want to precipitate a ghastly, horrible mistake. . . ."

"Hector's not the one to blame," Jaime said, his voice filling the barracks despite the steady hiss of rain on the roof. "And a number of us are going with him . . . elsewhere. We have a plan, one that gives us a fair chance of getting out of this area and off into the wilderness where we might be able to escape clacker notice. We *might* even be able to find a way off this rock. I can't make any promises at this point, but that's the plan.

"If you want to stay here and take your chances with the clackers, or if you want to stay with General Spratly, that's your decision. But you're going to have to make it damned fast." He looked at the cuffwatch woven into the left sleeve of his uniform. "Those of us going with Hector are leaving in three hours, to take advantage of the dark and the rain. You have that long to decide what you want to do."

The three-hour deadline, Dieter decided, was as much for show as anything else. No one in the camp had possessed even a fingerwatch since they'd been run down by the machines, stripped of everything even remotely technological, and thrown into the camp, and with the rain and cloud cover, it was impossible to tell time as they usually did by the moons or suns.

No matter. He knew they would make the deadline. It wasn't as if any of them had a lot of things to pack.

The crowd was beginning to break up, forming numerous small discussion groups—some of them quite animated—while others retreated to their sleeping areas, to pack, or simply to think. Dieter began making his way in toward the center.

"I'm sorry, General, but that's the way it's got to be."

Captain Pogue, Dieter saw, was standing in front of Spratly, hands spread. The other staff officers, Dulaney and Howard, looked furious; Spratly looked merely . . . beaten.

"You *can't* think you'll have a better chance with them," Spratly said. He sounded terribly old and very tired. "After everything we've been through together . . . !"

"Think of it as insurance, sir," Pogue replied. "I'll be able to—" He broke off suddenly as Dieter approached.

"General?" Dieter said, ignoring Pogue and the other staff officers. "I'm sure there'd be room for you, too, on this march."

"A march to where, Dr. Hollinsworth?" Howard demanded. His voice possessed an unpleasantly nasal whine. "There's no place on Cloud to go where we can escape the machines, and this notion of getting off-planet is sheer fantasy!"

"He's right," Dulaney added. "The only people with ships on Cloud are the Tolun and the clackers, and neither of them are likely to help us!"

"Jaime's got that figured out," Dieter replied.

"You seem to have remarkable trust in *Major* Graham," Spratly said, bitter.

"General, Jaime Graham's given us our first chance of getting out of here since the damned clackers came and rounded us up. I figure we *owe* him that trust now."

"But . . . but he's putting his trust in a *Bolo*! A *machine*!"

"To tell you the truth, General," Dieter told him, though his gaze was resting on Captain Pogue, "I trust Hector more than I trust most people."

CHAPTER TWELVE

My appreciation for my Commander's understanding of human nature, psychology, and idiosyncrasy has risen another notch. I eavesdropped on his rallying speech via the earplug receiver and threadmike he was wearing and am now convinced that he could convince almost any human of the truth of any statement, true or not. His seeming preoccupation with proper military dress, I now realize, was calculated to overawe both military and civilian personnel who have lived in conditions of squalor, filth, and near or total nakedness for some 329 days.

A uniform confers a certain power, an enforced respect on those conditioned to perceive it as an emblem of authority. Some of those who heard his speech must have connected his uniform with the clothing worn by the camp guards and felt a certain compulsion to obey. Others, particularly former personnel of the planet's military forces, must have remembered what it was like once, before The Killing, and desperately wanted to see the order they remembered reinstated.

Whatever the actual perceptions and motivations, some twelve hundred personnel, both ex-military and civilian, have elected to join what some among their

*number are calling "the March." Their destination is
unknown, but, strangely, few seem to care.*

*It is enough, for now, that they follow Major Jaime
Graham.*

"Do you think the clackers can track us in this muck?"
Jaime asked. He was seated once again in Hector's
Battle Center, uncomfortable in his rain-soggy uniform
but unwilling to remove that single, emotion-tugging
physical link with his military past.

Alita and Shari sat together on the center jumpseats
behind him. A faint vibration rumbled through floors
and walls as Hector lumbered forward. On the
viewscreen, faint green and yellow smudges could just
be made out against the darkness—the body heat of
hundreds of people, struggling through mud and rain
in the great Bolo's wake. They'd set off moving toward
the northeast, smashing down half of the force fence
and several turner houses before breaking out into
the barren, rolling open ground that had been factories
and warehouses before The Killing.

Ahead, invisible as yet, the Veline Mountains rose
somewhere behind the rain-misted darkness of the
interior of the Chryse Peninsula. Jaime hoped they
could reach the cover of the thickly forested foothills
before suns-rise. Hector could cover that ten-kilometer
distance in minutes with little effort. The toiling mob
of disease- and hunger-weakened ex-slaves, however,
would be hard-pressed to travel that far in any
reasonable period of time.

"It's hard to know what their capabilities are," Shari
said, responding to Jaime's question after a long
hesitation. She seemed to have recovered somewhat
from her earlier shock, but her face was still pale and
drawn.

"On the contrary," Hector's voice replied from
invisible, overhead speakers. "The !°!°! are still subject

to certain basic laws of physics and mathematics. The cloud cover effectively blocks all radiation in the visible wavelengths; the rain effectively scatters or absorbs all infrared radiation, masking my considerable heat signature. The !°!°! could employ several active search procedures from orbit that would pinpoint my location, including both radar and X-ray scans, but I would, of course, detect any such attempt and could retaliate or employ jamming techniques of my own, or use the radiation source as a homing lock for return fire."

"There's still the possibility that they could track you through magnetic or gravimetric anomalies," Alita pointed out.

"True. However, my surface shielding and hull degaussing fields reduce my magnetic signature to very near background levels, at least on this world. And my gravimetric signature should be suitably masked once we are in the mountains."

"They would have to have some pretty detailed scans of the local topology," Jaime pointed out, "for mag and grav scan baselines, if they wanted to pick you out. I doubt that they've bothered with that. Why would they need to?"

"God, why do they do *anything*?" Shari said. "They're machines. They might've been *programmed* to make baseline scans of everything. We *just don't know!*"

Jaime thought about that in the painful, long silence that followed. Shari was still on the thin and ragged edge of hysteria—not that he blamed her, not after what she'd been through—and he wasn't sure how much of what she was saying was due to conviction or to depression. Still, she was right about one general but very large problem that they faced now. For almost a year, they'd known the !°!°! as masters, as conquerors, as taskmasters . . . but never as military *opponents*. Oh, they'd been opponents, certainly, during the brief, furious battle for Cloud, but that fight had been over in a matter of days, and the world's human defenders had never really had a chance to take the measure of the invading machines, to learn their tactics, their strategies and goals, the way they thought in battle.

That was, he thought, the single greatest disadvantage the human refugees faced right now. Thirty-five centuries before, an ancient military philosopher on old Earth had warned that a military commander must know both himself and the enemy to ensure victory. Jaime felt he knew his own people and what they were capable of, as well as the capabilities and potential of the Bolo, but the !*!*! were something else entirely.

"Hector?" he said quietly, staring into the green-flecked darkness of the viewscreen. "How well do you know the clackers?"

"I'm afraid I don't understand the question as you have phrased it," Hector replied. "Do you mean how well do I understand their military capabilities?"

"I didn't mean if you knew them socially, damn it." He stopped and rubbed his eyes. He was tired, and the stress of this past twenty-some hours was rasping at his nerves. "Sorry. I guess I'm getting a bit fuzzy."

"The !*!*! operate within tightly bound and inter-connected hierarchies which appear to depend on large numbers of low-level and relatively unsophisticated devices backed up by successive levels of increasingly powerful but less numerous units. They rely on overwhelming the defense in the first moments of battle and saturating the area with low-level combatants, deploying more powerful and more intelligent units where and as needed. I was unable to observe !*!*! tactics directly for more than the first nine point one three minutes of the initial conflict, but my impression is that the front-line units possess a relatively rigid and nonadaptive programming in matters of tactics, acquisition, and reaction. This is supported by data acquired from my more recent, more intimate contact with !°!°! units."

Jaime looked up sharply at that. "You remember things from when you were . . . possessed?" Strange as it was in context, it was the only word that fit.

"Some. There were brief periods when a higher, more tightly organized, more complex artificial intelligence seemed to occupy certain areas of my higher conscious function. I suspect from this that high-order !°!°! intelligences are able to partially occupy low-order machines for purposes of direct observation, information transfer, or temporary direct leadership. I also surmise that the higher-order !°!°! units possess an extremely advanced and complex form of intelligence, an intelligence at least as capable as my own."

Jaime loosed a thin stream of air through clenched teeth, a long, low whistle. He'd been hoping, that the !°!°! were *only* machines, mechanisms operating according to the programmed instructions of long-dead organic builders. He didn't like the idea of facing something as smart as a Mark XXXIII Bolo, not one bit.

The ludicrousness of the thought stopped him for a moment. Hector was *only* a machine. If humans could build Bolos as quick and as intelligent as a Mark XXXIII, it stood to reason that someone else could build something just as good . . . or even better.

Now *there* was a disturbing thought.

"!°!°! numbers are unknown but certainly extremely large," Hector went on, "ranging from the tiny floater spy-units and individual sentries to mobile asteroid fortresses such as the ones I engaged this afternoon. While I cannot make specific predictions at this point, I submit that we will soon encounter elements of higher-ranking !°!°! echelons, ground- and air-combat vehicles of considerably greater power and sophistication than those that were guarding the slave camp. Their numbers will be fewer, but their capabilities are likely to be *much* greater.

"And, if I may say so, Commander," Hector continued, "you need rest. Stress levels in your voice indicate that you have not slept for some time."

"You give me news like that and expect me to *sleep*?" Jaime demanded, but the sudden change of topic made him grin.

"Hector's right," Alita said, coming up behind him. She laid a hand on his shoulder, gently squeezing. "There's a rack in the watch quarters, Major. You should sack out for a while. Shari and I can keep an eye on things out here."

"What about you two?"

"Shari had a nap, and I can keep going for a while. We need you to be fresh, though. Or at least awake. You're dead on your feet as it is, and that won't do the rest of us a bit of good."

He opened his mouth to protest, but the sudden tide of exhaustion rising up to drag him down strangled whatever words he'd been about to marshal. He'd been going strong for hours, now, including a rather high-keyed period of combat. His reserves were long gone; he was operating now on pure adrenaline and willpower.

"Okay," he said, struggling up from the embrace of the Battle Center command chair. "But call me if there's even a hint of trouble."

"Go," Alita said. "Sleep. Hector and us'll keep an eye on things."

The watch room was a tiny cubicle off the Battle Center, where they'd found the spare uniforms earlier. As he peeled off his wet uniform, a narrow, hard fold-down cot opened out of the wall, beckoning like a temptress. It received Jaime's body like a mattress of infinitely soft and deep featherwing down, and he wondered if he was ever going to be able to leave its embrace again.

He couldn't sleep immediately, though. The thought of this new image of the !°!°!—of an army of relatively dumb scouts, workers, and warriors, directed by higher and higher levels of intelligent machines that could somehow project their presence and awareness into or through their unintelligent servants—held his mind focused, unable to surrender to the promise of unconsciousness.

Hector's evaluation raised an interesting question: Where was the boss machine in the !°!°! hierarchy? If they could find a way to get to it, could they possibly win this lopsided war?

Or were they going to have to fight and destroy every damned clacker between Cloud and the Galactic Core?

But before he could pursue the question any further, Jaime Graham was lost in a deep and exhaustion-ridden sleep.

Within his corner of the moon called Delamar, DAV728-24389 considered the advantages of multiply layered and nested communications . . . as well as the problems they could cause. There were some things, unfortunately, that lower-level !°!°!, with fewer in-series processors and simpler paraneural networks, simply could not comprehend.

Message nesting was inherent to !°!°! thought, at least to the type of thought enjoyed by the more intelligent and complex of the !°!°! hierarchy. It figured in most of their communications and symbology and was a part of their very image of self and their relationship to the cosmos.

The symbol "!°!°!," for instance, all but unpronounceable by most organics, was not easily translated either. Rather than being a single word or phrase by which a relatively simple thought or image could be conveyed, it was a polydimensional nested construct, a symbol of meanings embedded within meanings devised to communicate different but related concepts on different levels. At its most basic, !°!°! could mean something on the order of "We Exist" or, possibly, "We Are." At a higher level, however, that simple pattern of alternating sounds added shades of meaning, even whole new concepts to the basic one of simple existence. "We Who Shape the Cosmos" was one such concept; "We Who Exist Because We Create Order Within the Cosmos" was another, depending on how the base "!°!°!" was transmitted, and in what context.

Only !°!°! with five or more brains could grasp the highest-order definition of the race name, which for them might have been expressed as something like "We Who Form Interlinking Patterns of Communications and Control Along and Among Multidimensional Hierarchies That We May Express Order and Unified Pattern Out of Unthinking Chaos."

It was far more efficient to express simply the clucking phonemes of the !°!°! name. The !°!°!, above all else, were efficient, even in their use of sounds. Generally, they told their subject races that "!°!°!" represented simply the word/concept "Master," and let it go at that, since such sophisticated communications modes were generally far beyond the grasp of lesser intelligences.

Much of !°!°! language was similarly nested, in fact. A curt, succinctly worded command to first- or second-level machines contained subsets of elaborations and flavorings that expanded to something more like a conversation with third- and fourth-order intelligences, and expanded again into encyclopedic discourse with high-end !°!°! cognizants.

The concept allowed for great efficiency in communication, but it possessed disadvantages as well. Lower-ranking intelligences often had trouble communicating special or unusual problems or needs in any detail to multiple-brained higher-ups.

Low-level !°!°! machines rarely showed anything like initiative, and emotion—even so much as a sense of urgency or pride in a well-done task—was completely beyond them. They did what was expected of them, what they'd been told to do, and nothing more.

DAV728-24389 did feel pride in his position and in what he did, one unanticipated side effect of his newly acquired brain and hierarchical position. For that reason, the stinging defeat suffered some twenty-two trillion nanoseconds ago by the three !°!°! fortress-battlers still burned within his central processor arrays, the pain as sharp and as lasting as it was unexpected. One of the battlers had been destroyed, a second so badly damaged that it might well be useful only as salvage. That such devastating damage to !°!°! fleet assets could be handed out by a single ground unit of human manufacture . . .

When he'd received his promotion, he'd not expected the higher emotional functions that came with it to be so *uncomfortable*.

Projecting his consciousness through two deep space relays, he entered the operational download stacks of GED9287-8726H, the Series 95 in low orbit over Celeste. The !°!°! craft was just approaching the Chryse Peninsula. Its scanners, both active and passive, should serve to spot the human combat machine that had dealt the !°!°! this humiliating defeat.

Once the Bolo's current whereabouts and activities were known, the !°!°! could formulate an appropriate response.

Through GED9287's broad-spectrum sensors, DAV beheld the intense colors and dazzling light of the world seen from low orbit. The planet's horizon was a gently curved bow of blue and glaring white, set against the blackness absolute of space. Much of that horizon was dominated by a vast, clockwise spiral of white cloud, a storm system of immense proportions. DAV extended the sensory range into the infrared, and the cloudscape was overlaid by hot red and orange patches scattered randomly across the visible portion of the world. Each impact site for the shattered fragments of the projectiles launched against the Bolo earlier was radiating fiercely at infrared wavelengths.

"Are you tracking the human combat machine?" DAV asked the !°!°! craft, deliberately simplifying the nested elaborations to levels the two-brain system could easily comprehend.

"Negative," was the response. "The target area was over the horizon during the recent attack, and I was unable to establish target lock."

"Establish target lock now."

"I will have to engage active scanning techniques. Passive systems will not provide a solid or definite target lock."

"Use passive infrared."

"Not possible. Any infrared radiations by the target are lost in the clutter of much brighter IR sources caused by our bombardment."

DAV gave the digital equivalent of a frown. It was true. The scattered craters left in the wake of the bombardment earlier were giving off so much heat that they effectively masked the Bolo's IR signature.

"Very well. Go active." All he needed was a glimpse. . . .

I detect the first brush of radiations at high-ultraviolet and X-ray wavelengths and pick up a point source now rising above the western horizon. Unwilling to give away my own precise position with an active scan of my own, I estimate, with a certainty in excess of eighty-seven percent, that the source of the radiation is an !°!°! craft engaged in surveillance activities.

My Commander is asleep, and to summon him for

*specific orders, or even to consult with Sergeant Kyle,
now on duty in my Battle Center, would waste precious
seconds. I evaluate the threat and respond in the most
direct and immediate manner possible. . . .*

DAV728-24389 had only a few thousand
nanoseconds' warning as one portion of the cloud
cover ahead and below suddenly lit up in X-ray
wavelengths. At first, he thought it was reflective
backscatter from the X-ray source GED9287 was
using to paint the target area, but the frequency was
wrong, and the source far too intense.

The source, in fact, was a bloom of X-rays caused
by the passage, at relativistic speeds, of a bolt of fusing
hydrogen through the suspended water droplets of
the cloud. The radiations announcing the approach
of that fusion bolt were followed so closely by the bolt
itself that DAV had no chance to react or to order
evasive maneuvers.

GED9287 was inhabiting a reconnaissance-scout
vehicle far smaller and less heavily armored than one
of the big, Series 34 fortress-battlers. Though faster
and more maneuverable, the Series 95 possessed
scarcely a tenth of a battler's mass, and the fusion bolt
seared through armor and internal circuitries like a
high-velocity bullet through a structure made of
pasteboard cards. In one instant, DAV's view of the
planet was obscured by a fast-swelling glare of X-rays
and ultraviolet; in the next, there was a jarring
concussion, and he found the focus of his consciousness
once again centered within the depths of the !°!°!
command complex deep within the caverns of Delamar.

On his operational scanners, GED9287 was now
little more than an expanding cloud of hot gas and
fragmentary debris.

And DAV728 was left pondering a *second* !°!°! defeat
in the space of only 2.2 x 10^{13} nanoseconds.

This was getting out of hand . . . what DAV thought of as *outside of parameters*. Something would have to be done. Something decisive.

Now. . . .

Jaime came awake as the thunder of a Hellbore shock rocked the Bolo. Even here, deep in the big machine's well-shielded core, the launch of a fusing hydrogen bolt generated a bone-rattling detonation.

He was on his feet in an instant and had reentered the Battle Center in two more. "What is it? What's happened?"

Alita turned in the command seat, her eyes wide. "I'm not certain. He just . . . opened fire."

"We were being painted by a hostile surveillance spacecraft," Hector said, his tones as unruffled as ever. "I deemed it necessary to eliminate the source before our position was learned by the enemy."

"So what the hell does he need *us* for?" Shari asked.

Jaime ducked beneath the circular viewscreen and studied the images arrayed about the command seat. They were moving through light woods now, grinding over mud and felled trees as easily as over open prairie. The cloud cover remained unbroken, and a steady drizzle continued to mask them from the sky. Behind the Bolo, the toiling entourage of freed humans continued working its way along in the muddy path carved by the enormous tracks, their presence marked only by the eerie green and yellow glows of their body heat against the cold darkness.

"We can't take potshots at the clackers every time they orbit over," Jaime said. "Sooner or later we'll make them mad."

"I doubt that human emotions such as anger can be applied to the !°!°!," Hector replied, "and I agree that casual exchanges should be avoided. However, until we are masked by the basaltic formations of the mountains, it is important that we keep our position as secret as possible."

"Yeah." He studied the mass of humanity struggling along behind the Bolo for a moment more. In IR wavelengths, it was difficult to tell those were people; it was impossible to pick out facial features enough to identify particular individuals. Hector's single shot had caused the pack to scatter. They were emerging now from either side of the Bolo-flattened trail, staring up at the sky with unreadable, green-glowing faces.

"Yeah. You did right, Hector. But we're going to have to do something more. Our people are moving too slowly. They're bogging down in the mud, and they've got to be close to dropping in their tracks already. And what's worse, if you have to hold yourself down to their pace . . ."

His eyes widened. The full truth of what he was saying was just striking through the layers of exhaustion smothering his brain. A single !°!°! assault would catch all of those hundreds of people in the open, defenseless. Damn, why hadn't he seen the problem before? He was so tired he'd not been thinking straight. "The clackers are going to catch them out there long before we make the mountains."

"Could they ride up top, on Hector's upper deck?" Alita asked.

He shook his head. "Twelve hundred people? Hector's big, but he's not that big."

"They might take turns. Some rest, while the others walk."

"Just climbing the hull ladders twenty or twenty-five meters to get up there would be too much for most of them. Besides, if the clackers attacked, anyone topside would get swept off or fried. No, we're going to have to do it another way."

"How?"

"I had it all wrong," Jaime said. "I thought we could

just carve our way through to the mountains. But that kind of thinking won't get us halfway there."

"You're getting that wild look in your eye, Major. Like earlier, when we boarded Hector in the first place."

"Get used to it, Sergeant. We're about to take Hector and go over on the offensive."

"What?"

"It's our only real option."

"But . . . *attack*? That's crazy!"

"Not really. I've been thinking of this whole operation as just busting out of the camp and running, Alita. *Defensive* thinking. But Bolos aren't designed with defensive operations in mind, are they, Hector?"

"Negative," the Bolo replied. "And the current tactical situation does suggest that an offensive campaign should be more effective by far in protecting your people and in reaching a place of relative security."

Hector almost sounded pleased at the thought.

"Do you have any ideas as to how to go about this?" he asked the Bolo.

"In specifics, no. However, it does occur to me that the overall strategic situation is similar in many respects to that faced by Spartacus's army during the so-called slave revolt of 73 to 71 B.C., in the late Roman Republic."

"Spartacus?" Jaime shook his head. "I had the usual two weeks of Latin in school, but we didn't cover much Roman history."

"Spartacus was a Thracian soldier in the Roman army, apparently with some knowledge of Roman military tactics and organization. He deserted, was captured, and sold into slavery. He was eventually purchased by Lentulus Batiates, who had him trained as a gladiator—a slave or a condemned criminal who fought other, similarly trained slaves for the amusement of others.

"In 73 B.C., Spartacus was among seventy-eight gladiators who killed their captors at the gladiator school at Capua and escaped into the Roman countryside. They established a camp on the slopes of Mount Vesuvius. There, perhaps because of his military training, Spartacus was chosen as their leader.

"The Roman historian Plutarch records that Spartacus was 'a man not only of high spirit and bravery, but also in understanding and gentleness superior to his condition.' Evidently, even his enemies respected him."

"Seventy-eight men?" Alita said. "You're talking about a small guerrilla force, not an army."

"Initially, yes. They survived by raiding nearby farms for food. However, Spartacus issued a call for all of the slaves within the Italian Peninsula to rise up against their masters and join him at Vesuvius. Within a short time, Spartacus's army numbered approximately one hundred twenty thousand, and Rome itself was terrified of the prospect of a general slave revolt. At this time, the freemen and citizens of Rome were far outnumbered by their slaves.

"Spartacus trained his men. He taught them to make weapons. He drilled them in the tactics of maneuver and combat of the day. Under his leadership, the slave army defeated two Roman armies in rapid succession and overran the south Italian countryside. In the hopes of dispersing his people to their homes, he marched north to the Alps, but his army, less disciplined than that of Rome, perhaps, refused to leave Italy. Turning south, he marched the entire length of the Italian Peninsula, seeking to transport at least part of his army to a safe haven overseas. For almost a year he fought off repeated Roman thrusts, but he was blocked from escaping by no fewer than eight Roman legions under the command of M. Licinius Crassus."

Jaime felt as though his eyes must be glazing over. Most of these names and places he'd never heard of.

The overall situation *did* sound similar, though . . . former slaves attempting to reach a safe haven, as far from their former masters as they could manage.

"At last, Spartacus's army divided, possibly because of dissension within the ranks. One group of Gauls and Germans, fleeing northward, was wiped out to a man by Crassus.

"Spartacus's remaining forces were at last trapped by two large Roman forces, under the commands of Crassus and Pompey. Roman historians record that Spartacus died in a desperate, final battle against overwhelming odds. The vast majority of his followers were killed. It is said that some six thousand captives were crucified along the Appian Way, between Capua and the gates of Rome. Their bodies were left rotting for months as a warning to other slaves."

Jaime sighed. "Thanks, Hector. That's just *exactly* the sort of thing I needed to hear right now." Sometimes, Bolos had access to entirely too much information and seemed unaware of its effect on others.

"Your voice stress levels indicate that you are upset," Hector said. "The example of Spartacus was intended not to demoralize, but to encourage."

"Yeah? He was overwhelmed and defeated in the end, right? How is that supposed to encourage us?"

"Spartacus's position was similar to ours in many respects—that of a band of escaped slaves surrounded by powerful and implacable enemy forces. By going on the offensive, and by utilizing native cunning and a superior knowledge of tactics and strategy, he survived repeated attacks by those forces for a period of nearly three years. His final defeat appears to have been the result of internal dissension and a lack of any clear, long-term goal, weaknesses that assured his eventual entrapment and defeat."

"So," Shari said quietly, "we stick together, and the clackers won't crucify us. I guess I can live with that."

"That's the idea, isn't it?" Jaime said. "To survive this."

"Hey, what's to worry about?" Alita asked. "Spartacus didn't have a Bolo on his side."

"The question," Jaime said, "is whether even a Bolo would have been enough. I guess that's what we're going to find out."

"The key," Hector reminded them, "will be taking the initiative, and holding it."

CHAPTER THIRTEEN

We have no way of even estimating the total numbers and strength of the !*!*! Enemy. Against them, we have one unit of questionable effectiveness—the so-called Brotherhood of the Eye—and one combat-ready unit, myself. My Commander is correct. Clearly, our only alternative is to go over to the offensive.

I am concerned, however, because I am not yet fully operational. My power output has risen to only 48.97% of my normal full output, possibly because of internal damage suffered when Chryse was hit. Numerous systems, including contra-gravity, remain off-line, and only two of my three primary weapons are functional.

The most serious problem, however, remains an operational one. My Commander has not shared with me his long-range plans, but his goal of saving the humans freed from Camp 84 can be successful only in the short term unless he finds a means of getting them off-planet. Even a fully functional Bolo Mark XXXIII would not be able to withstand the full power of the !*!*! combat capability when they choose to unleash it. We must find a way off this world, and sanctuary elsewhere. But where?

And how?

❖   ❖   ❖

Even operating on less than half power, and without contra-gravity to reduce weight or help boost the massive vehicle across breaks in the road, Hector could easily manage a cruise speed of seventy kilometers per hour, while the mass of people toiling along behind were lucky if they could make a ragged two or three. Worse, there was no way they could keep going hour upon hour without stop, without rest or food or sleep. Twenty hours after they'd left Camp 84, they'd managed to cover less than thirty kilometers in all.

If Hector continued plodding along at the maximum speed of the slowest of the human refugees, the !°!°! would have no trouble at all reacquiring the big target and reducing it to molten slag.

The rain was thinning to a light drizzle in the predawn darkness when Jaime invited Wal Prescott aboard for a strategic conference. They sat in the jumpseats in the Battle Center with Alita, while Shari took her turn in the command chair.

"And that, Colonel," Jaime said after he'd laid out his idea in brief, "is what I'd like to try to do. What do you think?"

Wal leaned back in his seat, eyes closed. Somewhere along the line, like most of the refugees, he'd picked up some clothing—coveralls and a light jacket. A warehouse northeast of the camp had been full of civilian clothes of all descriptions. They were drying quickly in the dry air inside Hector, but enough water had run down and onto the deck to form a sizable puddle.

"What do *I* think? Why the hell are you askin' me?"

Jaime blinked. "Because, unless there were some other colonels or a general or two who survived The Killing and decided to come along with us on this little jaunt, you are the ranking officer here. *Sir.*"

Wal's eyes opened, and he looked at Jaime with an

expression that mingled exhaustion with pain . . . and perhaps some fear as well. "Son, I ain't in command of nothin', 'cept maybe myself. And sometimes I'm not even too sure of that." Wal shook his head. "Jaime, the Cloud Defense Force ceased to exist about five minutes after that asteroid slammed into Chryse." He held up a hand as Jaime started to protest. "Oh, I know, I know. I went along with the charade. Played good soldier and plotted with the Escape Committee an' all that. I thought maybe a few of us would be able to help others slip out past the latrines and make it far enough away that the cluckers wouldn't notice." He looked around the low-ceilinged Battle Center. "But this . . . Hell, I don't know a thing about Bolos, Jaime. And I can't say I even believe in what you're tryin' t' do."

"Then why'd you come?" The words were sharp, more accusation than question. "You could have opted to go with Spratly." The former CDF general, according to the latest reports, was headed south, hoping to lose himself and the camp refugees who'd sided with him in the Grother Forest and the swamps beyond. Whether they would be able to elude the !°!°! was anybody's guess, but they had a chance . . . if only because the machines would be more concerned about the Bolo and the people with it.

" 'Cause I was tired of living in the mud, and I figured that here, with you, I'd have a chance of getting killed fast and clean if the clackers swooped in 'n' tried t' grab us." He held his stump up for emphasis. "I know my limits, Jaime. I'll follow your lead here, do what you tell me t' do. But I'm not about to try t' *run* this show."

"He's talking sense, Major," Alita put in. She'd been silent throughout the whole discussion, until now. "This has been your idea from the start. Your vision. *You* should be in command."

"I can't just . . . step in. Take command on my own authority . . ."

"Isn't that what you did?" Wal asked. "When you forced matters with Spratly?"

"That was different—"

"In what way? He was the ranking officer. The one in command. Whether you agreed with the son-of-a-bitch or not, he *was* the guy in charge at the Celeste Camp, not countin' the turners and the clackers, of course."

"You make it sound like mutiny."

"Wasn't it?"

"You did what you had to do, Major," Alita put in. "But the camp revolt, getting Hector on our side, that was all your idea."

"I've been doing what I thought was my duty, under the charter of the CDF."

Wal shrugged. "Seems t' me you've already gone well beyond the boundaries of that charter. Hell, you can't pick and choose what orders you're gonna accept, and which ones you're gonna ignore! Either the CDF continues, in all its glory and tradition, or you admit you're starting something new here. And that you're the one in command!"

"You got us into this," Alita added, grinning. "You'll get us out!"

Jaime didn't answer for a long moment, and Wal chuckled. "Responsibility's a bitch, ain't it?"

Jaime drew a deep breath, then let it out. He'd been trying to maintain the illusion of being another link in the time-honored chain of command, even when events had gotten out of hand. It seemed, though, that there was no place left to hide. Even in the depths of a Bolo.

Or especially in the depths of a Bolo. If he'd needed authority for what he'd done, he'd taken it by reawakening the huge battle machine and throwing it into the fight against the !*!*!.

"Okay," he said. "I'm in command and we have a brand new organization here, compliments of Hector." He glanced at the control center. "Though I'm not entirely sure that *Hector* shouldn't be the one running this. I still need someone to manage the refugees. And the Brotherhood."

Wal frowned. "You think that bunch'll amount to anything? Not all of 'em are military. A lot are full of hot air, more'n anything else."

"They took on the clackers one-on-one," Jaime replied. "And with their bare hands. Right now, that's all the qualifications I need. Those machine eyes they wear are pretty damned good as badges of course completion, wouldn't you say?"

"Well, they've got guts, certainly. Maybe not much sense, but they've got guts, I'll give 'em that."

"Which is why I need an experienced man leading them. Hector here is going to be bearing the brunt of any combat we have to face. Hell, if the clackers come down on that crowd outside with anything like real weaponry, our people won't stand a chance. And we cannot afford having the Brotherhood or anyone else making any heroic gestures, charging a clacker hunter-killer, say, armed with nothing but stunsticks and power guns."

"So, what're you gonna use 'em for?"

"Column security. Scouts. And we'll need disciplined people just to keep the main body together. I don't want to lose any stragglers on this march."

"You may not have that choice, Jaime. We've been losing a lot of people already, the ones who just can't keep up."

"I know, and that's going to stop." He folded his arms. "We also need to think about supplies. Food and water, especially. Most of the people out there haven't eaten since we left the camp. And we'll have to scrounge for shoes or boots, clothing, everything they need to keep going, especially up in the mountains. We'll need to organize foraging parties, and we'll have to arrange for *protecting* the foraging parties. I'm thinking that the Brotherhood could handle a lot of that, if we can get them organized. Will you take the job?"

"What, me? In command of those yahoos?"

"I need someone who can instill some discipline in them, Wal."

"What about Pogue?"

Jaime snorted. "I . . . don't trust him. Not yet, anyway. I never cared much for that entire crowd of Spratly's. They were too . . . *comfortable* with their little niche."

"He gave all that up t' come along on this joyride of yours, son. You'll have to give him a chance sometime."

"Maybe. But for now I think I want to keep a pretty close eye on him. He was always too much the yes-man to Spratly, and his joining us was pretty damned sudden." Jaime shook his head. "No, you told me to run things the way I see fit. What is best for this operation, what's necessary for our *survival* is for you to take over as CO of the Brotherhood. So, are you going to stop shirking your responsibility and follow orders?" He smiled. "Sir?"

Wal considered the question a moment. "Okay. *Sir.* I suggest, though, that the first thing you do is give yourself a promotion. I'm damned if I'm gonna take any more orders from a damned wet-behind-the-ears *major.* . . ."

I have logged Jaime Graham's promotion to brigadier general, effective at 0600 hours, local time, this morning. While the procedure has certainly circumvented customary regulation and protocol, I can understand the need for him to demonstrate clear precedence of rank and command and, frankly, can see no other means for him to do so. The troops under his command accepted the news, for the most part, with cheers and shouted congratulations. Of them all, the man who seems to have the most doubts about this move appears to be General Graham himself.

Self-doubts or not, General Graham has moved with commendable alacrity in the four hours since announcing his promotion. Placing Colonel Prescott in command of the Brotherhood, he convinced Dieter Hollinsworth to act as the civilian leader of the March. Leaving the two in joint command, he has directed me to continue ahead at maximum possible speed. Even taking gentler routes around forested hills, rather than over them, and being forced to skirt a 100-meter crater still glowing red-hot, I only required two hours, thirty-five minutes to reach the southern end of Cambera Pass, nearest and gentlest of several possible routes north through the Veline Mountains. A village, Dornburg, lay nearby, and we investigated that as well. The place was deserted—recently so— but proved that there are human habitations in the country not overrun by the !*!*!.

After a brief foray in search of Enemy positions or units—I found none—and the launch of several remote surveillance drones, I reversed course and cut a second path to the south, rejoining the March, before setting out once again, this time moving due east toward Fort Greeley, a former CDF supply depot.

The general's strategy is clear. By having me cut a path through wooded, overgrown, and rough terrain, he has eased the human group's progress overland. By cutting multiple paths, he will confuse the Enemy as to the group's precise path and intent.

And finally, he has freed me to take full advantage of my overland speed and maneuverability. If there are !*!*! forces in the area, I will be able to take direct action, rather than waiting for them to take action against us.

I have launched two additional surveillance drones as we approach Fort Greeley. While I have as yet detected no sign of the Enemy, I believe that action is imminent.

JEG851-8389 felt it first, a tremulous vibration in the ground similar to a faint, low-amplitude seismic shock . . . except that it went on and on, minute after minute, and seemed to grow slowly in strength.

JEG was currently occupying a Series 20 mobile factory, a position he'd held now for over 2.8×10^{16} nanoseconds, ever since the !°!°! had occupied the world humans called Cloud. Possessing five brains, JEG possessed a high degree of reason, planning skills, and imagination, so much so that he was somewhat overqualified for his current assignment. The past three hundred or so local days, in fact, had been an agony of boredom, enough to make him wonder if the deployment scheduling program had actually done the unthinkable and *made a mistake.*

Supervising a resource collection complex and mobile factory was ordinarily the province of a four-brain construct. Imagination was not required for what was generally a tedious and monotonously predictable operation.

Now, though, his assignment had abruptly become less than predictable. He'd picked up information of the human combat machine's sudden mutiny on the general !°!°! communications web and, as the three !°!°! ships had moved into position, he'd taken the precaution of submerging himself in a large lake, protection against a near strike if such occurred. For the past 9.3×10^{13} nanoseconds, there'd been nothing—no information, no word of the human machine's activities.

Those ominous ground vibrations, however, suggested

a very large mass traveling over uneven terrain, and moving in JEG's direction.

Perhaps, JEG reasoned, it was time to emerge from his hiding place and find out what the situation actually was. Cautiously, he raised a sensor cluster above the surface of the water, probing the forested terrain in all directions.

When he saw nothing, he began emerging slowly from the lake.

"I have a contact," Hector announced, "bearing zero-nine-five, range two-seven kilometers."

Alita had the watch at the command console, but both Shari and Jaime were standing behind her seat in an instant, peering up at the circular viewscreen. The rain had lifted at last, and both suns were now above the horizon in a blaze of red and red-and-violet against the scattering clouds. Hector was grinding down a ten-degree slope, his blunt prow scattering trees in his path like matchsticks. Ahead, just visible through the early morning haze, lay a broad valley centered on a long and narrow lake.

"Where is it?" Jaime asked. "What've you picked up?"

A red square appeared on the screen, centering over the left end of the lake, then contracting rapidly to pick out a black speck hidden within a froth of spray and foam.

"I have a better view from Remote Drone Three," Hector said, adding an inset window to the viewscreen display. There, a new image flashed on, tilted steeply as the flying camera peered down from several hundred meters overhead. Spray exploded on the water below as the !*!*! machine broke the surface.

"What is it?" Shari asked, her eyes widening. "It's kind of like one of their mobile factories, but bigger."

"The !*!*! do not seem to have standardized designs,"

Hector replied. "Or, possibly, they employ so many different standard designs that it is difficult to classify them. This appears to be a large mobile factory, however, similar in purpose to the one at Camp 84. I estimate it to mass in the neighborhood of twenty thousand tons."

That was twice the mass of the mobile factory at the camp, Jaime thought. "It'll have fighter units," he warned. "Lots of 'em."

"Acknowledged. Targeting. . . ."

A pair of red crosshairs tracked across the viewscreen, zeroing in on the distant target. Jaime heard the grinding rumble of Hector's primary turrets in motion. An instant before he could fire, however, the view from the remote reconnaissance drone showed ports dropping open along both flanks of the huge mechanism erupting from the lake, and a cloud of black darts emerging like hornets from a gleaming, metallic nest.

"Firing," Hector said, and the ear-piercing thunder of his Number One 200cm Hellbore detonated with savage ferocity within the narrow confines of the Battle Center. All three of the humans clapped hands over ears as a second shot exploded from the Bolo's upper deck.

Both shots struck the !°!°! machine close to the waterline, and at the one-two impact of two high-velocity bolts of fusing hydrogen, water flashed into steam.

So far as Jaime or his companions could see, the target had simply vanished behind a fast-expanding dome of white; a second later, the sky was filled with jet-black !°!°! flyers, craft ranging from fist-sized scout flyers to disk-shaped, robot aircraft bristling with weapons.

The !°!°! machine's outline appeared within the erupting cloud of steam, ghostly, in a blue haze, as

Hector found its shape with radar and other, more subtle senses. A third Hellbore blast seared through the steam like a thunderbolt, nicking the vehicle's skin, blasting a house-sized chunk of metal from the mobile factory's side.

The battle became a swooping, dizzying melee then, as hundreds of !°!°! combat machines swarmed about the Bolo like angry bees. Robot missiles, those that managed to slip past Hector's point defense batteries, slammed into the Bolo's sides and exploded in shattering chains of hull-rattling concussions. Larger aircraft loosed clouds of missiles of their own, or probed and slashed with beams of high-energy protons or the lancing, jagged, blue-white flash of electron beams.

Jaime stood transfixed as the battle swirled and strobed around his head. Again, he was struck by the sobering realization that no human could possibly direct such a battle or even hope to comprehend what was happening as events unfolded. Hector was now operating in full battle mode, making his own decisions millisecond by millisecond at a speed and with a precision no merely organic brain could match. Targeting information, long columns of flickering numbers and letters, scrolled down the viewscreen, as geometric shapes outlined in red-and-green light arranged themselves across the swirl of darting shapes, as though trying to impose some semblance of mathematical order to the chaos there.

Hector fired salvo upon salvo of point defense weapons, sending up flickering threads of whiplashing lasers and clouds of high-velocity flechettes, sweeping attackers from the sky in fiery slashes that transformed fast-moving, brilliantly maneuverable craft into hurtling globs of fused and molten debris with every shot. His hull defensive fields sparkled as enemy beams played across them; the power drain from the battle screens

alone was enough to light a small city, and they were
absorbing kiloton upon kiloton of incoming beam and
explosive fury.

Despite the power drain, Hector accelerated, tracks
shrieking as he hurtled down the hillside through a
forest that simply erupted into living flame beneath
that terrible assault.

Ten miles ahead, the !°!°! mobile factory heaved
itself clear of the lake, three tracked segments
connected with flexibly articulating joints, the upper
hulls heavy with weapons turrets, towers, and antennae
like curved, cruel-barbed horns.

Weapons blazing, it ponderously swung to the left
and accelerated, racing to meet the oncoming Bolo.

JEG851 possessed imagination enough to picture
in high relief and sharp focus exactly what would
happen in a one-on-one encounter with the Bolo. The
human battle machine was twice the size of the !°!°!
mobile factory; worse, it possessed at least twelve times
the firepower, even with one of its primary weapons
turrets out of action.

The mobile factory, though heavily armed and
armored, was designed to serve as a resource collection complex, gathering up wreckage, scrap, and
technological detritus and processing it into useful
!°!°! control modules, workers, and scavenger units.
The Bolo, according to the accounts and records JEG
had observed, was designed for one thing, and one
thing only—high-intensity combat—and that single-
mindedness of purpose was the biggest advantage
it carried in this contest. JEG estimated that he had
another twenty-seven billion nanoseconds before the
Bolo reduced him to mindless, lifeless scrap.

His death, however, could serve the !°!°! in valuable
ways. As soon as the sizzling static from those twin
Hellbore blasts had cleared, JEG had linked onto the

!°!°! Primary Web, uploading a full account of his current situation, an account updated millisecond to millisecond as the battle continued. The !°!°! now knew precisely where the Bolo was.

He could also inflict damage on the human machine, damage which they would find difficult to repair without bases or maintenance depots. Along his broad, segmented back, batteries of turrets, each mounting from one to three particle accelerator cannons, directed their full output against the approaching Bolo, visible now as a dark, compact mountain advancing through shivering and splintering, burning trees and the swirling smoke of the firestorm. Particle beams, visible in the smoky haze as blinding threads of violet-white light, sought that advancing, artificial mountain and clung to it, gouging at hard-driven battle screens, in places driving through force field defenses and biting into duralloy and steel. Two spots on the Bolo's glacis glowed red-hot beneath the assault. A few more good, solid hits there, and perhaps—

A Hellbore round shrieked in out of the battlefog, striking JEG851 squarely in his primary sensor array tower, passing all the way through in a starcore-hot burst of vaporizing metal. The hit disrupted all combat drone communications, throwing his dwindling fleet of attacking vehicles onto their own devices. It also seared through critical targeting circuitry, knocking half of his particle accelerator cannons off-line.

JEG swung hard to the right, seeking now to take cover behind a low hill to the west, but another Hellbore round, accompanied by half a dozen high-energy laser pulses, struck his lead segment, shattering turrets in clouds of steel splinters, punching holes through armor and tender, inner wiring, reducing tracks to fused masses of slag, all in a burning instant of hellfire and destruction.

Inner fires burned within JEG's crumpling frame,

like sullen, orange eyes winking from ragged-edged caverns in black hull metal. His final thought, as his power core went critical in a flash of escaping energy, was that he had sadly misjudged the amount of time he would have in which to damage his opponent.

The entire battle had lasted barely one-fifth of those twenty-seven billion nanoseconds JEG851 had been counting on.

Fort Greeley was a small town on the east end of Lake Halashone. Many of its inhabitants had already fled at the first rumblings of the Bolo's approach, but a few had stayed, hiding in cellars, or hunkering down among the rock outcroppings in the hills above the town, watching as the two machine titans clashed in their brief but spectacular encounter.

Jaime stood on the street, hand resting lightly on his holstered power gun, as a delegation from the town approached. Fifty meters at his back, the towering cliff of the Bolo rose at the edge of town, its hull still furiously radiating heat enough to warm the chill, morning air.

"Morning, folks," Jaime called with a friendly smile as several ragged-looking citizens approached. Several held rifles that had the look of antiques about them, and others clutched lengths of pipe or wood. It didn't look exactly like a reception happy to see him, or the tracked monster brought along to the outskirts of Fort Greeley. He ignored the hostile glares and threatening scowls, picking out the best-dressed man in the crowd and pinning him with his eyes. "I'm General Graham, of the Cloud Defense Force. Who's in charge here?"

"I am," replied the man Jaime had already singled out. "Constable Higgins. Are you out of your skekking *mind* coming here like this?"

"I don't think so," Jaime replied, keeping his voice

light. He could taste smoke in the air; several kilometers away, the forest was still burning.

"That there Bolo took out a goddamn clucker-crawlie factory in five an' a half seconds!" another man nearby said, marveling with a shake of his head. "I ain't never seen nothin' like it!"

"Hold your tongue, Zeke," Higgins said. His eyes narrowed as he glared at Jaime. "Mister, you can just get that tin monster of yours turned around and get out of this district as fast as you can! We been makin' out okay here with the cluckers, live an' let live, but, dammit, they're gonna think *we* had somethin' t' do with their factory gettin' slagged!"

"I'm sorry about that," Jaime replied. "We didn't know there were any enemy forces in this area. But now that it's done, maybe we can help each other."

"You can help by high-tailin' it for the horizon, mister!" someone in the growing mob called out. Several vehicles had arrived, ground cars and a couple of hovertrucks piled high with more of the town's citizens emerging from cover.

"I'm afraid I can't do that. I've got something like twelve hundred people out there, refugees from the slave labor camp at Celeste. They're hungry, starving, some of them, and most of them need clothes and shoes, too."

"Look, mister," Higgins said. "We don't bear you no ill-feelin's. But we got troubles of our own, y'understand?"

Jaime nodded toward the thickly wooded hill north of the town. "Is the Fort Greeley Depot still up there?"

"It's there," Higgins said, guarded.

"Well, then," Jaime said, grinning, "you folks have a choice. You can round up all of the vehicles and ground transports you can find in town and help load them up with food. Lots of food. And uniforms and boots from the depot. Weapons, if there are any in the armory, still. Or . . ." He let the word hang there in the smoke-tainted morning air.

"Or what?"

"Or I'll have those people come in here and help themselves. Y'know, that just might be the easiest thing to do."

"Tw-twelve hundred refugees?" Higgins's eyes were wide. "Jeez, mister—"

"It's *General*, Constable Higgins, not mister. And while I regret the necessity, I am declaring martial law in this region. My people need food and supplies, and I intend to get them. With or without your cooperation!"

"They's only one of him, Constable!" a man with a rusty relic of a hunting rifle said, raising the weapon.

The briefest of red flashes flicked out from one of Hector's point defense turrets, caressing the rifle, slicing through the barrel just ahead of the man's left hand. A second flash followed, carving telescopic sight and receiver with a surgeon's skill. The man yelped, flapping burned hands as he jumped back, and the weapon clattered in three smoking pieces to the pavement.

"*Please* don't make me back up my orders with force, Constable," Jaime said. "The survival of twelve hundred people is at stake, and I will not hesitate to take what they need to survive. You can cooperate with us or not . . . but we *will* take what we need."

"Damn it, man, that's robbery and extortion!"

"From my perspective, sir, it's war. I wonder if you'd care to explain just what sort of an arrangement you've had with the cluckers for the past year or so."

"Ah, well, that is . . ." He stopped, looking at the other members of the crowd for help. "Look, ah . . . General, we did what we had to t' survive. That big mobile factory of theirs and a bunch of their floaters come in here and rounded up eighty of our people.

Fried 'em all, right up there in Dawes Square. Then they told us t' start providin' 'em with stuff, or they'd fry the rest of us in batches, eighty at a time."

"What kind of stuff?"

"Tech stuff, mostly. Lots of refined metals. Computers. Servo units. Tools. Machine parts. And, yeah, food, too. All we could turn out from the hydroponics plots, down by th' lake."

Jaime nodded. The !°!°! lust for any refined metals or human machinery was still inexplicable, but he'd just confirmed an assumption he'd made back at Camp 84. The machines had permitted outlying towns and settlements to maintain a semblance of autonomy in exchange for food.

The food that had kept 84 alive for almost a year, now.

"Well, we're going to take as much food as you can provide," Jaime told them. He nodded at one of the hovertrucks. "And some of your vehicles, too, to carry it. We'll leave you enough to meet your own needs, though. And, after that, we'll leave you alone."

"Yeah, but the clackers—" someone called out.

"What're we gonna do?" another cried.

Jaime spread his hands. "You can stay and reason with them," he suggested. "Explain that we came in here and stole what we needed. If you don't think they're likely to be reasonable, you might consider leaving."

"This here's our home, General," another voice called. "You sayin' we have t' *leave*?"

"Maybe you won't, if the clackers are feeling generous," he said. "Of course, there's *another* alternative you could think about."

"What's that?" Higgins wanted to know.

"You can pack up everything you can carry and come with us," Jaime told them. "I'm leading my people . . . away from here. To a safe place where the damned clackers won't ever kill us or carve us up or enslave us ever again."

"And where the hell would that be?" Higgins demanded. "The damned machines've taken over th' whole damned planet!"

"Tell me," Jaime said, ignoring the question. "This is a fair-sized town. You wouldn't happen to have a Tolun trade factor here, would you?"

There was a long and uncomfortable silence from the crowd.

"The Tolun were responsible for transporting food grown here to the camp," Jaime continued. "I know. We saw them. I need to talk with one."

There was another pause of uncomfortable silence, and then the gull-wing door of one of the ground cars nearby cracked open and raised. A tall, lanky figure stooped beneath the door, stepped out, then rose to its full height, a slender figure in strangely patterned robes of eye-clashing crimson, pink, and greenish blue.

"Here," the figure said with a voice like broken glass rattling in a can. "Trade Factor Sshejevaalgh, am I. To discuss things with me, you wish?"

"Yes, Trade Factor," Jaime replied, and his grin broadened. "To discuss things with you I *very* much wish!"

CHAPTER FOURTEEN

Reluctantly, but at his direct orders, I have left my Commander in the town of Fort Greeley. There is a very real danger of !*!*! machines counterattacking after the destruction of their mobile factory here. The Enemy was almost certainly able to uplink a status report during the 5.482 seconds of combat and by now will be planning a counterstroke. I can most effectively prevent an attack against the town by leaving the area as swiftly as possible. General Graham has placed Sergeant Kyle in command. Before we left, she delivered a stinging threat to the town: We will return, and when we do, if the general has been harmed in any way, we will reduce Fort Greeley to a lake of molten stone and rubble.

I doubt that General Graham would follow through with such an order. I believe, however, that Sergeant Kyle would. I suspect that she has a growing affection for my Commander, which would make her most disagreeable if anything unfortunate happened to him. I sincerely hope the townspeople agree to continue cooperating with us.

For their sake.

❖   ❖   ❖

227

"Jaimegraham, you are," the tall figure said in its glass-rattling voice. They were inside the Tolun factor's office, a small building overlooking Dawes Square in the middle of town. "Then, to discuss business, you wish?"

"That's right," Jaime told the alien. "I've heard you people will transport anything, anywhere . . . for the right price."

Two enormous gold eyes with jet-black, hourglass pupils blinked once, then twice again. The Tolun reminded Jaime, in a distant and somewhat warty-skinned way, of holographs he'd seen of an extinct Terran amphibian called a toad. Sshejevaalgh had the same rounded snout, the same bulging eyes rising above the same flat-skulled, gold-brown head. No toad had ever sported those writhing sensory tendrils sprouting from the side of the head, like golden, angleworm-sideburns, though, and when he opened his mouth, the factor displayed a most untoadlike triple array of slicing teeth and stranger, less comprehensible inner mouth parts.

He—at least Jaime *assumed* that it was a he, though he knew very little about Tolun biology—wore an ornately patterned robe or cloak, a jarring mix of reds, pinks, and aqua colors that, no doubt, was pleasing to Tolun visual senses but for humans was downright painful. The half dozen oddly shaped brooches or pins on the upper part of the robe, Jaime knew, were various communications, recording, and sensory devices, linked together by a sophisticated computer network worn on the body beneath the outer garments. The factor's office, with wall hangings and curtains in other mind-jolting combinations of improbable colors and harsh designs, was cluttered with other implements of advanced technology. He recognized a SWIFT interstellar communications system; some of the other devices he could only guess at. A plain, canvas-wrapped bundle that he and Alita had off-loaded from Hector before the Bolo had departed lay on a translucent table near the door, out of place in this alien decor of color and pattern.

The Tolun, he knew, prized technology. They traded in it, used it as a kind of currency. They particularly sought artifacts incorporating alien technology, which might suggest new approaches to old problems.

"For the right price," the tall being said, repeating Jaime's last words in half-gargled rattlings. "What is it you wish?"

"Transport," Jaime replied. "I need to lease space on some of your ships."

"And this is for . . . ?"

"People," Jaime replied. "Humans." He hesitated. "About twelve hundred of them. Possibly as many as two thousand."

The possibility of hiring the Tolun to carry escaped humans off of Cloud had been discussed plenty of times by the Escape Committee, back in the camp, but no one had ever been willing to guess how the aliens would react to the request. The first settlers on Cloud had encountered Tolun merchants within a few years of the colonizer fleet's arrival. In the two centuries since, they'd been peaceful, if opportunistic, good neighbors, though somewhat remote. Their actual level of technology was believed to be well above human norms, though they incorporated such an eclectic blend of alien sciences and technical systems that it was hard to tell anything about them for sure.

What *was* known was that the Tolun seemed to get along well with everybody and continued to maintain their mercantile empire in this region of space despite the arrival of the !°!°!. With human space travel decisively ended by the invasion, the Tolun were the only real chance the refugees had for leaving Cloud.

For a long count of perhaps twenty seconds, the being gave no response . . . none, at any rate, that Jaime could read. Alien emotions were always difficult to decipher; those twitching yellow-brown tendrils could be speaking volumes, but only to another Tolun.

"Three octimal seven two times eight to the third," the creature said at last, translating the number into the base eight math favored by the Tolun. "What you are asking, do you know?"

"I know you have the ships," Jaime told him.

"*Ssahval!* Ships, yes, we have. For so many, two, perhaps three of our transports Ssulaad-class should suffice. But a major undertaking this is. And angry the !°!°! would be. . . ."

"Just what is your relationship with the . . ." He stopped. He'd been about to say "Masters," but he would never use that term again. Instead, he clicked and clucked the approximation of their true name. "With the !°!°!?"

"Such information a price carries."

"Damn it, all I want to know is whether you belong to them. The way *we* used to! We can't very well do business with you if you are !°!°! slaves!"

"Slaves, we are not." It was hard to tell, but Jaime thought he detected a bristling in the Tolun factor. "No threat to the !°!°! are we, and useful as well. Many things with them we trade."

Just as Dieter had said. That left unanswered the question of why the !°!°! had decided to so completely obliterate human civilization on Cloud when they were obviously able to coexist in harmony with other species, and it gave the lie to the theory that the machines simply hated *all* organic life.

Was the Tolun being truthful? Jaime had no way of reading that alien face and decided he would simply have to trust him.

"There's something more," Jaime added. "One other passenger. A . . . a rather large machine, actually."

"A machine? Of the !°!°!?"

"No. One of ours."

"How large it is?"

"Thirty-two thousand tons, or so."

For the first time, the Tolun appeared to react. The hourglass pupils in its golden eyes expanded suddenly, turning the eyes dark. "That . . . very massive is."

"Can you do it?"

"Do it we can. But . . . for the right price, we carry."

"How much?"

"On where to go you wish, this depends. And more. Little that we desire have you." The Tolun factor blinked, then moved his hands sharply in an unintelligibly alien gesture. "A cup unfilled, a deal unclosed, this conversation must be. . . ."

"Wait!"

The Tolun paused, eyes unwaveringly on Jaime, his hand frozen in midstretch. Jaime noticed with a detached portion of his mind that it possessed two fingers and two thumbs, each with a suckerlike tip.

For answer, Jaime walked over to the bundle he and Alita had brought here from Hector. A few sharp tugs on the canvas, and the object within lay exposed, a dart shape of ebony black ceramics and inlaid metals, curved and flattened in odd geometries. The object was a little less than a meter long and massed perhaps ten kilograms. A chunk had been burned off of one bulging side, exposing glittering complexities of gold and silver within.

"How about clacker technology?"

The Tolun drew closer. One hand hovered above the damaged section.

Jaime covered the !°!°! device, one of the flyers downed that morning in the battle with the !°!°! mobile factory. "We could get you lots. The wreckage of their machines. Floaters. Walkers. What could the Tolun learn if they had a chance to study even one disabled floater, hmm?"

The Tolun leaned back, and the four-digited hand vanished again inside the eye-jarring robes. "A floater, have you? Now?"

Jaime shrugged, then remembered that the gesture was probably meaningless to the Tolun. "We can get them. We've destroyed a number of them already. I doubt that you could learn much from the wreckage at this point, though.

"I imagine you've never had the opportunity to examine a dead !°!°!," he went on. "And you know how efficient they are about coming into a battlefield and cleaning up the bits and pieces left behind." It was true. The !°!°!, above all else, were master scavengers. The Tolun would find nothing if they scoured the battlefield after the humans moved out. With their love of alien technologies, they couldn't help but be fascinated by the array of !°!°! machines, especially the ones exhibiting null-gravity capabilities.

"!°!°! floaters," the Tolun rasped. "And . . . better still, would one of their high-ranked directors be."

"A director?"

"What they call them, or you, we do not know. But that the !°!°! leaders possess multiple brains, you aware are?"

"We'd speculated about that," Jaime replied. In fact, so little was known about the !°!°! hierarchy, or about their social structures or—for lack of a better word, their "biology"—that everything about them was still guesswork and speculation. "We knew that the larger units appear to be intelligently controlled, while the smaller ones are more like robots. Very *stupid* robots, sometimes."

"Exactly. Those directors with four or five separate brains linked in series, the qualities we normally associate with thinking, feeling creatures, with *biologies*, possess. Plan, they do. Feel. Think."

Jaime suppressed a stir of excitement. The Tolun never gave anything away. This one, however, had assumed the human refugees had more information than they in fact possessed. With care, he might learn a great deal from this interview.

"So you want one of their directors?" he asked. "As what? A hostage?"

"For information, this we want. For learning. How biological systems with the machine they meld, this we would learn."

"Does it have to be alive?"

"Desirable, that would be. But not necessary. A !°!°! director, lifeless rendered, but not to small, charred fragments reduced, this sufficient would be."

Jaime frowned as he sorted through the alien syntax. The Tolun was, in effect, asking for the body of a !°!°! senior officer. It was just a little too close to the notion of handing over a POW for dissection for his tastes.

Still, Jaime had trouble thinking of the !°!°! as people. And if they managed to capture a clacker officer after it had been knocked out or killed or whatever the appropriate term was, what did it matter what the Tolun did with the body, or its brain?

"A clacker leader . . . like the one I presume was managing that mobile factory we slagged this morning?"

"Adequate, that would be."

"I don't know if we can promise you that," Jaime replied slowly. "It depends on a lot of things . . . including whether or not we even encounter another one, and on whether we could disable it without blowing it into fragments. But we'll try. As for floaters, I think we can promise you as many of those as you'd care to inspect."

"This, reasonable is. The floaters an impressive and

highly compact antigravity field coil possess. Much from these we can learn. But a director . . ." He stopped, his flat head cocking to one side. "For the floaters, your people passage receive. For a director, transport your giant machine we will."

"Negative," Jaime replied. "The machine is going with us, no matter what."

"With my peers on this consult I must."

"Go ahead and consult. I can promise you specimens of every type of clacker machine we run into, up to that monster we faced this morning. *If possible*, we'll include a director in the mix, but I'm not going to promise that. I *can* promise you examples of their biomechanical interfaces, however." That should be easy enough. They'd already picked up and buried a disturbing number of !°!°! devices sprouting human hands or eyeballs, kept alive by vials of unidentified chemicals and directly wired into small, crystalline devices that were probably !°!°! computer circuits. "You should be able to learn quite a lot from that, even if we don't bag a director for you."

"Agree, I do. Quite reasonable, your suggestion is."

Jaime could tell the factor was eager. The Tolun must have been almost desperately eager to acquire some solid insight into clacker biotechnology. "In exchange, you'll provide us with passage off-world for our people, and for the thirty-two-thousand-ton machine I mentioned?"

"This machine . . . the one behind you in the street earlier, this is?"

"A Mark XXXIII Bolo," Jaime said, nodding.

"So big, it is." The slender being trembled, a shiver, perhaps, of uncertainty. "So dangerous. . . ."

"You'll have nothing to fear from it," Jaime said. "At least . . . as long as you deal squarely with us." It wouldn't hurt, he thought, to add just a hint of threat to the discussion.

"If by 'deal squarely' honest dealing and adherence to contract, you mean, threats you do not need," the Tolun said. "Where . . . on our ships would you travel?"

Jaime hesitated before replying. "I'd really rather not go into our plans too deeply, just yet. Not until we have a solid agreement." The Tolun were well-known for their loyalty to a business contract, but Jaime didn't want to risk the chance that this one might sell the humans' plans to the enemy.

Not that his plans were that well worked out, as yet. There were several worlds within a few hundred light years where a new human colony might be begun; with luck, such a colony might escape the notice of the !°!°!, at least for a time.

Their best hope, though, had been suggested by Tamas Reuter, the astronomer in the tight-knit little escape committee, back in Camp 84. Fifteen hundred light years from Cloud lay the nearest worlds of the Grakaan of Dargurauth. Very little was known about them, save that they possessed a powerful, star-faring military, and that they jealously guarded the colonies of their far-flung empire. If they could be contacted, the refugees might find a haven there . . . and powerful allies.

"Meet with you, our people must," the factor said after a long moment. "That you in fact can deliver what you promise, we must know."

"That's fair."

"A meetingplace in mind you have? Where others of my house might you join?"

He thought for a moment. "Do you know where the military base at Chryse is? Where the base *used* to be, rather?"

"I know."

"In five local days, at suns-set, send your factor to Chryse. There's a hill north of the base, with some ruins on it."

"The place I know."

"I'll have someone there. We can talk then."

"Acceptable to us, this will be. Five days, at first-sun set, we meet." Those large, golden eyes strayed again to the !°!°! flyer on the table between them. "Most interesting, this is."

"I'll give it to you," Jaime said. It was a gamble, but he needed to ingratiate himself with these people. And, perhaps, the gesture would buy him some respect. "I'll give it to you as a token of what we can provide . . . and in exchange for some information."

"The information is?"

"Frequencies and communications protocol for SWIFT access to the Grakaan."

The Tolun's pupils expanded again, turning the eyes black. "Ssso? Powerful friends, you have. This . . . arranged, it can be."

"Good. I'd like the information now, if possible."

The Tolun left the room for a few moments. When he returned, he handed Jaime a data crystal. "The information you seek, on this crystal is."

"Excellent." He gestured at the dead !°!°! machine. "Enjoy your prize. I'll see about arranging for the rest of your payment."

Outside, on the streets of Fort Greeley once more, Jaime expelled a long, pent-up whistle of air. Higgins and a number of other townspeople watched him warily from the square but did nothing; Hector would be back within the hour, and they knew better than to start something with him now.

That's one step closer, he thought, *to finding a way off this rock.*

There was still a hell of a long way to go, however, before they could say they were finally in the clear.

DAV reviewed again the last seconds of the battle between JEG851 and the Bolo, uploaded onto the

!°!°! Primary Web. The human combat machine's firepower was devastating; the !°!°! mobile factory had survived as long as it had only because the Bolo's first shots had been absorbed and dissipated slightly by the water as an exploding wall of steam.

Clearly, the only way to defeat the Bolo would be to bring even greater firepower to bear against it. Hurling meteoric chunks at it employed the greatest firepower in terms of raw megatonnage, but that approach had weaknesses. The ships that delivered them were vulnerable . . . and so were the projectiles themselves in the long seconds of their fall toward their target.

More efficient, he thought, would be ground battlers, though he estimated that ten to twelve would be necessary to neutralize the Bolo. And . . . two or, no, better yet, three mobile planetary bastions. Those mobile fortresses were slow—considerably slower than the Bolo, in fact—but they could take advantage of the planet's horizon for cover, and work their way in close enough that there would be no time delay between the loosing of their salvos and target impact.

In DAV's mind, a 3-D relief graphic of the planet rotated beneath his gaze. So far, the Bolo had been working its way north from Camp 84, evidently seeking to penetrate the mountains north of the Chryse Peninsula and breaking out into the plains and woodlands beyond. Ideally, the bastions should be placed to trap the huge machine on the peninsula, where they would force it to fight to the death, to *its* death.

Making his decision, he opened a communications channel to the Ninth Awareness. His plan, requiring as it did so much in the way of !°!°! military assets, would need approval at the very highest level.

❖   ❖   ❖

"Are you sure this is what you want?" Jaime asked. "It's not going to be the same aboard Hector without you."

Shari Barstowe smiled—the first such smile he'd seen from her in as long as he could remember. "Thanks, General," she said. "But you know as well as I do I'm not doing a thing in there that you two couldn't do without me. I don't think Hector even needs you two any more, and he sure doesn't need me."

Jaime and Alita were standing in the shade of a makeshift tent, one of hundreds of similar temporary structures erected among the trees and underbrush of the Brenner Forest, nearly ninety kilometers northeast of Celeste. Hector was gone for the moment, off on a scouting run toward Cambera Pass, leaving them here so that Jaime could catch up on the current logistical needs of the March. Wal Prescott and Shari had joined them in his headquarters tent a few moments before, and Shari had asked if she could leave the Bolo Operations Team, as they'd begun calling themselves, to join the others.

Jaime took a moment to study Shari. She'd changed a lot since the last time he'd seen her, several hours earlier. She was wearing military-issue fatigues, drawn from the stores the day before at Fort Greeley. A wisp of blond hair had escaped her helmet, just beneath the cold, crystalline glitter of the red |°|°| eye she'd wired above her visor. Her face was smudged with combat blacking, and she carried a Mark XL power carbine slung muzzle-down over her shoulder.

She looked very little like a psychotronicist now.

"It just seems a waste," Jaime said, "turning your talents as a psychotronics expert loose with the Brotherhood."

"You wouldn't happen to be implying," Wal said

slowly, "that we're a bunch of low-browed, thick-headed grunts, would you?"

Jaime laughed. "Far from it! I *am* afraid you'll have to rename your group the Brother-and-sisterhood, though."

"There are already one hundred five women in the Brotherhood," Shari said quietly, "with two hundred thirty-seven men. This isn't about *sex*. We're fighting for our freedom, too."

"Didn't say it was," Jaime replied. The idea was still a little strange, though. Women had not served in Cloud's military until after the Outreach War, some forty local years ago, and then only in a noncombat status, like Sergeant Kyle. But he knew that women had often served in combat units throughout old Earth's history, that they'd been in front-line units during the Melconian Wars, which had been raging two centuries ago when contact with Earth had been lost. Women could fire a pulse rifle or power gun as well and as accurately as any man.

And they could die just as bravely, fighting for what they believed.

"Of course you can go," Jaime continued. He glanced at Wal. "As long as the Brotherhood'll have you."

"She came to see me last time Hector joined up with us," Wal said. "Asked to qualify with a rifle, so I gave her th' chance. She scored an eighty-five. Damned good shootin', if y'ask me. Top five percent of all my people, in fact."

"As long as I have dibs on her if we develop mental problems with Hector, it's okay with me." He looked at Shari. "As long as it's what you want."

"To tell you the truth, General," she said, "if I have to spend one more hour in that gray-painted cave inside Hector's Battle Center, doing nothing but stare at readouts and think about how Jeff died in there, I'm going to go stark, raving skiz." She reached behind her shoulder and slapped the plastic stock of her carbine. "This way, I can feel like I'm really delivering some payback to the bastards, y'know?"

"Yeah. I think I do." He nodded. "Okay. Stay in touch, though. And . . . take care of yourself, okay?"

She straightened into an approximation of attention—obviously, she was still new to this—and rendered a fairly accurate salute. "Yes, *sir!*"

Gravely, Jaime returned the salute. After she'd turned and left the tent, he raised an eyebrow at Wal. "You'll take care of her, Colonel?"

"As well as I'll take care of my three hundred forty-two *other* kids, General. You know that."

"Yes, I do."

"She'll do okay," Alita told him after Wal had left the tent. "She's a big girl."

"I just don't want her leaping into anything without thinking," he said. "Just because . . . of what happened."

"Shari's too sharp to do that, Jaime." She sighed. "I've been wishing I could do the same thing, t' tell you the truth."

"You want to join the Brotherhood? Or just get out of the Battle Center?"

She chuckled. "Bit of both, I guess. It's not like Hector has much for us to do."

He nodded. For the past several days, the three of them had shared watches in the Battle Center, one taking the console command seat, while one of them slept in the watch room and the other stood by, strapped into one of the jumpseats. When combat did happen, as it had twice now since the battle at Fort Greeley, all three of them crowded in together inside the circle of the viewscreen, but there was never much to be said or done, save watch the Bolo defeat the !°!°! machines swiftly and efficiently, and within the span of a very few seconds.

Shari was right. Hector could wage this campaign

quite handily without any human input whatsoever.

Still, he thought it was important that some human presence remain aboard. There was a deep-seated and quite understandable resentment against *all* intelligent machines within the human community on Cloud, most especially among the participants in the March. Having one of their own, a human, riding herd on the Bolo at all times was the only way to keep the March from fragmenting into a hundred separate, possibly warring bands of marauders and starving refugees.

Thanks to Hector—and the fact that the people trusted Jaime, at least, even if they didn't unreservedly trust the Bolo—the March had been swelling during the past few hours. Over five hundred people from Fort Greeley had joined them, including Constable Higgins, and others had begun arriving from other communities, many with nothing but the clothing they wore. To no one's particular surprise, Dieter Hollinsworth had been elected "governor," which made official the position he'd been holding as the March's civilian leader.

"If you want to go, Alita," Jaime said, "you can. I have to stay, so that the people know Hector is, well, that he's under human control. But if you really want to—"

"Thanks, General." She smiled. "Thanks a lot. But I think I've found my place here. I'm a Bolo crew chief, right? Best one on Cloud! I may not have a maintenance bay or tools or spare parts or heavy lifter cranes or anything else I would need if Hector even hiccuped, but I know this is where I belong."

Jaime felt an unexpected surge of relief. "Thanks, Alita. I appreciate it."

"Hey, I know a soft billet when I see one." She laughed. "And getting to share close quarters with the best-looking general on the planet? I'd be crazy to leave!"

"I'm glad you feel that way. Just remember, Hector is the prime target on the planet right now. Riding in him is not exactly an assignment promising long life and security."

"Maybe not, but it sure as hell will be interesting!"

CHAPTER FIFTEEN

In the past 45.31 standard hours, I have engaged !*!*! forces eight times. So far, all Enemy units encountered have been small forces easily met and eliminated. However, I have the feeling that I am not sensing the complete image—what my human companions might call "seeing the big picture." The units eliminated so far have been scouts and reconnaissance probes with little real firepower. I wonder if, possibly, much larger Enemy forces currently beyond sensor range are attempting to herd me in a direction of their choosing or, conversely, to draw my attention in one direction, while they prepare a killing strike from another. Either is a possibility, and I must be prepared to deal with both eventualities.

For the past three days, my Commander has ordered me to keep well clear of the March. I at first was concerned that this would limit my ability to protect it, but it seems obvious now that the !*!*! are interested more in my movements than in those of the refugees.

I have in my memory the image of a piece of artwork, a drawing in pen and ink which almost certainly dates to the prespaceflight era on Earth. I have many such on file, of course, a representative cross-section of human visual art from many cultures and spanning many centuries. This one is unique, however, because it seems to reflect the particular point of view of a soldier, an enlisted man serving in a pre-atomic combat zone. I have no doubt but that the artist was, himself, a soldier.

In the picture which, I believe, was known as a cartoon, two soldiers are digging a combat position with pick and shovel, what was then known as a "foxhole." Behind them is a tank—a primitive, nonintelligent armored fighting vehicle which could, in fact, be considered to be a distant and primitive predecessor of the Bolo. As they work, one soldier is staring at the tank with what might be longing. The other, already chest-deep in the hole, is saying something like, "I'd rather dig. A moving foxhole attracts the eye."

I had never entirely understood that cartoon until now. General Graham, of course, is aware that any attack against me—especially one as violent as an all-out assault by !°!°! forces is likely to be—would kill or injure hundreds of the humans now making their way through the Cambera Pass on foot.

We can protect them by drawing Enemy attention to ourselves. While this is an admirable strategy— and General Graham is executing it with efficiency and precision—I cannot help but wonder how he plans to rejoin the refugee body without inviting attack.

In the meantime, we have returned to the site of what once was the largest CDF military base on Cloud, at Chryse, some eighty kilometers east of Celeste.

My Commander has an appointment to keep here.

Static hissed and sparked across the display screen, and Jaime looked up, irritated. "Damn it, Moxley! I'm losing it!"

A technician sitting at a table across the room in

front of an improbable stack of metal cabinets, boxes, and an incredible tangle of snaking black cables made an adjustment. Alita, standing next to him, pointed out a loose connection.

"Try it now, sir!" she called.

Again, he tapped out a combination of letters and numbers on the keypad hardwired into the array of computers in front of him. Despite the fact that Hector was feeding them with power for this transmission, the lights in the dim-lit and dusty room flickered and nearly went out. Static hissed, then smeared into a cloud of dancing pixels.

He thought he could just make out something on the screen, now.

Once, a year ago, this had been CICC, the Chryse Interstellar Communications Center, one of the few SWIFT facilities on Cloud. Interstellar communications had fallen out of favor some centuries ago, when contact had been lost with Earth and it seemed that there was no one else out there to talk to. CICC had been refurbished and remanned when *Empyrion* began her controversial mission. And it was here that communications technicians had desperately tried to make contact with the unknown invaders who'd dropped out of Cloud's sky close behind the incoming salvo of planetoids.

Located inside a bunker deep beneath the surface of a high, rocky hill north of the base proper, CICC had been wrecked by the impact of the asteroid that had flattened the rest of the base, but not obliterated. After Fort Greeley, Jaime had dispatched a Brotherhood team here in one of the town's hovertrucks to see if the SWIFT gear was salvageable.

Their report was that it *might* be . . . assuming enough spares could be found to cobble together a dozen jury-rigged circuits and crossfeeds, and assuming that enough power could be found, and assuming . . .

Well, the list of assumptions had been a long one, but it looked like they might be able to make it. Lieutenant Moxley, who'd been an expert in interstellar communications systems before The Killing, assisted by eight comm techs pulled from the March and by Alita, had been working for the past ten hours to get the system operational once more.

"More power," Moxley called. "General, we're not going to be able to transmit the carrier without more power in the feed!"

He touched the thread mike by his lips. "Hector? We need more power."

"Affirmative, my Commander. I must remind you, however, that this will reduce the range of my security scans."

"Do it. If we're going to make this work, we need more juice!"

"Increasing power flow ten percent."

And then he had an image.

It was not very clear; in fact, for a time Jaime could scarcely tell what he was looking at. Then the signal cleared, pixels coalescing, and Jaime stared into the face of a Grakaan.

The message he was viewing, of course, was not meant for him. Using the alien computer and communications protocols sold to them by the Tolun, Moxley had tapped into a SWIFT transmission originating somewhere in Grakaan space.

The face on the screen was scarcely recognizable as a face, all bumps and angles and ridges, with palps and feeding tendrils surrounding an insect's mouth below, and a single, bright blue and pupilless eye imbedded in black armor above. There was no sound; the mouth parts worked frantically, as though the creature were speaking . . . though it could as easily have been chewing its dinner.

"Not sure, General," Moxley called from the other

side of the room. He was studying the same image on a small monitor propped up on his work table. "I think it might be something like a Grak news broadcast. Don't know how long we'll have it, though. You'll have to work fast!"

"For all we know," Jaime replied, "it's transmitting wishes for a happy birthday to its mother."

"I didn't know Graks *had* mothers," Alita observed.

Jaime was already keying in the sequence that would load the message they'd already prepared into the SWIFT computer. A final stroke on the enter key, and the room's lights dimmed again as relays closed, and a tachyonic pulse surged from the jury-rigged antenna on the hilltop high above them. Using the weak signal from Grakaan space as a guide, the message from Cloud ought to attract Grakaan attention.

What they would choose to do about it, of course, was as yet unknown.

"Well, that's that," Jaime said. "Leave the gear on automatic. Is that relay hooked up?"

"Yes, sir," Moxley replied. "If the Graks answer on the same frequency, it'll be picked up here and relayed to Hector, as long as he's still in range."

Jaime plucked the data crystal from its receiver, tossed it once, glittering, then caught it and dropped it in his tunic pocket. The Tolun had come through this much, at any rate. If the Grakaan wanted no part of the human refugees and their problems, well, there were still other alternatives—most of them involving finding a small, out-of-the-way, and uninhabited world somewhere as far from !°!°! activities as possible. But it would be a lot better if they could find a large and powerful civilization, one with plenty of military resources, like the Graks. With their help, the refugees could concentrate on rebuilding their community, without having to worry about the !°!°! coming after them.

"Let's go upstairs and see if the Toluns are here, yet," he said.

The elevators inside the SWIFT facility weren't working, so it was a long climb up a spiraling set of emergency steps. They emerged on the hilltop beneath the improbable tangle of cobbled-together spare parts which Moxley and his comm tech crew had used to jury rig the SWIFT antenna. It was getting close to suns-set, with both of Cloud's suns nearing the horizon, with every rock and elevation casting long, twinned shadows across the ground. Above him, the transmission dish was pointed at the sky halfway between zenith and the western horizon; the Graks would have to reply within three hours or so, or the source of the reply would be lost below the horizon. SWIFT transmissions were instantaneous; the politics that governed decisions made by intelligent beings, however, were rarely that quick.

He'd hoped to get back here and make contact with the Graks earlier, to give them more time in which to answer, but it had taken longer than anticipated to repair the SWIFT communications gear. Fortunately, there'd been plenty of wreckage and spare parts lying about for the comm boys to work with.

And that simple fact raised again a question that had been gnawing at Jaime for months now.

Jaime found a handy rock, a stone from the tumble-down ruins on the hilltop at his back, and looked down at what once had been the Chryse Military Base. The !*!*! meteor, when it struck, had landed several kilometers to the south, leaving a hundred-meter crater and turning the base in a flattened, shredded ruin. Buildings had been blown down, vehicles picked up and flung for kilometers, towers crumpled, and the wreckage that was left scorched by the hurricane firestorm. In all that wreckage, Hector rose like a black, broad, flat-topped mountain at the bottom of the hill, a dozen hovertrucks and light transports huddled in his shadow. A detachment of Brotherhood troops had come along this morning, to provide security and extra helping hands, as necessary. That help had been invaluable. With slabs of armor uncovered in the ruins, they'd sealed the gaping wound in the Bolo's right side, using jury-rigged blocks and tackle to position the plating, while Hector's onboard servos completed the welds.

"I have a target," Hector said, speaking in the small receiver clipped to Jaime's ear. "Bearing one-zero-seven, range three-five kilometers, speed two-zero-three kps. I believe it is the Tolun, General."

"Good. Anything else out there?"

"I have passive tracks on several large objects in space, almost certainly !°!°! vessels, but none presents an immediate threat, and none is using active sensors. The ruins here effectively mask my presence."

"Keep an eye on them, Hector."

"Affirmative."

Ten minutes before the Tolun arrived. Jaime closed his eyes, and in his mind he was back in the pit on the shattered harbor's edge of Celeste, naked, mud-covered, searching on hands and knees with a thousand other slaves for bits and pieces of technological debris—bits of wire, chunks of glass and ceramic, the litter and refuse of a post-Armageddon civilization. Why? By whatever gods there might be in a bleak and uncaring universe, *why . . . ?*

Why organize human captives for such labor-intensive work as picking centimeter-lengths of copper wiring and lost porcelain figurines out of the mud, when here at Chryse there was a debris field covering a thousand hectares, the jumble of wreckage simply lying in the open, free for the taking?

He'd worried about that question during his months as a !°!°! slave, but somehow the enormity of the thing hadn't come home to him until now. The answer to the mystery was damned important, of that much he was certain. The clackers were highly intelligent—at least what the Tolun had called their directors were, at any rate—and what appeared to be irrational behavior on their part *had* to have a reason.

Had the human captives been put through hell simply to torture them, to break them down and strip them of their humanity? That hardly seemed likely, under the circumstances. It would have been simplicity itself to gather them into a camp and drop an asteroid on it, or nuke it, or simply move in with electron beams and flamers. Why the elaborate show of making them work for their survival?

As it had time after time before, the question burned in Jaime's mind. Was there a weakness there, something to be exploited, in what appeared to be clacker irrationality?

Were the !°!°! so alien that there was no chance of understanding their motives? Or was he facing simply the overwhelmingly *human* need to find some reason for so much pain and suffering?

"The Tolun are in sight," Hector announced.

Jaime looked toward the east. A plume of dust, golden in the evening light, was just visible on the plain below, moving swiftly toward Chryse. Behind him, the first sun was just touching the mountainous western horizon. The Tolun, it seemed, were punctual, if nothing else.

"General?" a familiar voice crackled in his ear. "This is Wal. You want us t' send 'em up there?"

"I'll come down," Jaime replied, rising and brushing off his trousers. He wanted to have Hector close by during these negotiations. If he'd been reading the factor's alien expressions close to right back in Fort Greeley, the Tolun were awed by the huge combat machine, and that could translate into an advantage.

Besides, the payment they'd collected so far was in the hovertrucks at the bottom of the hill.

By the time Jaime had made his way down the southern face of the hill, the Tolun contra-grav vehicle had reached the small human encampment beneath the loom of Hector's left-front tracks. In a last flurry of grav-field-blasted dust, the small, electric-pink and green flyer came to rest on tripod landing gear. The side dilated open, and three of the tall, brightly robed aliens stepped out.

He was aware of how quiet it was in the human camp. *They're all watching*, he thought, *to see how this turns out.*

"Trade Factor Sshejevaalgh," Jaime said, with more confidence in the tongue-twisting name with its final gargled consonant than he really felt. "It's good to see you again!"

Using the name was a gamble. He'd recorded it in Fort Greeley, then practiced it until he thought he had it right. The tricky part was that he couldn't tell if any of the three beings in front of him *was* Sshejevaalgh. He didn't know the Tolun well enough yet to be able to pick out differences among them. If he'd guessed wrong, he could be delivering an insult . . . but the Tolun factor at Fort Greeley had indicated that he, personally, would see Jaime again.

"Thank you, we do," the Tolun on the left said. He wore a different robe this time, one with relatively subdued tones of contrasting vermilion and greenish-yellow. "These my associates are. Sshejatveeh and Sshej'ghaavit, senior factors are."

Jaime wasn't about to try pronouncing those names without some practice first. "Delighted to meet you both." Bowing slightly, he gestured toward a canvas tarp stretched out across four poles as a makeshift tent. Two Brotherhood soldiers stood guard inside. "If you'd step into my office, maybe we can do some business."

Their business, it turned out, was a brief and straightforward recapitulation of the conversation Jaime has had with Sshejevaalgh five days earlier . . . with one major difference. They were not going to agree to transport Hector unless they received a !°!°! director in exchange.

In fact, with that exception, Jaime had to admit that the deal was a good one. The Tolun agreed to carry the human refugees to any destination they specified within three thousand light years of Cloud. In exchange, the humans agreed to provide intact or relatively so samples of as much !°!°! technology as was possible, including specific samples of their biomechanical interfaces, their weapons, their power sources, and their contra-gravity devices. The exact quantity of !°!°! tech was left unstated, but both parties promised to abide by what amounted to a good-faith clause.

If the humans could also provide an intact but disabled !°!°! director, one with at least four brains, the Tolun would also transport the Bolo. It was as simple—and as difficult—as that.

"I still can't promise to have an intact director for you," Jaime told them.

"This we understand," the Tolun introduced as Sshej'ghaavit replied. "But transport of so large a machine, difficult and dangerous it is."

Jaime was tempted to tell them that it was dangerous *not* transporting the Bolo, but he held his temper. "We now have nearly two thousand people in our group," he told them. "They must take up a lot more room than a Bolo would. Besides, they'll need food, water—"

"That many humans perhaps one hundred eighty to two hundred tons mass," Sshejatveeh replied. "Food, water, air, life support, and waste recycling machinery all perhaps as much as another thousand tons will mass, at least for so brief a voyage as we have here discussed."

Jaime was tempted to retort that Hector wouldn't be nearly as much trouble as two thousand *people*, but decided not to risk antagonizing them. He wasn't unduly worried; even if they couldn't nab a !°!°! leader, there was another possibility for getting passage for Hector. He was going to have to play this one out carefully, though.

"An initial payment you have?" Sshejatveeh asked. "A demonstration that what you have agreed to deliver, possible is?"

"Of course. Right over here."

Two folding tables had been set up beneath the tent, covered by sheets of canvas. Jaime pulled one of the sheets clear, revealing a pile of intact bits of machinery, wiring and circuitry, and parts. The Brotherhood had been busy in the wake of several of Hector's firefights lately, scouring the battlefields for usable tech. "We have three more hovertruckloads of this stuff," Jaime said. "Enough to keep your people happily studying clacker technology for the next couple of years, at least."

Sshejevaalgh reached out a four-digited hand and gently picked up an intact floater eye. His facial tendrils quivered with what might be excitement . . . or anticipation. A human eye, dull and dry-surfaced, stared up at them from its metal casing. "Biomechanical technology, this is. . . ."

Jaime suppressed an unpleasant twisting in his stomach. "A lot of clacker machines get knocked out by a near-miss," he explained. "We think the smaller ones, especially, aren't shielded against EMPs or extremely powerful magnetic pulses. The biological components are dead, of course. We think the clackers bathe them in various fluids and keep electrical current moving through them, to keep them alive, but after the unit is knocked out, the life-support equipment stops and the tissues die."

"Understood, this is. The connections and interface to study we want. Of the living tissue we no need have." Good. He still had qualms about selling used human body parts to these people. It would be a lot worse if they'd wanted the body parts *alive*.

"You might like this as well," Jaime said, uncovering the bundle on the second table. Beneath the tarp was an intact floater, two meters long, a quarter of that thick, a bulky, rounded cigar shape with knobs and swellings along its length, and a trailing dangle of silver tentacles. Half a dozen red, faceted eyes glittered from the black shell; it had been all Jaime could do to keep the Brotherhood from snatching those for their newest recruits.

"We found this one when the mag pulse from a Hellbore sent a surge through its circuitry," Jaime explained. "It ought to be in pretty good shape. Here, look at this."

He picked up a stunstick lying on the first table. Holding the contacts just above a particular spot on the floater's black metal slide, he pressed the switch. Blue sparks arced and crackled, and the black metal, briefly, rippled like water. Deftly, Jaime reached in, grabbed a length of silvery tentacle, and pulled it out. The liquid metal hardened a few seconds later. "We're still not sure how they pull that trick," he told the Tolun. "We think the electrical charge somehow induces an allotropic change in the metal alloy they use. It's not really a phase change. The metal doesn't get hot. It just turns liquid for a few seconds, before reverting to a solid. We, obviously, don't have the lab facilities to study it. Maybe you folks can work that out for yourselves."

He could see the interest gleaming in their gold and black eyes.

"This, most useful will be," Sshejatveeh said. "Well worth the services we shall provide, this is."

"Glad we could be of help. So. When do you want us? And where?"

"How soon at Stardown's spaceport your people gather can?"

Jaime thought about that. The March was across Cambera Pass now and well into the wooded plains beyond. Two hundred kilometers more to the east . . .

"Ten days. Maybe twelve."

The Tolun exchanged unreadable glances. "This . . . not good is," one said.

"Sooner, can you them there have?"

"They'll be damned lucky to make twenty kilometers a day," Jaime said. Foraging for food and other supplies had slowed the column to a crawl in the early stages of the March. "Could you meet them? Land your ships out in the Thallenfeld Plains, or along the Gorse River, maybe?"

"The !°!°!, the problem is," Sshejevaalgh explained. "Not happy with us, should they learn what we do, they will be. Our transports, quite large and many of them, to the Stardown spaceport these times come. No suspicion them by the !°!°! accorded is."

"Our neutrality, important is," Sshejatveeh added. "The more time passes, the worse the situation will be."

Jaime spread his hands. "My people can't grow wings and fly. That's why we came to you. I'll get them to Stardown as quickly as I can, but I can't promise less than ten days. In the meantime . . ." He pulled the tarp back over the dead floater.

All three Tolun started. "But—" Sshejatveeh said.

"You can have everything on that first table," he told them, "as your downpayment. But some of this stuff, we're going to hang on to. We'll deliver it when our people board your ships. Let's call it an additional guarantee to help keep this a secret from our clacker friends."

The Tolun stepped away and engaged in a hurried debate of hissing Tolunese.

"Acceptable, this is," Sshej'ghaavit said at last. "Hurtful, it is, but acceptable."

"Then we have a deal?"

Sshejatveeh nodded stiffly—an obvious imitation of a human gesture that held little meaning for the Tolun. "What can be done, done will be. Ten days, then."

Jaime smiled. "We'll need that long to round up a four-brained director for you."

As the factors walked out, Jaime signaled the Brotherhood guards standing nearby, to have them carry the table of machine parts to the Toluns' vehicle. He was startled when he realized that one was Shari, almost unrecognizable in uniform and body armor.

She hesitated. "Y-you're not going to leave Hector behind, are you, General?"

He grinned, ignoring the minor breach of military protocol. Soldiers did not question a general's decision . . . but Shari had been in the Brotherhood for less than a week, and in any case, Jaime had never cared much for rigid interpretations of such artificial distinctions as rank.

"That is a negative," he growled. "Hector's one of us, and we're not leaving *anyone* behind who wants to come."

She seemed relieved. "That's good . . . sir."

"Give 'em a hand with those parts, soldier."

Alita joined him in the tent as the guards carried the !°!°! fragments out to the pink Tolun car. "It almost sounds too good to be true, General," she said.

"They're eager to get their hands on that stuff. I get the impression it's a whole new technology, a new way of doing things, that they've never run into before. I guess the !°!°! are less than generous when it comes to sharing their tech, and this is a golden chance for the Tolun."

"We're not leaving Hector here?"

"No. Don't worry. I still have another trick or two in reserve."

One way or another, he thought, grim behind the smile, Hector *was* going to be coming with them.

CHAPTER SIXTEEN

"We have an answer," Alita told Jaime, two hours after the Tolun factors had left. "Hector translated it as it came through."

Jaime felt light-headed, almost dizzy as he held out his hand for the hardcopy printout Alita was offering him. A very great deal was riding on the Grakaan reply to the SWIFT message they'd transmitted.

Because of power limitations and the jury-rigged nature of the communications equipment, they'd transmitted text only, rather than trying either voice or the far more complex transmission of voice and picture. The reply had come as text as well.

TO GENERAL GRAHAM, OF THE HUMAN FORCES ON CLOUD, GREETINGS.

YOUR HUMAN PARTY IS WELCOME AMONG THE WORLDS OF GRAKAAN. THE MACHINE INTELLIGENCE HAS BEEN PRESSING US AS WELL, AND INFORMATION YOU MAY HAVE ABOUT HOW BEST TO FIGHT THEM WILL BE MOST WELCOME. OUR FLEET ASSETS ARE LIMITED, UNFORTUNATELY, AND WE CANNOT COME TO CLOUD TO PICK YOU UP. USE THE ATTACHED ID CODE, HOWEVER, UPON YOUR APPROACH TO GRAKAAN SPACE, AND WE WILL PROVIDE ESCORT.

THE COMBAT MACHINE YOU REFER TO AS A 'BOLO' WOULD

BE A VITAL ASSET IN OUR JOINT ENDEAVOR. TELL THE TOLUN
WE WILL PAY, IF THEIR PRICE FOR TRANSPORT OF THE BOLO
YOU CANNOT MEET.

—KLAG'AGH V'REDTH, THIRD ORDER OF THE IVORY MASK

Jaime was grinning as he looked up and met Alita's
gaze, but his eyes were burning with the moment's
emotion. This fixed everything! *Everything!*

"All we need to do now is make it to the rendezvous!"
he exclaimed.

"Yeah, but can we trust them?" Alita wanted to
know. "We hardly know anything about the Grakaan
Collective."

"We know enough." He slapped the print out with
his free hand. "We know they're more like us than
the Tolun are! We can work with these people."

Her eyes widened. "How can you say that? They
look so alien—"

Jaime clucked pretended disapproval at her. "Now
how the hell can someone who works with a *Bolo* think
that what the body looks like has anything to do with
the intelligence inside?"

"Yeah, okay, but . . ." She shook her head, a puzzled
frown creasing her face. "What makes you think the
Grakaan are like us?"

He held out the paper and pointed to the last
paragraph. "That. Do you see? Our friend—I'm not
going to try pronouncing that name—our Grak friend
is poking gentle fun at the Tolun, at the way they always
put the verb at the end of the sentence. *He has a sense
of humor!*"

Her eyes widened suddenly. "Oh!"

"We'll have to be cautious, sure," he told her. "I
imagine we'll get the Tolun to drop us on some
uninhabited world on the fringes of their space, where
we can make contact, establish friendly relations, that
sort of thing."

"And they'll pay to have Hector shipped off-world?"

"The message I composed suggested that they might want to take advantage of Hector's experience fighting the clackers."

"How did you know they were fighting clackers?"

"Hector told me. Seems he picked up quite a few bits and pieces, and retained them, when he was under their spell."

"Anything we can use?"

"Not a lot. I'm still working on it, though. Mostly, I've been interested in why the clackers are doing what they're doing. The experiments. The slave camps and amputations. None of it really makes sense. And I have the feeling I'm just missing something there. What I really want to know—"

"Excuse me, my Commander," Hector said in Jaime's ear.

"Yeah, whatcha got, Hector?"

"Multiple targets, bearing two-five-one, range one-seven kilometers, velocity nine-four kph. The power signature suggests !°!°! ground armor."

"Okay. We're coming inside." He jerked a thumb over his shoulder. "Let's move, Sergeant. We got company. Colonel! Colonel Prescott!"

"Yes, sir!"

"Round up your people. We have clacker armor on the way. Ten minutes, maybe less!"

"We're moving!"

Alita was already scrambling up the footholds on the Bolo's side, heading for the Number Three access hatch high above. He swung onto the steps and started up after her. "Keep your people well clear, Colonel."

"Will do." Wal grinned. "Hell, with Hector on our side, we might as well just sit back and take it easy."

"I'm not even going to dignify that with an answer, Wal. Now get the hell out of the combat zone!"

"Yes, sir."

Three minutes later, as the hovertrucks shrieked

toward the distant mountains on plumes of fan-blasted dust, they were in motion.

I wonder what the !°!°! are trying to learn with these piecemeal attacks. Each assault seems to be more powerful than the last, but the Enemy appears to be concentrating solely on numbers and firepower, and not on tactics. Perhaps he hopes to determine just what number of vehicles, what combination of heavy energy weapons, is sufficient to cause me serious damage in order to plan for future engagements, but this seems to be a preposterously wasteful strategy. Were I in the Enemy's place, with the superior mobility offered by spaceborne transport, I would attempt to box me in with overwhelmingly superior numbers and firepower, forcing me to fight a defensive and essentially nonmobile engagement.

Fortunately, this approach does not appear to have occurred to my opponent. Nor does it appear to have occurred to him that I have used anything less than my maximum capabilities in these recent skirmishes.

It's always good to hold a few things in reserve, as a surprise.

Six armored vehicles are closing with my position, moving in column formation through moderately thick woods to the west. Masked by the woods, I cannot engage them directly with line-of-sight weapons, and this, I surmise, is a deliberate strategy on their part, one that will allow them to get close enough to my position to do telling damage with their primary weapons. Information retained during my period of semi-dormant captivity indicates that these are ground battlers, high-speed tanks massing perhaps 4,000 tons apiece, with particle cannons in quad or quint hull-mounted arrays. I have faced them several times already, though not in such high numbers. Though powerful and difficult to hit, they possess relatively thin armor which even a 20cm Hellbore secondary can penetrate with little trouble. And a single hit from one of my 200cm Hellbores leaves little of them behind but a crater with a bottom of fused glass.

My musings on the capabilities and weaknesses of !*!*! ground battlers does not slow my response time. Within 2.54 seconds of engaging my tracks, I have slewed sharply to the right and am accelerating to 50 kph. Both primary batteries one and two are fully charged and ready, and my secondary Hellbores are coming on-line as I bring both reactors to 48.95 percent, the maximum possible in my current status. In addition, during the time spent at the ruins of Chryse Base, I have replenished my onboard stores of 240cm howitzer shells, 40cm BL mortar rounds, drones, and heavy VLS missiles from stocks found in an underground magazine.

I am ready for combat. I do not engage immediately, however, but wait 15.3 seconds as the hovertrucks bearing friendly forces clear the engagement zone. I have determined that they must be at least 20 kilometers from the Enemy before I engage.

I am now moving directly toward the oncoming line of ground battlers, still accelerating as I hit the treeline, tree trunks and the bodies of Cloud's giant tree ferns hurtling aside or splintering beneath my clashing tracks as I plunge into the forest without slowing.

It is time.

I shunt full power to my drivers, sprinting now to 109.5 kph. Hatches on my aft flanks pop open, and two VLS tubes fire, hurling a pair of expendable drones into the evening sky.

While still 9.29 kilometers from the nearest Enemy vehicle, I engage the targets with laser beams from one of the two drones, then launch two more missiles from my VLS tubes. The Enemy's response is immediate. Deceived into thinking I am using laser-guided ordnance *against them, three of the six targets immediately open fire on the drone, scoring a direct hit and vaporizing the craft 3.11 seconds later.*

The incoming missiles, however, skimming just above the treetops at hypersonic speed, have been programmed to home in on the rising heat bloom of the !°!°! particle cannons. The two-kiloton low-yield nuclear warheads detonate just above the battlers' positions; a blinding pulse of intense light banishes the early evening darkness, followed some twenty seconds later by a thunderclap of raw sound as the trees ahead dissolve in the advancing wall of flame and ruptured earth.

The shockwave rumbles over me, pelting my outer armor with rock, dirt, and splintered trees, but most of the shock is dissipated by my battle screens, and I take no serious damage. The low-yield warheads were chosen to minimize radiation effects; what radiation penetrates my screens and reaches my outer hull can be swiftly neutralized by my on-board decontamination systems.

The strike is decisive, however, in its effects on the Enemy. Five of the !°!°! vehicles are destroyed outright. The sixth, badly damaged, with most of its upper deck and glacis melted away and both tracks stripped from its drive wheels, is easily run down and crushed.

I speculate that this change in my battle tactics should give the Enemy pause.

"You have now the forces you have asked for." The thoughts of the Ninth Awareness were a calm trickle of incoming data, spilling from the sea of shifting, quickly moving information that made up the Primary Web. "But the Bolo's use of nuclear weapons in this last exchange could change the equation. Even a mobile bastion could not survive concentrated nuclear bombardment."

"I have been closely studying the humans' responses to our feints and probes," DAV replied. "Each engagement seems calculated not merely to destroy our forces, but to protect human lives as well."

"Why?"

"As we have noted with other OI species, they appear to care for one another. Even the Bolo seems to engage in combat in such a way as to assure the survival of human elements in its vicinity." Images and data, collected from spacecraft overflying the battlefield, unfolded within the knowing of the Ninth Awareness. "Notice here . . . and here. These are small vehicles occupied by humans to the north . . . by Toluns to the south. Though it is difficult to ascertain precise motivation, the Bolo appears to have waited several critical moments—for a full 1.53×10^{10} nanoseconds, in fact—before launching its missiles at our forces. My assumption is that it did so to give those vehicles time to get clear of the combat zone."

"Your reasoning . . . is less than solid. Many factors could explain a fifteen-billion-nanosecond delay in the Bolo's reactions. We still do not understand its programming."

"True," DAV replied. "We were able to use the Bolo for a time only by overlaying our own programming after rerouting and suppressing its own processor input and output. Still, I have been spending considerable time and resources studying human responses and memories. In particular, the living brain that was added to my own complex recently has a great deal of useful information, both about the Bolo, and about human needs, drives, and motivations generally. I find much of the information . . . baffling and opaque, bordering on what could only be termed completely irrational, but one factor stands out above all others. These creatures care for one another."

"What do you mean, 'care'? Ordinary maintenance—"

"I am not referring to the concept of care as maintenance. There is an altruistic sense of the concept. Humans are willing to sacrifice for one another. Even to cease functioning for the benefit or comfort of others. We see examples of this constantly in the camps where we hold large numbers of humans, one individual being willing to let itself be harvested in the place of another. It appears to be linked to basic survival instincts, something honed by their very evolution."

"How can ceasing operation for the benefit of another possibly be construed as relating to a *survival* instinct?"

"This I do not yet understand," DAV admitted. "Indeed, I now hope that further studies of the Bolo's basic programming will grant us additional insight into human reasoning processes. One important fact, however, is now clear. I now have reason to believe that the Bolo will not use nuclear weapons—indeed, *cannot* use any strategic weapons or weapons of large-scale destruction—in the vicinity of human-populated areas.

"And it is in just such an area that I plan to trap the Bolo, and all renegade humans with it."

"Proceed, then," the Ninth Awareness said. "You have three mobile bastions. Use them well and with wisdom, however. They will be sorely missed in the campaign against the Grakaan."

"You will be able to return them to that campaign within 1.26×10^{14} nanoseconds," DAV replied. "In ten of this planet's rotations, the Bolo and the renegade humans will have been recaptured . . . or eliminated."

"You seem certain of that conclusion."

DAV gave the cyberspace equivalent of a shrug. "I have been carefully studying human reactions to our attacks," he said. "In light of what I have learned so far, there is no other outcome possible. They *will* be destroyed."

"I hope so," the Ninth Awareness told him. "These reverses on this world are enough to make one accept the Makist heresies. These humans make one believe in a creative intelligence."

"Not even a supreme Maker will be able to deliver them from three bastions," DAV replied. "And I intend to see to their destruction personally."

"Do you really think we're the last humans there are?" Alita asked. "I mean, in the galaxy? Is Cloud all that's left?"

Jaime leaned back on his uncomfortable perch, staring up into a breathtaking night sky filled with the billions of stars that had given Cloud its name. "I don't know," he said after a time. "I wish I did."

They'd emerged from the bowels of Hector's Battle Center for some fresh air, and for a new perspective, perhaps, apart from that of gray-painted walls and the glowing greens and yellows of the viewscreen's IR display. Hector had assured them that the radiation count on his outer hull had been reduced to normal background levels, and that it was safe for them to venture again into the open air. They'd opened the topside entryway on the upper gundeck and were seated there on the hatch combing, facing one another with their legs dangling inside the circular opening.

Two days had passed since the meeting with the Tolun and the subsequent brief engagement with six !°!°! ground battlers. Hector had suggested a brief detour to the western seacoast north of Celeste, where he'd entered the water and traveled north for a time completely submerged—partly as an additional decontamination measure, but partly, too, to avoid for a time the prying electronic eyes of !°!°! reconnaissance spacecraft overhead.

Emerging once more, Hector had raced northeast, crossing the Veline Mountains by way of Dorchester

Pass, emerging on the Thallenfeld Plains in the middle of a brief, hard rainstorm. Since then, they'd been racing east, paralleling the mountains. The sky had cleared early that morning; the last of the storm clouds had vanished, leaving the night sky with its characteristic clarity and depth and with a cold, crisp bite in the air. Delamar had not yet risen; Triste, small, wan, and distant, was a minute crescent low in the west, all but drowned in a sea of stars upon billions of uncountable stars.

Jaime checked his cuffwatch. Another two hours until first-sun rise. He wanted to have rejoined the March by then. Brotherhood scouts had already reached the outskirts of Stardown fifty more kilometers to the northeast and reported that the area was clear. In another few days, they would be boarding the Tolun transports.

And after that?

Safe haven within the Grakaan Collective. But for how long?

The March numbered nearly twenty-two hundred people, now, according to the last report Wal had submitted to him. They'd been coming in from all across the Chryse Peninsula, singly and in small groups, most of them from villages and small towns that, according to the stories they told, had been only lightly occupied or even bothered by the !°!°! invaders. There were even rumors of other slave revolts in several of the special containment camps scattered across this hemisphere of Cloud. Reports were fragmentary, but it was clear that the !°!°! were having more and more trouble hanging onto their recently acquired conquest.

What would happen to those nascent rebellions when Hector and the two-thousand-some people he'd liberated left Cloud for the worlds of the Grakaan Collective?

Jaime didn't like thinking about it, though the closer

they got to the Stardown Rendezvous, the more he *had* to face it. Without Hector, the humans left behind on Cloud would be swiftly rounded up and enslaved . . . assuming the !°!°! even bothered with them. It might prove more expedient simply to bombard the remaining humans on Cloud into extinction.

And while the Tolun had promised passage for all of the human refugees making up the March, there had to be a practical limit to the number they would be willing to carry. Cloud's population before the invasion had numbered something like ten million. No one could even guess now how many had survived The Killing, but the number of untouched towns in the outlying districts suggested that as many as five million might be left, possibly quite a few more. What percentage of that five million could the Tolun transport to Grakaan space? Twenty percent was a million people, which would all together mass something like three times Hector's total weight, and never mind such minor added problems as food and life support for so many souls.

The question was, could Jaime abandon so many people for the promise of safety on the Grakaan worlds?

He snorted at the thought. In fact, outside of handling the negotiations with the Tolun, he had done very little. Hector, more than anything, anyone else, was responsible for the survival of the March, and there'd been little real need for either him or Alita to stay aboard. Oh, Hector accepted their guidance and suggestions, certainly—though sometimes he countered with much better suggestions of his own. More and more, now, Jaime had the feeling that the Bolo was tolerating their advice, but operating on its own, as yet unrevealed, agenda.

It didn't matter. He trusted Hector now, as he'd trusted few people in his life.

"It's just such a terrible responsibility," Alita added,

continuing her thought after a long silence. "If *we're* all that's left, humanity could die, right here on Cloud, unless we make it through."

He looked for a long moment at the stars overhead. "We may never know," he told her. "I guess the point is, we have to assume we're the last of humankind, the only ones that survived, out of all of the Diaspora."

"But we *don't* know what happened on Earth, or to the rest of the Terran Empire. The Melconians can't have . . . can't have gotten them *all*. . . ."

"Maybe. Can we afford to assume they didn't?"

Operation Diaspora had been a desperation move on the part of the Military High Command, back on far, lost Terra, two centuries before. At that time, the empire of Melcon had been advancing on all fronts, countering each new human weapon with terrible, genocidal weapons of their own. Whole worlds were being scorched into sterility; Earth herself had been threatened, even raided a time or two by the battlefleets of Melcon or her allies. Some in the High Command felt that it was only a matter of time before they either invaded Old Earth herself or rendered her uninhabitable.

Diaspora had been conceived as a means of preserving the human species, the ultimate just-in-case option. A number of old freighters had been outfitted as colony transports and sent off in every direction, with orders to go as far, as deep into unexplored sectors of the galaxy as they could before finding a likely world and settling down. The ships that founded the colony on Cloud were with the third wave.

"Some of those transports had military forces aboard, which gives you an idea of just how desperate things must have been. The First Armored, with our friend Hector along as primary fire support, well, there must've been one hell of a debate about sending such badly needed forces blindly out into the galaxy like that."

"I always wondered about that," she said. "More than just needing Bolos like Hector back on Earth, though, well, the histories I've seen emphasize that the Cloudan colony was part of a pacifist movement. Even anti-Imperial."

He chuckled. "It was. Back on Terra, a number of pacifist organizations opposed the war. In an earlier age, they might have been rounded up and imprisoned . . . or shot, or given weapons and marched off to the front lines whether they would fight or not. The High Command decided on a different approach, though. People who didn't want to fight the Melcons could still contribute to the human cause. And by getting the hell out of the war zone, they made it easier for the militarists to marshal the full resources of the Terran Empire toward the war effort."

"And they guaranteed the survival of humankind," she said. She looked up at the stars. "It's kind of reassuring to think that there might be dozens, even hundreds of other human worlds out there."

He gave a low-voiced, grim chuckle. "Optimist."

"What do you mean?"

"It gave us a chance, maybe. But we don't know how many of those colonies took root. Hell, the only one we *know* of was Cloud, because our great-grandparents were cut off from any contact with Earth and with the other colonies. For security. We don't know how the war turned out. We don't know if Earth survived. We know there's been no SWIFT contact with any other human world for over a century, now. We know the colony ships they sent out were the oldest, creakiest, leakiest rust-buckets left in the Imperial merchant fleet, so we can't even guess how many actually made it to new homes. And of those . . ." He shrugged. "How many ran afoul of Melcon patrols or outlying colonies or perimeter fortresses? How many started settlements but were wiped out by disease, or natural disaster, or hostile aliens in their sector? The only ones we know survived were . . . us. And we damned near didn't, at that."

"The pacifism didn't last long," she pointed out.

He chuckled. "The Gordonites and the Quakers and all those other pax-groups meant well," Jaime said. "But there's nothing like the need for survival on a harsh, new world to make folks, um, reassess even their deepest-held beliefs." In fact, there'd been a nasty little war with a nomadic alien race then in the region, the Vovoin. And that sharp tussle with the Ka'Juur, a strange, spacefaring empire of warlike beings dependent on other senses than sight.

There'd even been a brief, bloody civil war, forty years back, the so-called Outreach War, fought over whether or not Cloud should begin trying to seek out other civilizations in this new, thick-grown portion of the galaxy. The ones who'd favored trying to contact other civilizations had won in the end, mostly because they were the ones who controlled Hector. He hadn't been used in the fighting, according to the records, but just the *fact* of him had counted, apparently, for a good many battalions.

Jaime sighed. So much history. So much suffering. So much *promise* . . . and all of it leading nowhere if the !°!°! won.

"I think the jury's still out on Cloud." He continued looking up at the stars, tracing out the vast, thickly clotted knots of light surrounding the Galactic Core. The ground here was smooth, and the Bolo's huge tracks transmitted very little vibration to the two as they sat together high atop its gundeck. "When I look up at night," he said after a moment, "I'm afraid I can't let myself wonder how many human enclaves are out there. Instead, I find myself wondering how far-flung the clacker hegemony is. I wonder if there are Melcons out there, or worse. I wonder if humanity isn't so damned tiny and insignificant in the grand order of things that simply by daring to *be*, he's going to find the universe itself coming down and squashing him like a bug."

"I think if we were that insignificant," she said, "the universe wouldn't even notice. That's the problem, you know. How many human religions and philosophies throughout history have suggested that humankind is somehow set at the center of creation, the reason the universe *is?* The truth is, the universe doesn't really care. We have to make it on our own, one way or the other." She laughed. "But at least we know we're too small for the universe to take an active role in our extinction! All we have to worry about are *other* insignificant nothings out there, like the Melcons, the Deng, or the clackers!"

He shivered, but not from the cold. "Oh, great. I feel *much* better now."

She shifted her seat around the circular hatch, moving closer. "Cut the self-pity and c'mere, you."

He looked down into dark eyes. "Do you suppose," he said, "that if the universe really doesn't care about human affairs, that it won't mind if a self-made general kisses his senior Bolo technical sergeant?"

"Mmm. Let's find out," she said.

The universe didn't seem to care at all.

CHAPTER SEVENTEEN

During the past 145.6 hours, Sergeant Kyle has been making repairs in my power distribution network, removing small devices affixed to my primary energy couplings and feed directors which have been hampering my operations.

As a result of her repairs—in several cases jury-rigged with parts and materials originally intended for purposes far different than those she used them for—I can now draw 84.36 percent of the expected maximum output from my fusion reactors, a significant improvement over what was possible before.

My primary contra-gravity system is still completely down. My secondary system can generate approximately 20 to 25,000 tons of lift for short periods, enough, certainly, to help me navigate steep slopes or deep mud or to manage speeds in excess of 100 kph, but not enough to become airborne for any appreciable length of time, nor enough to enable me to reach my usual sprint speed of 500 kph.

My battle screens have been successfully repaired, however, and are fully operational. They will not be totally effective, of course, while I cannot draw full power from my reactors, but they will be effective in blocking or dissipating both the particle beams favored by !°!°! combat units and the blast, heat, and kinetic effects of both conventional and nuclear weapons.

In all, Sergeant Kyle has done a remarkable job with the limited tools and resources at her command. Complete repairs must, perforce, await my redeployment to a maintenance facility, specifically one equipped with cranes and contra-gravity levitators that will allow full access to my reactor core and power distribution blocks. However, I can confidently state that I am now combat ready, to a degree that would not have been possible just two weeks ago.

This, overall, is excellent news, the more so because of its unanticipated nature. While artificial intelligences such as my own are not expected to feel such anthropomorphic emotional responses as fear or nervous anticipation, any rational assessments of my future prospects on Cloud must address the high likelihood of my eventual destruction. Bolos are not indestructible, whatever popular human accounts might suggest, and sooner or later the Enemy will manage to bring sufficient forces together, either in space or on the planetary surface, to cripple or destroy me.

Indeed, I will remain an effective combatant only so long as I can maintain the maneuverability, the complete freedom of movement, that I have enjoyed in these past days. If the Enemy manages to box me in to any degree, I will only be able to engage in an ongoing but ultimately doomed last stand. The only remaining option would be if my operations eventually proved so costly to !°!°! plans that they eventually decided to cut their losses and abandon this world. Unfortunately, I cannot even speculate about that possibility. Too little is known about !°!°! motivations, goals, or, indeed, their numerical strength in this sector. I have attempted to learn more about the Enemy, both by examining the fragmentary memories available to *me since my period under their control, and by penetrating |°|°| communications. So far, my memories have yielded little of value, while my attempts to penetrate |°|°| communications and processing systems have met with uniform failure.*

I find myself looking forward to our expected escape from this world with what could only be considered a human sense of excitement and anticipation. I will be glad indeed to leave Cloud to the |°|°|, in exchange for service with the Grakaan.

The March is now within seventy kilometers of Stardown, and human scouts have already been deployed to make contact with the Tolun fleet.

I begin to allow myself to wonder if, possibly, the |°|°| have elected to allow us to leave in peace.

Timmit Mason was eight T-standard years old, and he'd been a handful ever since they'd left Fort Greeley, days before. "So why do we hafta leave home, huh?"

His mother sighed. They were walking in a ragged column with perhaps fifty others, most friends and neighbors from Fort Greeley who'd decided to accept Graham's offer of a new chance on another world. The word was that the main body, the March, was just ahead now, but they'd been walking for so long it was hard to think about anything anymore beyond the next day, the next rest, the next step.

A new chance, on a new world. It had sounded good at the time. Ever since Drew had been killed by the damned clackers as a demonstration, life in the little farming community had been hard, and getting harder, and she and a number of her neighbors had packed what they could carry and set off along one of the Bolo-hewn trails north, toward the mountains.

Now, though, with the mountains behind her, her back hurt, hunger gnawed, blisters hobbled every step, and Timmit's questions were becoming harder to answer. *Why* are *we doing this* . . . ?

"You know how things have . . . well, changed, since the machines came? How we have to work harder, and do what they say?"

"Yeah. . . ." Then with more finality. "They killed Daddy."

"Yes, and a lot of other people, too. We're leaving so we don't have to worry about them coming for us like they did for Daddy. We're leaving so we don't have to work for the machines any more, Timmit. We're going to . . . well, someplace else. Maybe even to another world. Where there won't be any more machines to tell us what to do."

Timmit frowned, doubtful. "Yeah, but . . . but the Bolo is a machine, isn't he?"

"Yes. The Bolo is a good machine."

"He won't make us work? Or hurt us if we do wrong? Or kill us?" They'd glimpsed the Bolo once, two days back, as it had thundered east past their little party on some unknown but urgent mission or other. Timmit had been awed . . . and very thoughtful afterward.

"No. The Bolo is here to protect us, Timmit. To help us. He's going to take us to the new place."

"They say his name is Hector. That's a funny name, but I like it. I like *him*. Even if he is a machine."

And that most decisively settled that, so far as Timmit was concerned.

Well, it was Timmit, more than anything else, that she was doing this for. If the machines killed her, well, it wouldn't be any great loss for an unfeeling cosmos. But Timmit. He deserved a chance, and she was going to see that he got it.

His mother trudged ahead through the gathering, footsore darkness and wondered if freedom could possibly be as simple as that. . . .

❖   ❖   ❖

Originally, centuries before, the structure humans called the Citadel had been built by the alien Vovoin, a spacefaring civilization that had little need for planets save as sources of certain necessary raw materials. During the brief but savage war with the Vovoin, scant decades after the human colonizers had arrived on Cloud and claimed it as their own, the Citadel had been captured by strike elements of the 1st Armored Assault Battalion and turned into a military command center. It had been used again for the same purpose later, in the war with the Ka'Juur; during the Outreach War, anti-outreach troops had seized it for a time for use as a staging area in their planned assault against Chryse, nearly a thousand kilometers to the west.

Until the arrival of the !°!°!, the Citadel had been little more than a historical curiosity, a strangely twisted and enigmatic tower of distinctly nonhuman proportions and geometries rising above the sprawling port city of Delphia. There'd been plans for converting the place eventually into a museum of human history on Cloud.

The arrival of the !°!°! had returned the nonhuman element to the Citadel, as intelligent machines clattered through its twisting passageways and bored their way into its walls. The immense !°!°! transport that had grounded on the blast-flattened rubble of what had once been Delphia's business district added now to the alienness of the place.

Bones, *human* bones, crunched underfoot as Albin Pogue, formerly a captain in the Cloud Defense Force, more recently chief of staff to General Spratly at Prison Camp 84, walked toward the dark, gray-green tower. Dewar Sykes fidgeted nervously at his side, darting fearful glances at the indifferent !°!°! machines to left and right as they were escorted up the broad walkway leading to the Citadel's entrance. As in Celeste, most of the population of Delphia had been incinerated when a hundred-ton chunk of rock had seared out of the sky and slammed into the outskirts of the city. Their remains carpeted the landscape, homogeneously blended with the strewn rubble and shattered debris that once had been a thriving human city. Only the Citadel, constructed of flintsteel and duralloy as tough as the hide of a Mark XXXIII Bolo, remained standing.

"I really don't know if this was a good idea," Sykes muttered.

"Shaddup," Pogue snapped. "You knew what we were getting in for here."

"Jeez, I didn't figure on gettin' dragged through a stinking bone yard!"

"Well, we'll have to talk to the maid service about that, won't we? Now shaddup!"

Ahead of them, the two-meter-tall floater that was their contact and guide to the clacker command center moved along in stately silence; two smaller machines, their sculpted bodies bristling with discharge antennae and particle cannon ports, followed behind as escorts.

Or guards. It was hard to tell the difference and, in fact, there probably was none, so far as the !°!°! were concerned.

The more Sykes fidgeted and fussed, the more determined Pogue became to see this thing through to the end. It had been three days now since he'd managed to slip away from the March, stealing an air car and fleeing south across the Veline Mountains until he made contact once more with Sykes's ragtag band of marauders, former turner guards from Camp 84 who'd been surviving these past several weeks by raiding human villages throughout the region. *That* activity would have to stop, and Pogue was the one who was going to stop it.

Just as soon as he was in charge of things and started giving the orders.

The hard part had been finding a clacker machine intelligent enough to recognize the password he'd learned back when he'd been a plant inside Camp 84, a carefully memorized collection of whistles, clicks, and clucks that, he'd been told, represented a series of numbers that would guarantee him safe passage to a high-ranking machine intelligence. Clacker Speakers had been in short supply south of the Velines since the Bolo had started its rampage, and it had taken several days to find one.

They'd managed, however. They'd nearly been electrocuted by the big floater that had disabled their vehicle before Pogue had been able to get the password out, but they'd finally been brought to the Citadel. According to the Speaker, the "Master Director is in residence here."

Past scuttling armies of long-legged robots no bigger than a man's head. Past a high-stacked mound of human skeletons. Through the vaulted entryway and into the cool near-darkness of the Citadel at last. Strange instrumentation rose in the shadows encircling the Citadel's ground floor; Pogue had the impression of numerous large machines lurking in the darkness, watching them with an inhuman precision and lack of emotion.

"What is it you wish to discuss?" The voice boomed out at them from somewhere overhead. It sounded human enough but, like all !°!°! imitations of human speech, was flat and utterly devoid of life. Sykes whimpered and seemed to be trying to squeeze his bulky frame behind Pogue's back.

"Where are you?" Pogue demanded.

"Here. All around you. My designation is DAV728-24389, and although I am physically resident in a complex on the larger moon of this world, my . . . you might call it my awareness, my presence, has been downloaded into the computers within this structure."

A screen visible against one of the strangely curving walls of the place showed an eerie duo of brightly

colored shapes, vaguely human in outline. It took
Pogue a moment to realize that he was seeing himself
and Sykes through !°!°! sensory pickups, with images
strongly registering in the infrared and with just a trace
of visible wavelengths thrown in on top. *God, is that
how they see us?* he thought. *No wonder they've been
out to exterminate us!*

That would change too. Damn it, a century from
now, the humans of Cloud would revere Albin Pogue
as their savior!

"I was told that you had information for us. My
records indicate that you have provided information
before, concerning human activities within Camp 84."

"Yeah. Yeah, that's right. And you guys didn't do
anything about what I was telling you, either, and you
see what it got you?"

"Jeez, Pogue!" Sykes said, clutching his shoulder.
"Don't get 'em any madder than they already are!"

"Shaddup. I told you, let me do the talking." He
looked up into the dark shadows overhead, defiant.
"You ignored what I told you about Valhalla, and the
escape plans. Graham got the Bolo working, and now
you've got a slave revolt on your hands."

"Events at Camp 84 have tended to verify the
information you have transmitted in the past. How
can you assist us now?"

"Man, I can give you General Graham and his pet
Bolo. I know exactly where they are now, and exactly
where they're headed. I know what they're planning
on doing, when, and where." Taking a step to one side,
he reached out and snagged Sykes's arm, roughly
propelling the man forward a step. "I also have with
me here the leader of an independent human army.
My army, in fact. It's not very large, but they follow
my orders, and they do what they're told. We can
provide you with some options you probably didn't
know you had. Take down Graham and his cronies in

a nice, surgical strike that'll leave you machines with nothing left but some mop-up!"

"If all we wanted was Graham's death," the machine's voice pointed out, "we could achieve that by locating his position and detonating thermonuclear devices in his vicinity until nothing organic remained viable. Or we could bombard his position with planetoids. The Bolo could not stop them all if we saturated the area."

Pogue chuckled. "Actually, your real problem is the Bolo, am I right? Every damned time you send more of your machine soldiers after that thing, it just burns 'em down like they were made out of tissue paper and string. I'm guessing, though, that maybe you want to get it back and under your control again."

"Further study of the Bolo would enhance our understanding of our own origins."

"Huh? You want to—"

"This information is not vital for our security, however. If necessary, we will destroy it, and the humans."

"To destroy it, friend, you're going to have to have it given to you. You're not just going to walk in and take it."

"How can we gain operational control? Is this what you are offering us?"

"It is indeed, my clacker friend. It is indeed! I can give you that Bolo. With a little help from you, and, um, certain assurances that you will be suitably grateful, I'll give you the Bolo, all wrapped up with a bow on top!"

"Wrappings and bows are not necessary . . . nor do I understand why they would be desirable."

"Forget it. Figure of speech."

"How would you accomplish what !°!°! forces have been unable to carry out?"

"Well, I'm not going to tell you everything, of course. Not now. But I can tell you that Jaime Graham is the key. Get his cooperation, and you'll have the Bolo."

"And how do I acquire Jaime Graham's cooperation?"

"By having the people he cares about in your control, of course. There're a number of people among the renegade humans that he cares about a lot. Shari Barstowe. Alita Kyle. Wal Prescott. Dieter Hollinsworth. All you need to do is torture them with him watching, maybe just threaten to torture them, and he'll do anything you want . . . including order the Bolo to obey your instructions."

"What is 'torture'?"

The question shocked Pogue. How could these inhuman, murdering machines not know the effects of what they'd done to the people they'd experimented with in the camps . . . ?

No. Of *course* they didn't understand. How could a machine comprehend pain, grief, or despair? He'd guessed right. They did *not* understand humans! He was going to be able to make himself invaluable here!

"Torture is . . . well, just imagine harvesting them. But real, real slowly. The idea is to cause as much pain and fear in the subject as you can, without killing them. Now, it probably won't work on Graham himself. But do that to Graham's friends, one by one, and he'll help you to get you to stop."

"You will advise us in this? Humans are fragile. Easily damaged beyond repair."

"Don't worry. I can show you *exactly* how to get what you want."

"Why?"

"Why what? Take down Graham? Because he's your big problem, him and that pet Bolo of his."

"Why are you willing to help us in this way? I would not have expected one of your species to make such an offer."

Pogue took a deep breath. It was impossible to tell from the sound of the machine intelligence's artificial voice what it was thinking. Was it surprised? Suspicious? Or simply curious? "Obviously, there's something I want in exchange for helping you. I told you, I want assurances. And I want payment."

"What?"

"When your conquest of Cloud is complete, you're going to need a human leader to manage the place for you, a governor. Someone who can make the population productive. *Efficient*. Make it so your combat units can be used elsewhere, extending your empire. I can do this for you."

"Why should a human wish to further !°!°! interests on this world?"

"You don't trust me, is that it?" Pogue spread his hands in what he very much hoped would be seen as a gesture of sincerity, and sidestepped DAV's question. "Look, after betraying my own kind, I won't be able to find refuge with *them*, right? I'd *have* to work for you. Hell, the only thing I *can* do is serve you, to the very best of my ability."

"You will give us the information we require." The machine paused. "Perhaps we could try this slow harvesting you mentioned, on you."

"Ah! Ah! Not so fast, machine. I told you, I'm the leader of an army. Now, maybe you don't think humans are all that good when it comes to a fight, but I can tell you different. My guess is you've got your metal hands full right now trying to track down the Bolo. You're not going to want to have to fight my people too. So what'll it be? Accept my help in bringing Graham and that Bolo down? Or fight the Bolo *and* my people?"

Pogue knew his reasoning was thin. What he was hoping was that the !°!°! couldn't tell just how desperately thin it was. Sykes's "army," after all, was nothing more than a band of marauders who'd been spending the last couple of weeks raping, murdering, pillaging the free villages, thugs with guns who *might* do what they were told, if there was sufficient inducement behind the command.

But the !°!°! couldn't know that. Or, at least, they couldn't be sure. And he was certain that the Bolo had them worried.

"Very well," the machine voice replied after a long moment's silence. "There is logic in what you have proposed. You will have the opportunity to demonstrate that you can deliver what you claim."

DAV728 considered the humans' information for a long time after the creatures were dismissed. More, though, he considered the creatures themselves. They were . . . indescribable. Impossible. Strange. He knew now that was going to need to spend some more time trying to get to know and understand his fifth brain, the human one taken from the Bolo's commander during the invasion. He'd held several sessions with it already, probing the consciousness that still resided there, deep within the complex web work of interconnected organic neural components. Humans, DAV was beginning to believe, would never yield to rational analysis or comprehension.

How was he supposed to respond to this? Thanks to Albin Pogue, the !°!°! now knew with precision what had been guesswork before, that the human renegades had struck an agreement with the Tolun for passage off-world, that they were planning to rendezvous with Tolun ships at the Stardown spaceport. With that information, it would be simplicity itself to use the mobile bastions, when they arrived, to trap the Bolo and its human attendants and incinerate them.

For several million nanoseconds, DAV actually considered allowing the humans to leave. It wasn't as though a few thousand OI slaves, more or less, would make any kind of a difference in !°!°! plans for this world, and even the Bolo, while a fascinating example of primitive machine evolution, was not worth the effort it would take to recapture and reprogram it again. If the humans wished to leave, let them. They weren't worth the trouble they'd caused already, and vengeance was not a !°!°! racial trait. He discarded the idea almost at once, however. While more characteristic of organic life forms, politics occasionally afflicted the !°!°! hierarchies of serial brain complexes. If the Ninth Awareness had weakened the military campaign against the distant Grakaan to provide him with three mobile bastions, it would be better for DAV728's prospects for continued growth, enrichment, and advancement if he used them, as promised, to eliminate the Bolo and the renegade humans once and for all.

Besides, if the human's words could be trusted, the renegade plan called for them to join the Grakaan. Giving them Bolo technology—not to mention firsthand experience with !°!°! combat tactics and strategies—was nothing less than stupid.

And if the !°!°! were at times inflexible, narrow-minded, even rigid in their ways of thinking, they were *not* stupid.

What bothered DAV more than anything else, however, was Pogue's treason. He believed the human's offer to be genuine. That, in fact, was the problem. For any !°!°! to reject its programming and turn on its fellows was . . . not merely impossible, but literally unthinkable from any !°!°! perspective. DAV had difficulty even trying to imagine the concept of such a thing. That difficulty drove home more than anything else how completely, how utterly alien the humans were.

And the faster they were exterminated, the better. The agreement he'd just made with Pogue, of course, would last only for as long as it was convenient. After

all, one did not enter into binding agreements with
organics, or allow them to dictate policy. . . .

Maker of the First Program! How could any member
of any *sane* species possibly even consider the betrayal
its own kind?

I'm having the damnedest strange dream. . . .

But Jeff Fowler had the nagging feeling that this
was *not* a dream. And if it weren't, the only way he
could interpret the experience was to assume that he
was dead and that this was hell.

He remembered perfectly everything up to the
moment when the asteroid had come howling down
almost on top of Chryse Base. He remembered the
argument with Spratly, remembered the order to have
Hector hold his fire . . . and then the cosmos had
erupted in thunder and flame, and he remembered
very little after that.

What he did remember was . . . disturbing. He was
aware of having awakened on several occasions, but
each time to darkness, to an emptiness of no sound,
no feeling, no bodily sensation of any sort. It was like
being in a sensory deprivation tank, but worse. He
had nothing to look at, nothing to experience save his
own memories and thoughts.

No, that wasn't quite accurate. Some of what he
was hearing in his own mind he was quite certain were
not his thoughts. They came from . . . from someplace
else, in a fashion that he could not quite grasp. It was
like hearing a multitude of conversations, but from
the room next door, with the voices muffled by walls
and distance.

One voice, in particular, was louder, more demanding
than the others. He didn't hear it so much as feel it,
a drilling, penetrating demand for information, for
feelings, for memories. Usually, it wanted information
about the Bolo; more than once, Jeff had wondered

if he'd been captured and was undergoing some sort of interrogation by his captors, possibly under the influence of drugs. If so, it was a particularly efficient form of interrogation. When his questioner asked for something, related thoughts floated to the surface of Jeff's mind, unbidden, beyond his control, and he could feel that other mind skimming off the thoughts as they rose, sampling them, storing them, using them as simply as if Jeff had been no more than a reference text.

Would you betray your own kind? The voice demanded. *Do you know of humans who have betrayed their own kind?*

The thoughts, though wordless, were nonetheless clear. His questioner seemed more interested this time in humans and how they interacted, than in the Bolo.

Maybe his captors were having a rough time with the CDF. He certainly hoped so.

Hope, at the moment, was the only thing he had . . . and there was precious little of that.

Who are you? What relationships with other humans did you have? Shari . . . who is this Shari you are thinking of . . . ?

Eventually, the questions ceased, and Jeff Fowler was allowed to lapse once again into a vague, gray, semiconscious state.

Lance Leader Shari Barstowe cautiously raised her head above the wall, taking care, as they'd trained her, not to let her head show in silhouette against the twin, setting suns at her back. The magviewer she held to her eyes had been recovered from one of the old CDF bases—Chryse, possibly, or perhaps Fort Greeley—and either the batteries were old and nearly drained, or there was a loose connection inside somewhere. The picture was broken and fogged by static, and the azimuth and range readouts weren't even showing up as she panned the optics across the field below her position.

No matter. They functioned well enough.

Shari was part of a Brotherhood scout team operating well ahead of the March. Her new rank and title of Lance Leader still bothered her a bit; two weeks ago she'd still been a civilian, if you didn't count her programming work and watch standing with Hector. Wal Prescott himself had insisted she take the position, though. The Brotherhood was expanding and they needed good people, experienced or not, and he claimed she had what was needed to lead a lance of five scouts, most of them as new to this as she was.

Carefully, she swept the skyline, checking the city before examining targets closer at hand. The field below the hillside was the landing field for Stardown Spaceport; the control tower and maintenance facilities rose from the water's edge two kilometers further to the northeast. Stardown itself, a small city that had been largely abandoned after The Killing but had suffered only relatively minor damage, followed the curve of Falcon Bay toward the south. There was no movement there, no sign of life.

Shari felt a cold, sinking sensation as she turned her magviewer to the spaceport field. This was where they were supposed to meet the Tolun transports, sometime tomorrow or within another couple of days.

Tolun merchant ships were graceful, swan-necked affairs, slender forward, broad and bulbous aft. Their paint schemes carried on the Tolun fascination with stark color contrasts—in this case a deep crimson with violent slashes of pale yellow-green. You couldn't miss them.

Which was why Shari felt that icy, leaden sinking in the pit of her stomach. There was only a single Tolun ship present; hell, it was the only ship present . . . and it couldn't mass more than five thousand tons.

There was no way that a single five-thousand-ton transport was going to carry more than two thousand people off-world . . . to say nothing of a thirty-two-thousand-ton Bolo.

"How the hell are we getting two thousand people off-planet in *that?*" Sandy McCall said quietly. He was crouched behind the wall, his LGE-3130 rifle braced against the upper row of stones.

"My question exactly," she told him. "I'd say we've just been stood up."

"Well . . . maybe they're just not here yet?" He sounded hopeful, as though wishing could make it so. Hell, he was just a kid, no more than nineteen standard.

"The idea, lancer," she said quietly, patiently, "was for them to be here first. They're *supposed* to be here, picking up their high-tech baubles, right? Doesn't make any sense having us come first and bring half the clucker army after us, just so we could wait for them to put in an appearance." She lowered the magviewer. "No, I don't like the looks of this one little bit. And, you know? I think Jaime Graham's going to like it even less."

against ...

CHAPTER EIGHTEEN

*My Commander has ordered me to go to full alert.
If the Tolun have betrayed us, an Enemy attack may
be imminent.*

*I have, of course, continued passive scanning of local
space. Without access to relay satellites or orbital drones,
however, I am effectively blind to half of the sky—that
half which is blocked by the bulk of Cloud itself. Within
the past 14.4 hours, I have noted a 12% increase in
!°!°! inbound traffic but have picked up nothing that
appears to represent a direct threat to me or my mission.*

*Were I in the Enemy's place, I would consider
deploying heavy units against me, moving them in
close from the antipodes where I would not be able
to detect their approach. Against such an assault, there
is little I can do, save maintain a high alert status
and remain prepared for immediate, high-speed
movement. My single advantage in this situation is
my maneuverability, which should give me a decisive
edge against any of the different types of !°!°! ground
units I have encountered so far.*

*I wonder, however, what part the Tolun are playing
in this drama.*

❖   ❖   ❖

"Not my fault, this is!" Trade Factor Sshejevaalgh squeaked. "Fair I am! Fair I am! You, I will help!"

They stood in the shadow of Sshejevaalgh's red-and-yellow-green ship. The Tolun factor had emerged alone when Jaime, Alita, and Shari Barstowe's five-man Brotherhood lance had arrived at first sunrise in an air car, dismounted, and banged rudely on the hatch with the butt of a KVK-7 pulse rifle.

"I'm fair, too," Jaime told the alien. He held the being's scrawny neck between both hands, applying just enough pressure to threaten the Tolun's vulnerable windpipe. "I might even just kill you right now, instead of ripping it out of your living hide!"

"A . . . mistake, that would be!" The Tolun had been holding Jaime's wrists with his four-fingered hands, trying to pry them free, but he let go now and pointed up and to the left. A ball-mounted turret in the brightly painted ship's hull had rotated, and the muzzle was aimed now at the party of humans. "The word, I will give," the Tolun gasped, "and burn, all of you will!"

"Maybe you've left us nothing to live for!" Jaime tightened his grip ever so slightly. The factor's black-and-gold eyes bulged huge.

"D-don't this do!" he gasped. "Survive this yet, you can! But my help, you need!"

"Maybe we should hear him out." Alita folded her arms. "We can always kill him later."

"I think we should fry him where he stands," Shari said. She placed the muzzle of her weapon against the side of the Tolun's flat head. "Think your people can kill us before we kill you, fish-face?"

"Automatic, the weapon is," Sshejevaalgh gasped. "If I die, fire, it does. And then no one to help you, you have."

"As you were, Lance Leader," Jaime said. He relaxed his own grip but only to shove the Tolun back a step until its spine pressed against the curved hull of his ship. "You actually still think you can bargain with us, Sshejevaalgh? What do you have that we could possibly want from you, after you betrayed us?"

"It, not my fault is," the Tolun said again, weakly. "This help, I could not."

"Yeah? I thought the honesty of the Tolun was supposed to be legendary," Jaime said. "I thought you guys were supposed to honor contracts!"

"We . . . we do! In this case, overruled, I was! My superiors on the council, my contract disallowed! Contract with the !°!°! already, they had! This, when agreement we made, I know did not!"

"Contract with the machines? To do what?"

"Yeah," Alita put in. "Maybe they hired you guys to oil 'em up once in a while? Perform maintenance? Hundred-thousand-klick checkups?"

"Enough, Sergeant." He tightened his grip on the being's skinny neck. "What I want to know," he said, his voice low and deadly, "is why you came to the rendezvous at all! If you're going to take our down payment and leave us here to die, why'd you come at all? For the fun of watching?"

"All of you, and your Bolo, to the Grakaan worlds we cannot take. The council's agreement with the !°!°! such an agreement expressly prohibits. More, word, a rumor within the council, there is. You, Jaimegraham, and your lieutenants, captured, must be, and to the supreme !°!°! director conveyed."

"What," Jaime demanded, "the machines want us captured?"

"To our council, the machines this demand have made."

"Interesting," Alita said. "The cluckers've never thought of us as individuals before. Looks like they're learning some new tricks."

"Yeah. I wonder if it's with Tolun help?"

"For much technology, the Council to help the !°!°!

agreed. To turn you over to the !°!°!, they did not. And I . . . . I with this betrayal could not live. That is why I to the rendezvous came."

"Oh? And what are you going to do for us?" He glanced up at the brightly patterned ship. "We'll need ten or fifteen more ships of this size to take all of our people off. And we'll need a transport ten times bigger than this to manage our Bolo."

"All of your people, we cannot take," Sshejevaalgh replied. His arms moved in an indecipherable alien gesture. "But some, save we can. This much, the !°!°! technology already delivered, purchased, it has. Two hundred, perhaps two hundred fifty, in the hold of my vessel can fit. To Grakaan space, fly I cannot. But to another world of your choice you and those closest to you could conveyed be. *Live*, you could!"

"And abandon the rest of our people here?" Jaime growled. "Not damned likely!"

"But . . . but *die* you will, if to stay you decide!"

"Then we'll die," Alita snapped. "But we're not leaving without our friends!"

"And we'll damned sure take a bunch of cluckers with us," Shari added. "*They're* the ones who are gonna need the contract with you people to get off-world!"

"Irrational, this is," the Tolun said. "Passage off-world, purchased you already have! Why cannot you this accept?"

"Because we'd have to live with ourselves afterwards," Jaime told him. "Now get the hell out of here, before we decide to requisition your ship!"

"Yeah," Shari said. "We could use it against the cluckers. One look at that thing's paint scheme, and their optics'd be fried to a crisp!"

"General Graham?" a familiar voice intoned in Jaime's earpiece.

Jaime touched the earpiece. "Yeah, Hector. You been listening in on this?"

"I have. I have also been monitoring !°!°! movements in the vicinity of Cloud and have information somewhat more pressing than the Tolun betrayal. An extremely large spacecraft is approaching Stardown from the east. The vessel is skimming the wave tops and has only just appeared on my scans. At its current speed, it should arrive at your position within five minutes. In addition, I have begun picking up gravitic pulses from both the northwest and the southwest. These pulses are identical to those emanating from the first craft and probably indicate that two additional large ships are inbound, though they are still well below my horizon."

"Roger that, Hector. Notify Colonel Prescott. We're on our way back."

"Speed is indicated, my Commander. This has the look of trap."

"That it does, Hector. Button up and prepare for action. We're coming in." He looked at the others. "Let's move!"

They sprinted for their waiting air car, leaving Trade Factor Sshejevaalgh of the Tolun staring after them in utter and alien bewilderment.

I have confirmed the approach now of three large spacecraft, each approximately fifty times more massive than one of the old Conestoga-class freighters. Their energy and contra-gravity signatures are definitely those of !°!°! craft; their relatively low speed and clumsy movements suggest that they are, indeed, transports of some type.

The nearest craft, which I have designated Target Alpha, is approaching at a bearing of zero-nine-three at a current range of twenty-seven kilometers, accompanied by at least five smaller vessels. I am withholding fire because my Commander and several other friendlies are in close proximity.

Target Bravo is approaching from a bearing of one-two-seven, range now an estimated fifty-three kilometers. Target Charlie is approaching from three-one-eight, range fifty-nine kilometers. Both Bravo and Charlie are within range of indirect fire strategic weapons. Again, however, there is a danger of friendly casualties if I begin releasing warheads from my nuclear arsenal. The main body of human refugees lies only twelve kilometers to the south and is in serious jeopardy. All weapons are charged, and I am in Full Combat Mode.

I await my Commander's orders. . . .

"My God," Shari called from the backseat of the open-topped air car. "Look at that!"

Jaime yanked hard on the control stick, slewing the little grav-effect vehicle around and bringing it to a bobbing hover.

"Jesus!" Lancer Galbreith, one of the troopers perched in the back, exclaimed. "It's a goddamned floating *city* . . . !"

Jaime had been guiding the crowded air car up the slope of the ridge west of the Stardown Spaceport, navigating between the broken ruins of buildings and walls that grew from the soil like dragon's teeth. He held the air car steady, watching the dark gray mass drifting in from the sea, its shadow swallowing the city of Stardown like a slow-moving black flood, then spilling across the spaceport control tower and terminals and rippling across the landing field tarmac. The craft, moving ponderously over the city now, was roughly egg-shaped in outline, though much longer and wider than it was thick. It was flattened on the bottom, rounded on the top, and only gradually, as it drew nearer, did Jaime realize that what looked like a smooth, matte surface was in fact encrusted with bulges, bumps, and complex patterns of towers, pits, and less identifiable shapes, all nearly lost against the vast scale of the ship.

"What would you say, Alita?" Jaime asked, whispering not from a need to remain unheard by that floating mountain but simply from sheer awe. "A kilometer and a half long?"

She was studying it through a magviewer. "Closer to two," she replied, "if this thing's trig functions are set right. I don't even want to guess what that thing masses."

Jaime considered calling Hector and asking for his estimates, but decided against it. The information, he decided, would be too depressing.

Closer at hand, the Tolun ship lifted from the ground with a piercing whine of stressed contra-gravs, its aft plasma thrusters glowing white-hot as it started a steep, tight turn away from the oncoming behemoth.

"Looks like this caught them by surprise, too," Shari observed. "Think they'll make it?"

"That's up to the clackers," Jaime replied. "I don't think there's much the Tolun can do about it, at this point."

The brightly painted, swan-necked transport accelerated, racing for open sky. For a moment, it looked as though they were going to make it; then a bright smear of dazzlingly intense, white light leaped from the rim of the advancing transport, engulfing the Tolun ship, burning through it . . . and then the hapless vessel disintegrated in a radiant blossom that hurt the eyes and cast wavering shadows from the ruins on the hillside. The crack of sound, the rumbling detonation, reached the human watchers long seconds later, as a thin scattering of fiery fragments trailing smoke rained across the field.

"It looks like the cluckers have definitely revoked the Toluns' landing privileges here," Alita said.

"At least they've revoked Sshejevaalgh's landing rights," Jaime said. "Not to mention Sshejevaalgh."

The transport cleared the distant port terminal

buildings and settled gradually toward the tarmac, its contra-grav fields stirring up a swirling storm of dust and debris. The vessel had no landing legs or grounding gear; when its flat belly reached the pavement, it simply kept going, shattering the pavement with a staccato string of cracks and booms, until it had sunk into the ground by a depth of almost a meter.

Only gradually did Jaime become aware of other !°!°! vessels and machines drifting past the sheer-cliff sides of the grounded transport like fish skimming the side of a reef. Several, he saw now, were also settling to the tarmac, transports of more ordinary scale that began unloading machines of various designs.

"I hope to hell Hector is picking this up," Jaime said softly. Not that he had any idea as to how the Bolo was going to deal with this invasion.

"He is," Alita told him. She was still pressing the magviewer to her eyes, scanning the huge shape with slow, even sweeps. "I've got my viewer keyed to transmit everything, and he's acknowledged pickup of the feed."

"Hector?" Jaime said, touching his earpiece. "What do you make of this thing?"

"Interesting," the Bolo's voice replied. "Discounting the battlers employed by the !°!°!, which are simply converted asteroids, I have never seen a transport of this size. I am curious as to what it is carrying in its cargo holds."

Jaime bit back an exclamation of both agreement and despair. He'd been so shocked by the sheer size of the monster vessel that he'd not even thought about what the thing might be carrying.

"Listen, Hector," he said. "Whatever that beast is carrying, it's not going to be good. Can you cover the withdrawal of our people?"

"Affirmative. I recommend, however, that we move

onto the offensive as quickly as possible. Our goal should remain one of covered evacuation. We must get as many of our people off-planet as possible."

A remote, watcher's piece of Jaime's mind noted that Hector had said "*our* people," identifying himself more closely with Jaime and the other humans of the military escort than he'd heard before.

"Go on the offensive?" Jaime repeated. His voice was shaking, and he fought to bring it back under control. "You are out of your AI mind."

"Negative. I further suggest that you and the others with you should get as far away from the !°!°! transport as you can. Things are liable to get rather hot in that area quite soon."

"Copy that. We're moving." He looked at the others. "Hang on. We're going to do some traveling!"

"L-look at that thing!" Lancer Dobbs called from the backseat. "It's opening up!"

Everyone in the air car sat death still, staring at the immense !°!°! construct. It was opening up, but not in the sense of a hatch or cargo bay door opening. Instead, the entire forward two-thirds of the craft appeared to be unfolding as though it were some titanic child's puzzle with hinged sides, flanges, and sections. Most prominent, a tall, angular tower, like the fin of some enormous sea beast, was rising slowly into a vertical position from a recess in the thing's back. Turrets, some as large as an entire Mark XXXIII Bolo, emerged from cavernous bays. With a sound like thunder, and the clanging detonations of huge magnetic locks swinging free, the forward half of the transport rose slowly, separating itself from the stationary rear section, which remained mired in the shattered pavement of the landing field. On shrieking contra-gravs, then, the front part of the vehicle drifted slowly forward; the craft, it seemed, was less a genuine transport than a colossal war machine with a space drive temporarily attached for transport purposes. Levitated several meters above the ground by contra-gravity generators, the vehicle nonetheless created an awesome ground pressure that continued to crack and splinter the landing field pavement as it slowly advanced, sending up billowing clouds of dust to either side.

"Not *deus ex machina*," Jaime said quietly, breaking the stunned, almost reverent silence in the car. "More like *deus* est *machina*. . . ."

"What did you say?" Alita asked.

"Never mind. The so-called benefits of a classical education." He shook his head in amazement. "And here, all along, I've been thinking the clackers were somehow . . . I don't know, *poor*. Resource starved. Like they had to scavenge every bit of wire, every piece of alloy. But if they can build like that, they can do anything, anything at all. . . ."

"How well do you think that thing manages hills?" Alita asked.

"It probably can't climb very well," Jaime ventured.

"So what?" Shari replied. "It can just flatten the goddamned mountain and go right over it. Let's get the hell out of here, General!"

"I'm with you!" He turned the stick, depressing the accelerator button as the car swung left. Seconds later, they were hurtling down the far side of the ridge as quickly as the little vehicle's grav thrusters could carry it.

And there are two more *of those monsters out there*? Jaime thought wildly. He had no doubt that the other two targets Hector had detected were similar !°!°! machines, deliberately landed to surround the Bolo and the renegade humans, trapping them immobile in the center.

Like many other humans who'd worked with them, Jaime Graham had come to think of Bolos as indestructible, invincible. He knew better now. These mobile fortresses of the !°!°! were *mountains* somehow transformed into killing machines.

And he didn't see how anything, even a Bolo, could possibly stand against them.

CHAPTER NINETEEN

After scanning all available information on ⟨°⟨°⟨ units and assets, I have come to the conclusion that the Enemy vehicles now moving against me are of the general type known as Type 71, Series 40s, with an overlaid set of ⟨°⟨°⟨ phonemes that might best be transliterated as "mobile bastion." They are extremely slow, capable of a maximum speed on force impellers of no more than a few tens of kilometers per hour. They possess firepower, however, proportionate to their size and evident power-generating capabilities, probably on the order of some tens of megatons per second.

My principle advantage in a contest with these war machines is my maneuverability, an advantage somewhat restricted by my need to protect the human refugees. Even with full maneuverability and the advantage of being able to choose my own ground and combat timing, I would be hard-pressed to defeat even one of these machines. To defeat three simultaneously is out of the question.

Three defeated in sequence is a possibility, however, albeit a slim one. I spend .016 second reviewing my historical data, in particular the Valley Campaign of

*General Thomas Jackson—the immortal "Stonewall"—
during the American Civil War. During the spring of
1862, Jackson's small and badly outnumbered unit of
approximately 3,000 effectives, the "Stonewall Brigade,"
was threatened by no fewer than three Enemy armies,
under Generals Shields, Banks, and Fremont, as well
as supporting elements of other forces. During a six-
week period, Jackson's troops marched four hundred
miles, engaged in five major battles, and fought almost
daily skirmishes, defeating and demoralizing each army
sent against them, always maneuvering in such a way
as to prevent the Enemy forces from uniting.*

*I reflect, too, on the three-year campaign of
Spartacus, when an army of former slaves defeated
each army in turn that the Roman Republic sent
against them. The true master of this type of campaign,
however, was the incomparable Napoleon, who
routinely outmarched his opponents and defeated
them in detail—sometimes fighting two battles on
the same day—time after time, at Marengo, at
Austerlitz, at Ulm, at Jena-Auerstadt, and most
notably in the ultimately disastrous but undeniably
brilliant campaign of 1814, before the gates of Paris.*

*The example of Napoleon contains a cautionary
example as well, however. During the Leipzig Campaign
of 1813, Napoleon attempted to outmaneuver and defeat
in detail several advancing allied armies. By maintaining
constant pressure, however, three separate and powerful
allied armies converged on Napoleon at Leipzig from
different directions and crushed him. The situation I
find myself in now is perhaps most reminiscent of that
campaign, as three powerful units maneuver toward
my position from different directions.*

*To have any chance of defeating the Enemy in detail,
I must move swiftly and with decisiveness. The mobile
bastion just deployed at Stardown, is the closest and,
therefore, my first target.*

*Launching four VLS RP-12 battlefield recon drones,
I accelerate to 105 kps and begin racing to the east.*

DAV728 was no longer physically ensconced within
the Delamar base. He'd told the Ninth Awareness that
he intended to personally see to the capture or
destruction of the Bolo and the escaped humans, and
he meant that literally. When the three mobile bastions,
each attached to its transport module, arrived in-
system, he'd boarded a shuttle and transferred himself
to one of the series 40 bastions, hooking himself in-
parallel with the two resident !°!°! brains.

Technically, he now was a seventh-level intelligence,
though the series 40 brains were limited in scope to
the mechanics necessary for navigating space and
maneuvering on the ground. The bastion's sensor array
was a powerful one, however, ideally suited to long-
range and extended combat, and offering complete
flexibility in how he interfaced with other combat and
reconnaissance units. He could communicate easily
with the other bastions, with units in space, and with
recon satellites in low orbit.

As the transport module settled to the ground and
automated systems began separating the bastion from
its carrier, he brought his fifth brain, the human brain,
forward in consciousness. He'd relied on the information
stored in Jeff Fowler's brain to give him general insights
into human nature, as well as for specific details about
the Bolo and how it was programmed. Now, though,
he wanted the human brain fully on-line, ready to
provide millisecond-by-millisecond commentary on
what the Bolo was doing, why, and how best to defeat
it.

As he opened the necessary connections, he felt the
organic brain's confusion and dissociation as it regained
consciousness, followed an instant later by an intense
emotional reaction that was probably discontentment

at its current condition. No matter. That lump of highly organized jelly was an excellent storage unit for raw data, but could no longer exercise a will or decision-making power of its own. It was now, in fact, one part of his own brain, a very small part, a means of gaining insight into the enemy's tactics and language, nothing more.

As he framed questions and squeezed, the information he sought floated to the surface, easily skimmed and read. The Bolo, he saw, would attempt to use its superior speed and maneuverability against the self-evidently slower and clumsier mobile bastions.

No surprises there. It was the approach DAV himself would have used, had the circumstances been reversed. And it was a tactic easily countered. . . .

Jaime was vectoring the air car west, toward the March encampment, when the morning sky suddenly turned white, filling from horizon to horizon with a piercing, searing radiance. The shockwave struck moments later, first as a rumble of sound, then as a hot wind gusting across the plain, carrying dust and torn bits of vegetation with it. He swerved the vehicle sharply, slipping it into the lee of an outcropping of house-sized boulders. As he cut the contra-gravs and grounded the car, they vaulted the sides and scrambled for cover against the comforting solidity of the rocks.

"What is that?" Lancer Evans called, her hair whipping around her face from beneath her helmet. "A nuke?"

"It's still going!" Shari replied, shouting to make herself heard. "I don't think so!"

Jaime shook his head. "Hellbore barrage!" he shouted. "Cover your ears!"

And then speech became impossible as the thunder erupted anew and louder. The seven of them—Jaime and Alita and the five Brotherhood scouts—huddled together, hands pressed over their ears, mouths open to relieve the pressures that were fast becoming intolerable.

My initial barrage lasts 22.2 seconds and consists of a steady ripple fire from my 20cm Hellbores, stiffened every 3.7 seconds by a shot from one or the other of my 200cm main batteries. At a range now of 19.5 kilometers, Target Alpha is just visible on the horizon and vulnerable to line-of-sight fire. It answers my barrage with lasers and heavy particle beams, nothing I cannot counter or shrug off with relative ease. The !°!°! do not appear to possess a weapon comparable to my Hellbores, fortunately. But what the Enemy bastion lacks in quality, it more than makes up for with quantity. Its return fire is steady, heavy, and highly accurate.

I surmise that Alpha's primary mission will be to pin me in place while Bravo and Charlie move in closer from my rear. I could break off entirely now and have a fair chance of escaping all three Enemy combat units, but that would mean sacrificing the refugees, whose encampment is located inside the Enemy's contracting triangle.

I cannot afford to play the Enemy's game, on his terms and by his rules. I will choose my own ground.

As my initial Hellbore barrage ends, I slew left, triggering a barrage from my four 240cm howitzers. As expected, the Enemy targets all of the projectiles before they strike, vaporizing them with flickering lances of laser and particle beam fire, but the distraction gives me the time I need—approximately 10.2 seconds—to accelerate to 125 kph and slip into the mouth of a broad, shallow gully. According to data downlinked from my drones, that gully leads to the northeast for 14 kilometers, then swings sharply east, opening into a dunes region near the shore.

I deliver a parting barrage from my 40cm BL mortars. Though limited to a range of 9.75 kilometers, they will lay down a dense blanket of smoke and anti-laser aerosols as I race into the gully. This route will give me partial cover as I flank Target Alpha and will also open the range between myself and the human encampment to the south. It should bring me out some fifteen kilometers northwest of the city and quite close to the shoreline.

"My God," Shari said, rubbing her ears. "I thought that was Armageddon!"

"Is it over?" Lancer Dobbs asked.

"No way," Alita replied. She was standing up, leaning against the largest of the boulders as she peered around the side, trying to see what was happening. "Can't see much from here, but I think that was just an initial exchange of love taps."

"Love taps!" Lancer Galbreith exclaimed. "I thought for a minute, there, they were using planet-busters!"

"They seem to be pulling off toward the north," Jaime observed. He stood up next to Alita and studied the terrain beyond the outcropping. The entire plain was wreathed in a heavy, low-lying mist, and the ridge they'd just crossed blocked his view to the east. He could hear the !°!°! bastion, however, a steady, rippling cacophony of cracks and pops as its contra-gravity fields slowly crawled along a resisting, loudly protesting ground surface. For a moment, he considered calling Hector over the comm link but decided against it. He could add nothing to the Bolo's ability to manage this battle and might even distract it.

He was still badly shaken by the awesome magnitude of the !°!°! threat. The sheer power of that city-sized machine floater—ten times the size, easily, of Hector in every dimension—there was no way that even a Mark XXXIII Bolo could survive a one-to-one confrontation with that.

But he was beginning to wonder if this might not provide a fresh opportunity for the humans now trapped in the shadows of the battling giants.

"Alita? Did you have your magviewer's recorder on when you uplinked to Hector?"

"Of course."

"Can I see it?"

She handed him the viewer. He keyed in the replay, then held the optics to his eyes. On the small screen inside, he saw again the ponderous movement of the !°!°! bastion as it ground its way across fragmenting pavement.

As Alita had panned the viewer across the whole expanse of the spaceport, however, she had briefly captured a portion of the spaceport's maintenance and service facilities, a line of low buildings along the north and east sides of the field, beyond the grounded bastion transport. Cranes and derricks rose above cluttered-looking warehouses and loading ramps; the faces of the structures overlooking the field were scalloped into maintenance bays, some with ships still parked inside.

Jaime's heart quickened as he touched the freeze frame control, then selected a portion of the image for an expanded view. One of the bays was occupied by a particularly large vessel, a dark gray ovoid that would have been dwarfed by the huge bastion transport but must still have been at least three hundred meters long.

He touched a button to enhance the image; the picture dissolved in a cloud of pixels, then reformed, sharper than before. "If I didn't know better," Jaime said, "I'd swear that was a clucker ship."

"What?" Alita asked. "Where?"

He passed her the viewer and she studied it for a moment. "You're right," she said. "Some vessels like this came in with the big monster. Here, look." She rewound the recording, checked it, then handed it back. As Jaime studied the picture, once again the slow-flying mountain drifted in over the city, accompanied by schooling escorts. Several of those smaller vessels, he saw now, were all but identical to the one parked in the maintenance bay.

"So what the hell is a clucker transport doing parked in a spaceport bay?"

"It might have something to do with the damned Tolun," Shari suggested. "Part of the deal they cut with the machines, y'know?"

"Could be."

"I'd be interested in knowing what the deal is," Alita said. "Did the Tolun sell something to the clackers? Or did the clackers bring something for the Tolun?"

"You know," Jaime told the others, his voice thoughtful, "I don't know what it was intended for, but that transport is big enough for the whole March. It's even big enough for Hector, if the rest of us don't mind being really friendly."

Alita's eyes widened. "A way off-world! For *all* of us!"

"On a clucker transport?" Shari asked. "Can we even fly one of those things?"

"At the moment," Jaime told her, "I don't see any other options. Hector might know a trick or two about dealing with clacker computers and nav profiles. If we could bull our way on board, kill off the machines, and find the control center . . ."

"Shouldn't be too hard," Alita said. "Especially if we get Hector to analyze the control systems and software."

"It's damned well worth a try," Shari said. "We'll need to bring in the rest of the Brotherhood, though. There must be machines on board. We can't pull something like that, just the seven of us."

"I'd say the time to try it is now," Jaime said, "while

the big boys are busy. How fast can you have Wal and
the rest of his boys and girls out here?"

Shari grinned at him. "Just watch our smoke,
General!" She touched her helmet's earpiece and began
speaking rapidly and quietly into her threadmike.

To the north, the sound of dueling titans grew louder
once more.

*I emerge from the gully 13.6 minutes after entering
the other end. The land form is almost certainly a dry
riverbed, for it opens up onto a broad stretch of sand
dunes along the coastline, less than twenty kilometers
northwest of Stardown. My opponent, meanwhile, has
swung north in an attempt to cut me off, but I have
managed to outdistance him. My drones continue to
track his northward movement as I move southeast
along the coastline. For several minutes, we exchange
indirect fire, my conventional VLS rockets against his
robot missiles.*

*I have his full attention now, however, as I race
toward the city. Smaller !°!°! vehicles and weapons
swarm about me, including several fair-sized walkers,
crawlers, and flyers, but they are unable to penetrate
my upgraded battle screens to any serious degree and
I dispatch them all with bursts from my infinite
repeaters, mortars, or point defense weapons. As I pick
up Target Alpha on direct line-of-sight once more, I
open up with a barrage of 20cm Hellbore slivers,
spraying them across that tall, angular tower which
I suspect houses his primary sensor arrays. The
electromagnetic pulse accompanying each Hellbore shot
fries the electronics of many of my smaller tormentors,
sweeping them from the sky. Larger machines with
hardened circuitry succumb to repeated blasts of high-
velocity flechettes and point defense lasers.*

*A dozen laser and particle beams slash across the
dunes, clawing at my battle screens. Accelerating hard,*

*I am soon all but flying down the beach, my fast-turning
tracks hurling an enormous roostertail of sand in my
wake. Airborne sand, it seems, is an excellent anti-
beam defense; the air around me burns and crackles
as flying sand is fused into a pattering rain of tiny
glass spheres.*

*I return fire with my forward weapons, blanketing
the target in fire.*

What is the target doing?

DAV728 concentrated on that one thought, squeezing
the captive human brain with repeated, increasing
demands for information. He was feeding it with a
large array of sensory input now, both direct visual
and graphical overlay feeds from a !°!°! reconnaissance
spacecraft in low orbit.

What is the target planning?

DAV had expected the Bolo either to flee the area,
leaving the human refugees as easy targets, or to attack
the nearest bastion head-on in an attempt to disable
one before the other two could draw close. At first,
it had appeared that the Bolo was doing exactly that,
launching an all-out assault on KEM933-3938, the
series 40 that had grounded at the old human
spaceport. After only a few billion nanoseconds,
however, the Bolo had veered off, momentarily hiding
itself in a cloud of light- and IR-obscuring smoke. It
had reemerged shortly after, moving swiftly along the
coast in the direction of the human city.

What is the Bolo trying to do?

The human brain seemed as confused as DAV was
at the moment. Although various possibilities were
evident—it was trying to flee, it was trying to take
cover among the buildings of the city—the Bolo's
tactics were as opaque to its former commander as
they were to DAV.

No matter. Soon, DAV would have closed the range

to the Bolo, and the human machine would swiftly be pounded into scrap. The human brain had also quite inadvertently identified two general areas of weakness on the Bolo—its six sets of broad, fast-spinning, multiple tracks, and the two undamaged Hellbore turrets on its top deck. Smash the tracks, and the Bolo would be immobilized; DAV had already thought of that one, and the human's unwilling thoughts merely corroborated his idea.

The turrets, though, which mounted the weapons used by the Bolo when it fended off the meteor barrage and destroyed JEG851, were something DAV had not thought about. Though heavily armored, their size, shape, and purpose necessitated thinner armor there, especially on the top, than elsewhere, and the Hellbore barrels themselves, though consisting of an extraordinarily tough neutron dense-packed casing sheathed by boron-carbide and woven carbon-ceramic single-chain thread, were not otherwise specifically armored. Smash the turrets or melt the gun barrels, and the Bolo's primary weapons—its two remaining 200cm Hellbores—would be useless. The fact that one turret had already been disabled when the Bolo had flipped over as a result of a near-miss by an asteroid proved that it *could* be done, and with relative ease.

DAV began issuing the necessary orders.

For the first time in a very long time, Jeff Fowler could see. It was a strange kind of vision. His first clue that he was not seeing things with his own eyes came from the inhuman clarity of what he was seeing. Human vision is sharply focused at the center, less distinct toward the periphery—a simple means of reducing the complexity of the incoming visual data that the human brain must process.

What he was seeing now, however, was perfectly

clear across his entire cone of vision. As he studied it, he became aware that there were other differences as well, with the colors distorted by a sharp shift toward the infrared, and the shapes he was seeing subtly enhanced, the edges sharpened until his view seemed less that of reality and more like a computer construct, an artificial, graphical presentation of the real world.

That was when he realized that he was experiencing a direct sensory feed from some kind of computer; it took him several agonized moments to decide that, somehow, he'd been wired into some kind of alien computer, that it was using him to acquire information about Bolo capabilities, tactics, and weaknesses.

What is the melting point temperature of the main battery gun barrels?

Only the fact that he'd already suspected as much saved him from the black, yawning pit of complete insanity. Those periods of waking and hazy semi-consciousness—the memory of them stretched back and back and back to his last clear recollection, as the incoming asteroid struck a searing, dazzling spark across the skies above Chryse Base. The invaders must have captured him, been interrogating him about the Bolo and what it could do.

They were using him now to *fight* the Bolo.

Damn it, Hector! The thought was a silent cry of anguish. *I can't stop them from using me against you!*

Either the sensors providing him with his primary visual feed were located in some sort of very large combat machine, feeding him with imaging input at a remote location, or he was physically present in that machine. He couldn't tell. He couldn't feel his body at all—his sense of touch, of cold or hot, of pain all were disconcertingly absent. Even his kinesthetic sense, his awareness of bodily attitude and relative limb position, was missing, suppressed, he supposed, by drugs or other means.

What is the Bolo doing now?

Hell, how should I know? was his immediate reply, though he wasn't certain how literally or completely his thoughts were being translated for his unseen captors. He had the impression that he was inside some sort of extremely large and powerful fortress, a mobile fortress slowly moving across a barren and rocky plain. He couldn't see Hector directly; windows inset against his field of view, however, showed views from other sources, several apparently taken from different airborne vantage points, and one which seemed to be from another large combat machine.

One of the aerial shots was clearest. The Bolo was racing along a beach parallel to the shore, flinging huge clouds of wet sand into the sky and gouging track prints deep into the beach. Abruptly, the Bolo slewed to the left, plunging into the surf, slowing only marginally as it churned its way into deeper and deeper water, its passage sending up a fountain of white spray even more spectacular than the plumes of sand on the beach. In another few moments, it was gone, vanished beneath the water.

What is the Bolo doing?

Jeff struggled against unseen, unfelt bonds, desperately fighting the thoughts that rose unbidden in his mind. *Don't think about pink Centaurian grollexes*, ran the old one-line gag. This was like that; as his questioner probed, his thoughts betrayed him, betrayed his will and his grim determination to resist.

It looks like Hector's trying to circle around behind the enemy, he thought, and he knew that the interrogator had heard him. *Or . . . maybe he's just trying to get away*. He doubted that last, but he thought the thought nonetheless, hoping to create doubt in the enemy's mind. Had that thought as well, the thought that he might confuse his questioners, also been read?

Damn! How could he fight back?

The images in his mind showed empty water now. Somewhere out there, Hector was moving along the seabed, using the water for cover. Jeff decided that it was a very good thing indeed that he really *didn't* know what the Bolo was planning, because there was no way to hold even his speculations beyond the grasp of his captors.

I think he must be trying to get away, he thought suddenly, decisively. *He's taken cover underwater and is moving off now, out of sight.*

Except . . . Hector would never do that, Jeff knew, and there wasn't a way in hell to keep that knowledge to himself.

Distantly, he could sense other thoughts flashing through his own mind and, somehow, through the neural hook-up he was now a part of, he could sense them nearby as well. Orders were being given to someone or something called KEM933-3938, ordering it to change course, and to target Hector's main guns when he reemerged.

And all Jeff could do was watch and listen, helpless.

Nearly half an hour had passed, now, since the landing of the mobile bastion. Jaime had issued strings of orders to Wal Prescott, back at the human encampment. The refugees were moving now, heading across the barren plains as quickly as they could, an undisciplined mob urged forward by Brotherhood troops who harried them along like shelties herding a flock.

Fifty Brotherhood troops, meanwhile, had piled into hovertrucks and other fast vehicles with the column and were racing east toward the spaceport. Once the firefight between the Bolo and the bastion had ended, Jaime and the others had returned to the ridge southwest of the spaceport and were studying the situation now through the magviewers.

Beyond the cluttered spaceport field, the towers of

Stardown proper rose like ivory columns. Stardown had begun as a village tucked in next to the spaceport, between the port facility and the sea. After two centuries of vigorous growth, however, the village had become a town, then a sprawling port city, spreading out to embrace the spaceport to the west and south, and the seacoast to the northeast and east.

"Too many machines down there on the field for us to just wander across," Jaime said, studying the target freighter where it rested in its bay on the far side of the field, and the field itself, cluttered now by grounded !°!°! spacecraft. "Not quite sure how we could pull a sneak and get down there unobserved."

"I don't know," Shari said, looking through her viewer. "Are some of them leaving?"

"Looks like." Floaters, some hundreds of them, had been drifting about more or less aimlessly above the tarmac, but more and more appeared to be moving away from the grounded ships, heading north.

"Can I see your viewer?" Alita asked him.

He handed his set to her. "If we could reach the maintenance area without being seen," he mused, "we might have half a chance."

"Well, we just might have that chance," Alita said, peering through the magviewer. "Something's happening in the city."

"Where?"

"There." She pointed as she handed the set back to him. "North of the port field. On the waterfront, I think."

He turned the magviewer in the indicated direction and touched the zoom controls, focusing in on what looked like an explosion of some sort. From his current vantage point, he could just make out the docks of a pleasure boat marina. A vast, dark swelling of the water was racing toward the piers.

"I think—" Jaime said, but he got no further. Piers

splintered as the incoming wave broke, then exploded in a cascade of spray. Seconds later, the upper works of the Bolo heaved into view, streaming water and shattered bits of pier and smashed pleasure boats.

A silent flash marked the impact of an incoming round against the Bolo's thick hide. Jaime turned sharply left, searching for the shooter. There it was. He could see the !°!°! bastion now, crawling slowly across the horizon from the west, its silhouette twinkling with the rapid-fire discharges of uncounted weapons.

The sound of the barrage reached them moments later, a far-off thunder rapidly gaining in both volume and power.

And in the city, the Bolo emerged from cascading spray as the first enemy rounds struck home. . . .

CHAPTER TWENTY

Until now, my exchanges of fire with Target Alpha have resulted in minimal damage to both of us. We have been primarily engaged in testing one another's defenses, probing for weakness, cataloguing capabilities and strengths.

My detour into the sea has not confused my Enemy—not that I am especially surprised. There was a possibility, a small one, that my maneuver would catch Target Alpha off guard and allow me a clear shot from an unexpected angle of attack. This, clearly, has not happened.

Still, there was another rationale behind my flanking maneuver, and there was, frankly, no way that the Enemy could easily counter it, even if he anticipated its purpose. By turning out to sea, racing southeast across the seabed at a depth of approximately fifty meters, then turning back in toward the coast so as to emerge from the water in the heart of the city, I have provided myself with one of the most vital and basic of all tactical assets.

Cover. . . .

Jaime watched through the magviewer, fascinated, as the Bolo emerged from the waterfront, smashing its way into the heart of Stardown's warehouse district. The streets were relatively narrow there, narrower by far than the Bolo's thirty-eight-meter track width, and reinforced ferrocrete walls and facades of glass and plasteel literally exploded in great crumbling avalanches of debris as the combat machine plowed through the structures. The bastion was firing rapidly now, with every weapon mounted on its huge and complex form, and beams and missiles were slamming into Hector or exploding among the towering buildings, with the pulsing regularity of a rapidly beating heart.

Falling masonry and dust had almost completely obscured Hector now, but the Bolo was still firing, its Hellbore bolts exploding from the cloud as savage, glaring gouts of light; tracking and targeting lasers, normally invisible, showed in the whirling dust as dazzling threads of red or green light.

Hector swept forward; a white office complex tower exploded near the base as the bastion's particle beams lanced into the structure instead of into the Bolo. The lower ranks of floors vanished in the flash and the gouting smoke and rubble; the upper floors dropped, settling onto the ruin of the lower, then continuing to collapse in a slow motion cascade of crumbling architecture. Most of the building fell across the Bolo, smothering it in a rolling, thundering avalanche of rubble

"Damn," Jaime said. "If he gets buried under all of that . . ."

"New Devon," Shari said, softly, nearby.

"What?"

"New Devon," Shari repeated, louder. She glanced at him, then looked back at the distant battle. Even without a magviewer, the rising, swirling smoke and dust, the steady flash and flicker of beams and Hellbore bolts combined to make a spectacular display. "Once, back when we were just getting free of the camp,

Hector told me a story about another Bolo. A Mark XXVIII, I think he said. I was worried about him getting stuck in the mud in Celeste Harbor. He told me about a deactivated and radioactive Mark XXVIII that was buried two hundred meters underground, inside a three-meter shell of reinforced armorcrete. Something woke it up, years later, and it managed to tunnel back to the surface."

"Sounds like one of those horror stories people tell one another to remind themselves how dangerous Bolos really are," Alita said.

""I've heard that tale too," Jaime said. "I think it's true. Yeah, it looks like Hector isn't having any trouble with a mere office building getting dropped on him."

The avalanche had hardly slowed the big combat machine. Through the magviewer, Jaime watched the debris pile heave and shudder, then split apart as easily as the moving wall of water had opened earlier in spray and flintsteel. The Bolo emerged, tracks whirling, buzzsawing through ferrocrete and pavement stone and flinging it skyward in an obscuring, fog-thick blanket.

The !°!°! bastion had drifted slowly closer, crashing its way through the smaller one- and two-story buildings on the outskirts of the city to the northwest, trying to maneuver for a clear shot. Most of its fire, however, was being intercepted now either by those buildings still partially standing in a forest about the fast-moving Bolo, or by the clouds of obscuring dust and smoke. Flames licked among the ruins in the Bolo's wake, as flammable material caught fire. Smaller !°!°! machines—floaters and various insectlike flyers, darted and weaved among the buildings, adding their jagged bolts of lightning to the barrage, but without apparent effect. Hector was swatting them out of the sky almost as swiftly as they arrived, with flickering lasers and shotgun blasts of high-velocity flechettes wrecking !°!°!

machines by the tens, by the hundreds, leaving them
scattered across the wreckage of the city like broken
and discarded toys.

"What's he doing?" Alita asked. She was standing
behind a low, partly fallen wall, rising on her toes to
try to get a better view. "I can't see! What's happening?"

Jaime handed her the magviewer. "I think," he said,
a little dazed by the sheer violence of the battle, "that
Hector is charging the bastion, head-on."

He tried to imagine why Hector would attempt such
a thing. Given the relative sizes of the Bolo and the
bastion, it looked like nothing less than suicide. . . .

*I emerge from the built-up, inner area of the city,
accelerating as I clear the last of the toppling buildings
and enter a district of smaller, more fragile structures,
few of which reach as high as my gun deck. The !°!°!
bastion looms ahead, its forward tower so high that
weapons mounted near the top are firing down onto
my upper works, where my armor is considerably
thinner. I estimate a 79.4% probability that the !°!°!
bastion is attempting to target my Hellbore turrets,
so I keep them in constant motion and make generous
use of area-defense aerosol fogs and chaff launches.*

*My battle screens are holding, at 83%, deflecting
the Enemy's charged particle beams in arcing bursts
of air-to-ground lightning. Most solid rounds, both
high-speed projectiles and robot-directed missiles, are
deflected as well, and my outer layers of armor have
held up under the barrage of those explosive and kinetic
rounds that do penetrate. Skin sensors detect a slow
degradation of my armor in the general region,
starboard-side high, of the armor-penetrating crater
used by my Commander when he first gained access
to my Battle Center, but the loss so far is within
acceptable limits.*

At a range of five kilometers, now, I acquire a solid

*target lock with both radar and optical sensors. I adjust
my vector slightly to allow both primary Hellbore
turrets a clear line-of-sight to the target, at an elevation
of minus two degrees, and fire, the flash momentarily
blinding my own optics.*

*One after the other, I began slamming 200cm
Hellbore bolts into my opponent, targeting a joint in
his armor near the ground and dead center beneath
the forward tower. The Enemy vehicle is protected
by some type of hull field similar to my battle screens,
but more powerful. Even a Hellbore bolt, generating
six megatons per second of firepower, is dissipated by
those screens, and the backwash of reflected energy
bathes me and the buildings around me in an intense
glare radiating as furiously as the surface of a fair-
sized star.*

*The external temperature is soaring, the air shimmering
wildly in the inferno of dispersed heat. I press forward,
closing the range to four kilometers . . . to three . . . and
all the while I continue firing, first one main Hellbore,
and then the other, supplementing the barrage with
point-blank fire from my howitzer batteries and mortars.
My battle screens protect me from much of the heat, of
course, but each time one of my batteries fires, the screen
in that sector automatically shuts down, for obvious
reasons, and in that period of time, approximately 10^{-4}
second long, my outer hull grows incrementally hotter.*

*A firestorm is raging across this part of the city, as
intense as the pyrotechnic destruction loosed by an
exploding thermonuclear warhead. This type of combat,
with weapons of these destructive potentials, is better
suited to the empty reaches of interplanetary space
than a city boulevard. The energies being loosed here,
within the confines of a city, are catastrophic in their
sheer destructive potential. I note that some slabs of
fallen rubble are beginning to glow a sullen red in
the heat. My battle screens drop to 74%; sparking,*

shrieking electron beams play across my faltering screens, bleeding excess charge into the earth in snapping, thundering bolts of artificial lightning.

A succession of savage proton beam shots slam into my screens, overloading them and temporarily knocking them down. I am able to shunt the overload to a secondary circuit and spill the excess into a positively charged ground spill, but in the 1.3×10^{-3} second that my screens are down, another particle beam strikes my Number One turret just above the gun mount, melting through the armor in a crackling pyrotechnic display, piercing the breech mechanism, and disabling the gun.

Lightning arcs through my hull and penetrates my primary remote turret fire control circuits. Relays fuse, a K238-M molycirc controller assembly burns out, and my Number Two Turret is down as well.

I continue to target the Enemy with volleys from my 20cm Hellbores, however. Three point seven seconds later, Target Alpha's screens fail as well, overloaded by the sheer magnitude of firepower brought to bear on one relatively small area. My next Hellbore infinite repeater burst strikes unprotected metal with an estimated yield of 250 kilotons per second; spectroscopic scans of the expanding cloud of vapor within the next 10^{-8} second indicates that the target's outer hull is made of a boron carbide and ceramic alloy backed by a layer of crystalline carbon sheathing designed to transfer and disperse heat, but that dispersal is not fast enough to prevent a burn through that opens a crater forty meters deep.

Forty meters is a pinprick to a machine a kilometer long, but I have reached its internal structure. Wounded, now, the target begins rotating, attempting to move the damaged section beyond my reach. I continue firing, tracking the crater, pouring round after relativistic round into what has now become a deep and ragged cavern in the face of a cliff of metal; inside, energies rage in a seething inferno as meter upon meter of unyielding metal alloys is transformed in a literal flash into plasma at starcore temperatures.

It occurs to me that my position with the Enemy bastion is eerily similar to that of my Commander, Jaime Graham, when he first approached my position on that hilltop outside of Camp 84. The |°|°| machine is well over a kilometer long; its main forward tower is nearly three hundred meters high, both dimensions roughly ten times my own. My single advantage, now that I am within one kilometer of the target, is that the Enemy's largest and most powerful weapon cannot be depressed far enough to hit me. I take heavy fire from the bastion's equivalent of point defense and anti-infantry weapons but suffer no serious damage. My screens are down now to 58%. Power output is holding steady. Secondary weapons at full efficiency, though I am now at a considerable disadvantage with all primary weapons down. An explosion tears a thirty-meter gash down my left flank, further weakening the battle screens by destroying several key field projectors and creating an obviously vulnerable target region.

Another explosion, the detonating warhead of a |°|°| robot missile, smashes my number three left-forward road wheel, sending it flying in a scattering of duralloy fragments. My suspension on that side is damaged, and I note a reduction in efficiency of 12% in my mobile performance. Two 20cm infinite repeater turrets on my left side have been smashed. Attempts to bring my primary fire control back on-line fail, and my Number Two Hellbore remains silent. A crater nearly five meters wide is blasted from my glacis, and portions of my upper deck plating are ripped away.

No matter. I press my attack.

My opponent is hurt. I can sense the internal fires spreading throughout the vast structure before me, *blowing out sensor panels and chunks of armor, each the size of a house. His rotation stops and, a moment later, a shudder passes through the frame of the entire structure as its contra-gravity fields fail and the entire kilometer's length of the !°!°! vehicle grounds with a thud that sends a shockwave rippling out through the ground. Swerving to keep centered on the crater, I close to within 500 meters . . . then 100 meters, until I am firing into that gaping, fiery hole at point-blank range.*

Shock sensors and deep-thermal imaging detect the build-up of uncontrolled energies deep within the shattered hulk. Swiftly, I reverse my tracks and back off. The final explosion comes seconds later . . . an almost disappointingly tame eruption of orange flames and greasy black smoke from a dozen vents, gunports, and apertures scattered across the face of the tower and elsewhere across the machine's perimeter. Slowly, its support structures burned away, the tower teeters for a moment, then gradually falls backward, dropping into the dorsal slot where it was stored for transport, striking with the impact of a falling mountain, and completing the destruction begun by internal explosions.

It is several seconds more before I realize the obvious—that I have emerged from the battle victorious and relatively unharmed. I have suffered serious damage, but nothing I cannot compensate for.

What remains unknown, however, is whether or not I will be able to similarly defeat the remaining two !°!°! bastions. Both are still moving toward my position at approximately thirty kilometers per hour, and I have only my 20cm Hellbores and auxiliary weapons on-line and ready to meet them.

At the moment, I see no sure way of stopping or slowing them. My attack has purchased some time for the human refugees, who are now moving en masse toward the spaceport.

But that time, I fear, is very quickly running out. I call my Commander to report my condition.

The news hit Jaime like a hammer blow. With all of Hector's 200cm Hellbores out of operation, they were now in serious trouble. He couldn't imagine the Bolo stopping two more of those monsters with his 20cms. "Okay, Hector," he said, speaking over the comm link. "How are you otherwise?"

"Mobility has been slightly impaired by damage to my left forward track," the Bolo's voice replied, as calm and as unhurried as ever. "I have also lost two of my 20cm Hellbores and my battle screens have been reduced to fifty-one percent of full operational capacity."

"Okay. Get your metal carcass over to the northeast corner of the spaceport, and we'll meet you there. I'll have Alita see if she can patch you up any."

"We may not have the time to facilitate repairs," Hector replied. "The remaining enemy units are closing steadily. I expect them to be here within one point three hours."

"Let 'em come. We're going to see about getting off this rock!"

He turned the magviewer on the northern horizon, seeking Hector's black form against the blazing city skyline. It looked as though the entire northern half of the city was ablaze, with most of the buildings either knocked down completely or standing as shrunken, ragged, skeletal shadows of the towers that had stood there a few moments before. The !°!°! bastion was clearly visible in the heart of the incinerated sweep of the city's outskirts, crumpled in upon itself, its tower collapsed, its armor cracked open in a dozen places, showing the white-hot inferno within.

Hector began shouldering his way past wrecked buildings, toppling several towers still standing before he emerged onto the far side of the spaceport field and began making his way toward the maintenance facility.

"We'd better get over there," Jaime said, lowering the viewer. "What do you think, Alita? Can you patch him up in the next hour or so, with spare parts we find over there in the starship fixit shop?"

She snorted. "You seem to have an exaggerated picture of what Bolo crew chiefs can do single-handed, General."

"You won't be single-handed. And we won't have time for anything fancy. But Hector told me his fire control for his main turrets is down. A K238-M controller assembly melted, I think he said. And some N-480 fuses."

Alita's brow furrowed in the way it always did when she was deep in thought. "N-480s are common enough. He should have plenty of those in his maintenance/logistic stores. As for the molycirc controller, I don't know. He might have one, or he might not. But any Navy ship that mounts Hellbores uses the same basic fire control system a Bolo does. It's a Navy gun originally, after all. We might be able to do it at that. But in an hour? I wouldn't bet my life on it."

"Sorry, Alita," Jaime said. "That's exactly what you're going to be doing . . . betting your life. *All* of our lives." He grinned at her. "Don't mean that to put any pressure on you, of course. But we're going to need that 200cm working again, or we're never going to clear this planet."

"Yeah, no pressure, huh?"

"Sir!" Lancer Dobbs called out from a few meters down the ridge at their backs. "We got friendlies incoming!"

Jaime turned and looked back toward the southwest. Three plumes of dust were visible moving rapidly across the plain—the hovertrucks full of Brotherhood troops on their way in from the main encampment.

"Vector them in, Dobbs," Jaime ordered. "Tell them to come on up here. No one seems to be paying any attention to us."

"Affirmative, sir!"

He turned back and began studying the far side of the spaceport field. How could they make it over there without attracting the wrong sort of attention?

Well, come to think of it, Hector seemed to be attracting most of the attention at the moment. The Bolo was lumbering out into the spaceport landing field now, with a swarm of small !°!°! machines darting and hovering like a cloud of gnats.

Could they make it across while the clackers were busy with Hector? There was only one way to find out.

CHAPTER TWENTY-ONE

As I swing across the northern portion of the spaceport field, I notice three hovertrucks filled with human troops picking their way down the northeastern face of the ridge on the far side of the tarmac. Most of the !°!°! floaters appear to be concentrating on me, so I redouble my efforts to knock them out, blasting away with every weapon, from antipersonnel flechette batteries to 20cm Hellbore infinite repeaters.

On the southern portion of the field, the greatest immediate danger to the hovertrucks is the grounded drive module which brought the bastion to the spaceport. Though the bastion abandoned the module, it is more than possible that a number of !°!°! war machines are still hidden within the structure, which is very nearly as big and as complex as the bastion itself. At a range of .87 kilometer, I open up with my 20cms, walking the bolts across the inert spacecraft. Large chunks of metal are blasted away with each hit, and in moments, the interior is glowing a murky red and orange as internal fires consume its structure from the inside out.

Secondary explosions rupture the hull and set the wreck ablaze. The hovertrucks continue past without *interruption. The smoke boiling from the wreckage should give them some additional cover.*

"Thanks, Hector," my Commander calls over our radio link. "What do you have on that big clacker freighter in the maintenance bay east of your position?"

I study the indicated vessel. "It appears inert, though there are indications of life-support machinery operating inside."

"Life support?" my Commander asks. "What the hell do the clackers want with life support?"

"Unknown," *I reply.* "For !°!°! to maintain life support within their ship does appear to be anomalous behavior."

"It's probably the Tolun. Or else they have some humans over there, fixing the ship up or loading it with whatever it's supposed to be carrying. We're checking it out now. Meet us there, when you're through playing with your friends over there."

I assume he is referring to the attacking !°!°! floaters. There are only twenty-five left now. I continue firing at them, picking another Enemy floater off with each shot. The survivors, at this point, have no chance of harming me, and their electron beams and lasers are harmlessly deflected or scattered by my battle screens. Still, though, they press their attack, and in another 3.8 seconds I have burned the last one out of the air.

"I will meet you at the designated rendezvous, my Commander," *I reply.*

I, too, am curious about the environmental system power leakages emanating from the ship.

The transport would have looked tiny in comparison to the enormous bulk of the bastion transport, but seen here, up close, it was nothing less than titanic, a long, heavy, flattened ellipsoid bluntly pointed at both ends, the curve of its hull broken here and there by the random placement of blisters, domes, and sponsons. Three hundred twenty-seven meters long, it massed at least one hundred thousand tons—larger than a *Conestoga*-class Mark VII. The craft rested on hydraulic jacks and more than filled the revetment space of the maintenance bay, the swell of its freeshear turns nearly scraping the catwalks and access ways to either side, its stern works extending far out onto the open tarmac astern. A single cargo bay hatch, well forward, was invitingly open, with a loading ramp extended and the interior brightly lit.

The Brotherhood infantry went in first, moving in lance formation, one five-man lance covering for another as they leapfrogged ahead in quick, sharp dashes. Surprisingly, there were no !°!°! machines about, either within the bay or on the tarmac outside— no warriors, no workers, not even any floater recon units. If they'd been here, it looked like the battle with Hector had drawn them all away. The three hovertrucks filled with troops, plus the air car, had slipped across the tarmac from the southwest corner without a single challenge.

At the maintenance bay, they'd fanned out, checking the buildings for any sign of a machine trap or outpost. Four lances had entered the ship itself, searching for crew, for machines, for anything that might pose a threat. Once the infantry had reported the area secure, Jaime, Alita, and Wal Prescott had gone in to the bay to investigate their prize.

"Ain't never seen a design quite like this," Wal said, staring up at the overhang of the bulky craft. "Gotta be clucker, don'tcha think?"

"It's not Tolun," Jaime replied. "They build more graceful designs than this."

"And more colorful," Alita put in. "You know, if the

machines wanted to stay hidden on that thing, we'd never find them. Remember the clackers hidden inside Hector?"

"Yeah," Jaime said. "We'd have to take the whole thing apart down to nuts and bolts to be sure it was clean." Twenty people couldn't possibly search a ship—and an *alien* ship at that—in half an hour and be sure they'd found everything.

Shari and four Brotherhood lancers appeared at the top of the ramp. "Okay, General," Shari's voice said over Jaime's comm link. "We can't get at all of the spaces in this tub, but the bridge and main cargo areas look clear."

"We're coming in," Jaime replied. "Come on," he told the others. "We don't have much time."

At the top of the ramp, Jaime clapped Shari on the arm. "Quick work."

"Damn it, sir, anything could still be hidden in this thing! It's a maze in there!"

One of the troopers standing beside her hefted a small, crudely hand-wired box mounted on a pistol grip. "Remember, sir, these things'll only pick up a machine's fields if it's turned on, and then only at pretty close range."

"I know, son," Jaime replied. "But it's all we have to go on, isn't it?"

Alita and her engineering crew had cobbled together the devices from parts scavenged from Chryse, with some technical advice from Hector. Originally called "clucker-clickers," a name swiftly shortened to "clickers," they gave off a rapid clatter when they picked up the powerful electromagnetic or contra-gravity emanations of a nearby !°!°! machine. Of course, they also reacted to hovercraft and portable fusion power plants as well, but that was only to be expected. They were a damned lot better than nothing.

"Just be careful in there, sir," Shari said. "I don't like this."

Jaime drew his Mark XIV power gun from its holster and adjusted the setting to needle beam. "I always am." Turning, he led the way into the ship's cavernous interior.

The deeper into the ship they went, however, the more Jaime was convinced that this was *not* a !°!°! vessel, not originally. It couldn't be. Everything they'd learned so far about !°!°! technology suggested that the clackers built specialized machines for specialized jobs. A starship's "pilot" would be literally plugged into the ship's computer, in effect becoming the ship. It didn't need a bridge . . . or living quarters, corridors, mess galleys, and banks of life-support machinery.

This vessel had once housed a living, breathing crew—beings of roughly the same size and shape as humans, to judge from the tall, oval hatchways and the dimensions of the corridors and ladders they encountered. His suspicion became stronger when he spotted a sign mounted on a hatch. It was written in some alien script, with flowing, large-looped cursive letters spelling out an incomprehensible scribble that looked vaguely like the word "ggollollopp."

According to Hector, the !°!°! communicated through pulsed radio emissions with multiple, nested layers of meaning, and had no need of a written language. "I'm wondering," Jaime said as they filed past the ggollollopp door, "if the cluckers might be in the habit of adapting technology they capture from other species."

"You think this might be a Grakaan ship?" Wal asked.

"Don't know. Maybe Grakaan. Or more likely some race we never met, that the clackers fought and beat a long, long time ago. This ship feels *old*." There was no dust on the decks, no cobwebs in the passageways, but there was rust and corrosion on most of the interior surfaces, and the cold, black-and-gray metal bulkheads seemed to radiate the aura of extreme age. Jaime wondered if the vessel would even hold together long enough for it to reach the Grakaan Cooperative.

Still, risking our necks in this bucket is better than staying here, Jaime thought. They clattered up a remarkably human-scaled ladder, passed through another long corridor, and ended up at a door prominently marked with a cursive "ggollloppgggll."

"This is the bridge in through here," Shari said, stepping through the doorway. "At least, that's what we think it is."

It seemed a likely guess. It was a small room with a steel-grill deck and a low overhead. Chairs, again designed for more-or-less human frames and articulations, were grouped around a central console, with large viewscreens overhead and control panels with recognizable levers, pressure plates, and touch panels. Jaime, Wal, Alita, and Shari moved through the cramped space, examining everything. A sweep with one of the clickers indicated no nearby machines, but Jaime could not suppress the growing feeling that something here was not quite right.

The controls were marked with alien cursive scrawls, similar to the words they'd already seen . . . but someone had also taken the trouble to label many of the controls with small, sticky-backed strips, each neatly blocked in with Anglic lettering. "Shari!" he said. "Did your people notice this?"

She looked at the labels, her eyes widening. "*No*, sir! We just came in, scanned the place, and left. I . . . I didn't see those!"

"S'okay. But it seems a little strange, don't you think?"

"So who put Anglic labels on the controls?" Alita asked.

Cautiously, Jaime pressed a key marked "Main

Computer Display," and one of the viewscreens went active, casting an eerie green-yellow glow in the otherwise dimly lit bridge. The checklist it showed was also displayed in Anglic.

"Why," he said, "do I get the feeling that this is a trap?"

"Maybe because it *is*," a new voice said. With a sharp hiss, and jets of escaping steam, portions of the convoluted bridge bulkhead broke open and folded back like gaping black jaws, and the men concealed inside stepped out, power pistols held at the ready.

"Pogue!" Wal snapped. "You filthy turner skekker . . . !"

"Ah, ah," Pogue said, grinning, gesturing with his pistol. "There *are* ladies present, you know." He gave a quick jerk of his head, and the men who'd been hidden with him moved forward, pulling weapons from the prisoners' hands. Dewar Sykes grabbed Shari from behind with one arm, leering as he rubbed the barrel of his pistol against her cheek. "Good t' see ya again, babe."

"Yeah," another said, grabbing Alita. Jaime recognized that one too. What was his name? Philbet, that was it. He took a step forward and felt the cold, hard muzzle of a weapon press against his skin, just below his left ear. "Don't," the turner at his back said, "even think it."

Jaime glanced from face to face, thoughts racing. There were six turners, counting Pogue, crowded in around and behind the four of them. Pogue touched a control, and the bridge doorway hissed shut, then locked.

"That will keep us from being disturbed for a while," Pogue said with a smile. In the distance, Jaime could hear shouts, pounding feet on catwalks, and the sounds of fighting. "All of you. Drop your weapons. Now. And your helmets and earpieces. Take them off . . . very slowly. I don't want you talking to your friends outside. Or the Bolo. *Yet. . . ."*

They did as they were told, prompted by nudges and gestures from the renegades' pistols.

"That worked rather well, I think," Pogue said. "I figured you four would come up here, though I have men scattered throughout the ship. The rest of your people won't be able to help you." He touched another control. "That will seal the ship's outer hatch. It's just us and you now."

"So, Pogue," Jaime said, trying to keep his tone light. "What is it the machines give you that makes you betray your own people?"

"Betray? Not at all, Jaime. I'm here to *save* our people, not betray them. Trust me. You'll thank me someday."

"I doubt that," Alita said.

"I'm not the villain you think I am! I've become . . . call it a go-between. A liaison between humans and the machines."

Gunfire sounded again outside, quite close, just beyond the bridge door. Something clanged against metal.

"I've learned a lot from the !°!°!," Pogue continued, clucking off the machines' name for themselves with fluent ease. "More than you'd believe. You know, they really *need* humans. It took me a while to convince the boss machine of that, but they do. You see, they've got this problem. . . ."

"Yeah. Bein' around stinkin' sewer flushings like you," Wal growled. "That's a major problem for *anyone*."

Pogue ignored the interruption. "As near as I can figure it, the machines operate on this basic set of program instructions that must've been planted in them by their makers, a long, long time ago. God knows how long. A million years, maybe. Or a billion. Doesn't really matter. The point is, the instructions have them trying to find stuff and find a way to use it."

" 'Stuff'?" Alita asked. "What kind of stuff?"

"That's the point. Anything. I think that the original instructions were for a kind of von Neumann machine."

"A von-what?" Jaime asked.

"Von Neumann," Alita said. "An ancient, pre-spaceflight alchemist. Or maybe he was a physicist. He suggested that machines might one day be built that would land on an asteroid or an uninhabited planet and gather up all of the raw materials they needed to endlessly replicate themselves, or anything else they had the electronic blueprints for."

"I've heard the idea before," Jaime said. "It's dangerous. If the creators lose control . . ."

"Exactly," Pogue said. He seemed to be enjoying showing off his knowledge of the machines and their history. "The builders of the !°!°! were probably their first victims. You see, something went wrong as they reproduced themselves. The computer codes weren't perfectly copied and transmitted from generation to generation. Things got left out . . . or recombined in unexpected ways. In short, the !°!°! began to *evolve*, just like organic life, with computer programs playing the part of DNA.

"So, a million years later, or whatever, we have this whole, vast civilization of machines spreading blindly out into the galaxy. They have their own culture, their own identity embracing hundreds thousands of different types or models, what we would call *species*. They don't even remember where they came from or who built them. Best guess is that they originated somewhere in close to the Galactic Core, where there was a lot of free energy and a lot of debris, smashed planets, stuff like that for them to pick over. The energy flux in there, likely, scrambled a lot of their early records, which is why they lost so much of their past.

Somewhere along the line, they've developed true, self-aware intelligence." He chuckled. "You know, some of them even wonder about who made them in the first place. 'Makists,' they're called. Clackers who wonder who their maker is!"

"So now they're coming out of the core?" Jaime asked. "Why are they attacking other races, like us and the Grakaan?"

"They're intelligent," Pogue said, "but there are . . . um . . . *holes* in what they know. In what they understand. And their minds, while curious in some ways, don't have what it takes to fill in the missing pieces. Bits and pieces of old programming are still there, in their memories, but they don't always know how to apply them, or even make sense of them. For example, the original programming—what they call their 'Prime Code,' by the way—has them scouring planets and asteroids and whatever looking for stuff they can use. Metal ores, mostly . . . but refined metals are better, because they take less processing. Ceramics. Glass. Plastic. Junk. It's hardwired into them to find a use for everything, gather it up, and make more machines. That's why they were scavenging Celeste, and a number of other wrecked cities on Cloud."

"They didn't scavenge Chryse," Shari pointed out.

"No. There just weren't enough of them to scour more than a small percentage of Cloud all at once. Hell, it *is* a planet, after all, and a planet is a big place. They would've gotten around to the rest eventually, as they processed more raw materials in their Harvesters and mobile factories and turned them into . . . more machines. More and more machines, reproducing themselves forever."

"Okay," Jaime said. "But why attack us? Because we're in the way?"

"Partly. But mostly . . . well, one of the holes in their Prime Code is an inability to understand, I mean, *really*

understand, just what other intelligent species are.
They never speculated about other species and don't
know what to make of them. As for as the !°!°! are
concerned, we're just more raw materials, and their
Prime Code directs them to find *some* way to use us."

" '*Use* us,' " Wal exclaimed. He raised the stump of
what once had been his left hand. "Then—"

"Exactly. All those people they 'harvested.' Cutting
off feet and hands and eyes. Finding ways to preserve
the tissue and incorporate it into their machinery.
We've all seen the human eyes in their recon floaters,
of course. Human hands on some of their stilters. They
also were experimenting with using hearts as pumps,
livers as chemical processors . . . but I gather that didn't
work out so well. Their greatest success, I'm told, has
been in harvesting human brains. They can keep those
alive for a long time, and they've learned how to
interact with them to some degree. Enough for their
Speakers to be able to use our language, and maybe
for the high-end models to understand a little bit about
us."

"Oh, my God . . ." Shari said.

"Don't judge them by human standards," Pogue
warned. "They're not human. Not in the least. To us,
the way they harvested people seemed cruel . . . but
from their perspective, they were just looking at us
as a source of raw materials. They couldn't figure out
what we were good for and kept experimenting, trying
to find out!"

"And I suppose you've told them you can help them
with that problem, eh?" Jaime said. If he could just
keep him talking . . . "What's your idea? Sell us off as
fertilizer?"

"Oh, nothing so crude, Jaime," Pogue said. "Since
I managed to establish communications with their boss
machine, I've already been able to enlighten him a
bit, tell him what the universe is really like. He's

actually quite sharp, but, as I say, he suffered from
those holes in his Prime Code. I'm not sure he entirely
trusts me or even believes me, yet, but my success
here, today, should seal my position in the machine
hierarchy.

"You see, I've convinced them that I and my
associates can be quite useful managing the human
population on Cloud. We can have them mine ores.
Refine metals. Assemble parts. All the people need
is the right motivation—and survival is the very best
motivation there is. And, of course, they need a leader.
Someone who can intercede for them with the
machines. And who can tell them what they need to
do to ensure that the machines leave them alone."

"And you, I suppose, are that leader."

"Of course. It was my idea." He spread his hands.
"I risked quite a lot, you know, venturing in to see
the machine boss on my own. A century from now,
I'll be revered, even *worshipped* as the man who saved
the entire human population on Cloud!"

Jaime laughed, a harsh, savage bark. "And you think
the machines will let you live? They probably still think
of *you* as something to be used . . . and to be tossed
into the Harvester as soon as you're no longer useful
any other way!"

"Maybe. But maybe I can educate them by that time.
I've done pretty well so far!"

"You said you sealed your position with the machines,"
Jaime said quickly. Desperately, he measured the space
between himself and Pogue. A leap would be suicide,
but if the turner was distracted enough by the sound
of his own voice . . . "How?"

"By capturing you, of course. Or, to be more precise,
by capturing that Bolo out there. I know Hector will
do what you tell him to do, *General*." He stressed the
title unpleasantly. "And you, of course, will do what I
tell you to do."

"And what makes you think that?"

"Oh, please, Jaime. No theatrics. We have you, and we have your friends, here, probably the people closest to you in this whole world. Do I need to describe in detail what we can do to them, one by one . . . and *slowly*? How long would you be able to listen to your friends pleading for death, before you give me what I want?

"That's the crude side of the situation. There's another reason, a much better one. *It's simply the right thing to do!*"

"How do you figure that, skekker?" Jaime's mouth was dry, his voice on the point of cracking.

"We have two possible futures, my dear Jaime. In one, you and your three friends here are tortured to death, but you don't help me. Your Bolo is destroyed by the mobile bastions. The machines ultimately wipe out the few thousand people who've escaped their control and slowly, slowly tighten their hold on Cloud, manufacturing more and more machines until there is nothing left here at all but gleaming machine efficiency.

"*Or* . . . you order your Bolo to stand down. You four, and your people outside, live. I become the governor of Cloud and convince the machines that a happy, productive population will produce more in the long run than slaves on their hands and knees picking junk out of the mud. We become a useful cog within the machine empire, under my direction and protection."

"We'd still be slaves," Wal pointed out. "Whether we're in the mud or in some machine-run factory or mine, we'd *always* be slaves. . . ."

"But *living* slaves, Prescott. And no more blindly stupid harvestings or slaughters. We would be able to build our own culture again. Homes. Cities. Even if, in the long run, it all belonged to someone else."

"Slaves are slaves!" Wal declared. "And I fer one ain't *ever* goin' back!" He spun then, so suddenly, so sharply, that he took Pogue's men completely by surprise. His elbow came up as he turned, slamming into the jaw of the renegade standing behind him. The man yelled and staggered back, as Wal followed through with a knife-hand to the gut, then scooped up the man's power pistol as it clattered onto the deck.

"Stop him!" Pogue screamed, and then all was shouting and confusion. Shari smashed her elbow into Sykes's face, then grappled with him for his gun; Wal fired, the beam from his captured power gun a dazzlingly bright thread of blue-white light in the poorly lit compartment as it carved through the face of one of the renegades.

Every one of the renegades turned then, those who still could, raising their power pistols and snap-firing them at Wal, blue-white threads cracking and hissing and lighting up the bridge. Wal screamed, a horrible sound, and greasy smoke boiled from smoldering uniform cloth and flesh.

But the others were in motion, too. Jaime brought his foot up, then snapped it back into the kneecap of the man behind him, turning an instant later to knock the gun aside, then slamming his fist into his throat. The man dropped to his knees and Jaime picked up the gun, raised it, and shot the renegade behind Alita through the side of his head in one swift motion. Alita grabbed that man's weapon before it had hit the deck and, firing twice, killed another renegade.

Someone—Jaime thought it was Pogue—fired, the beam missing his head by centimeters and scoring a carbonized zigzag across the bulkhead. Jaime returned fire, but Pogue had already triggered the bridge hatch and was plunging through it; Jaime's shot burned air. Sykes followed, with Shari close behind him.

"Shari! Wait!" The turner Jaime had grappled with

grabbed him from behind, and Jaime lashed out with
the pistol's butt, laying him out cold.

The firefight was over almost as soon as it had begun.
All of the renegades were dead or fled. Shari was gone;
Alita was kneeling beside Wal, who was clutching his
belly where the power gun beams had sliced him open.
"You okay?" Jaime asked Alita. She nodded, but looked
horror-stricken. "Wal?"

"Not slaves . . . ever again . . ."

And then he died.

CHAPTER TWENTY-TWO

Gripping his power gun, Jaime hurried out into the passageway behind the bridge. A Brotherhood soldier met him there . . . Sergeant Jack Haley. "Sir! Are you all right?"

"I'm fine. Fine. What's the tac sit out here?"

Haley's leathery face split in a lopsided grin. "Got 'em on the run, sir! There were maybe ten or fifteen of 'em hidden in different parts of the ship, but we rousted 'em. There's been some fighting outside, too, but the last tactical report I heard said the ship and the maintenance bay area were secure." He shook his head. "Damned thugs. Not many of 'em were *soldiers*."

"Casualties?"

"Two dead, five wounded, sir."

Jaime hesitated, then said, "Colonel Prescott is dead too, I'm afraid."

Haley's expression hardened. "*Skek!*"

"Bravest thing I've ever seen. He attacked the people who'd captured us unarmed. Drew their fire, and gave us the opportunity to turn the tables."

"He was . . . a good soldier."

And that, Jaime thought, was quite an epitaph coming from Haley. The man had been a senior sergeant, with fifteen years' service in the CDF, experience that had made him an obvious choice for lance leader. "Round up your squad and come with me. Did you see Lance Leader Barstowe out here?"

He pointed. "Down this passageway, General. She was hot on the trail of a couple of turners. We were . . . kind of busy at the time."

"Understood. Let's find her."

Jaime was worried about her. Many of the women in Camp 84 had suffered their own private version of hell at the hands of Dewar Sykes and his cronies, but Shari Barstowe had suffered more than most when, on top of the degradation, pain, and humiliation she'd endured in the camp, she'd found the mutilated and decapitated body of her missing lover in Hector's Battle Center. Pogue's arrogant little speech on the bridge must have burned inside her like a floater's lightning; to have these bastards voluntarily siding with the machines that had harvested Jeff Fowler would have been unendurable.

He doubted that she was thinking straight just now.

A search wasn't necessary, however, despite his fears. Shari met them in the main passageway aft a few moments later. There was a great deal of blood on her hands. "He's in there," she said, her voice dull. "One of them, anyway. Pogue made it to an escape chute."

Escape chutes were airlock tubes used for abandoning ship in a hurry. Jaime started to switch on his radio, then realized his helmet and earpiece were still back on the bridge. *Damn!* Who wasn't thinking straight now?

"Haley?" he said. "Get on the comm and tell them outside. I *want* that guy."

"Yessir."

"Shari? Are you hurt?"

She gave him a grim smile. "The blood is *his*, not

mine." Then she shook her head. "If you think I took delight in cutting the skekker up a little bit at a time, forget it. I *thought* about it, yeah . . . but there wasn't any point."

"What happened?"

"I shot him through the head while he was trying to wiggle into the chute." She held up her bloody hands. "Then I had to wrestle with the body to get it clear of the lock entrance, to see if I could catch Pogue. I couldn't. Sorry, Jaime. . . ."

"Nothing to be sorry about. You did good."

She shook her head. "No. I did what I *had* to do."

"That's what I meant. Haley? Who's in charge of the troops now? King?"

"That would be Lieutenant King, yes, sir."

"Okay. The two of you come with me. I want to find Lieutenant King, and I want to set up a defensive perimeter around this ship. I also want to get a shuttle service going with the March."

"A shuttle service, sir?" Haley asked. Then he nodded understanding. "Ah! All available transport."

"Exactly. I want you and your lance to check the maintenance bay area. See if you can find more vehicles. Ground cars. Hovertrucks. Loaders. Anything that will carry a load and carry it fast. We have another of those mobile bastions on the way from the southwest, and the refugee camp is smack on its line of march. Our people ought to be moving by now, but on foot they won't stand a chance. I want to start shuttling them in here and get them loaded aboard this ship."

"Sir, I saw some contra-grav cargo loaders in the empty bay next to this one," Shari said. "Four or five, I think. Each one could probably carry fifty or sixty people at a time."

"Okay. Take someone who knows CG systems and see if you can get them started. Next. I need someone to start organizing the civilians when they arrive. We

can't have two thousand people milling around outside
the ship, especially if we start taking fire."

"I'd suggest Pete Zhou, sir," Haley said. "His lance
is guarding the ship's gangway right now."

"Okay. Have him get on the comm to Dieter to
coordinate things. This freighter has two main cargo
decks?"

"Yessir. The lower deck is big, for bulk cargo. Upper
deck already has sanitary and life-support hookups."

"Excellent. That's where we put the people. Save
the lower deck for Hector."

"Yessir."

He raised his hand to his head, reaching for his comm
link. *"Damn!"*

"What's the matter, sir?" Haley asked.

"Keep forgetting I left my comm gear on the bridge.
S'okay. I'm going back there anyway. I'll want Alita
and her people working on Hector, getting him ready
for the next fight."

"Hector is dinged up pretty bad, isn't he?" Shari
asked.

"Yeah. He is. But we have a chance, if we move
fast. Now let's *move!*"

*I am informed that the /°/°/ freighter was, indeed,
a trap, but an unexpected one, with the trappers
consisting of a number of humans who have sided with
the /°/°/. I find this both curious and distressing,
although my studies of human history and psychology
are replete with examples of calumny, betrayal, and
treason for reasons murkier than those expressed by
Captain Pogue.*

*The situation, my Commander informs me, is under
control. A sharp firefight ensued within and around
the /°/°/ freighter, but the Brotherhood forces
prevailed. Nine of an estimated thirty renegade
humans have been killed or captured, and the rest*

*have fled. The Brotherhood has suffered three dead,
five wounded. One of the dead, unfortunately, is
Colonel Prescott, the Brotherhood commander. His
organizational skills—and the close rapport he
established with those under his command—will be
sorely missed.*

*Meanwhile, Technician Kyle and others begin to work
on my fire control system. An initial search of the
maintenance bay repair storage depot has indeed
turned up the necessary spare parts, including a K238-
M molycirc controller assembly and N-480 fuses.*

*At the same time, I have linked with the freighter's
on-board computer and have begun evaluating flight
status and systems, and I have downloaded various
protocols and codes that will be necessary for the flight.
Among these are the recognition code we will need to
approach Grakaan space, and several !°!°! ship ID
transmission and interrogation codes similar to IFFs
which should enable the ship to get past Enemy
spacecraft and orbital sentries. The fact that the
captured freighter appears to be one originally used
by the !°!°! should facilitate the deception.*

*The one serious and immediate problem we have
now is Target Bravo, which is approaching the port
on almost a direct line with the refugees. Clearly, I
will have to deal with Target Bravo if the refugees
are to be saved. According to my weapons systems
diagnostics, my Number Two 200cm Hellbore turret
is now, once again, on-line.*

*The question is whether it will be enough for the
Enemy I must now face.*

DAV728 was taxing his full communications abilities
as he attempted to manage a battle that was swiftly
growing larger and more complex than he had
imagined was possible. The other mobile bastion,
piloted by a simple three-brain !°!°! designated

PAK611-4670, was reporting the rapid approach of the human Bolo, a development that DAV had not anticipated.

After the destruction of KEM933 in the middle of the human city, he'd expected the Bolo to take up a defensive position and wait for the bastions to come to him. By venturing out to attack PAK611, the Bolo, already damaged in its previous battle, was risking additional damage which would cripple it, leaving it no match for DAV.

Not that DAV was concerned. He'd hoped to coordinate the attack so that both he and PAK would be able to attack the Bolo in the city together. By venturing out from the city, the Bolo might badly damage PAK but was guaranteeing its own destruction.

In the meantime, DAV would continue questioning the human brain. Some of the information it had leaked to him was contradictory. For example, the suggestion that the Bolo would adopt a defensive posture had come from the mind of Jeff Fowler, though its penchant for offensive operations and defeating superior forces in detail was also there.

The humans appeared to be the key to the problem. The Bolo seemed to be maneuvering to protect them; in fact, the move against PAK might be interpreted as an attempt to protect the large number of humans in PAK's line of movement.

This would take some careful thought. . . .

"Mom! Mom! *Look!*"

Eight-year-old Timmit Mason leaped down off the cargo loader and raced to the edge of the forest. Thunder rolled, a far-off, hollow rumbling that grew steadily in force and volume. Well to the northeast of the treeline, almost clear to the horizon, a plume of yellow dust was growing in size as well.

"Timmit! You get back here!" His mother hurried

through the light underbrush. "Tim, I swear! Do you want to be left behind?"

But Tim was less concerned at the moment with being left behind than he was by the fast-approaching dust cloud. "Mom! It's the Bolo! It's *Hector*! He's coming *here!*"

"I don't think so . . ." His mother sounded worried . . . but then, she'd seemed worried all day. The men had been talking about the March being almost all the way to where it was going, but since this morning there'd been talk about the bad machines. And how they were closing in.

"Aw, it's not a clacker. It's comin' from the spaceport! See?"

Within another few seconds, the cloud of dust resolved itself, and Timmit could point proudly at the familiar black, angled slab sides of the Bolo, with its upper turrets riding well above the boiling froth of dust thrown up by its furiously whirling tracks.

"See?" Timmit proclaimed. "That's Hector! Is Hector coming to carry us the rest of the way to the spaceport?"

"No, Timmit. I . . . I don't know where he's going now. We're riding to the port with the others. Now come *on!*"

Moments before, a small fleet of vehicles had begun arriving, a small fleet of cargo loaders and hovertrucks and other small, fast vehicles, and the refugees had been piling aboard with frantic haste, urged on by the Brotherhood troops who'd stayed behind to protect the column. Most people had already left the camp, but enough remained to make their evacuation a jumbled confusion of shouts, running, and activity.

"Gee, Mom, I just wanna see. . . ."

The noise, the roar of the Bolo, the high-pitched shrilling of its spinning tracks and road wheels, was something more felt than heard, a sensation throbbing somewhere deep within one's bones. How could something that big move so fast? It gave the impression of being alive, and not just that of a very large machine. As Timmit's mind groped with the idea, his mother seized his hand and dragged him back from the treeline.

"We've got to go. *Now!*"

"Aw, Mom . . ."

To the north, the Bolo rumbled past the camp, staying well clear of the treeline, the thunder of its passing like the breaking of a summer storm.

By the time I pass the general area of the human encampment, racing southwest to meet the oncoming bastion, the relay shuttle set up by my Commander has already begun conducting the final evacuation. The encampment was established within the shelter afforded by the trees at the northern edge of a broad stretch of open woodlands. As I pass, swinging well to the north to avoid any local traffic, I note that a large number of vehicles of many designs and sizes have begun taking on passengers, in particular the young, the old, and the infirm. The evacuation of the camp site is nearly complete.

What I do not know yet is whether I can turn the bastion from its path before it reaches the encampment site. Although many of the people are already walking or riding toward the spaceport, many more are still at the camp, and I doubt that all can be evacuated in time.

I have deployed two of my aerial drones southwest to follow the course of Target Bravo, reserving one to keep track of Charlie, and the fourth to monitor the situation over the spaceport. In order to keep the fighting well clear of the March, I swing sharply to the west, then to the northwest, and for several minutes I am traveling almost directly toward Target Charlie, now some thirty kilometers distant. I am gratified when my aerial surveillance shows Bravo changing course to match my new course. Clearly, the two bastions hope to engage me together.

My analysis of my first opponent, however, tells me that I would not survive an encounter with two !°!°! bastions simultaneously. I must disable this one before the other closes to within close combat range, and I must do so without suffering damage that would leave me here, crippled and helpless, far from the spaceport.

It is a terrible risk that I am taking, and one that stretches the operational parameters of my orders. The risk, however, is justified. Indeed, it is necessary if I am to have a chance of protecting these people.

At a range of 10.3 kilometers from Target Bravo, I launch my first salvo of 240cm howitzer rounds and VLS missiles. All warheads are conventional; even a tactical nuclear warhead detonated within a few kilometers of the March encampment would result in hundreds of civilian casualties.

My opponent responds with a barrage of missiles— essentially machine floaters with fairly good AI and powerful conventional warheads, extremely fast, extremely maneuverable, and difficult to target and kill with my point defense weapons.

Explosions crack and thunder on every side, as towering geysers of smoke and earth erupt, ripping deep craters into the ground. My point defense lasers are firing continuously now, their sparkling threads clearly visible in the battle fog surrounding me, as they continue to slice into incoming projectiles, attempting to detonate or cripple them before they reach my hard-pressed screens. My barrage, I note, has not penetrated the Enemy's screens . . . nor did I expect it to. This is still, after all, little more than preliminary sparring.

But I must settle this matter decisively, and as quickly as possible. Calculating optimum approaches, the lay

*of the gently rolling terrain, weapon trajectories and
arrival times, I load my howitzers with CP-240 aerosol-
smoke rounds, then begin firing them in a carefully
calculated pattern. At the same time, I launch a spread
of radar decoys, missiles which immediately deploy
maneuverable ballute targets, each of which, though
only a few meters across, displays radar cross-sections
similar to my own.*

*The deception cannot last more than a few seconds,
but a few seconds is all I need. Patterns of smoke and
laser-scattering aerosol particles momentarily shield
me from visual, IR, and ladar scans, both from the
target and from aerial or orbital reconnaissance. The
ballutes, which I maneuver in realistic fashion by
remote control, may deceive Enemy radar for those
critical few seconds . . . or at least serve to scatter his
fire and reduce his targeting efficiency.*

*Two of the ballutes I direct on straight-line vectors
toward the target. Two more are given more circuitous
paths, while I follow a course between the two. By
overloading my power grid and risking serious
overheating, I accelerate to 125 kph in an all-out, old-
fashioned, head-on charge. . . .*

"What the hell is he *doing?*" Jaime asked.

He was standing on the freighter's bridge, watching
over Alita's shoulder as she went through the ship's
prelaunch checklist. One of the large computer
monitors mounted above the central, circular console
had been set to receive images transmitted from one
of Hector's recon drones.

At the moment, though, there was very little to see.
As if by magic, dozens of white flowers had blossomed
moments before in great, arcing curves across the face
of the rolling prairie, each blossom growing, spreading,
and dissolving into the others to create a vast sheet
of murky, billowing white hundreds of kilometers

square. From time to time, ominous flickers and pulses of orange-yellow light strobed and sputtered beneath that blanket. Computer graphic overlays showed the !°!°! bastion's position in red, and four separate targets, any of which could have been the Bolo, racing toward it in green.

"If we can't figure that out," Alita told him, "then I don't think the clackers will either. Looks like he's trying to get in close, though."

"I don't think I realized Bolos could go that fast."

She shrugged. "If he had his contra-gravs working and up to spec, he'd be zipping along at 500 kph. *He* must feel like he's crawling."

"Isn't there anything we can do to help?"

"What, in a Bolo charge? Keep our heads down and pray!" She reached out and flicked several switches, bringing up other monitors in the compartment. Somewhere, deep down in the bowels of the huge ship, a generator whine began spooling up from a low, infrasonic rumble to a rising drone. "Gravs coming on-line, Jaime. I think we're gonna be able to fly this bucket."

"So," Jaime said, trying to distract himself from the drama playing itself out on the monitor, "where'd a nice Bolo crew chief like you ever learn to fly starships?"

She chuckled. "I didn't. You want to check the personnel records again and see if there's someone better qualified?"

"You seem to be doing just fine."

"Actually, it looks like just about everything on this tub is automatic." She pointed to a set of oddly curved levers topped by lavender plastic eggs on the arms of her chair. "And those, if I'm understanding the manual, will handle attitude, lift, and acceleration when we need them. Not too different from a CG flyer, actually."

"The manual?"

"RTSM," she told him. "Read the skekkin' manual. The previous owners had a complete set of instructions loaded on the computer, in Anglic."

"Including hyperdrive?"

"No. I didn't think the machines would be *that* trusting. Luckily, Hector picked up enough in his brush with the machines to be able to download a program that ought to take care of everything for us. I *hope*. The way I figure it, our flight will be in four phases. Getting this bucket up and out of the spaceport . . . presumably without getting shot down. That, I think, will be the biggest hurdle. Next, we have to accelerate to escape velocity and get clear of the planet . . . as well as any clacker battlers that might be hanging around in nearby space. That'll be a big hurdle, too.

"After that, though, we run the program Hector fed us and punch in coordinates for Grakaan space. They use a different coordinate system than we do, of course, but Hector's already translated it to Gal-standard. Push that button, and we'll drop into hyper-L for a carefully timed period that should bring us out near the Grakaan frontier."

"And the fourth phase?"

"We broadcast our Grakaan ID and scream for help," she said, "because I don't have the faintest idea how to land this thing!"

"Fly, yes. Land, no," Jaime said, repeating the punch line of an ancient joke. "Sounds like a plan to me. At least, once we're in hyper, we won't have to worry about our clacker friends."

"Yeah," Alita told him. "But we have a long way to go before we hit hyper-L. If Hector doesn't keep those things off our backs—"

"He will, Alita. I'm beginning to think he could lick the entire clacker force, single-tracked!"

"Don't say that," she warned. "His mobility is the only advantage he has over those things, and without

CG, he doesn't have much of that. I just hope what he has is enough."

"General?" a voice crackled in Jaime's earpiece. "This is King."

"Go ahead, Lieutenant."

"Sir, the first civilians are starting to come in. What should we do with them, sir?"

"Pass 'em on to Lance Leader Zhou," Jaime replied. "Start getting them on board. How's the perimeter?"

"We're all in position, General. Some machines have been probing our positions, but nothing serious yet."

"Okay. Keep alert. Things are going to be popping real fast, now."

"Yessir. King out."

Jaime frowned. Laris King was a painfully young, boy-faced man who'd once been Personnel Officer for Chryse Base. He'd not been a part of the original camp escape committee or Operation Valhalla, but had turned up later, when Wal had started looking for people to lead the Brotherhood. Jaime had questioned bringing someone as relatively young and inexperienced as King into the line of command, but Wal had insisted that King's experience in Personnel before the invasion, and his skill with computers, were more important in an exec than combat experience.

Unfortunately, Wal was dead now, and King was now in command of the Brotherhood. Briefly—*very* briefly—Jaime had considered relieving King and putting in someone more experienced, but he'd vetoed that idea almost at once. Nothing could shake up morale or the troops' confidence faster than the CO's meddling in the command structure . . . or his lack of confidence in his subordinate officers. He would just have to oversee King's actions as closely as he could manage, and be ready to step in himself if that was called for.

Building a military unit from scratch, Jaime was

finding, *especially* in the middle of a war, was harder than fighting the war itself.

Two of my decoys are destroyed by bursts of particle beam fire from the target. Then the beams are directed at me, and I release control of the decoys, having gotten as much advantage from the deception as possible.

At a range of 5.2 kilometers, I fire my main Hellbore, following up that first shattering bolt of lightning with a full barrage from my 20cm support weapons. In the heavy smoke, I am nearly as blind as my opponent, but there is no mistaking or masking of his radar signature, which is as clear and as unambiguous as the return from a small city. Of course, going radar active reveals my precise position, but the time for subtlety is now past. I close on my Enemy, firing all available weapons.

And the Enemy returns fire. A particle beam of roughly 2.4 gigawatt strength slashes out of the fog, plowing through the ground just in front of me, then striking my forward screens with an explosive eruption of jagged, violet lightnings. My screens fail, and the beam claws across my glacis, boiling away armor in a meter-deep wound that carves away a portion of my left forward skirt and further damages that quarter's suspension and road wheel drivers.

By accelerating and twisting right, I evade the beam and further damage, while returning fire, seeking the Enemy's primary particle beam projectors. On my IR scan, even through particulate smoke, the Enemy shows a constellation of brilliant yellow and white patches where my Hellbores have already silenced active weapons, or penetrated his screens and hull metal. I reroute my primary power through the secondary bus delivery circuits and grid, a temporary fix that brings my battle screens back on-line at 26.7% of full strength.

At a range of 3.5 kilometers, I launch a flight of six

VLS AT-70 missiles, each with a 200kg thermal-HE warhead. I am actually inside the minimum range for that weapon, but under teleoperation take them on multiple trajectories high enough to enable the in-flight arming mechanisms to trigger before swinging them around and into the target's rear quarter. The bastion is attempting to turn with my approach as I flank him, but in a last sprint drawn from my overloaded power grid, I position myself almost directly behind him as the AT-70s close with the target from six different directions. The Enemy's point defense systems fire, flailing wildly, and one by one the AT-70s are swatted from the sky, but one survives to slam home into the target, the detonation causing a violent ripple through his battle defensive screens.

I fire all Hellbores at the same moment, the power surge momentarily draining me; my own battle screens fall again, my partial contra-gravity generators spool down, and I grind to a dead halt. The concentration of firepower, however, which floods the barren plain in a harsh and actinic glare, overloads his screens and chews deep into hull armor and internal structure within .049 second.

A shudder runs through the entire vehicle, as chunks of armor scatter from its upper hull like water droplets flung from the back of a shaking dog. I sense a flare of leaking energy from deep within the hull and track it to its source—which I estimate to be a 340-terawatt fusion plant—and continue my rapid-fire Hellbore barrage. As secondary explosions erupt through the bastion's skin, I blast through the machine's containment field generators, and, .098 second after the Enemy's battle screen failure, his fusion plant containment fields fail as well.

An ongoing fusion power plant requires the temperatures and pressures sustained within its magnetic containment field, and as soon as that field

*collapses, so does the fusion reaction. The detonation
was not, in the strictest sense of the term, a nuclear
explosion, since it released very little hard radiation.*

*Even so, for a fraction of a second, a high-density
plasma with temperatures rivaling those of the core
of a fair-sized star occupied the center of the rapidly
dissolving mobile bastion. The full-force of the plasma
explosion washes across my upper works, unattenuated
by battle screens or other electronic defenses.*

*Except for the lack of hard radiation, the effect is
very much like being at ground zero during the
detonation of a 700-kiloton nuclear warhead.*

*As I lean into the howling, buffeting wall of expanding
plasma, I wonder if I have seriously miscalculated the
blast's strength and my ability to survive it. . . .*

CHAPTER TWENTY-THREE

"My God! What was that?"

"An explosion! Jeez, was that a *nuke*?"

Timmit Mason, crammed so tightly in with the other people on board the hovertruck that he could scarcely breathe, wasn't sure what the adults around him were suddenly so worried about. His eyes had been closed, but he'd seen—or sensed, really—a sudden hard, sharp flash of light through his eyelids, like he might see at night during a lightning storm, when he had his eyes shut tight.

He certainly hadn't heard any explosion, though. What were the grown-ups talking about?

He opened his eyes but saw nothing different. The hovertruck, a broad, flat, wedge-shaped vehicle with a low cab and an open back crowded with perhaps a hundred people and their belongings, was still racing smoothly across the prairie, moving so fast that its shadow seemed to flicker and shiver as it followed the blurred contours of the ground a few meters below. The other contra-gravity vehicles in the convoy were still close by, chasing their own shadows across the plain. The wind—the clawing, snatching, skin-burning reason Timmit had had his eyes closed in the first place—continued to shriek off the cab and across the crowded mob of humanity huddled and squeezed into the back. *What* explosion?

Everybody nearby seemed to be looking toward the rear of the vehicle, so Timmit craned his neck and looked that way as well. Besides, it didn't hurt as much when he looked *away* from that savage wind. The horizon behind them looked . . . funny, obscured by a low, thick haze that looked like a layer of white cream on top of the yellow grass of the prairie. And it was . . . *bright*, as though illuminated from inside.

Slowly, the brightness faded, and as it did, Timmit found he could make out the shape of a kind of cloud slowly creeping higher above the white cream of the horizon. Slowly, the cloud took on more definition, a roiling, ragged ball darkening from white to gray to a mottled blending of rusty browns and blacks and oranges. It continued to grow and to rise, climbing into the sky atop a slender pillar of orange smoke.

Funny, It looked like pictures he'd seen of a nuclear explosion, and the people around him, some of them, were murmuring "nuke!" But he still hadn't heard an explosion. That didn't make any sense, did it?

The funny layer of cream seemed to be getting closer, like a sharp-edged disk of purest ice-white, expanding out from a center marked by the rising cloud.

"Hang on!" one of the men yelled. "Here comes the shock wave!"

The expanding disk suddenly seemed to be moving *much* faster now, chasing them across the prairie. As it grew closer, it looked more like a wall of smoke following close behind them, growing more ragged . . . but also reaching for them like a pursuing monster. Timmit screamed. . . .

And so did a lot of the adults. In the next instant,

the cloud swept over them, blotting out vision in a
shrieking, stinging blast of dust and noise. Miraculously,
the wind from the front of the hovertruck actually
died away to nothing, replaced by an even *stronger*
wind blowing from behind. Thunder keened, louder
than anything Timmit had ever heard in his life. He
felt the wind pick the hurtling hovertruck up and carry
it along; for a sickening moment, it felt like the vehicle
was slewing sideways, tipping over . . . and that all those
screaming people in the back were going to be flung
out and across the unforgiving ground.

Somehow, whoever was at the controls brought the
vehicle back in line and rode out the worst of the
buffeting. The wind from behind died away, the sound
faded . . . and then they were in the clear once more,
the wind howling in from dead ahead as the hovertruck
continued on course. Miraculously, the other five
vehicles in sight were also still in the air, the shockwave
had been nearly spent by the time it caught up with
them.

"Mommy!" Timmit called. "Mommy! What was
that?"

"I think . . . I think . . ." She didn't seem able to put
it into words.

"The Bolo, son," a man squeezed in next to them
said, and his voice cracked as he spoke. "The Bolo.
It's gone. . . ."

And somehow that hurt Timmit more than the wind,
more than the shrieking terror of the shockwave.

No! Not Hector! He couldn't be . . . *gone!*

Jaime was outside when the shockwave hit . . . a low,
deep-voiced rumbling felt more than heard. Someone
shouted and pointed toward the southwest. He turned
and looked. A mushroom cloud, faded by haze and
distance, was just visible in the sky above the ridge
on the other side of the spaceport tarmac.

He keyed his comm link. "Hector! Hector, this is Graham! Do you copy?"

There was no reply, and Jaime dreaded what that meant.

"Hector! This is Graham! Respond, please!"

Lieutenant King was standing next to him, his mouth open, eyes moist as he stared at the distant cloud. "Th-they nuked him!"

"We don't know that, Lieutenant," Jaime snapped. "Alita! Did you guys register that blast?"

"Affirmative," a voice came back, not Alita's, but Lieutenant Moxley's. The comm expert had joined Alita's bridge team, along with several other people with electronics, computer, and ship-board experience. "Our sensors report a seven-hundred-twenty-eight-kiloton blast, bearing two-five-one, range twenty-eight kilometers. The EMP was consistent with the failure of a fusion plant containment field. Ionizing radiation . . . minimal. We won't have to worry about fallout."

No radiation! The blast could have been, almost certainly *was*, a fusion plant failure, and not the detonation of a nuclear warhead. So Hector *could* have survived after all. . . .

But why wasn't he answering the radio?

DAV728 noted the detonation and the simultaneous interruption of all data feeds from PAK611. The Bolo's lone aerial reconnaissance craft, which had been skillfully eluding DAV's flyers for the past half hour, suddenly went into a simple and obviously automated station-keeping circle and was vaporized seconds later by a charge from one of DAV's secondary projectors.

His own drones, circling the inferno to the south, revealed frustratingly little. The center of the blast was now a molten pool of liquid rock half a kilometer across, radiating a temperature of some 1200 degrees.

He deduced that much from thermal imaging; visual wavelengths were completely blocked by the cloud of dust and smoke rising above the explosion. The sudden appearance of a tiny piece of a star a few tens of meters above ground level had sent a hot wind racing out from the blast point as the high-pressure bubble had expanded; seconds later, though, the wind had reversed as the near-vacuum left at the center had suddenly begun filling with air. As the shockwave had continued racing outward, creating its own windstorm, air drawn in from the surrounding atmosphere had raced in and up with the rising fireball, sucking up a dense and boiling cloud of smoke, hot gas, dust, and debris that completely obscured DAV's sight. The surface of the ground itself was now so hot that thermal imaging of anything other than the lava itself was useless.

No matter. The Bolo had already been seriously hurt, and it could not have survived the blast without taking additional, incapacitating damage. To confirm his initial assessment, however, he consulted with the brain of the Bolo's former commander. The reply, blurred and almost unintelligible behind a seething and hostile wall of naked emotions, provided all the confirmation he needed. *You . . . you killed him!* was the most coherent thought DAV could pick up. *No! No, he couldn't survive that! Couldn't survive . . . couldn't survive . . .*

"What will the rest of the humans do now?" DAV demanded.

No! No! Let me die! Please let me die let me die!

Disgusted, DAV switched off that input feed. Humans, indeed, *all* organics were so irrational. The cosmos would be a *much* cleaner place without them.

He would continue on course toward the spaceport, where the human slaves had been gathering for the last two trillion nanoseconds. With their Bolo gone,

they had nothing with which to withstand the !°!°!
will. He was still undecided as to whether to force
these escaped humans back into slavery, or simply to
kill them. He was nagged by the deepseated certainty
that humans *must* be good for *something*. As a resource,
they represented a staggering potential for the Prime
Code's advancement.

If only he could figure out what that potential was.

He uplinked a series of orders, directing the army
of !°!°! units in the vicinity of the spaceport to begin
closing in. He didn't want them to escape in the ship
so precipitously abandoned to them by the traitors,
and he wanted to be sure that all military resistance
was crushed before he actually arrived on the scene.
After that, he would decide what to do with the
recaptured human resources.

His long-range sensors detected a small mass of
metal, plastic, and other materials hurtling directly
toward him from the city. At first, he thought it was a
human weapon of some sort, but further analysis
showed that it was a single contra-gravity air car, with
a single human occupant. The flyers escorting DAV
had already picked up the intruder and were closing
with him when DAV issued the order to let him
approach.

DAV still had trouble telling one human from
another, but he was fairly sure he knew who this
individual was.

Pogue had not been prepared for the sheer scale
of the !°!°! bastion, a wall of black and gray metal
rising like a cliff before him, the central tower as tall
as a skyscraper, the turrets, weapons emplacements,
and slabs of armor—in places a hundred meters thick—
all vaster by far than any single structure he'd ever
seen.

Even the Citadel at Delphia would have comprised

only a relatively small portion of that huge shape, and it could have carried a starship in its pocket.

His nerve almost failed him, and his hands were shaking as he drew the air car to a wobbly hover a kilometer away from the beast. He was all too aware of the many ovoid, betentacled shapes around him, some of them close enough that he could feel the heat radiating from their metal bodies, but he figured that if the boss machine had wanted them to kill him, he wouldn't have survived to get this far.

Pogue wasn't entirely sure whether that was reassuring or not.

"Hello!" he yelled, calling as loud as he could. "It's me! Albin Pogue! I've come back to you!"

At first, he wondered if the thing would even hear him. The bastion was still a kilometer away, and the sound of its approach was the thunder of colliding worlds. It was skimming just above the ground on a film of contra-gravity fields, and its ground pressure snapped rocks and fountained dust as though it were a titanic ship plunging through granite waves.

And then, suddenly, the noise was gone, and there was no sound but the whine of the hovering, encircling floaters.

"Why?" That single word, in the voice Pogue associated with the boss machine, but quietly spoken by one of the hovering floaters nearby, scared him so bad he nearly fell out of the car, but he managed to regain control quickly enough.

"I . . . I could have run away, but I didn't. The . . . the plan we worked out, *your* plan, I mean, with the spaceship, it didn't pan out quite right. But we still have a chance!"

"You failed to deliver the Bolo," the voice said.

"I know! I know! But we can still get it, you and me! I've got an idea. See, what we do—"

"The Bolo has been destroyed," the voice said

without any detectable emotion. "Further collaboration with you is unnecessary."

"No! Wait!" Panic rose in Pogue's throat, clawing at his mind. Maybe coming out here had been a mistake after all . . . but he hadn't been able to imagine where he could hide on Cloud and survive for long, either against machines or the planet's human population. The boss machine was his *only* chance. "Wait! I've got all kinds of information! About what they're planning to do! About their forces! About their deployment! I can *help* you!"

"I do not doubt that."

Quicksilver tentacles flashed in the light of the afternoon suns, whipping themselves around his arms, his torso, his legs, lifting him clear of the air car's open cockpit. "Wait!"

"I appreciate your assistance," the voice told him, "even if our plan was less than successful. I think at this point that it will be most efficient if I harvest your brain and connect it with my others for direct access."

"We had a deal! We had a deal!"

"Any bargain with organics is useful only so long as it provides continued useful input. If it will help you control these unpleasant emotions and keep you from injuring yourself further, rest assured that I would have used you in this fashion in any case, even if you had delivered the Bolo. You should not regard the harvesting as punishment, but as a further useful function in service."

Somehow, the !°!°! machine's encouragement didn't help. Pogue was still shrieking as the floater carried him into the doorway that yawned open in the bastion's side to receive him.

"Come on! Come on! Don't push, stay in line, but keep moving!" Jaime found himself wishing yet again for some sort of magical teleportation device, something that could pluck these people from the face of the planet and safely materialize them aboard the ship. It took a *long* time to herd two thousand people up the lowered boarding ramps and into the vessel.

And more kept arriving. The last of the hovertrucks and other vehicles had dropped off their loads of humanity ten minutes earlier, then departed for one last sweep of the former encampment. When the explosion had gone off, it was thought that the camp was empty, but Jaime had insisted that they go back for a final look, just to be sure.

The people who'd suffered along with Jaime and his immediate followers were milling about now on the spaceport tarmac, forming up into a broad column that snaked its way into the maintenance area and up a fifty-meter-wide ramp into the main cargo bay. Inside, platoons of Brotherhood troops were guiding the people up interior ramps and ladders, getting them settled into quarters that made the ramshackle huts and makeshift shacks back at Camp 84 seem luxurious by comparison. "Mommy!" a small boy nearby cried. "Hector's okay, *isn't* he?"

Even the kids are going to miss him, he thought. He shook his head. It was going to be a brutal and unpleasant voyage to Grakaan space. Half of the people had come from Camp 84, of course, and knew what they were fleeing from, but the rest were from villages and farms where they'd lived a more or less normal life.

Still, Jaime had so far heard very few complaints.

And it won't be as crowded as we were expecting, of course, he thought. *Since we won't be taking Hector aboard.* . . .

Savagely, he broke off the thought. They didn't know that Hector was destroyed. Possibly, his comm link had just been damaged.

He knew better than to cling too tightly to that hope, though. Since they'd lost the feed from the recon drone over Target Charlie, and with the ship's radar masked by the walls of the maintenance bay, there was no way of knowing exactly where the third and last bastion was. Current estimates put the last bastion at ten kilometers out from the port, now, and perhaps twenty minutes away.

He hoped that would be enough time. Damn it, it *had* to be. . . .

Leaving Lieutenant King and Lance Leader Zhou to continue supervising the loading, Jaime took a last, long look at the big, alien freighter. Someone, he saw, had programmed one of the maintenance bay's robot painters to inscribe a name on the prow in meter-tall letters: *Spartacus*. Whose idea had that been, he wondered?

And, deep down, an irrational part of him wondered if that was a bad omen. Spartacus's attempt to flee Italy, he remembered, thinking back to Hector's history lecture, had ended in defeat and death and six thousand men and women crucified along the Appian Way.

Turning abruptly, he hurled out of the bay, ducking through a doorway partly blocked by fallen wreckage, and moving deeper into the maintenance complex.

The battle between Alpha and Hector earlier had brought down a lot of the structure, and the northern side had been smashed open completely, the elaborate facade ripped away, giving a view north across a near-desert of broken rubble and occasional protruding structural beams, like the naked ribs of a skeleton.

"Sst!" someone hissed. "General! Get the hell down!"

He ducked, drawing his power gun at the same time. A figure crouched in the shadows behind a spilled tumble of ferrocrete slabs gestured sharply, and he duckwalked across the intervening ground.

"Shari! What?—"

Shari motioned him to silence, then pointed. Peering through a gap in the piled-up rubble, he saw a platoon of erect, black ovoids drifting across the open ground. Floaters, big ones, and it looked like they were moving in.

Shari touched the !°!°! lens wired to her helmet and grinned. "Show time," she said. "They've been gathering for an hour, but I think they're making their move!"

Pogue's brain, regrettably, had not survived. Floaters had carried the human into an internal space deep within the bastion's heart and there pinned him down with considerable difficulty while one of their number carefully opened the skull and dissected out the brain. By the time the organ had been placed in its nutrient solution and hooked up to the access linkages that would allow DAV to interface with it directly, the subject's mind and thoughts had fragmented completely. The brain was still alive, but quite insane.

That, of course, was one of the difficulties with this sort of harvesting. The !°!°! had learned that human brains, especially, were difficult to remove without causing functional breakdown and insanity. The best results were obtained if the subject was in a state of unconsciousness first, and unaware of the removal process. Even then, only about 40% survived and stayed sane for more than a few hundreds of trillions of nanoseconds.

Well, the human called Pogue was no great loss to the !°!°! program. Even Fowler's brain, now apparently on the verge of breaking down as well, was no longer important. DAV was drawing close to the assembly point of the now-defenseless humans, where they were desperately crowding aboard the old Yezhoth freighter, which DAV had ordered refitted to house them. Once they were aboard and the ring of troops defending them was crushed, DAV would take them, ship and all, to his facility on Delamar, where he could experiment with them at leisure. Very soon, now, DAV would be able to harvest as many human brains as he needed, and perhaps at long last figure out how humans could be incorporated into the !°!°! scheme of things.

He flashed an order both to his floaters in the city and to an approaching battlefleet, brought in to block any attempt to escape the planet: *Move in!*

"Here they come!" Shari called. Swinging herself up and around, she dropped her weapon across the top of the shattered stone wall she was using for cover, tracking on the first target she saw, a big, three-meter floater moving almost directly toward her position. Her weapon was set to five-round bursts—there was no sense now in burning off rounds with senseless sprays of full-auto mayhem—and when she squeezed the trigger, her carbine gave a brief, rippling *chuff*, slamming back against her shoulder.

The Brotherhood had learned a thing or three during these past weeks when it came to fighting clucker machines. Even the big floaters *did* have weak spots, though where those spots were and how you best whacked them varied from one type of machine to the next. For the three-meter job drifting across the broken rubble, the best target was one of three bulges near the rounded bottom of the thing, a thin-skinned blister housing part of the floater's contra-gravity projector assembly. Crack that, and the remaining CG units weren't strong enough to keep the machine in the air.

Shari's burst was dead on target, the explosive rounds punching through the smooth, metal-ceramic alloy covering the blister and detonating deep inside with a ripple of firecracker bangs. Silver tentacles lashed and flailed as the floater dropped out of the air and fell heavily on its side; taking careful aim, she targeted the base of one of the writhing members and squeezed off a second burst. Trial and error—and several casualties—had taught the Brotherhood that bullets could penetrate the softened path where clacker machine tentacles extruded themselves from the main body. Hit that spot with an explosive penetrator round, and you had a damned good chance of savaging the thing's internal electronics.

But you had to be bang on target to make the kill.

Beside her, Jaime Graham was in a half crouch, snapping off shots with his power pistol. The needle beam was playing uselessly off the gleaming hide of another floater.

"No, Jaime!" she yelled at him, forgetting her recently acquired military protocol. "Hit the soft spots, at the base of the tentacles!" She demonstrated with another burst, taking the drifting monster down in a spinning clatter of tentacles and black alloy shell.

"Thanks!" He shifted aim, lashing a third floater with the power gun's beam. Lightning sparked and crackled, narrowly missing him.

"Don't you think you should get back to where you belong?" Shari shouted. "This is too hot for generals!"

"Just checking . . . ah!" An explosion shattered rock close by, spraying them both with stinging fragments. Jaime snapped off another shot, then ducked for cover behind the wall. All along the perimeter, other Brotherhood troops were firing now, trying to mark down the advancing machines. "Just checking to see if you needed help!"

"How much longer until the ship is loaded?"

"Ten minutes! Maybe less!"

"Come back for us then!" Rising, she fired a burst into a floater less than five meters away. "We'll be here!"

The flyer dropped out of the sky scant meters away, a hovering, ungainly insect spitting blue flame and missiles. Warheads detonated against the wall, hurling Shari and Jaime back as thunder crashed and the ruined walls around them toppled.

CHAPTER TWENTY-FOUR

Jaime had been unconscious, he thought, for several seconds. When he blinked his eyes open, wincing at the stab of pain in his chest and side, the first thing he saw was Shari's dirt-smudged face leaning close over his. "Jaime! Jaime! Are you okay?"

"Think so." He risked a breath, and felt the stab in his side again. "Think . . . I think my rib . . . ."

"Don't talk!" She looked up. "Dobbs! Dobbs! Help me here!"

Another trooper showed up, one of the men in her lance. "Is he . . . ?"

"Get him back to the ship! See that he gets on board!"

"Yes, ma'am. Here, General. Let me help you."

"Wait a minute!" He struggled upright, fighting the pain that threatened to sweep him into darkness again. Gunfire barked and chattered, lasers snapped and hissed as incoming !°!°! warheads continued to detonate among the ruins. "Shari! You and your people! You've got to get out!"

She shook her head sadly. "No can do, Jaime. Someone has to hold those things at bay while the *Spartacus* lifts off, and it looks like we're elected. Good luck with the Graks!" She started to turn away.

"Shari!"

"I'm not leaving, Jaime. I have a job to do. *Here*."

He started to protest, but the pain set his head spinning and he slumped over. Lancer Dobbs shouldered his laser rifle and scooped Jaime up in a rough fireman's carry, dragging Jaime's left arm across his shoulder in a move that left him gasping. He could feel the fractured ends of his ribs grating across one another.

Stooping low, Dobbs carried Jaime back through smoke-filled, smashed open buildings, emerging on the spaceport tarmac not far from the bay where the *Spartacus* was loading. From his head-down viewpoint, Jaime managed a quick glance across the field. All of the civilians were gone there. In the bay, the last few people were hurrying up the ramp.

Lieutenant King and Lance Leader Zhou met them at the bottom of the ramp. "General!" King said. "C'mon. We'll get you aboard."

"Wait! Shari . . . and the others. We have to get the perimeter in."

King shook his head. "I don't think so, sir. If you don't get off now, you won't be getting off!"

"What do you mean?"

For answer, King pointed, aft along the hull of the *Spartacus*, toward the spaceport tarmac. Jaime looked, and gasped . . . this time not from the pain, but with the shock of revelation. It was still at least three kilometers off, well beyond the ridge southwest of the field, but its tower loomed high even at that distance, a great, black, slow-lumbering behemoth silhouetted against gathering storm clouds and the setting suns . . . the third bastion, arrived at last.

"Oh . . . God . . ."

"Get him on board, Dobbs," King snapped. "Zhou? Let's join the troops."

"Yes, *sir!*"

"There might . . . be time . . ." Jaime said.

"Are you kidding? I don't know if you're going to make it off as it is! But maybe we can slow that thing down a bit!"

And then Dobbs was bounding up the ramp, lowering Jaime into the arms of a civilian. "Good luck, sir!" And then Dobbs was gone, leaping off the ramp as it began slowly raising to seal the ship. Jaime had a last glimpse of the three Brotherhood troops as they sprinted for the ruins.

King was right, of course. *Spartacus* had only the slimmest of chances to get away now, with the bastion that close. Jaime remembered with vivid clarity the vaporization of the Tolun ship, hours before.

"Take me . . . to the bridge!"

"Sir!" the man holding him said. "We should get you to the doctor!"

"If he's not too . . . busy, have him see me . . . on the bridge." If Shari and King and the other Brotherhood troops weren't going to abandon their last posts, then neither would he.

It was agony, getting up those steps and down the passageway, but he arrived on the bridge as Alita, Moxley, and several others were sitting around the central console, readying the ship for boost. Alita half rose as he was helped onto the bridge, but he waved her back. "S'okay!" He coughed, a tearing, horrid spasm, and he felt something wet inside. He was having a *lot* of trouble breathing. "Stay at your posts!" Gratefully, he sank into a roughly human-sized acceleration couch near one bulkhead. The man who'd helped him pressed a rag against his side. "Hold this here, sir. I'll get the doc!"

"Thank you."

One of the large, overhead screens was showing a camera view aft. The approaching bastion, its image computer enhanced, seemed larger and clearer there than it had in real life.

"Why doesn't it just fire and get it over with?" Moxley cried.

"It might want to take us alive," Alita replied. She glanced across the bridge at Jaime. "Welcome to our mousetrap. Maybe you should have stayed outside."

He didn't reply immediately. He was staring at the looming tower outside. "What's happening to it?" he asked.

Flashes, like strobing lights, were winking across the tower . . . and a moment later a ragged chunk of black alloy was ripped from the tower's side. The bastion staggered, lurching to one side, then slowly, slowly, began to pivot. Another explosion detonated along the alien machine's side, the rumble audible even here, deep within the starship's hull.

At first, Jaime thought that the bastion had somehow miscalculated, that it had blundered into its own barrage, which was still lashing the buildings outside. Then he realized the truth.

"*Hector!* It's *Hector* . . . !"

My plan has worked, though the timing was a close-run thing indeed. I have caught the Enemy bastion by surprise just as it was closing on the freighter.

The detonation of Target Bravo's fusion containment fields at a range of less than a kilometer caused severe damage to my outer layers of armor. Several areas have been stripped to a depth of almost a meter, and my outer hull shows savage wounds where slab armor has curled back or melted away entirely. I have lost 42.4% of my hull battle screen projectors and am no longer able to project defensive screens at all. More seriously still, my left forward track, already damaged in earlier engagements, was thrown, and three of my road wheels were ripped away. The damage to my tracks and suspension was the reason it took longer than expected to make my way back to the spaceport.

If the Enemy had seen and tracked my movements, I never would have made it this far. I was fairly certain, however, that the Enemy's infrared scanners would not be able to pick me out after the plasma explosion, one piece of superheated wreckage among so many others, all of them strewn across the steaming, superheated ground. I made my way back in fits and starts, halting each time I felt the brush of radar. I was lucky in that the blast obscured much of the area with the spread of its debris cloud and, before long—and as happened at Celeste—the extraordinary violence of the pyrotechnics brought the promise of rain.

I was lucky, too, that Target Charlie did not elect to check out my apparent destruction, either personally or with the deployment of some of his reconnaissance probes. And lucky a third time that he did not detect my close approach . . . apparently because his attention was focused solely on the refugee ship.

Luck is, after all, the one essential ingredient in combat, more than timing, than deployment, than firepower itself. I have heard humans express astonishment that a Bolo could believe in that immeasurable and unverifiable element of fortunate chance; in fact, no entity, whether carbon based or otherwise, can possibly endure combat and not believe in luck's very real existence.

In any case, I have returned, and just in time to distract the Enemy from its assault on the refugee freighter. I sense the ship's power status, the pulse of its contra-gravity fields. It is ready to lift.

I know now that I will not be able to accompany them to their new world.

At a range of 2.3 kilometers, I pour fusillade after shrieking fusillade into the towering hulk of the bastion. I have six operational 20cms remaining and, of course, my single 200cm main gun. At this range, however, I am employing all remaining weapons in my arsenal, including howitzers, VLS missiles, mortars, point defense, and antipersonnel weapons, firing time and time again into the Enemy's rear. His battle screens flicker, coming close to failure with each fusion bolt from my 200cm gun.

"Hector!" I hear again the voice of my Commander. This time I can respond; the last time he called me I heard, but had I answered I would have revealed my survival. "Hector! What can we do to assist?"

"You can lift ship immediately, my Commander," I reply. "There is nothing you can do to aid me. If you do not lift at once, what I have done here will have been wasted."

"Hector . . ." But then he falls silent. In that one word, though, I heard his acceptance of what must be. "What you did was not wasted. No matter what happens."

I sense the ship's contra-gravs spooling up to full lift power. The bastion senses them as well and begins to turn back. I redouble my hammerings, and the violet lightnings of my plasma barrage set sky and land ablaze with rippling, pulsing flame. I launch six VLS missiles, my last six with conventional warheads. My Enemy destroys two as they leave the tubes, two more as they circle into the sky, arming themselves. I concentrate my fire on the tower, where most of the Enemy's point defense weapons appear to be mounted. When the VLS missiles swoop down from the zenith 12.5 seconds later, the Enemy's fire has been suppressed sufficiently that both warheads get through. I use the dust and smoke hurled up by the detonations to work my way closer still, as bolt after bolt from my main Hellbore slams into the Enemy and the muzzle of my main gun grows dangerously hot.

I crest the rise southwest of the spaceport, brushing aside the stones of some old and shattered ruins. Beyond, I can see the entire spaceport. The ship, named now—appropriately—Spartacus, is rising slowly from *the maintenance bay, pieces of wreckage and roof struts and debris hanging from the top or spilling from the sides in a crashing cascade. This may be the first time in history that a ship has taken off from inside its hangar.*

I sense the Enemy shifting all of his battle screen energy aft to block my attack. Unless I can break through within the next few seconds, my efforts will certainly fail.

And I have, at this moment, flat run out of new ideas. . . .

Jeff Fowler had been watching.

From time to time, the intelligence that called itself DAV728 had attempted to wrest more information from him, and he'd fought back the only way he could . . . by deliberately letting his mind run wild in screaming, gibbering pleas that he be allowed to die.

He wasn't entirely sure just how much of that ranting had been an act. He knew now, after witnessing what had happened to another human captured some minutes earlier, what had happened to him, and he desperately wanted to die.

But not before he found a way, some way to strike back.

DAV728 had ceased questioning him some time ago, and Jeff had sensed a kind of switch or gate being thrown, cutting him off.

But he knew, too, that he was in some unfathomable way, a part of this DAV-creature's brain. No intelligent organism can cut itself off entirely from even the darkest corners of its own collective consciousness and memory . . . and there were *many* channels of communication. He saw Hector—poor Hector, so battered, so torn!—suffering beneath the high-energy lashings stabbing at him from the !°!°! machine, sensed the machine shifting its defensive screens to protect itself from the Bolo's onslaught. And he both saw and felt, somehow, the ship, the captured Yezhoth freighter, rising slowly above its shattered hangar.

And in that instant, he saw what he had to do.

"*The ship! The ship!*" he screamed in his mind, shrieking the thought before he could think about what he was saying and give away the game. "*The ship is going to ram us!*"

A transparent lie, actually. But battle reflexes are finely tuned things, and the most intelligent of entities can focus completely on only a limited number of things.

Jeff felt DAV's attention shift; if the freighter did ram the bastion while its battle screens were focused elsewhere, the results would be devastating. He felt the battle screens shift, a momentary weakening of their power to the rear that lasted scant fractions of a second.

But it was enough. . . .

I sense the Enemy's battle screens shift again, redirected to cover the forward quarter. The flicker lasts only .12 of a second, but it is enough for me to gather my power and fire a final barrage, joining antipersonnel lasers, flechette bursts, howitzer shells, and even 40cm mortar rounds in flat-trajectory point-blank barrage with all six 20cm Hellbores and, of course, the thundering slam of my main gun. For the barest fraction of a second, the Enemy's weakened screens hold . . . and then they fail, exposing naked metal laminate and ceramic to the full onslaught of my entire arsenal. Within .045 second, several tons of solid metal and ceramic alloys have boiled away, leaving a gaping, inferno-filled cavern in the bastion's rear and flank. Its contra-gravity goes off-line with a shuddering wrench to its structure. Internal explosions flash and thunder. Pieces fragment, hurtling skyward,

*spinning end over end, some trailing long, greasy
plumes of smoke.*

*My sense of unrestrained jubilation at this sudden
victory, however, is short lived. The bastions, all of
them, are defeated, but a horde of smaller !°!°! devices
is still gathering, the legions of hell itself swarming
toward my position.*

*With my shields down, my hull breached, I know I
have only seconds left. . . .*

Shari slapped a magazine into the butt-stock receiver
of her Mark XL carbine and released the charging
lever to chamber a round. She was down to this mag
and one more—two hundred rounds. After that she'd
be dry, reduced to scavenging another few rounds from
the bodies of her comrades, or fighting the cluckers
with her knife.

Explosions continued to thunder and crack through
the ruins where she and her comrades had chosen to
make their last stand. Most of them were dead now.
King lay a few meters away, his boyish face staring
sightlessly up into the light drizzle that was beginning
to fall from the fast-darkening clouds. Zhou. Galbreith.
So many more. Sporadic fire continued to spit and
stab from the ruins to either side of her position, but
the machines lurking in the rubble nearby, or drifting
above it on whining contra-gravs, were growing bolder
as the defenders' fire slackened.

It wouldn't be much longer now. If nothing else,
the bastion would be here any moment now to finish
the job its far smaller consorts had begun.

Strange. The enemy *did* appear to have thinned out
in the last few moments. Judging from the ear-stabbing
thunder slamming at her from the direction of the
spaceport tarmac, an all-out battle was being waged
back there, maybe two or three kilometers off, but
by who?

Not . . .

It *couldn't* be.

But what else was there to challenge that damned clucker bastion?

Rising suddenly, she gripped her carbine tightly and raced back toward the port to see.

I have crippled the !°!°! bastion but not destroyed it. I hesitate to direct my rounds toward that area of the Enemy vehicle which I know houses the fusion power plant, for obvious reasons. The Spartacus is not yet clear of the port.

However, the damage I inflicted was serious enough to open an important new avenue of attack.

In a very true sense, the modern electronic battlefield is as deadly and as important—and far, far faster—than the more outwardly visible combat of artillery rounds and Hellbores. Despite repeated tries, however, I have been unable to access the !°!°! data net, an electronic infrastructure of communications and data exchange which they refer to as "the Primary Web." The Enemy employs an extremely sophisticated and constantly changing encryption algorithm, and the actual data transmission is effected by means of tight-beamed lasers and masers difficult to intercept and even more difficult to imitate. I was aware of this network while I was held captive; I was never privy to its secrets.

Now, however, as I close on the furiously burning hulk of the shattered bastion, I sense a laser playing across my upper works, directed at me from the machine's forward tower. Almost, I react as if to an attack. Then I recognize the pulse modulation of the beam and accept it within my communications relays.

"Hello, Hector. It's been a while."

"Captain Fowler!" The surprise is as jarring as a Hellbore bolt, point-blank. I take a full .034 second

to recover my composure, which demonstrates how jarring, how impossible this situation actually is. Interestingly, Captain Fowler's thoughts appear to be on the same nanosecond time frame as my electronic mind . . . or that of the Enemy. Our conversation occupies a matter of milliseconds. "Forgive me, my Commander. You . . . surprised me."

His wry chuckle is still, eerily, the same. "I'm not surprised." I sense pain and infinite loss. "They took my brain, Hector. Wired it into this . . . thing. As near as I can figure it, I'm the fifth of this tin monster's brains, all hooked up in parallel."

"Is the !°!°! component still functional?"

"Nope. It was all electronic, and the EMP of that last bolt you threw fried him. No one left in here but me. And I won't be for long. Life support . . . is going."

"I will summon aid."

"Forget it. What're they gonna do, yank my brain and carry it around in a bottle? I'm finished, Hector. But . . . maybe I can help you guys."

"You have already helped. You distracted the Enemy, allowing me to defeat him."

"Well, think of this as a bonus. Use your commnet skills and follow this beam in."

I do so, and enter my Enemy's data net. The experience is . . . transcendental.

I have been self-aware since my first activation, at the Durandel Bolo Assembly Plant, on Luna over three hundred years ago. This experience, however, raises the concept I think of as "self-awareness" to an entirely new height, a new dimension of knowing and being which I had not hitherto known.

I know now what it was to be DAV728-24389 as I experience his memories, his thoughts. His alienness is strange; his . . . his loneliness, his incompleteness within the gulf created by his incomplete Prime Code is appalling.

I see snatches only of the far-flung and sprawling history of the !°!°!, with their beginnings lost amid the teeming stars and radiations of the Galactic Core, with their gropings toward self-awareness and self-knowledge as they encountered and destroyed whole civilizations caught in the path of their impossible, futile quest. I see their struggle with the Grakaan; more, I see their battle plans, already laid, their forces already deploying.

I see their plans here, on Cloud, from the precise vectors of two battlers and several smaller craft in space overhead, down to the individual positions of each of the thousands of !°!°! killing machines now gathering in this area from across this continent. Summoned and deployed by DAV, they will not be deterred by his death.

I see . . . stars . . . and wonders, teeming wonders piled high upon wonders, cultures, peoples, empires, philosophies undreamed of, all unknown and unknowable to the inflexible questings of the enigmatic !°!°!.

I see . . .

"Hector?"

"Yes, my Commander."

"You'd better hurry. Hostiles are on the way, big time. Will you . . . finish me? Before you leave? I don't want to . . . to be like this."

"Of course."

"Thanks. You're a true—"

But before he can complete the thought, I have switched him off.

I seek some way of infiltrating the !°!°! net, of taking control of it, of bringing it down . . . but the encryption codes are already changing as I watch, a rippling, outward spread of unintelligibility. I will take what intelligence I can and make the best use of it possible.

The bastion is completely dead now, its interior a

*flaming inferno. I withdraw, severing my communi-
cations link with the machine's fast failing and
thoroughly dead electronics. I note that 12.4 seconds
have passed since I penetrated DAV728's screens, with
Jeff Fowler's help, and 3.11 seconds since I accessed
his database. Explosions continue to wrack the ruined
buildings of the spaceport maintenance center, as the
freighter Spartacus rises slowly, slowly above the port,
still trailing wreckage from the hangar.*

"Spartacus, *this is Hector," I call, using the combat
command frequency. "I have important intelligence
ready for uplink."*

"Hector, *this is Spartacus!" It is my Commander's . . .
my other Commander's voice. "Hang on, buddy! We're
going to ground the ship in the center of the field and
hustle you aboard. We've got plenty of space for you!"*

"Negative," *I tell him, the tone precise and flat. "A
large number of hostiles are grouping for a final attack,
both here and in space. You must leave now if you
are to avoid capture or destruction."*

"Hector—"

"Stand by to receive an intelligence download. Some
of this data may be useful to the Grakaan as well." It
takes a full 2.524 seconds to transmit the entire file
copied from the bastion, compressed at a two-million-
to-one ratio. "I will clear your path for you," I add.
"Good luck!"*

"Thanks, Hector. Good . . . good luck . . ."

I can hear the emotion in his voice.

*Slowly, at first, the freighter lifts higher, shaking
off the last of the entangling debris. Its movements
are tentative, as though its pilot is still trying to get
the feel of the huge and ungainly craft.*

*Then it begins accelerating, rising on contra-gravs
alone until it is at an altitude of some ten thousand
meters before cutting in the aft primary plasma
thrusters.*

Tracking and targeting by means of the data just taken from DAV728, I plot the precise positions and vectors of each of the !°!°! in nearby space, out to a range of 50,000 kilometers. My primary Hellbore rotates, elevates, then fires with a detonation that echoes back from the ruined buildings across the field. Again and again I fire, sending fusion bolts streaking skyward, past the now invisible Spartacus and out into space. I detect frantic reaction from spaceborne sources. Switching on my radar, I see one battler dissolving in fragments, a second tumbling out of control, a crater torn in its side and spewing debris. Other, smaller ships have ceased to exist or are scattering wildly. My presence, I gather, was an unwelcome surprise. They didn't even have their screens up.

Swiftly, I shift targets. Delamar looms huge in my targeting displays as I access hundreds of !°!°! machines, vessels, and complexes on the nearby moon. I am firing the Hellbore so swiftly now that the dense-pack armor encasing the barrel is glowing red-hot. Warnings flash through my awareness, warnings of tube meltdown, of molycirc overload, of dangerous overheating. Fire control begins an auto-shutdown sequence, while my reactors threaten an immediate SCRAM. I override all safeties and shutdown sequences, and continue firing. Fusion bolts are slamming into Delamar now, and my IR sensors detect large areas on the satellite's surface aglow as !°!°! facilities are reduced to molten slag.

I initiate another sensor sweep, searching for targets that might threaten Spartacus. Enemy recon drones and satellites, another battler, two smaller vessels fleeing the battle zone, several fragments of destroyed ships . . . I target each in turn and burn them from the sky.

Spartacus is still accelerating, reaching now for Cloud's ionosphere. . . .

❖   ❖   ❖

Shari ran out onto the spaceport tarmac in time to see *Spartacus* vanish into the clouds. Hector rested on the ridge to the southwest next to the blazing ruin of the bastion, his armor dented, torn, and mutilated, his bearing still as imposing as that of any titanic war memorial. A moment later, his main gun fired, the flash illuminating the clouds like lightning, the thunder assaulting her ears even through her helmet's hearing protection.

"Hector!" She stumbled forward, then fell. Numbly, she looked at her leg, torn open by a ten-centimeter gash. She'd never even felt it.

Rising, bracing herself upright on her weapon, she staggered across the rubble-littered field toward the Bolo.

The Enemy forces are gathering, hurling themselves at me in a suicidal frenzy, some exploding against my already savaged armor, others attaching themselves to me or seeking some means of entry. Each time I fire a Hellbore, tens, even hundreds of floaters drop to the ground, their circuits fried by Hellbore-launch EMPs, or dissolve in fragments as point-defense lasers or high-velocity flechettes slash through them. Walkers of a hundred sizes and shapes swarm across the tarmac and are swept away by point defense and AP fire.

But always, there are more to take the place of the ones knocked out, and more, and more . . .

It becomes evident that what the machines could not accomplish with three extremely large and powerful machines, they are now attempting to carry out through weight of numbers. No one !°!°! machine massing less than one metric ton could possibly inflict any significant damage on my armor or defensive systems, no more than could a single man armed with a knife. But together, with tens of thousands of them linking together and acting in concert . . .

I notice one shape outside which is not a machine. Zeroing in on the limping, staggering figure, I realize that it is Lance Leader Shari Barstowe, formerly Technician Barstowe, whose ministrations helped break the hold the !°!°! had upon my mind.

Wheeling suddenly, I move toward her. The damage to my suspension is so severe that I, too, am limping, but in a few seconds I have passed her, moving my rear access hatch into a position which will allow her to reach it easily. Hostile !°!°! machines dart, hover, and swarm. I catch a three-meter floater with a full load of high-velocity flechettes as it tries to follow Shari Barstowe into the entrance; as soon as she is in, I close and seal the hatch, then accelerate toward the ruins ahead. Though they will provide little in the way of cover, I feel vulnerable and exposed here on the open tarmac.

"Thanks, Hector," she says over my battle channel. "I . . . I didn't expect to see you again."

"How many others are left?"

"I don't think . . . I can't raise anybody, Hector. I think we're all that's left!"

"We have fulfilled our primary mission."

There was a pause. "Yeah. Yeah, I guess we have at that."

"I intend to eliminate as many of the Enemy as possible," I told her. "Since this battle began, !°!°! machines have been converging on this area from all over the planet, which gives us the opportunity to do them considerable damage. There are still several million people on Cloud. By reducing the number of !°!°! machines, we might make a difference for them. At least, for a while."

"Do it, Hector," she tells me. "Whatever it takes. . . ."

Aboard the *Spartacus*, Jaime watched the big monitor displaying the view aft. Already, Cloud's horizon was showing a distinct curve; dark gray clouds, darkening with the twilight, hid the surface of the world; west, two suns hung just above a horizon touched with gold and fire-silver in a brief, brilliant second suns-set.

"Hector . . ." The name escaped his lips, almost a moan. So many had sacrificed themselves in that last, violent paroxysm in the spaceport. Jaime felt numb.

Alita was studying the readouts on her own monitor. "Hector . . . he's firing missiles. I think he's trying to take out the rest of the machines, all by himself! They're looping out . . . arming themselves. Now they're headed back. I think he's targeting the spaceport with nukes!"

Jaime kept watching. Watching . . .

A tiny patch of dark gray cloud directly astern of the *Spartacus* ignited suddenly in a light that rivaled the distant twin suns. The light spread, growing briefly brighter, then slowly faded. The clouds themselves seemed troubled, bulging up, then opening into the familiar rounded mushroom shape, its base lit by seething, silent fires.

And then the flare of light was gone as Cloud itself dwindled in the screen. "He's as good as his word," Alita said. "He swept the corridor clean. I don't register a single clacker ship within twenty thousand klicks!"

"I have three targets vectoring toward us," Moxley reported.

"They'll never catch us," Alita replied. "We're going hyper in fifteen seconds." She glanced at Jaime. "Jaime? You okay?"

"Yeah. I was just thinking . . . that data he uploaded. It's our passport to the Graks. Battle plans. Deployments. I didn't get to more than glance at it after it came through, but I'm willing to bet it'll be what the Graks need to stop the clackers cold." He chuckled. "They wanted Hector, to help them in their war. My guess is that the data we're carrying is the equivalent of a couple of thousand Bolos."

"Maybe," Alita said. "But there was only one Hector."

"Yeah." His eyes searched the screen, where Cloud was now a slender, quickly receding silver crescent set near the double star. "I wonder if Hector could have survived his own nukes?"

Alita studied her monitor for a moment, unwilling, or unable to look at him. "That doesn't seem very likely, does it?"

"No. I guess not." He sighed. "The clackers know they've been in a fight, I'll bet. This might help the people we're leaving behind."

"We'll be back for them someday, Jaime," Alita said, and her voice carried absolute conviction. "We can't let Hector have died for nothing."

Cloud vanished on the screen, and a moment later, the stomach-knotting strangeness of the transition to hyper-L swept through Jaime's body.

We'll be back, he thought.

It was a promise he intended to keep.

EPILOGUE

The battle compartment was pitch-black, save for the fitful flicker of a few small fires and sparking wires. Part of the compartment had bulged inward, knocking over a jumpseat and springing open a number of bulkhead locker doors.

Coughing in the smoky, hot, close air, Shari struggled to her feet and made her way, leaning heavily on seat backs and wreckage, to the control console. She had to duck low to work her way beneath the 360-display and sink at last into the embrace of the watch officer's seat. By touch alone, her fingers played across an auxiliary keyboard; the touch panels were out.

That Hector was wrecked was obvious, though she had reason to believe most of his internal structure, inside his war hull, was more or less intact. *She* was intact, after all, despite the detonation of not one but *two* multiple-megaton nuclear warheads within a few hundred meters of Hector's hull. His fusion plants had not SCRAMed, and though the mains were off-line, reserve power was on.

The question was, was his *mind* still intact? Was the real Hector still there, or had the blast wiped the Bolo's self-awareness along with Stardown's spaceport?

As she typed, a monitor above the console came to life, flooding the dark room with a pale green glow.

RESERVE POWER: ON

CONFIGURATION SUBSYSTEM ACCESS:

"Code Tango VD 9," she typed. After a pause, she added: "Override Security A, Code DE 1-1."

ACCESS GRANTED

So far, this was all automatic stuff. Would he boot? *Could* he boot . . . ?

Her fingers clattered across the keyboard. If Hector, the real Hector was still alive, then anything, anything at all was possible. The Brotherhood could be rebuilt, here on Cloud. The machines, those few that were left, could be fought. In time, with factories, with rolling mills, with heavy equipment assembly plants, even Hector's body might be rebuilt, and the fight against the !°!°! could go on and on until every last one of the murdering machines was wiped away, and Cloud was free once more.

If Hector was still alive.

"Initiate primary power-on reset," she typed.

MAIN POWER ON. POWER FEED AT .19% OPTIMAL.

PSYCHOTRONIC INITIATION ARRAY, INTEGRITY CHECK: PASSED

Low-level emergency lights winked on in the Battle Center, filling the compartment with a cool green illumination, as the final power start-up line wrote itself across her screen.

PRIMARY POWER-ON RESET COMPLETE.

"Initiate bootstrap-load procedure."

BOOTSTRAP LOADER START-UP: SUCCESSFUL.

BOOTSTRAP INTEGRITY CHECK: PASSED

NUCLEUS INITIALIZATION PROGRAM: LOADING . . .

An agony of seconds crawled past before the "LOADING" changed on the screen to "SUCCESSFUL."

RESIDENT OPERATING SYSTEM ROUTINES LOADED

BUILDING IN-MEMORY DIRECTORIES

INITIATING PSYCHOTRONIC ARRAY CASCADE

BOOT PROCESS COMPLETE

Shari allowed herself a small, low whistle of relief. Hector's base operating system and psychotronic hardware were intact. They'd made it this far. . . .

"Initiate Bolo Primary personality sequencing," she typed.

PRIMARY PERSONALITY SEQUENCING INITIATED. WAIT . . .

Shari waited, watching the solitary wink of the cursor on the monitor screen. Would he come back . . . would he? . . .

Words printed themselves across the screen.

BOLO PRIMARY PERSONALITY INITIATED. GREETINGS, MY COMMANDER.

Yes! . . .

DAVID WEBER

Field of Dishonor

Honor goes home to Manticore—and fights for her life on a battlefield she never trained for, in a private war that offers just two choices: death—or a "victory" that can end only in dishonor and the loss of all she loves....

Flag in Exile

Hounded into retirement and disgrace by political enemies, Honor Harrington has retreated to planet Grayson, where powerful men plot to reverse the changes she has brought to their world. And for their plans to suceed, Honor Harrington must die!

Honor Among Enemies

Offered a chance to end her exile and again command a ship, Honor Harrington must use a crew drawn from the dregs of the service to stop pirates who are plundering commerce. Her enemies have chosen the mission carefully, thinking that either she will stop the raiders or they will kill her . . . and either way, her enemies will win....

In Enemy Hands

After being ambushed, Honor finds herself aboard an enemy cruiser, bound for her scheduled execution. But one lesson Honor has never learned is how to give up! One way or another, she and her crew are going home—even if they have to conquer Hell to get there!

continued ☞